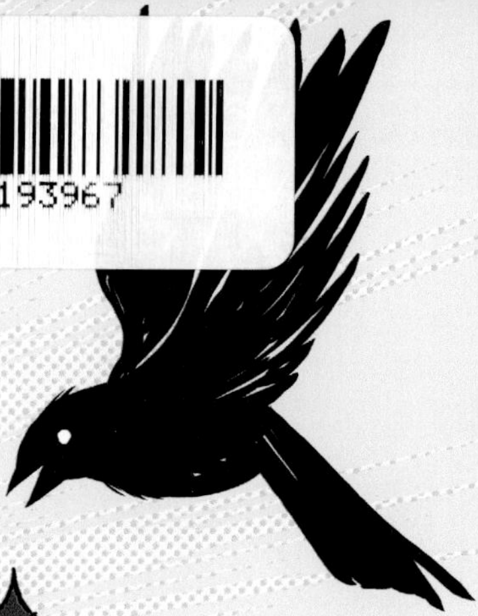

BLACK CANARY IGNITE

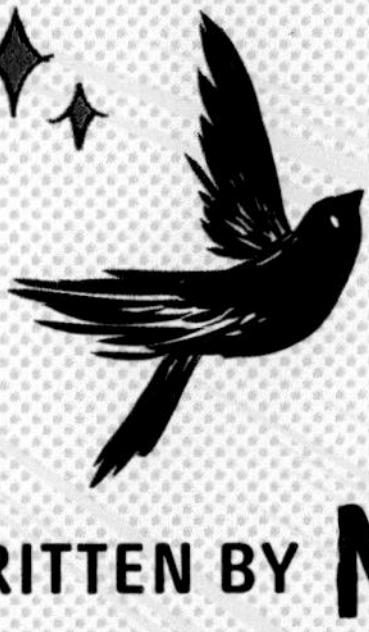

WRITTEN BY MEG CABOT
ILLUSTRATED BY CARA McGEE
COLORED BY CAITLIN QUIRK
LETTERED BY CLAYTON COWLES

SARA MILLER Editor
LIZ ERICKSON Assistant Editor
STEVE COOK Design Director - Books
AMIE BROCKWAY-METCALF Publication Design

BOB HARRAS Senior VP - Editor-in-Chief, DC Comics
MICHELE R. WELLS VP & Executive Editor, Young Reader

DAN DiDIO Publisher
JIM LEE Publisher & Chief Creative Officer
BOBBIE CHASE VP - New Publishing Initiatives & Talent Development
DON FALLETTI VP - Manufacturing Operations & Workflow Management
LAWRENCE GANEM VP - Talent Services
ALISON GILL Senior VP - Manufacturing & Operations
HANK KANALZ Senior VP - Publishing Strategy & Support Services
DAN MIRON VP - Publishing Operations
NICK J. NAPOLITANO VP - Manufacturing Administration & Design
NANCY SPEARS VP - Sales

BLACK CANARY: IGNITE

DC Comics, 2900 West Alameda Ave., Burbank, CA 91505

Printed by LSC Communications,
Crawfordsville, IN, USA.
9/20/19.

First Printing.

ISBN: 978-1-4012-8620-0

Library of Congress Cataloging-in-Publication Data

Names: Cabot, Meg, writer. | McGee, Cara, illustrator. | Quirk, Caitlin,
    colourist. | Cowles, Clayton, letterer.

Title: Black Canary : ignite / written by Meg Cabot ; illustrated by Cara
    McGee ; colored by Caitlin Quirk ; lettered by Clayton Cowles.

Description: Burbank, CA : DC Comics, [2019] | Summary: Thirteen-year-old
    Dinah Lance is in a rock band with her two best friends and has a good
    relationship with her mom, but when a mysterious figure threatens her
    friends and family, she learns more about herself and her mother's secret
    past.

Identifiers: LCCN 2019013353 | ISBN 9781401286200

Subjects: LCSH: Graphic novels. | CYAC: Graphic novels. | Rock
    groups--Fiction. | Friendship--Fiction. | Mothers and daughters--Fiction.
    | Family secrets--Fiction.

Classification: LCC PZ7.7.C33 Bl 2019 | DDC 741.5/973--dc23

TABLE OF CONTENTS

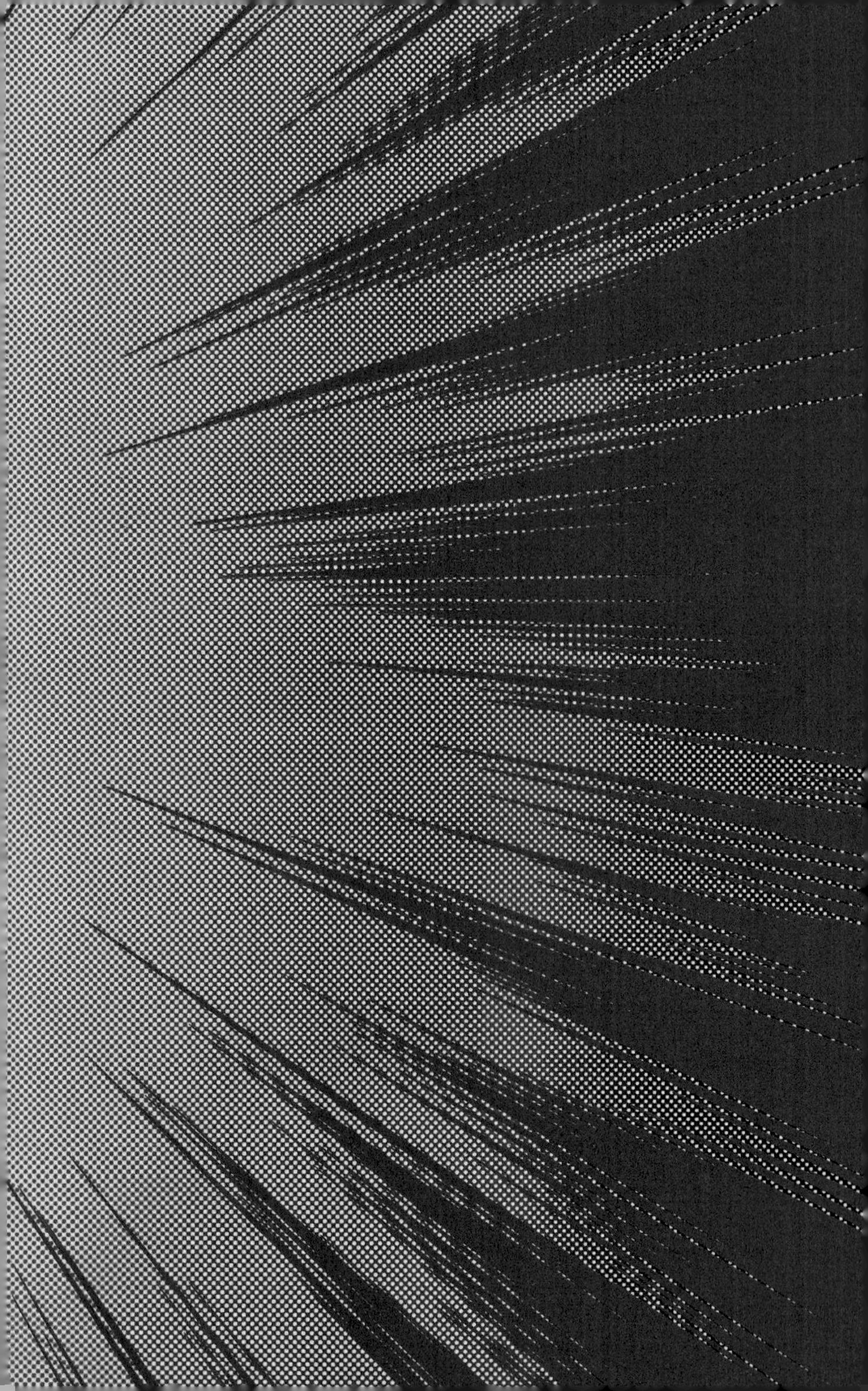

CHAPTER 1
JUST AN ORDINARY GIRL

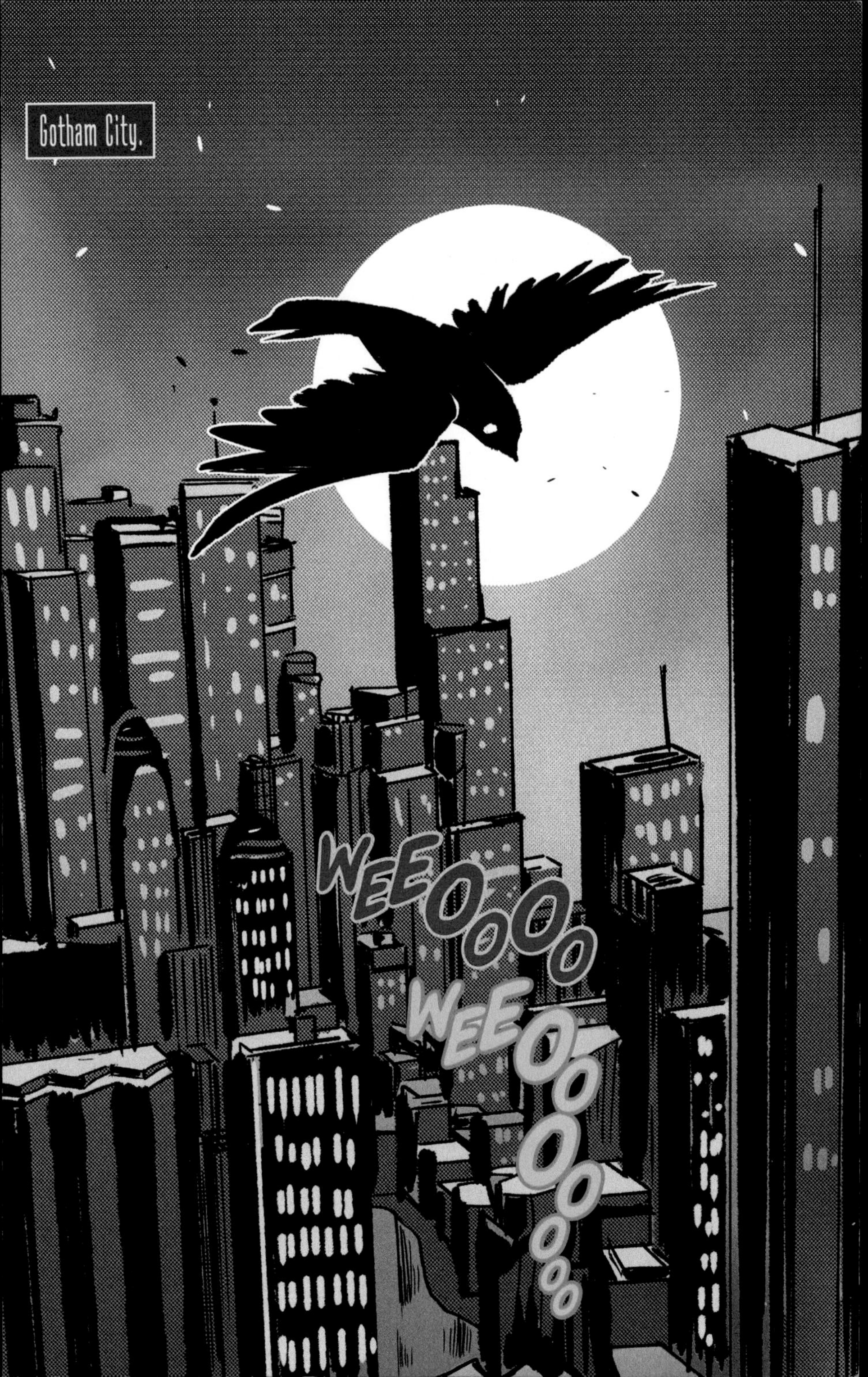
Gotham City.
WEEOOOO
WEEOOOOOooo

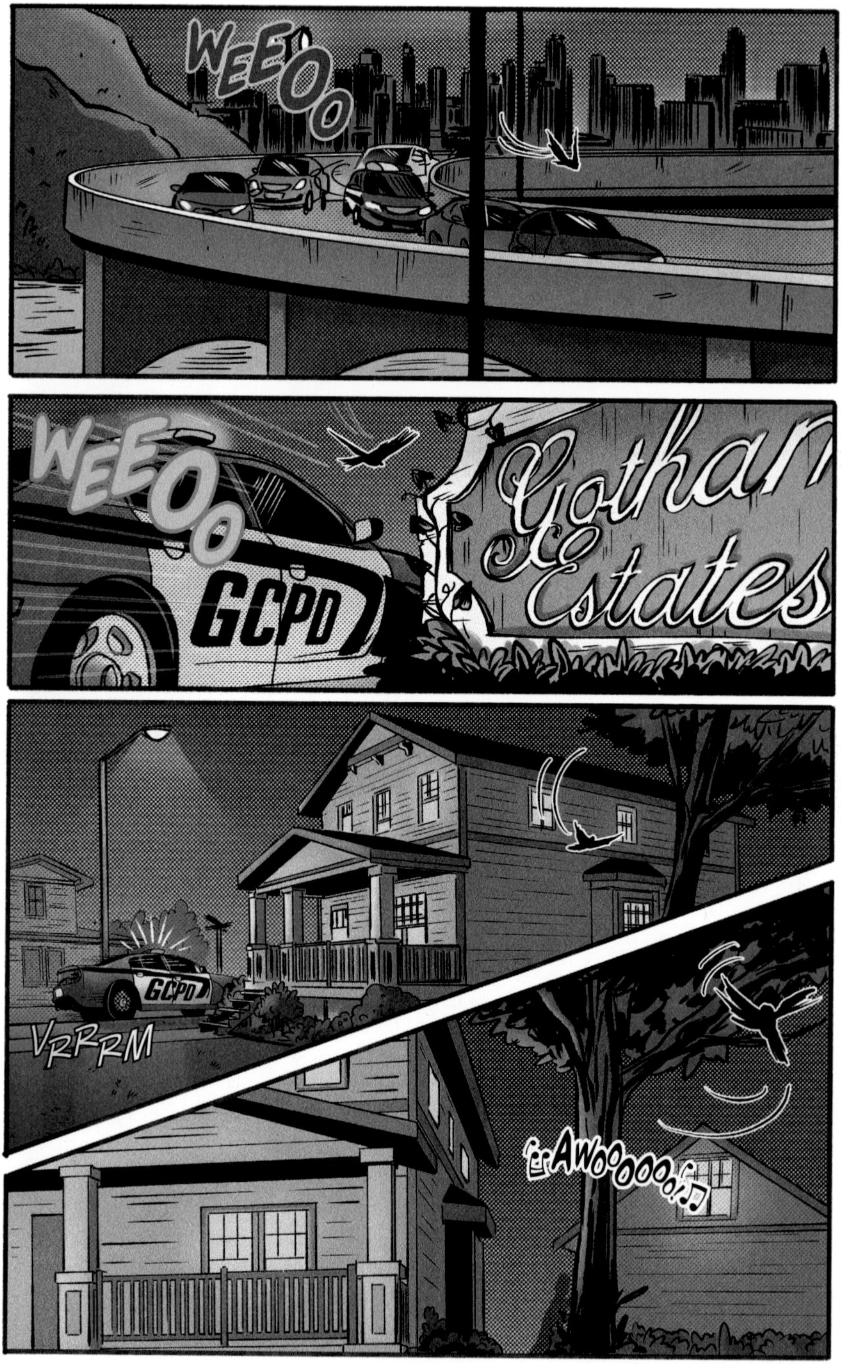
WEEOO
WEEOO
GCPD
Gotham Estates
GCPD
VRRRM
AWOOOOOO!

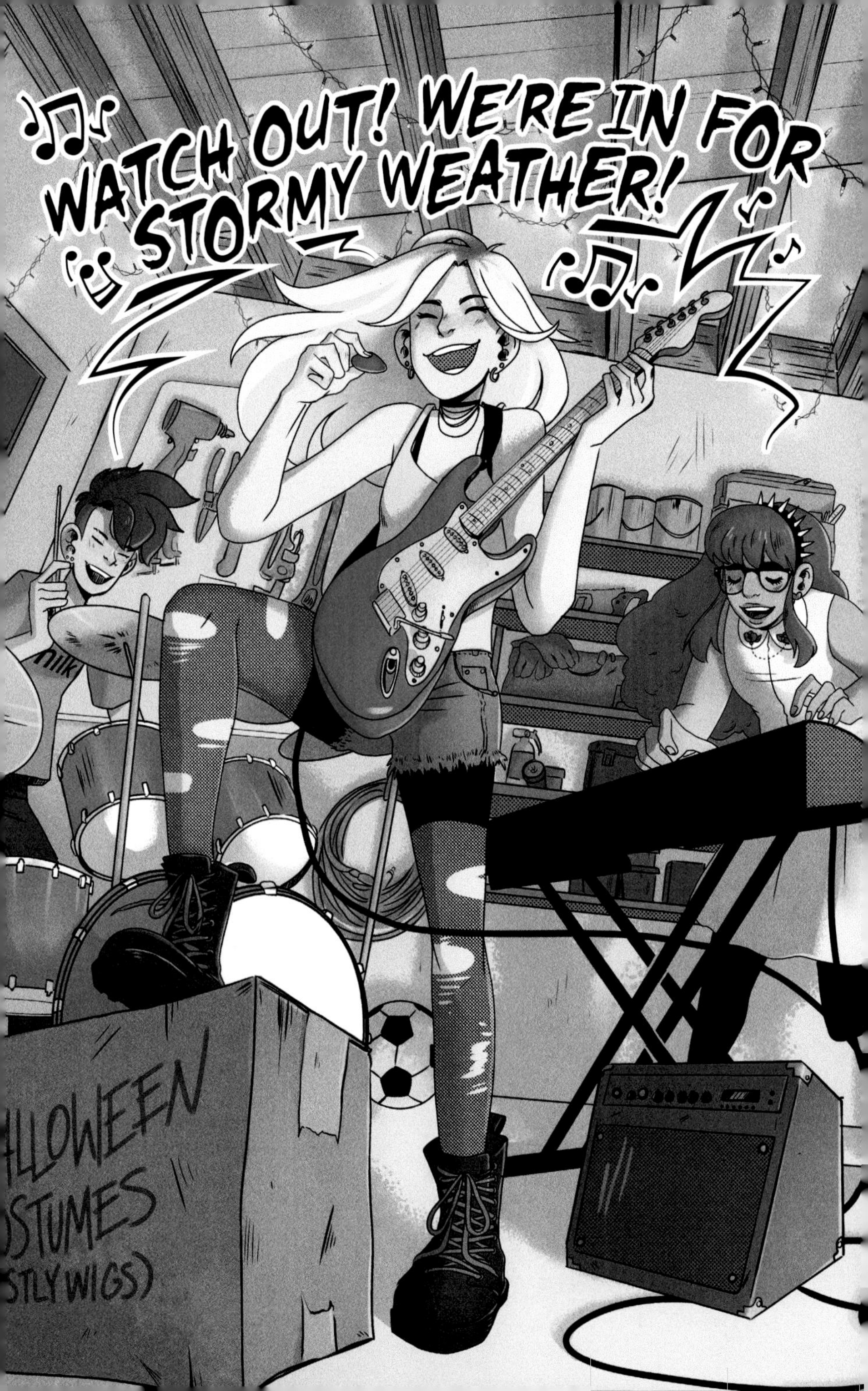
WATCH OUT! WE'RE IN FOR STORMY WEATHER!
LLOWEEN
OSTUMES
STLY WIGS)

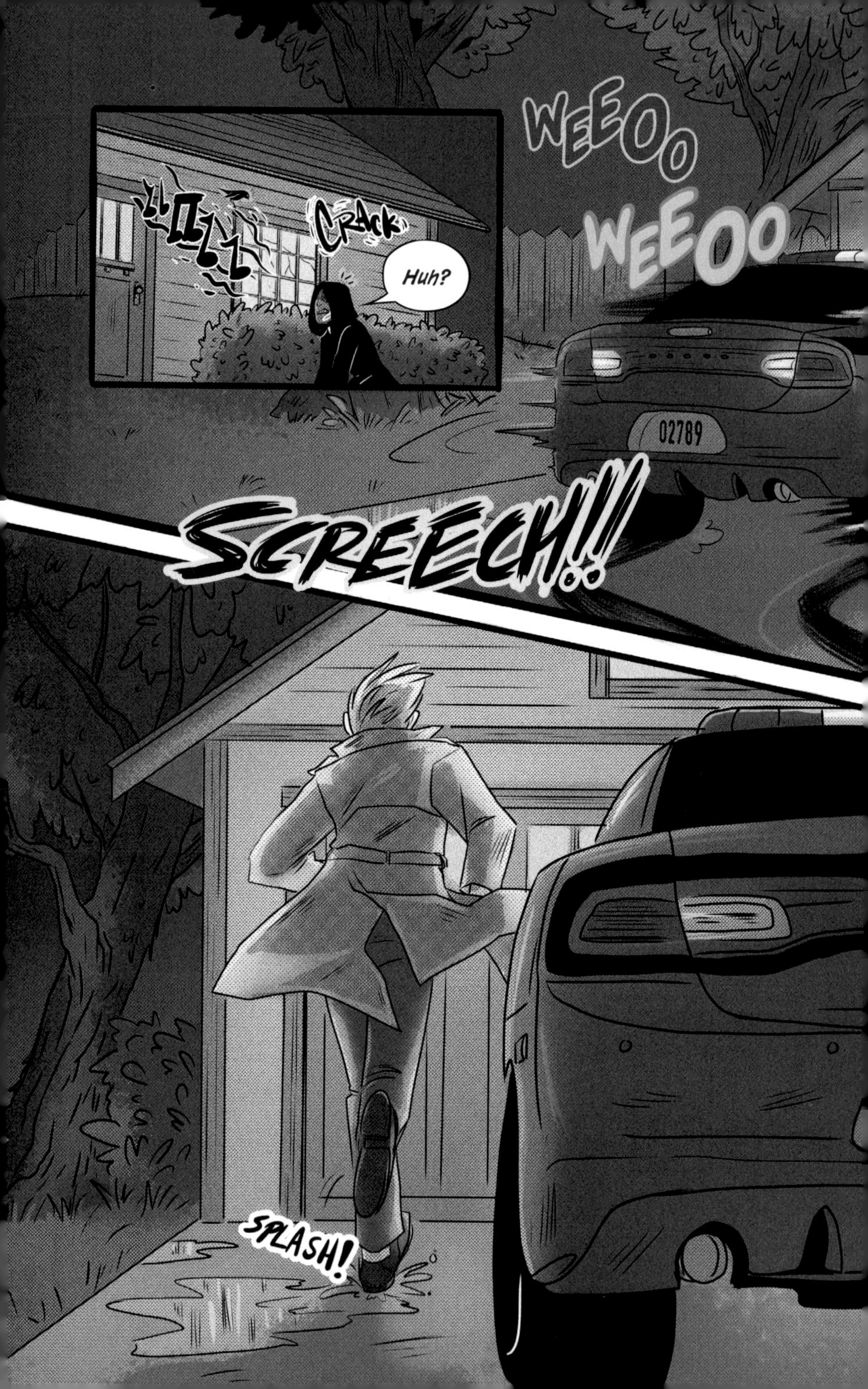
WEEOO
WEEOO
CRACK
Huh?
02789
SCREECH!!
SPLASH!

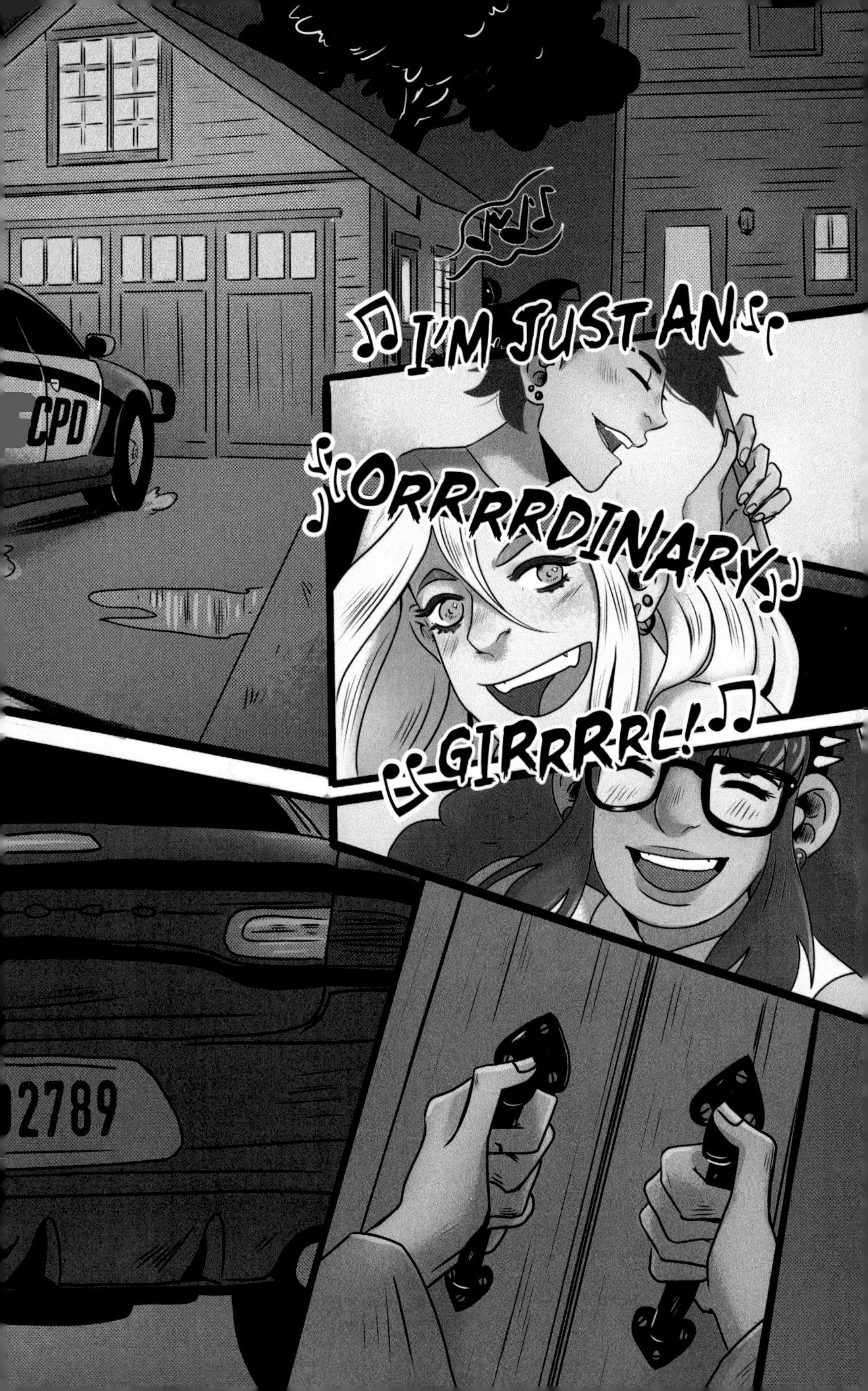
CPD
♫ I'M JUST AN ♪
♪ ORRRRRDINARY ♪
♪ GIRRRRRL! ♫
2789

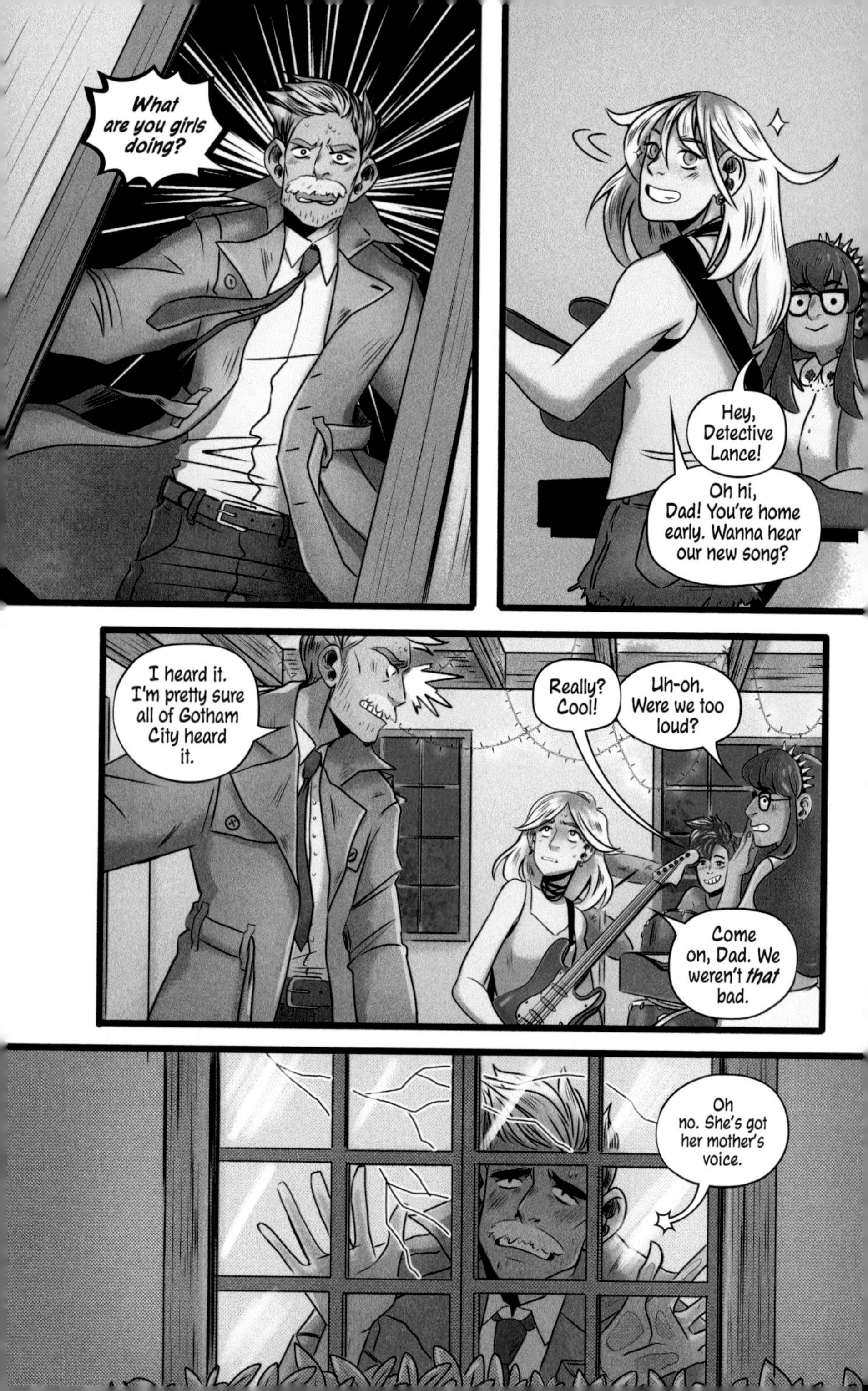
What are you girls doing?
Hey, Detective Lance!
Oh hi, Dad! You're home early. Wanna hear our new song?
I heard it. I'm pretty sure all of Gotham City heard it.
Really? Cool!
Uh-oh. Were we too loud?
Come on, Dad. We weren't *that* bad.
Oh no. She's got her mother's voice.

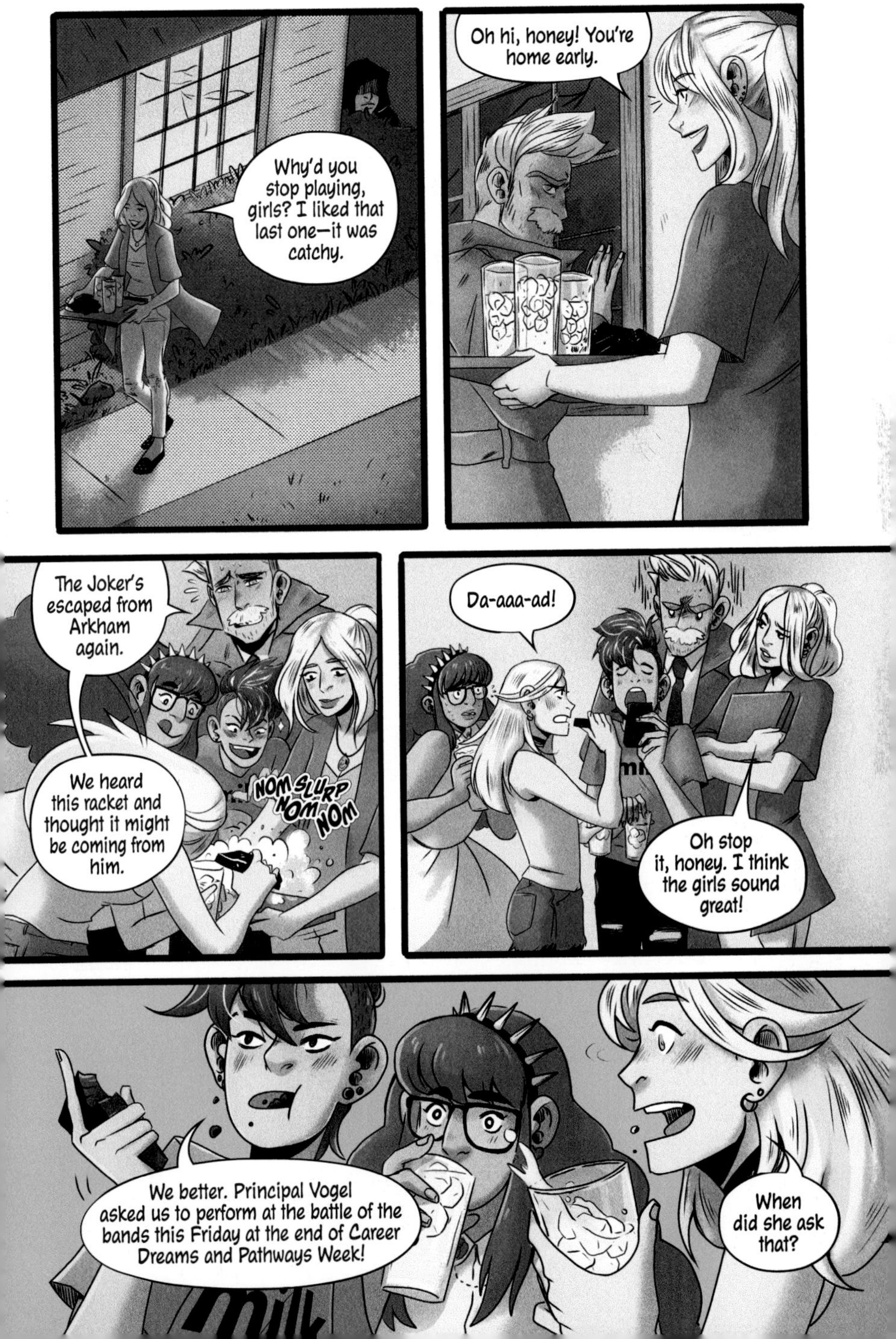
Why'd you stop playing, girls? I liked that last one—it was catchy.
Oh hi, honey! You're home early.
The Joker's escaped from Arkham again.
We heard this racket and thought it might be coming from him.
NOM SLURP NOM NOM
Da-aaa-ad!
Oh stop it, honey. I think the girls sound great!
We better. Principal Vogel asked us to perform at the battle of the bands this Friday at the end of Career Dreams and Pathways Week!
When did she ask that?

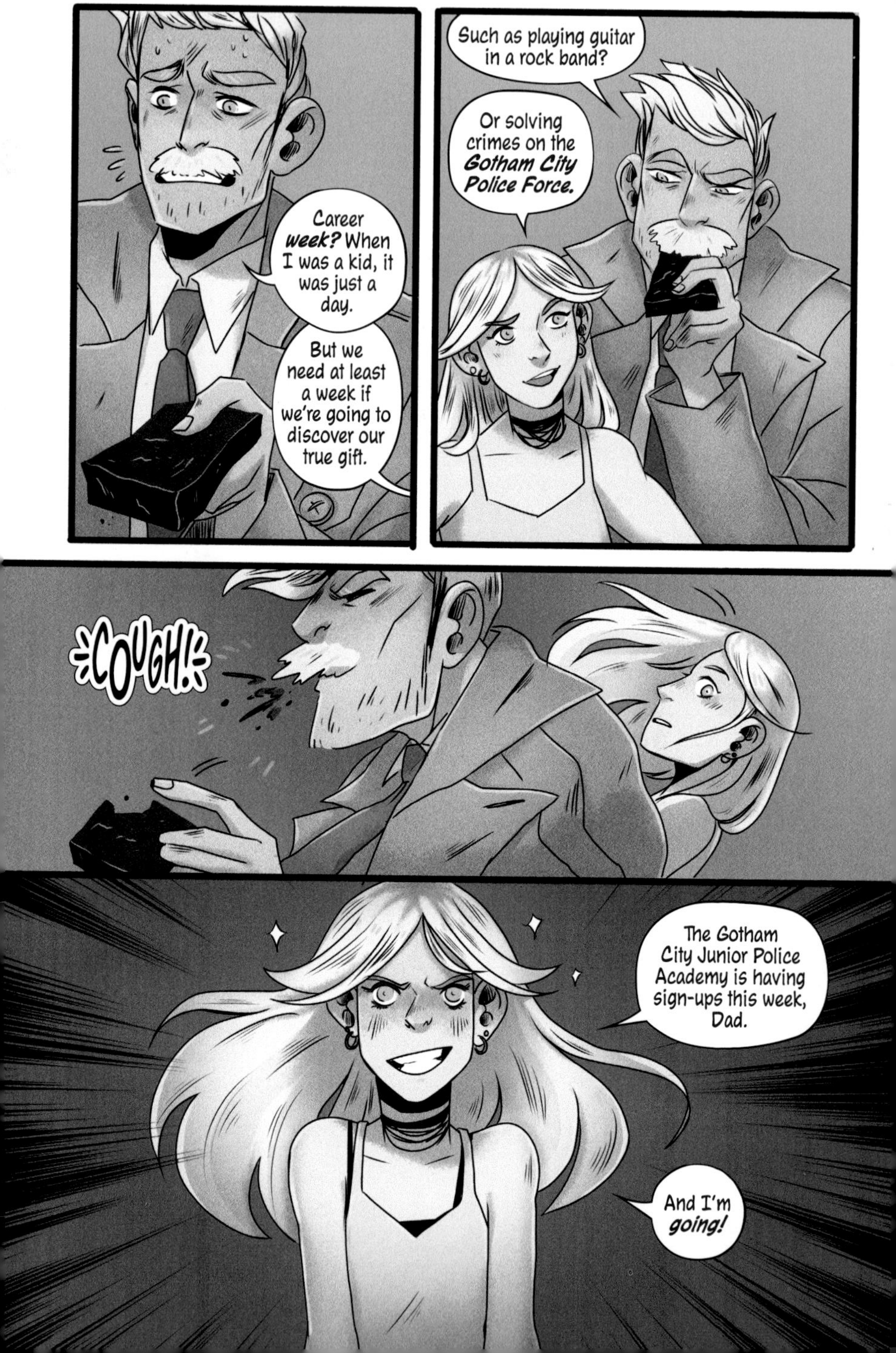
Career *week?* When I was a kid, it was just a day.
But we need at least a week if we're going to discover our true gift.
Such as playing guitar in a rock band?
Or solving crimes on the ***Gotham City Police Force.***
COUGH!
The Gotham City Junior Police Academy is having sign-ups this week, Dad.
And I'm *going!*

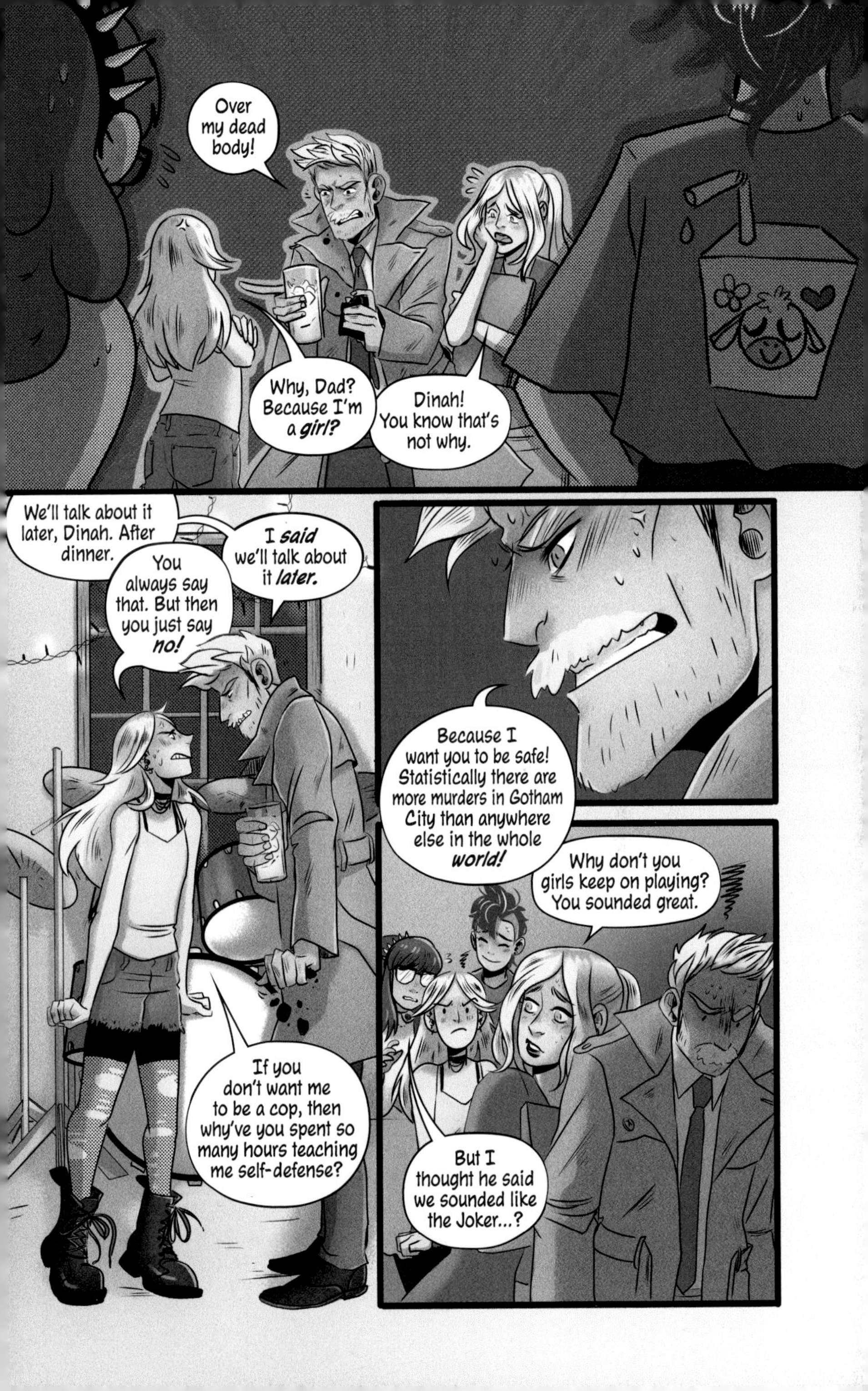

Over my dead body!
Why, Dad? Because I'm a *girl?*
Dinah! You know that's not why.
We'll talk about it later, Dinah. After dinner.
You always say that. But then you just say *no!*
I *said* we'll talk about it *later.*
If you don't want me to be a cop, then why've you spent so many hours teaching me self-defense?
Because I want you to be safe! Statistically there are more murders in Gotham City than anywhere else in the whole *world!*
Why don't you girls keep on playing? You sounded great.
But I thought he said we sounded like the Joker...?

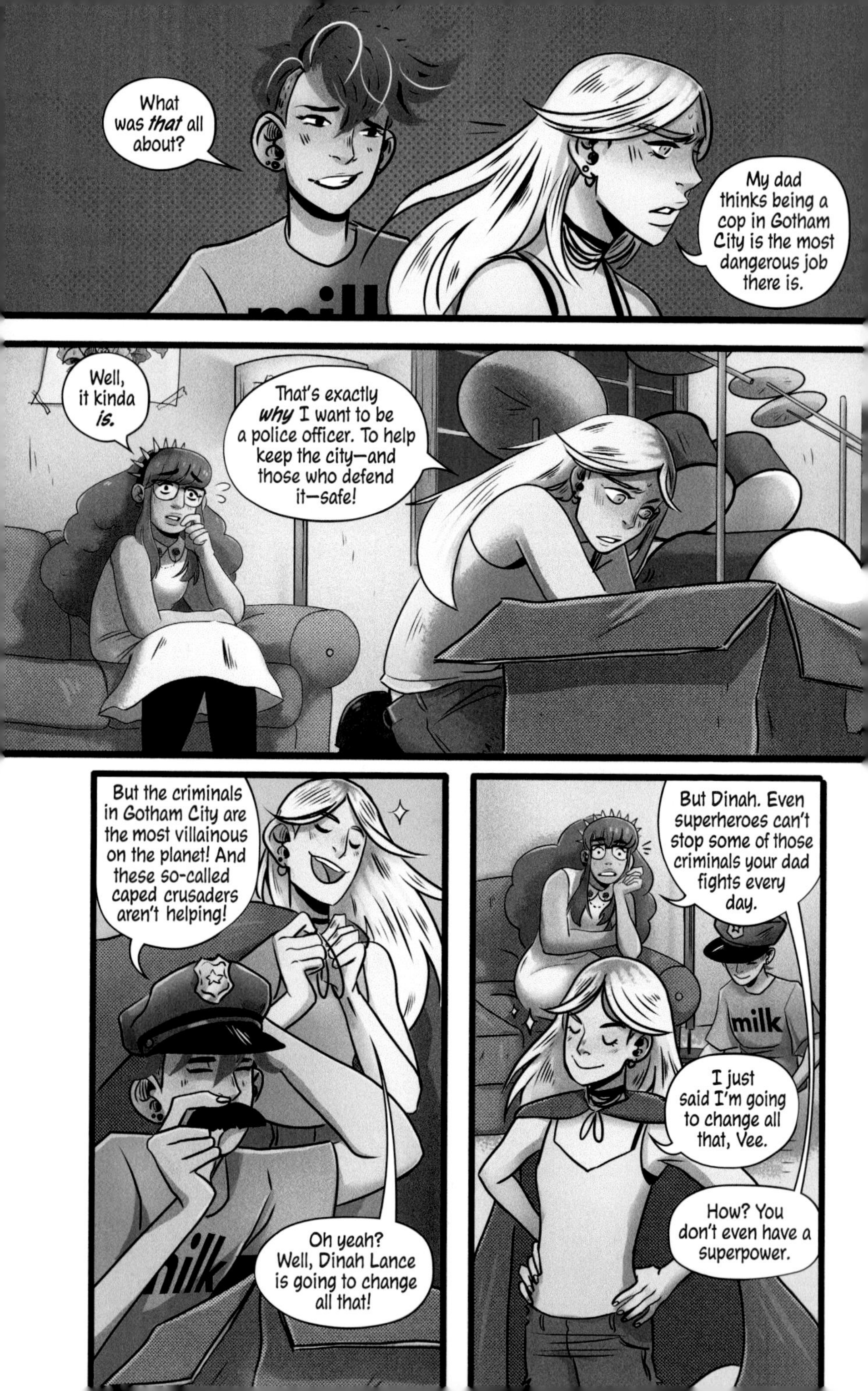
What was *that* all about?
My dad thinks being a cop in Gotham City is the most dangerous job there is.
Well, it kinda *is.*
That's exactly *why* I want to be a police officer. To help keep the city—and those who defend it—safe!
But the criminals in Gotham City are the most villainous on the planet! And these so-called caped crusaders aren't helping!
Oh yeah? Well, Dinah Lance is going to change all that!
milk
But Dinah. Even superheroes can't stop some of those criminals your dad fights every day.
milk
I just said I'm going to change all that, Vee.
How? You don't even have a superpower.

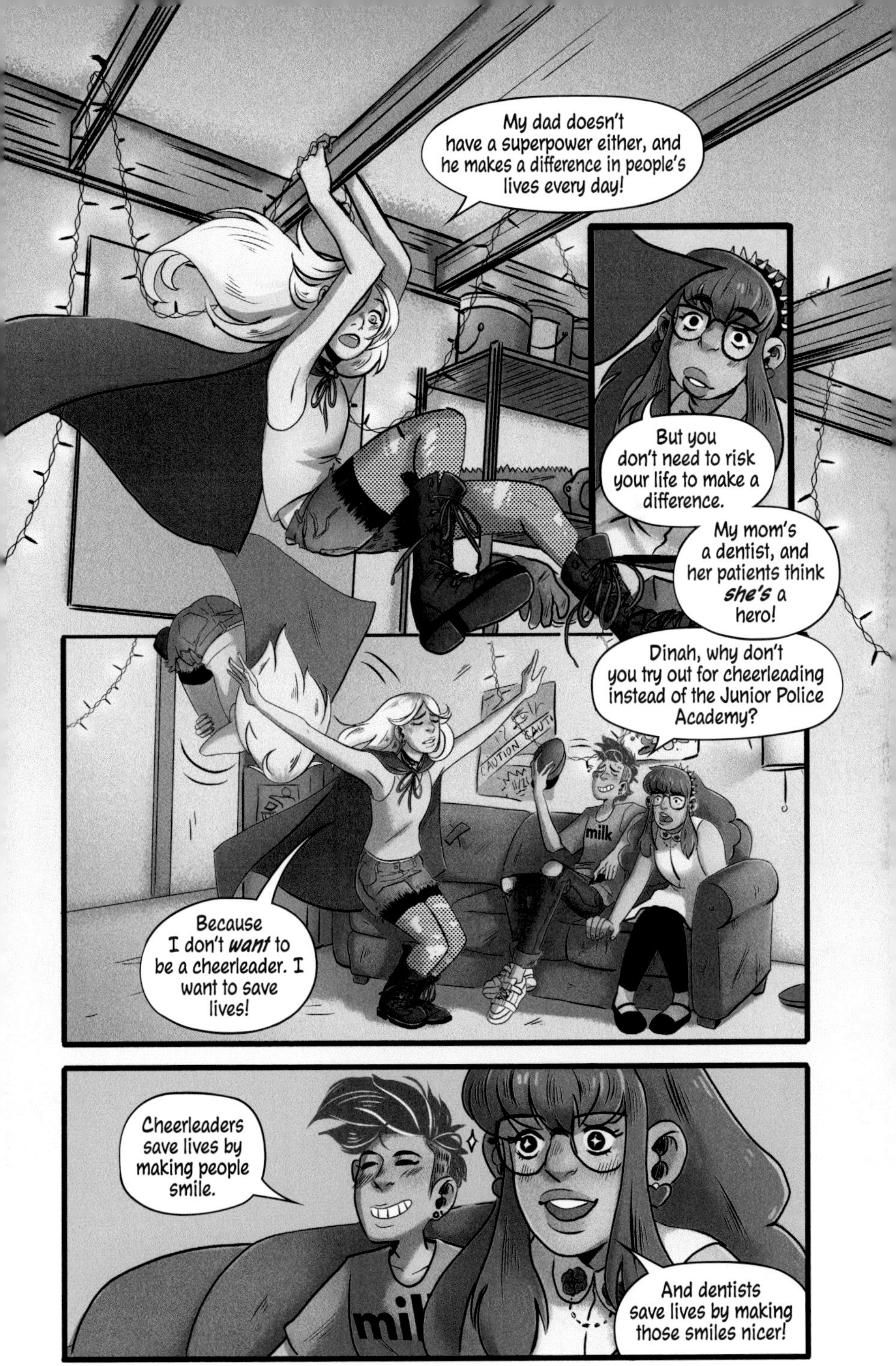
My dad doesn't have a superpower either, and he makes a difference in people's lives every day!
But you don't need to risk your life to make a difference.
My mom's a dentist, and her patients think *she's* a hero!
Dinah, why don't you try out for cheerleading instead of the Junior Police Academy?
Because I don't *want* to be a cheerleader. I want to save lives!
CAUTION CAUTI
milk
Cheerleaders save lives by making people smile.
And dentists save lives by making those smiles nicer!

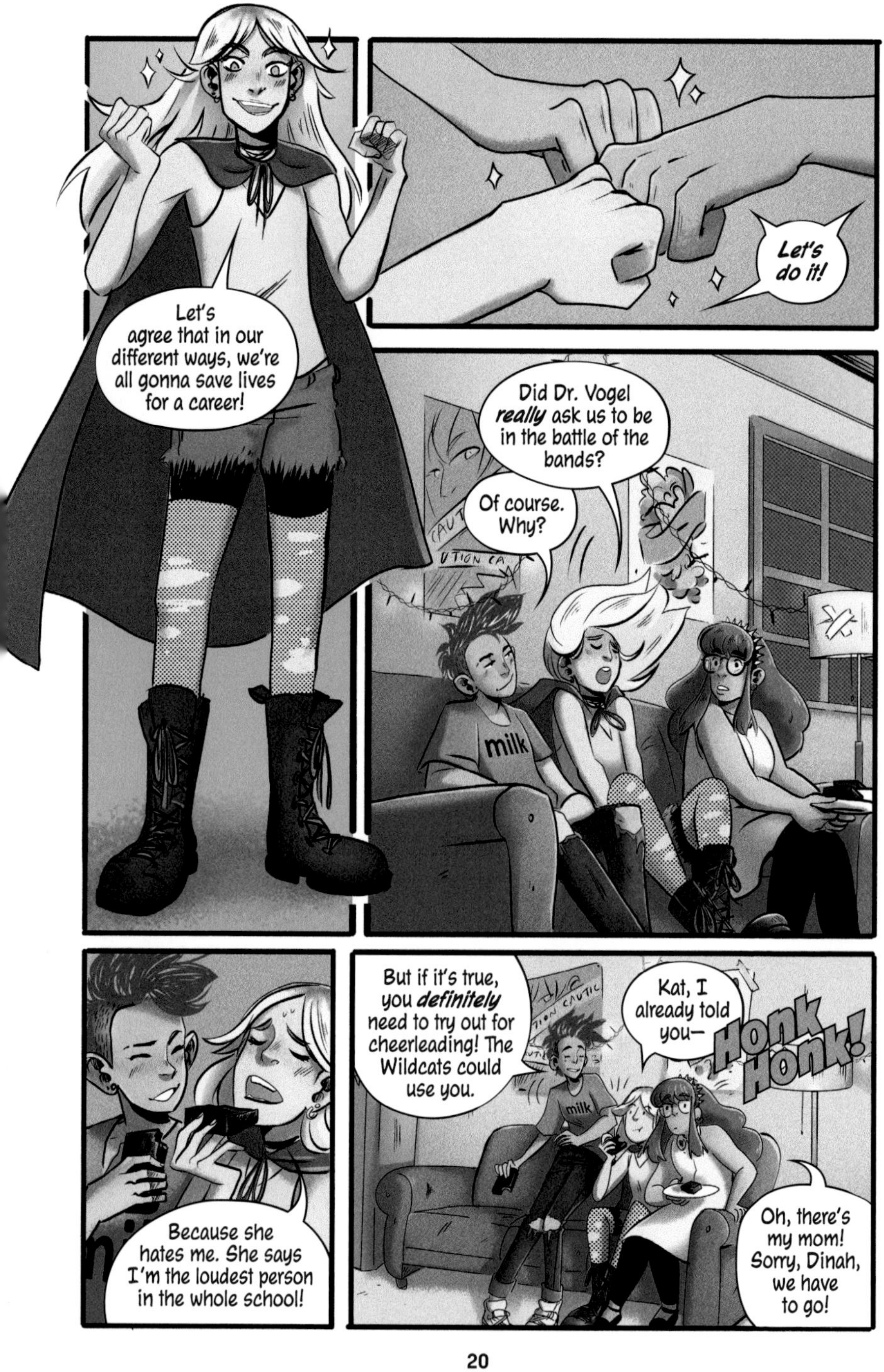
Let's agree that in our different ways, we're all gonna save lives for a career!
Let's do it!
Did Dr. Vogel *really* ask us to be in the battle of the bands?
Of course. Why?
Because she hates me. She says I'm the loudest person in the whole school!
But if it's true, you *definitely* need to try out for cheerleading! The Wildcats could use you.
Kat, I already told you—
HONK HONK!
Oh, there's my mom! Sorry, Dinah, we have to go!
milk

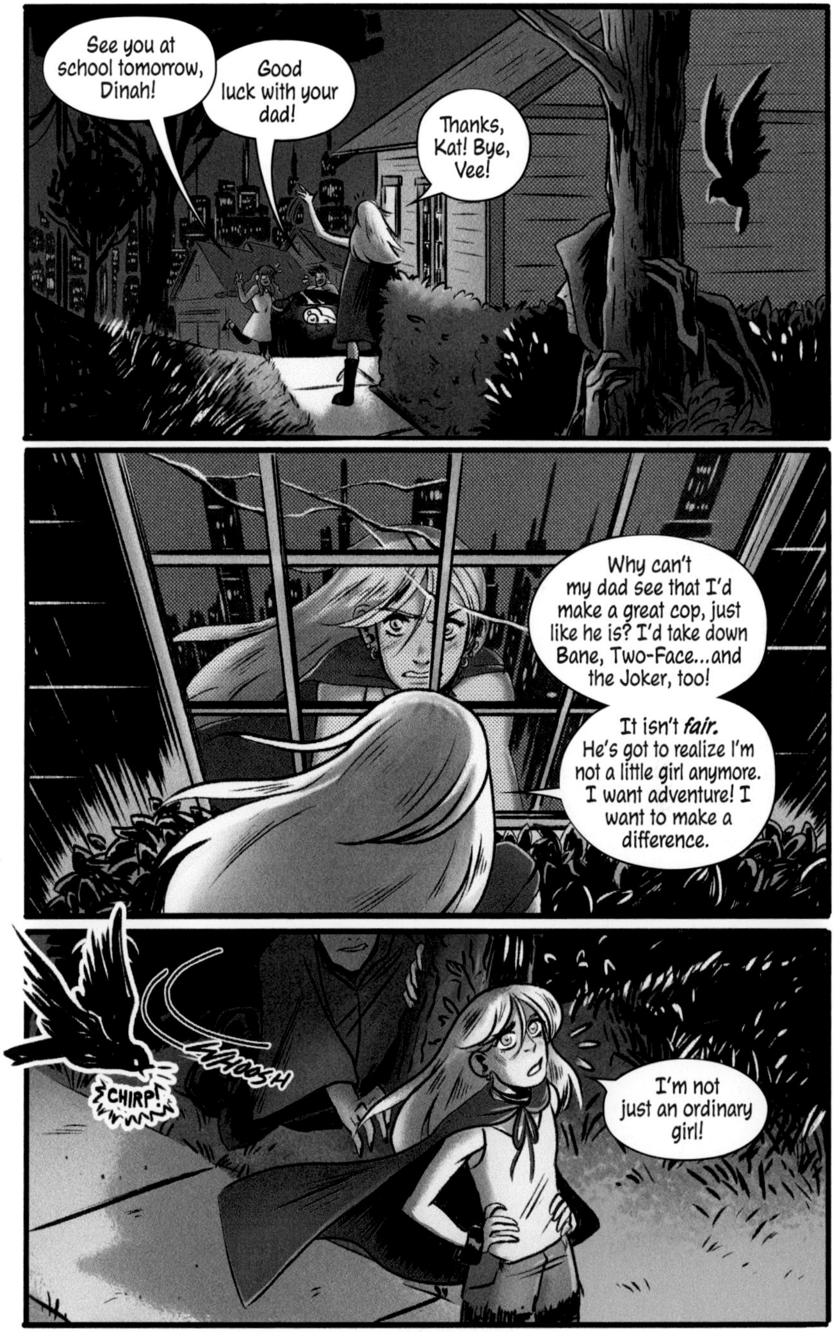
See you at school tomorrow, Dinah!
Good luck with your dad!
Thanks, Kat! Bye, Vee!
Why can't my dad see that I'd make a great cop, just like he is? I'd take down Bane, Two-Face...and the Joker, too!
It isn't *fair.* He's got to realize I'm not a little girl anymore. I want adventure! I want to make a difference.
CHIRP!
WHOOSH
I'm not just an ordinary girl!

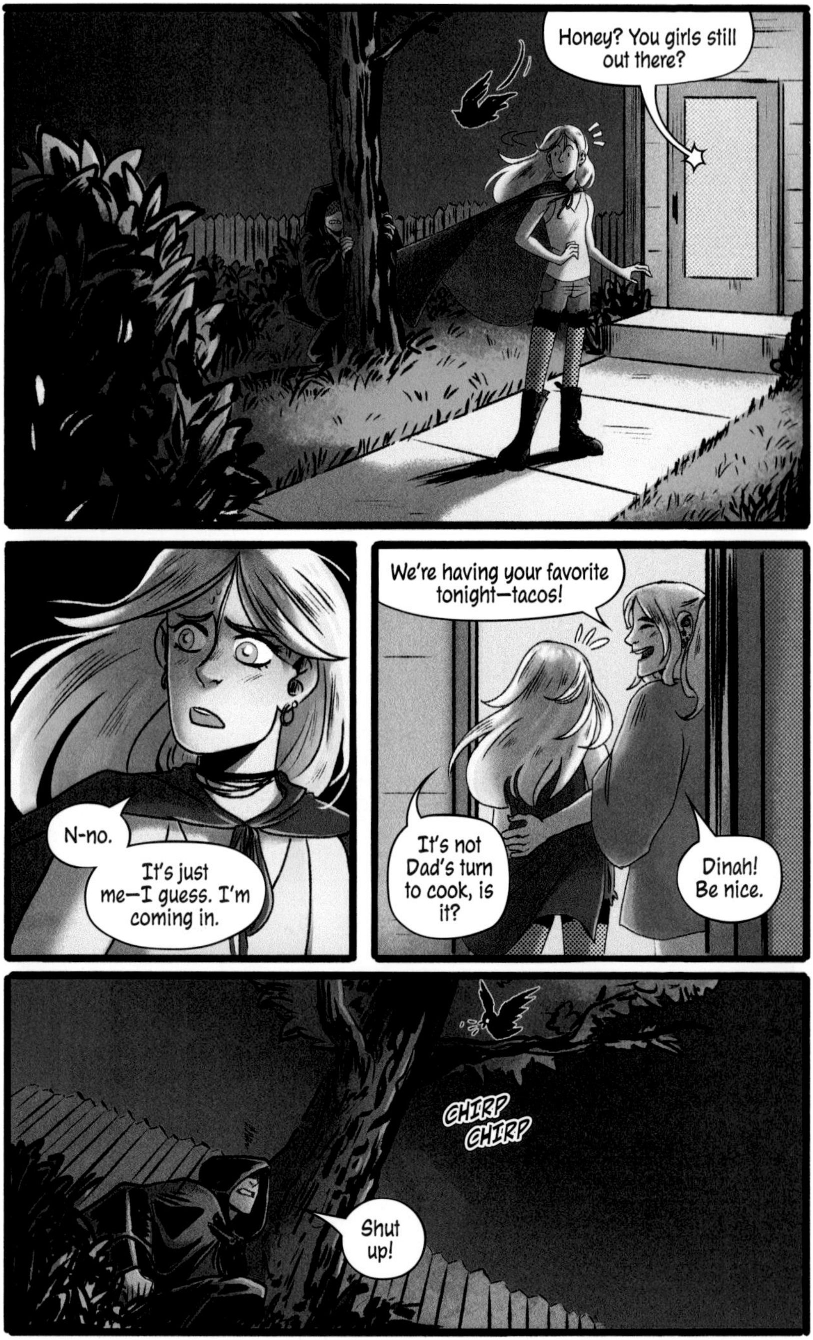
Honey? You girls still out there?
N-no.
It's just me—I guess. I'm coming in.
We're having your favorite tonight—tacos!
It's not Dad's turn to cook, is it?
Dinah! Be nice.
CHIRP CHIRP
Shut up!

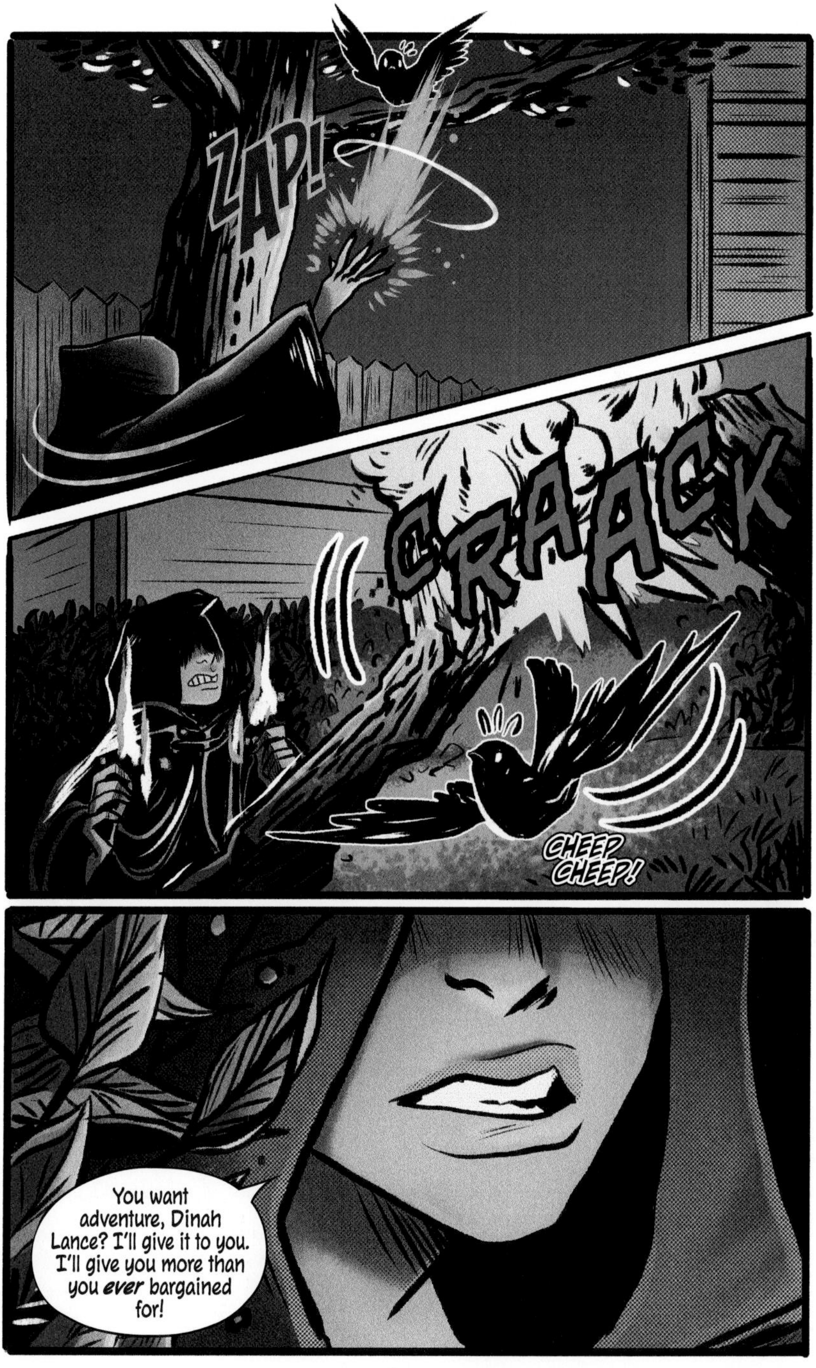
ZAP!
CRAACK
CHEEP CHEEP!
You want adventure, Dinah Lance? I'll give it to you. I'll give you more than you *ever* bargained for!

CHAPTER 2
DON'T WANNA HURT NOBODY

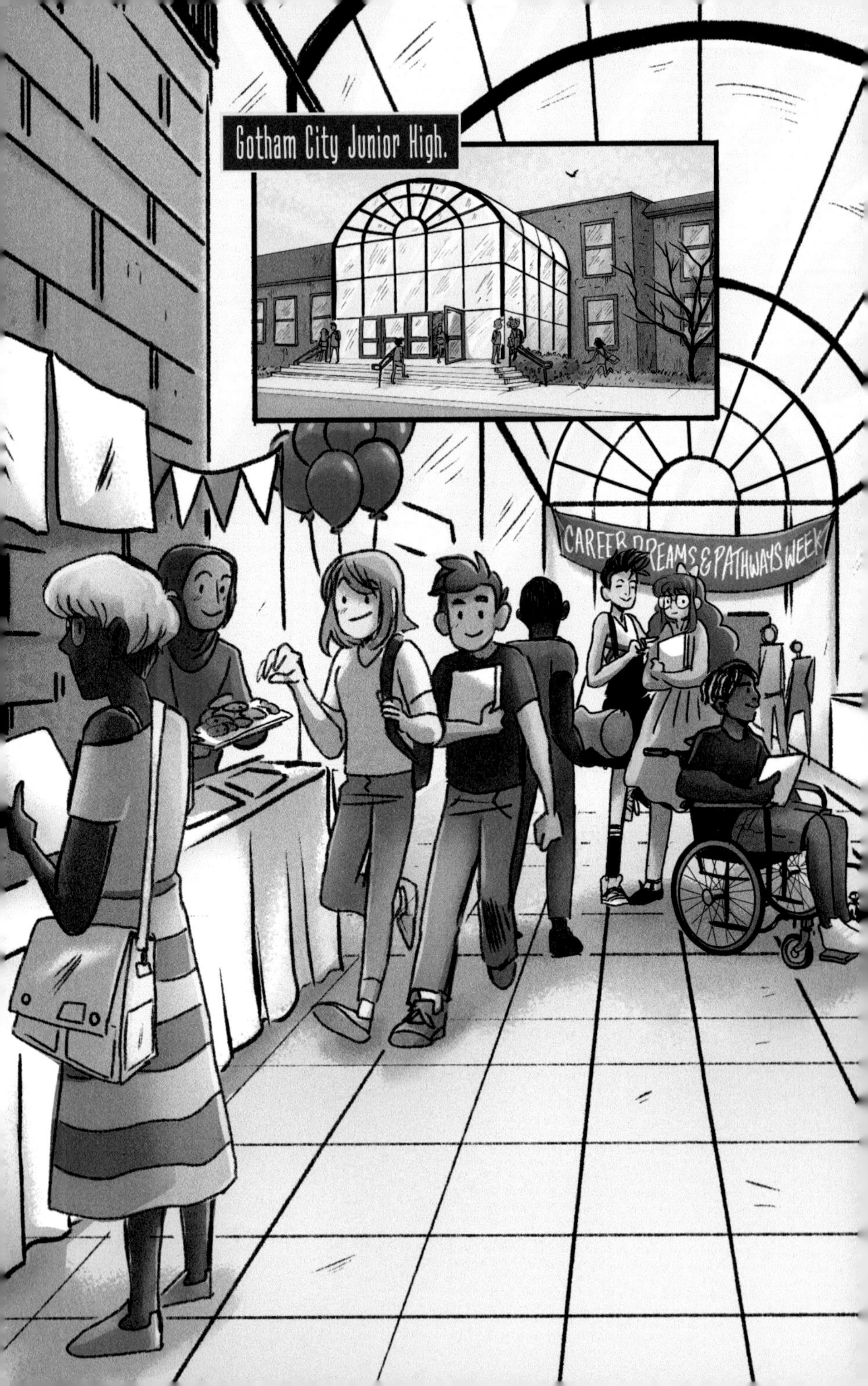
Gotham City Junior High.
CAREER DREAMS & PATHWAYS WEEK

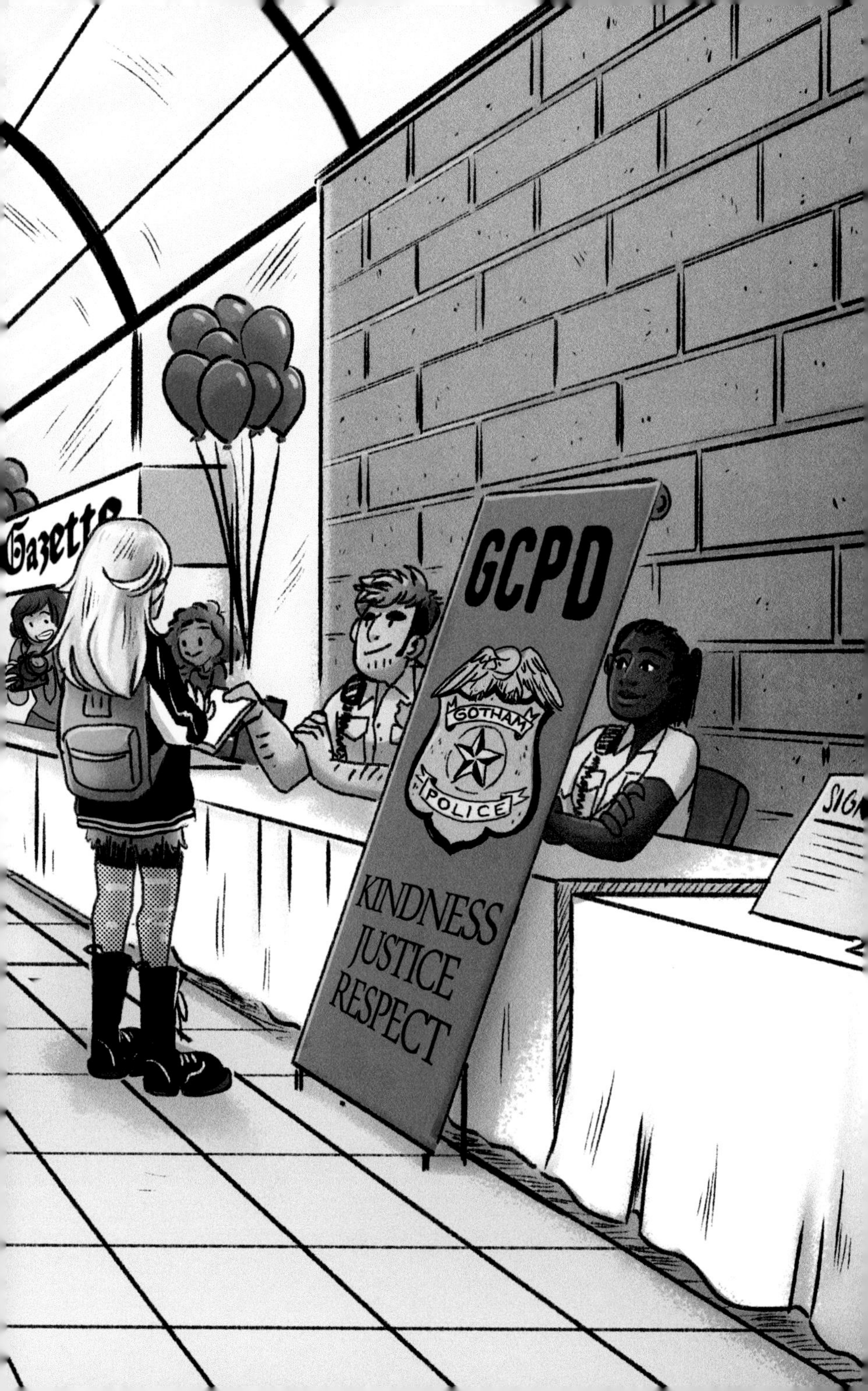
Gazette
GCPD
GOTHAM
POLICE
KINDNESS
JUSTICE
RESPECT

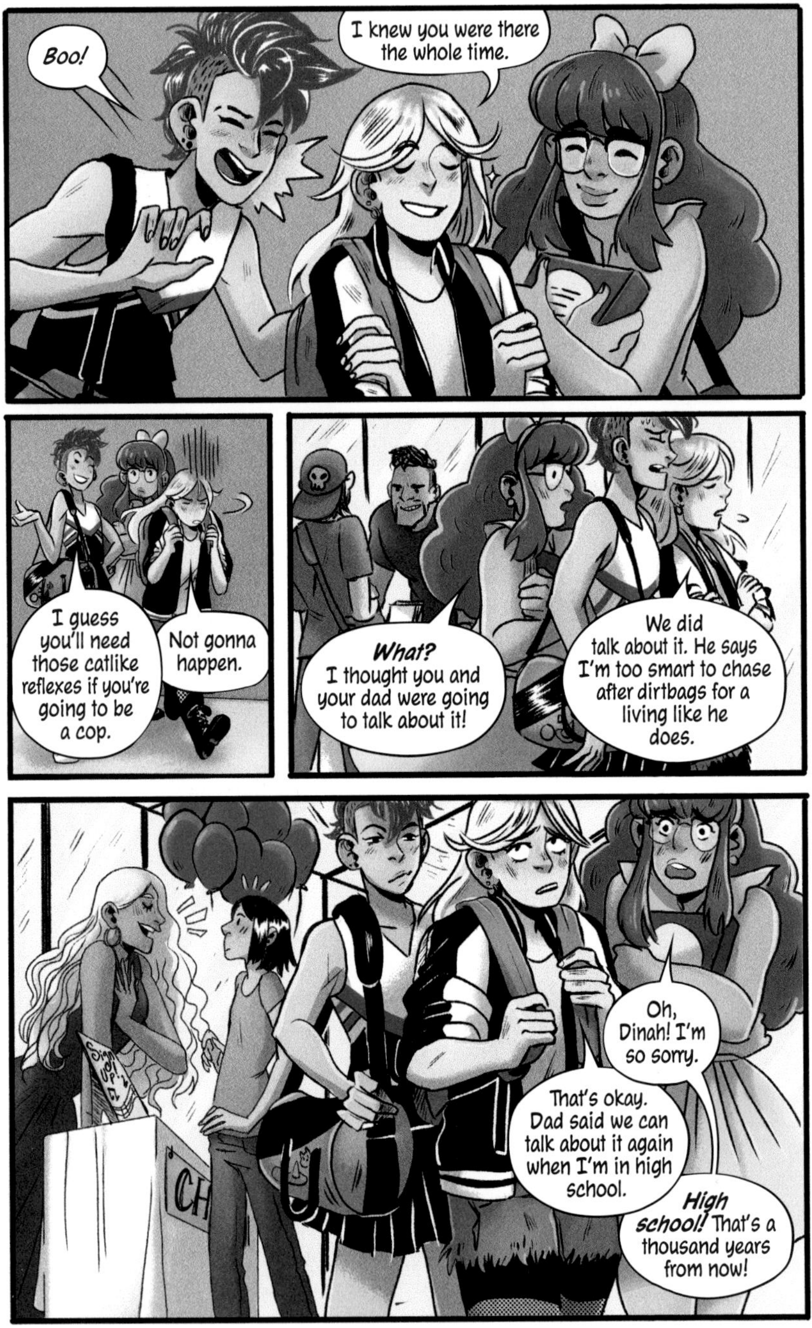
Boo!
I knew you were there the whole time.
I guess you'll need those catlike reflexes if you're going to be a cop.
Not gonna happen.
What? I thought you and your dad were going to talk about it!
We did talk about it. He says I'm too smart to chase after dirtbags for a living like he does.
Oh, Dinah! I'm so sorry.
That's okay. Dad said we can talk about it again when I'm in high school.
High school! That's a thousand years from now!

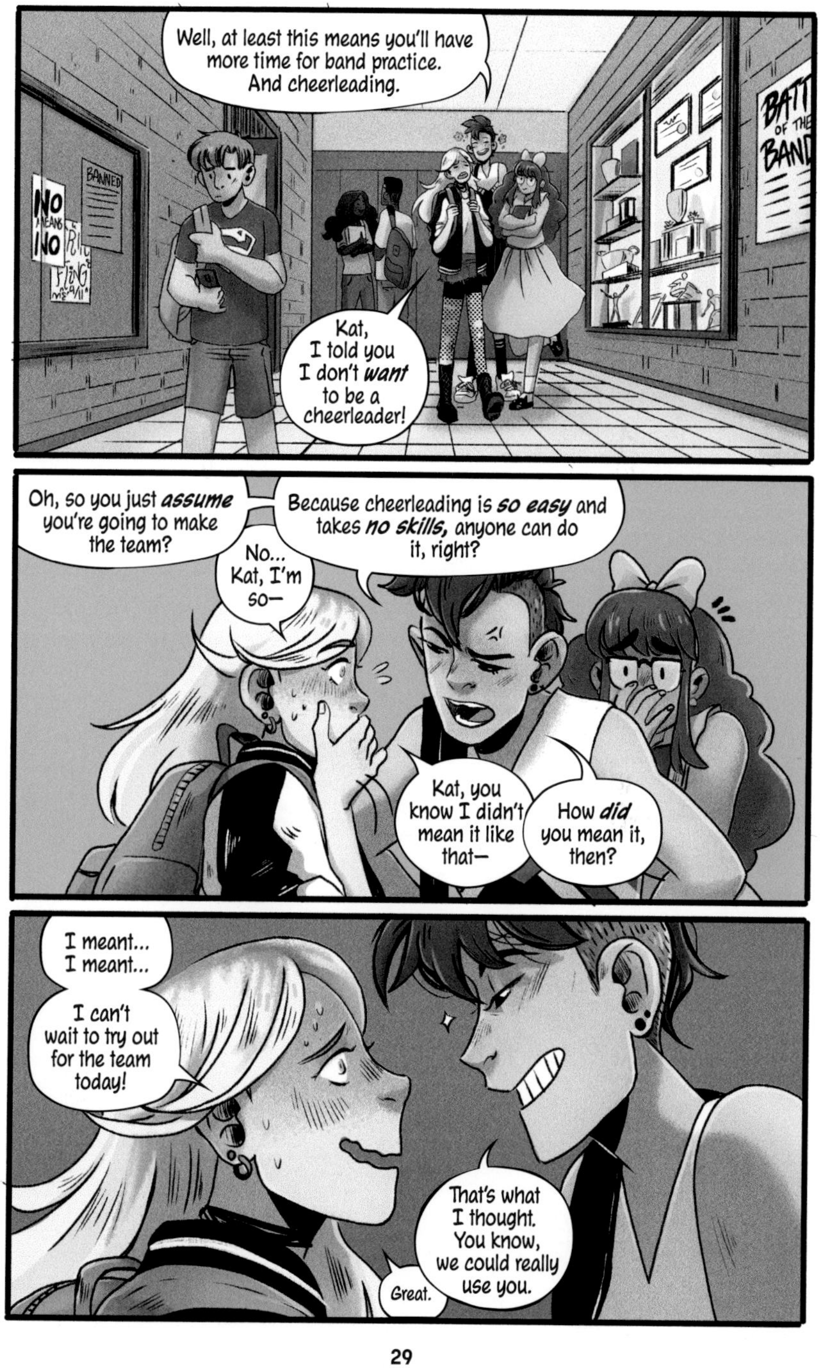

Well, at least this means you'll have more time for band practice. And cheerleading.
Kat, I told you I don't *want* to be a cheerleader!
Oh, so you just *assume* you're going to make the team?
Because cheerleading is *so easy* and takes *no skills,* anyone can do it, right?
No... Kat, I'm so—
Kat, you know I didn't mean it like that—
How *did* you mean it, then?
I meant... I meant...
I can't wait to try out for the team today!
That's what I thought. You know, we could really use you.
Great.

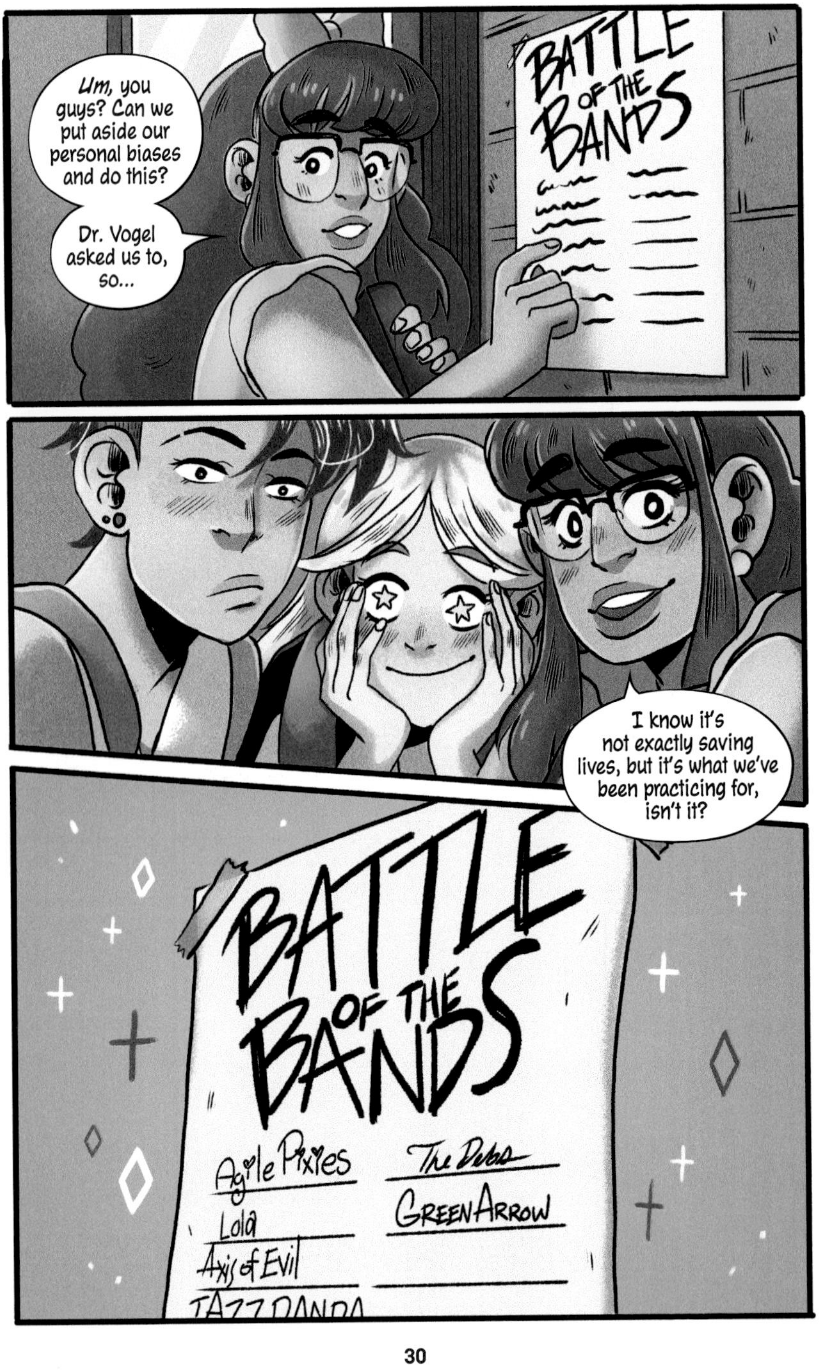
Um, you guys? Can we put aside our personal biases and do this?
Dr. Vogel asked us to, so...
BATTLE OF THE BANDS
I know it's not exactly saving lives, but it's what we've been practicing for, isn't it?
BATTLE OF THE BANDS
Agile Pixies
The Debs
Lola
Green Arrow
Axis of Evil

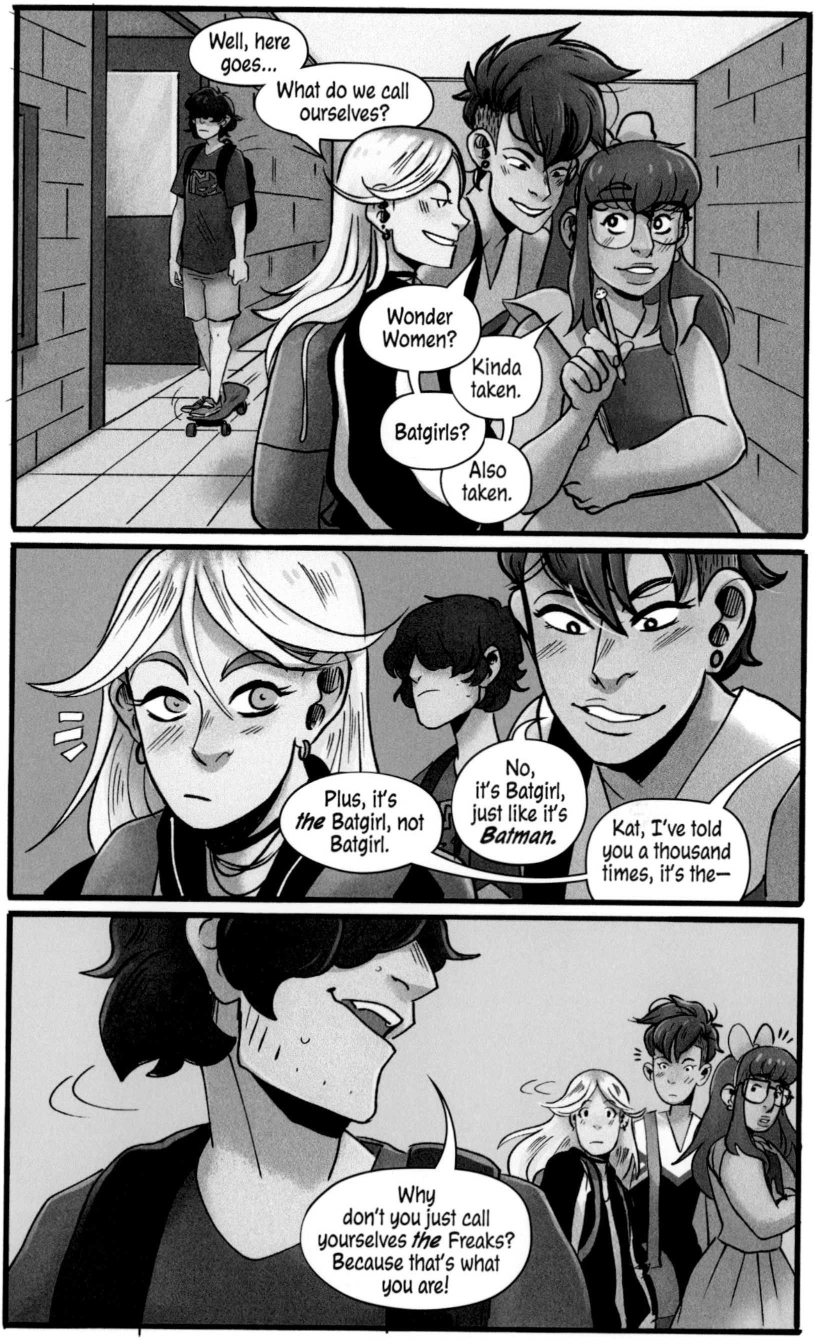
Well, here goes...
What do we call ourselves?
Wonder Women?
Kinda taken.
Batgirls?
Also taken.
Kat, I've told you a thousand times, it's the—
No, it's Batgirl, just like it's *Batman.*
Plus, it's *the* Batgirl, not Batgirl.
Why don't you just call yourselves *the* Freaks? Because that's what you are!

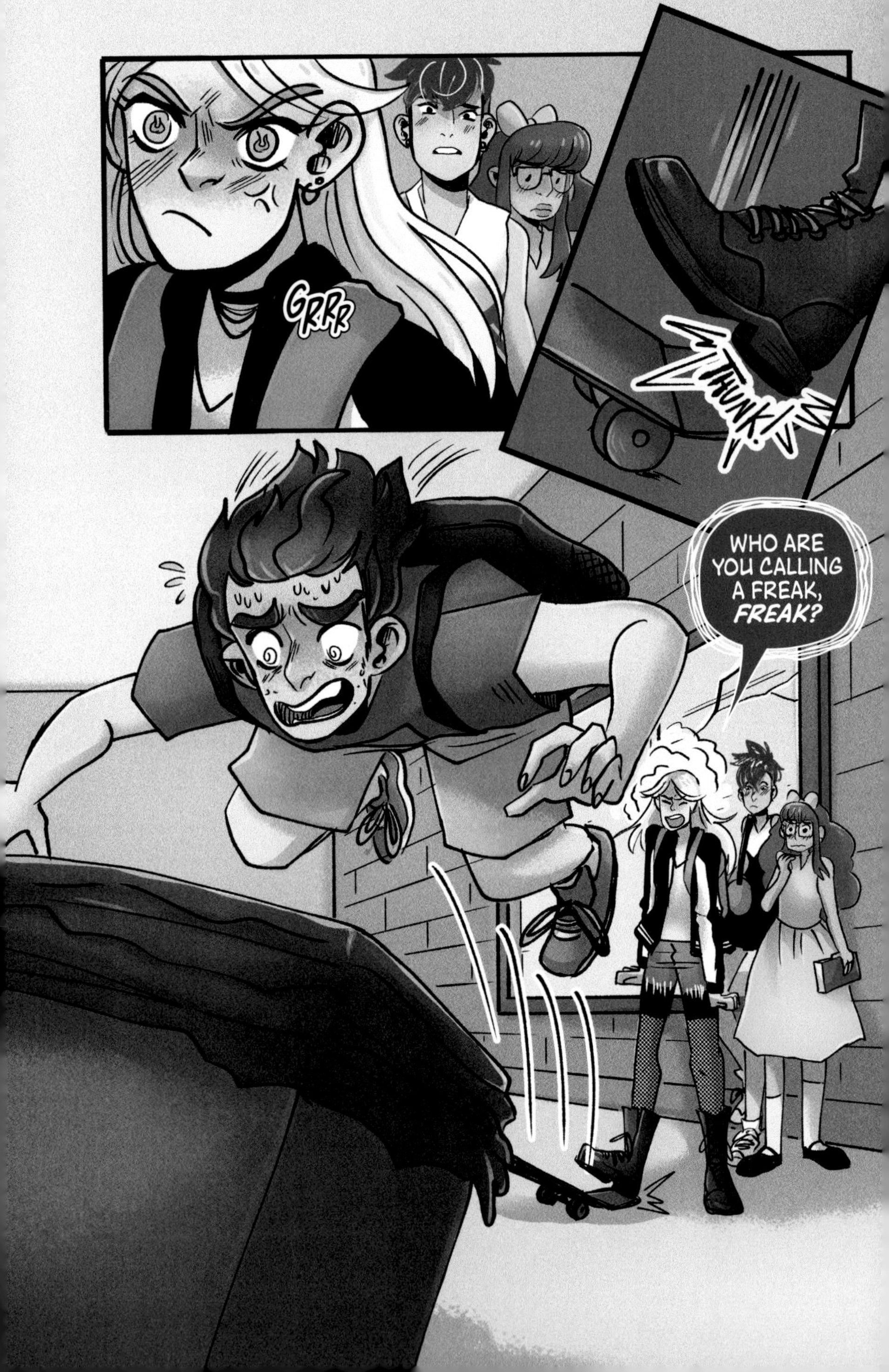
GRRR
THUNK!
WHO ARE YOU CALLING A FREAK, *FREAK?*

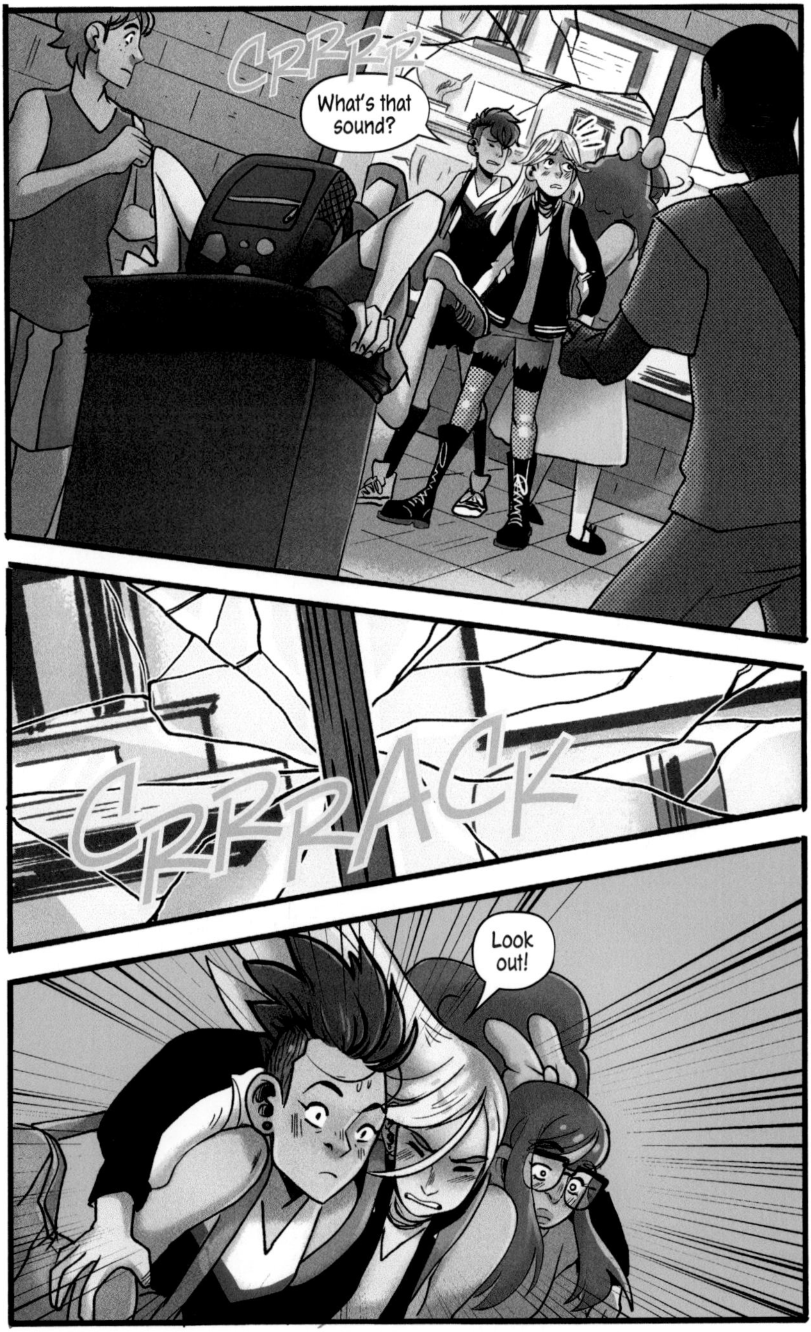
CRRRR
What's that sound?
CRRRACK
Look out!

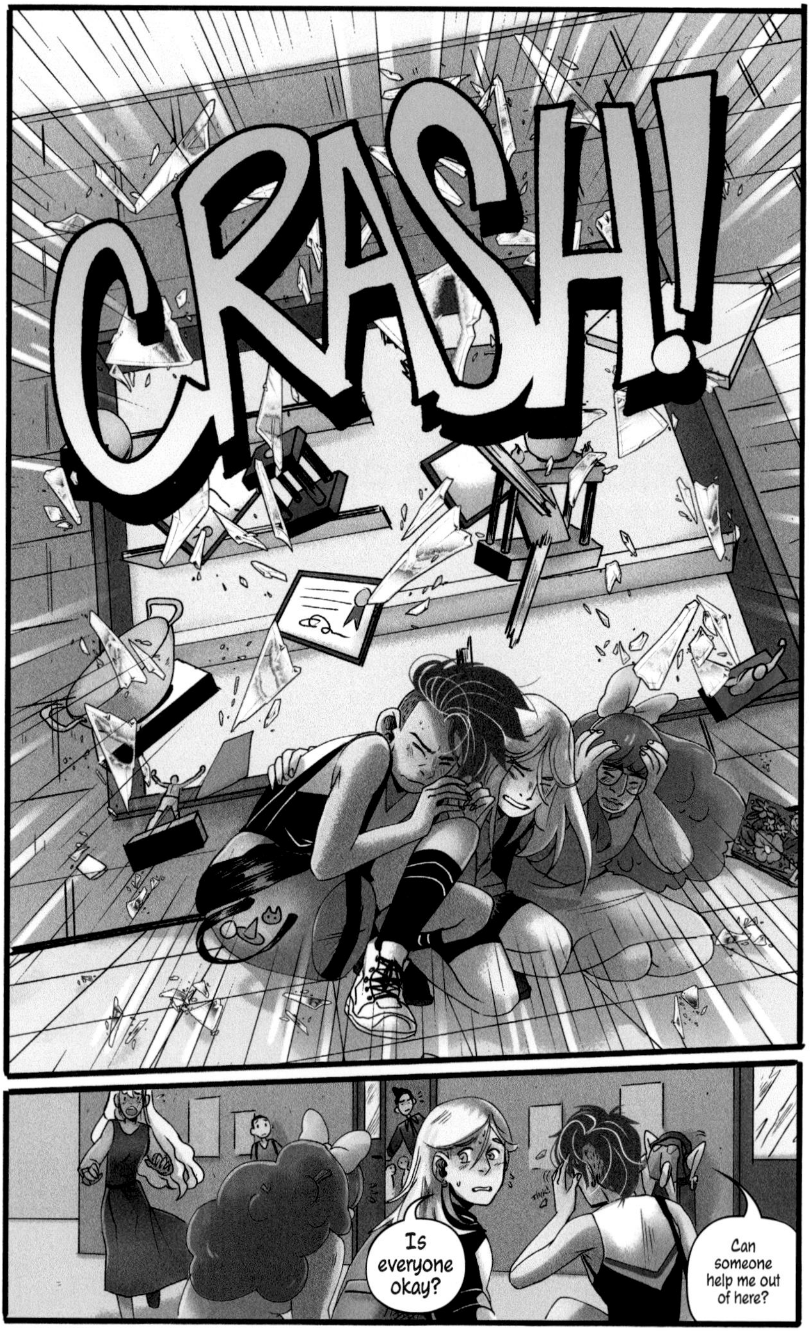
CRASH!
Is everyone okay?
Can someone help me out of here?

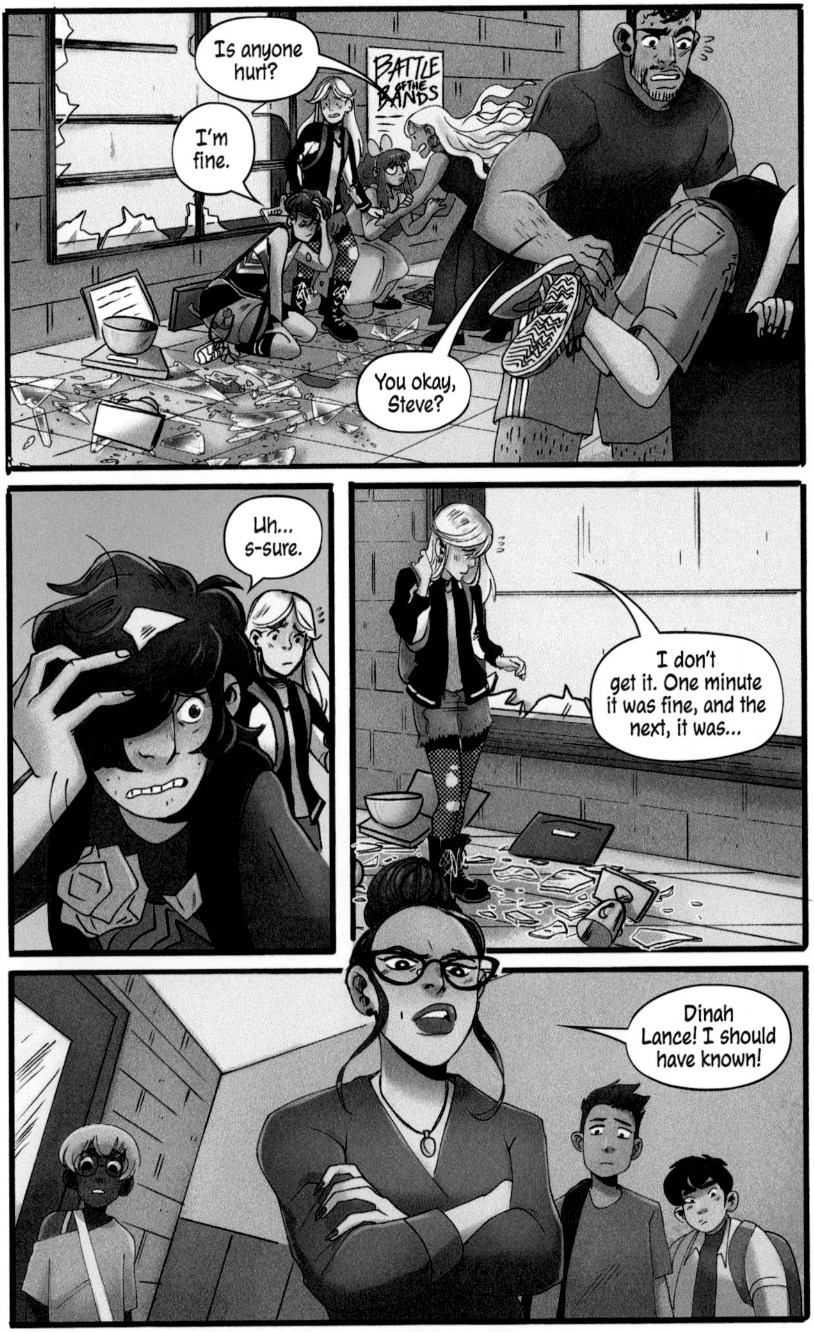
Is anyone hurt?
BATTLE OF THE BANDS
I'm fine.
You okay, Steve?
Uh... s-sure.
I don't get it. One minute it was fine, and the next, it was...
Dinah Lance! I should have known!

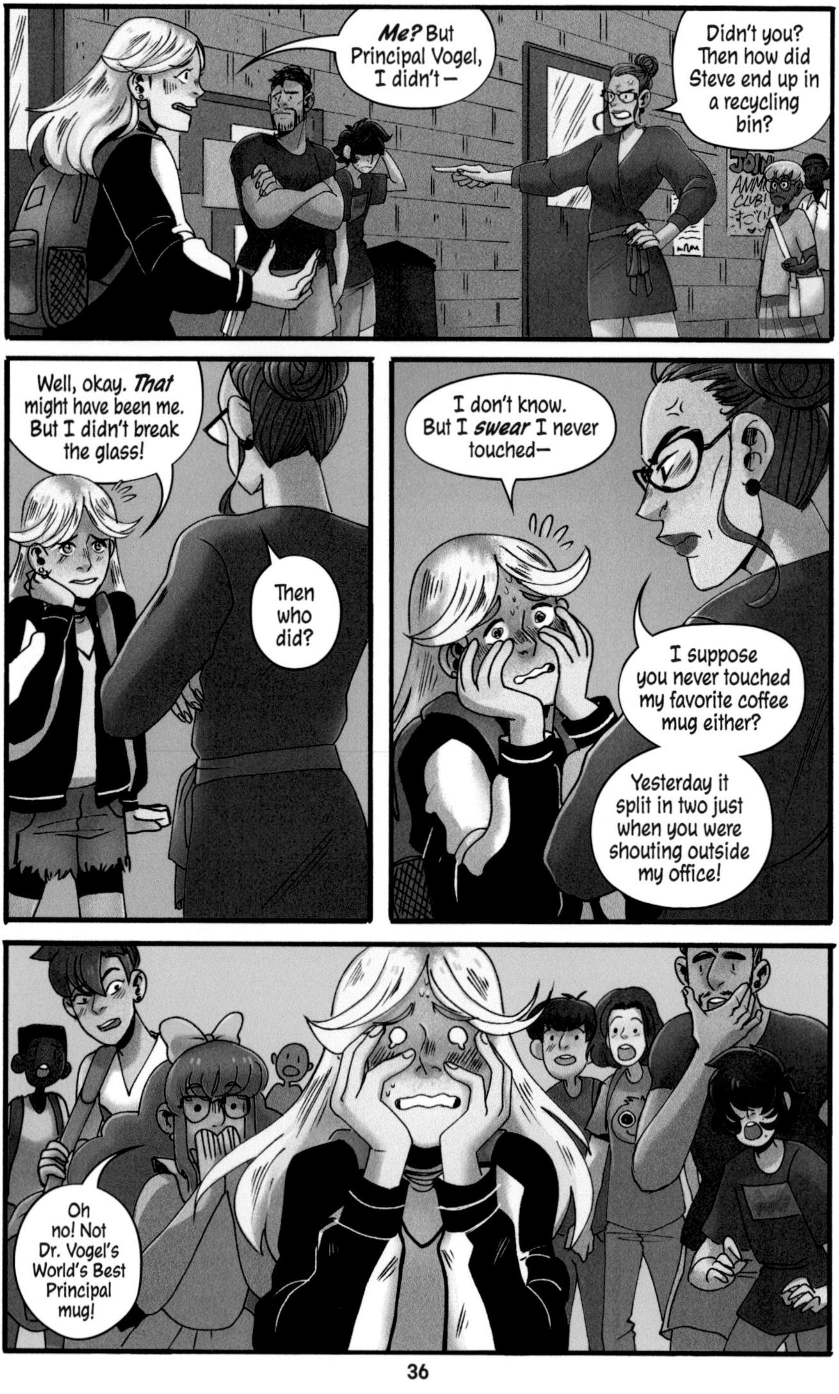
Me? But Principal Vogel, I didn't—
Didn't you? Then how did Steve end up in a recycling bin?
Well, okay. *That* might have been me. But I didn't break the glass!
Then who did?
I don't know. But I *swear* I never touched—
I suppose you never touched my favorite coffee mug either?
Yesterday it split in two just when you were shouting outside my office!
Oh no! Not Dr. Vogel's World's Best Principal mug!

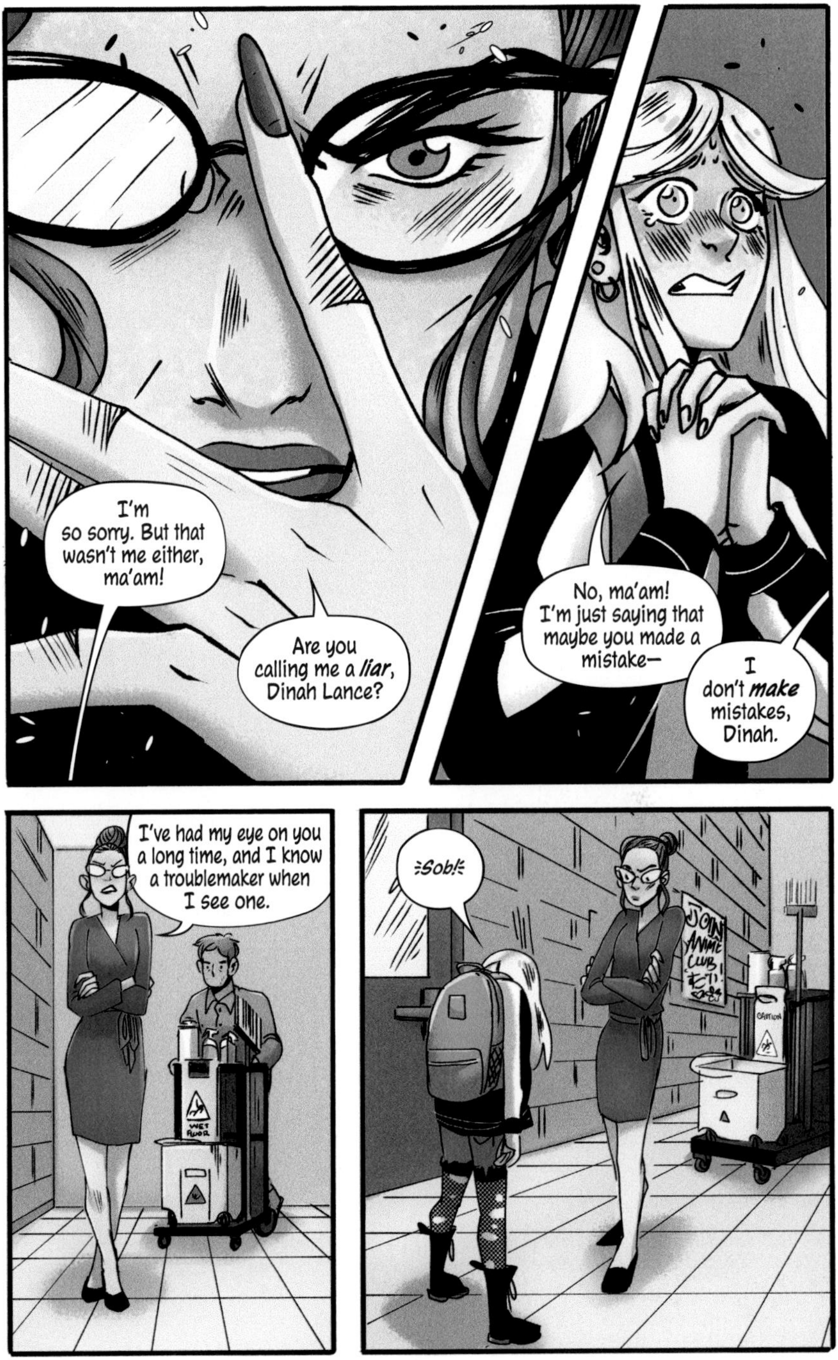
Are you calling me a *liar*, Dinah Lance?
I'm so sorry. But that wasn't me either, ma'am!
No, ma'am! I'm just saying that maybe you made a mistake—
I don't ***make*** mistakes, Dinah.
I've had my eye on you a long time, and I know a troublemaker when I see one.
WET FLOOR
Sob!
JOIN ANIME CLUB!
CAUTION

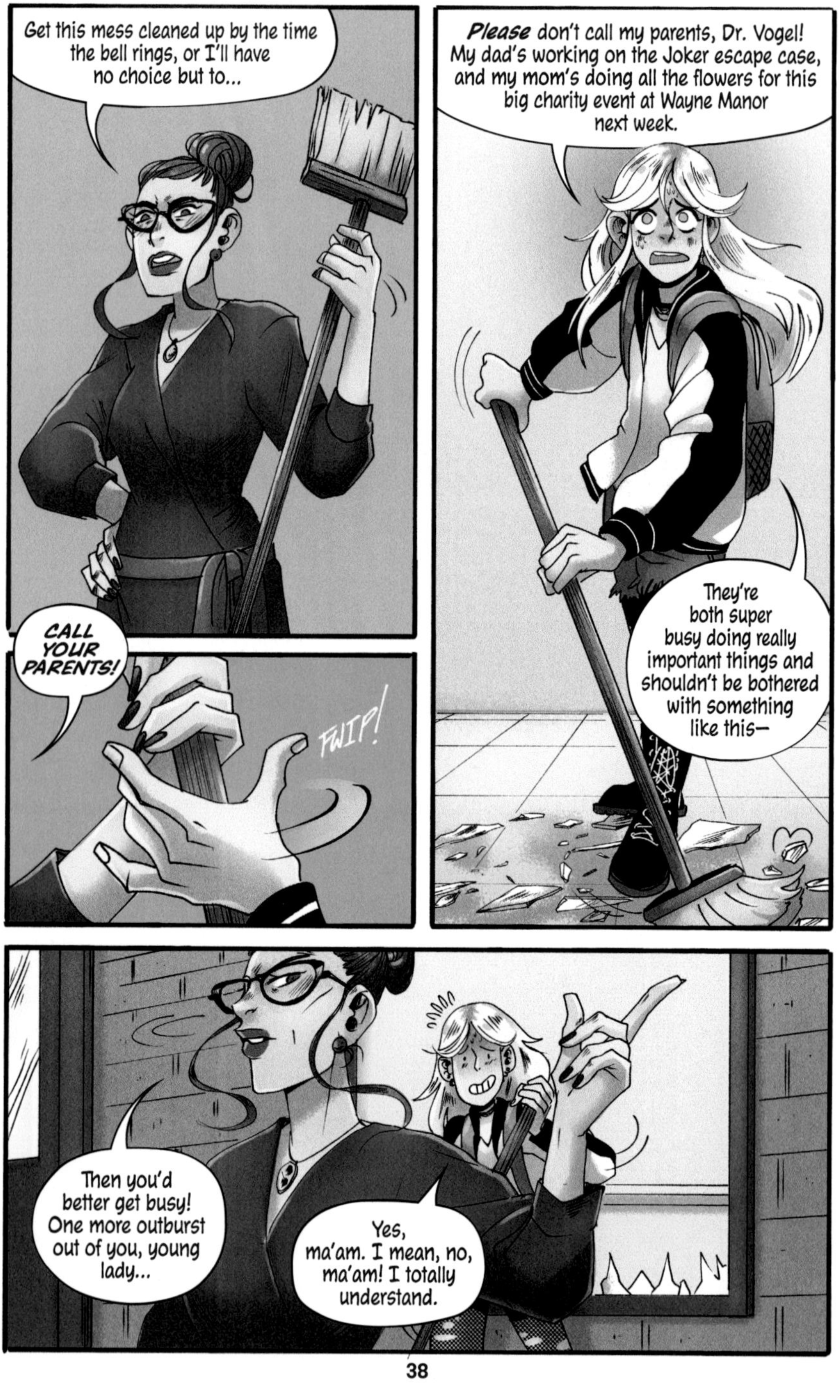
Get this mess cleaned up by the time the bell rings, or I'll have no choice but to...
CALL YOUR PARENTS!
FWIP!
Please don't call my parents, Dr. Vogel! My dad's working on the Joker escape case, and my mom's doing all the flowers for this big charity event at Wayne Manor next week.
They're both super busy doing really important things and shouldn't be bothered with something like this—
Then you'd better get busy! One more outburst out of you, young lady...
Yes, ma'am. I mean, no, ma'am! I totally understand.

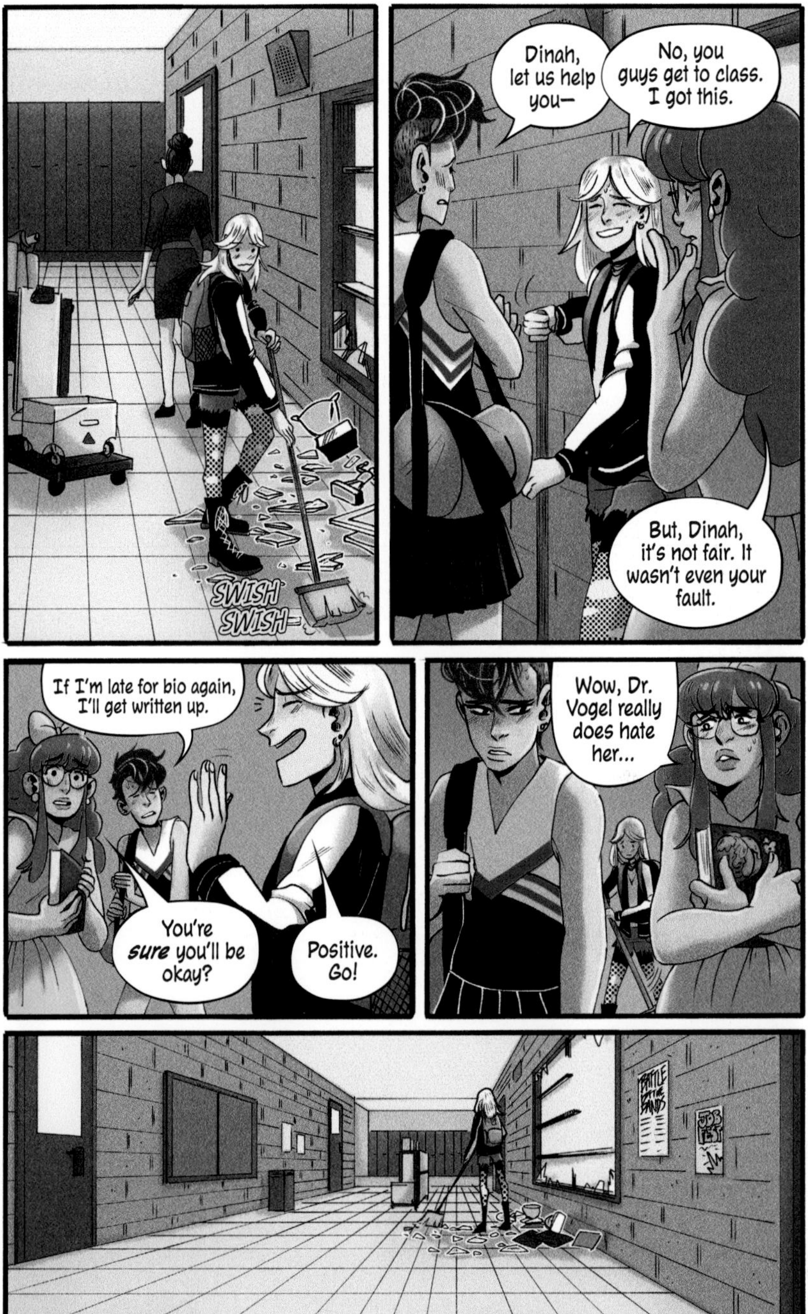
SWISH
SWISH
Dinah, let us help you—
No, you guys get to class. I got this.
But, Dinah, it's not fair. It wasn't even your fault.
If I'm late for bio again, I'll get written up.
You're *sure* you'll be okay?
Positive. Go!
Wow, Dr. Vogel really does hate her...
BATTLE OF THE BANDS
JOB FEST

CHAPTER 3
WATCH OUT!
WE'RE IN FOR STORMY WEATHER

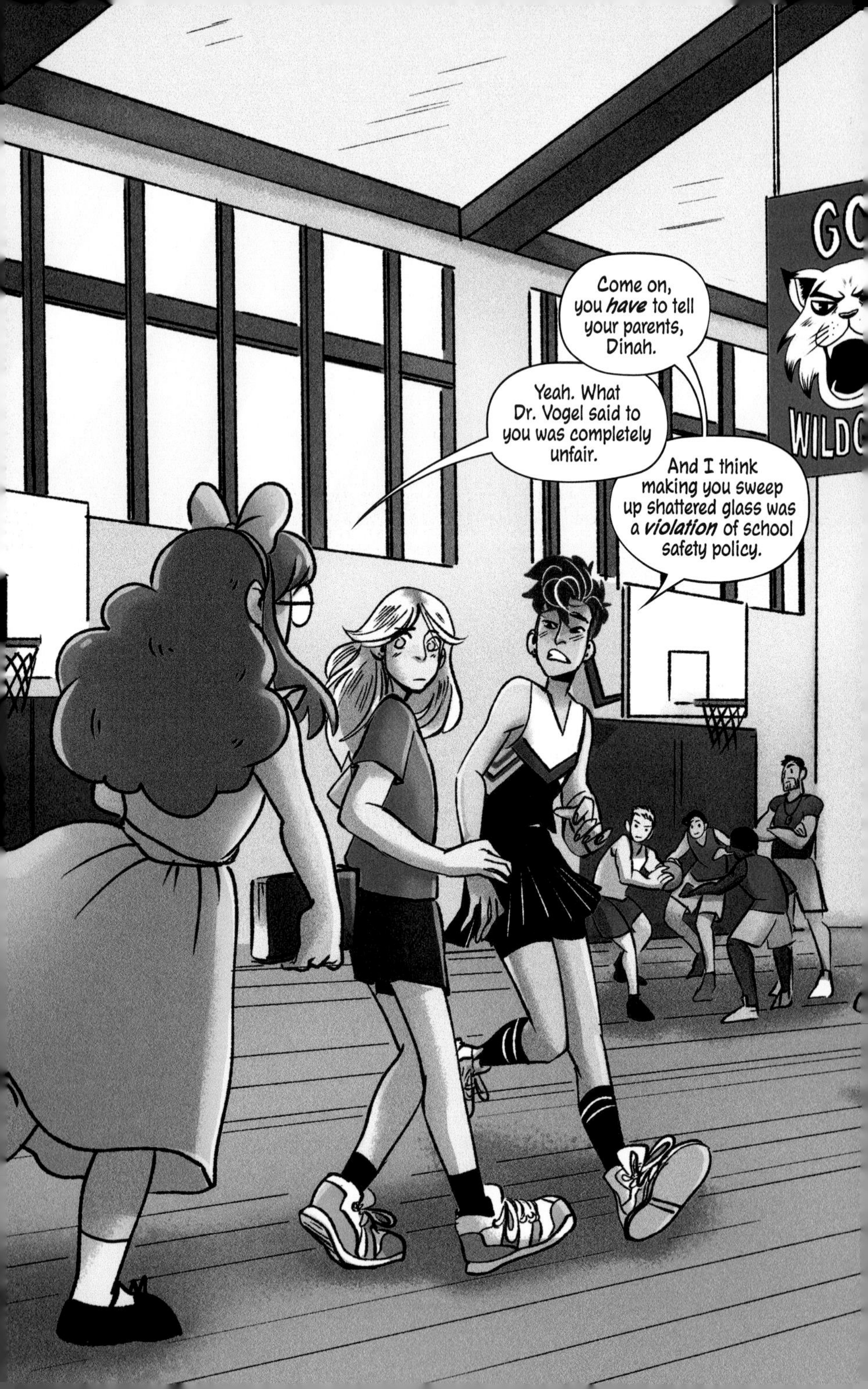
GO
WILDC
Come on, you *have* to tell your parents, Dinah.
Yeah. What Dr. Vogel said to you was completely unfair.
And I think making you sweep up shattered glass was a *violation* of school safety policy.

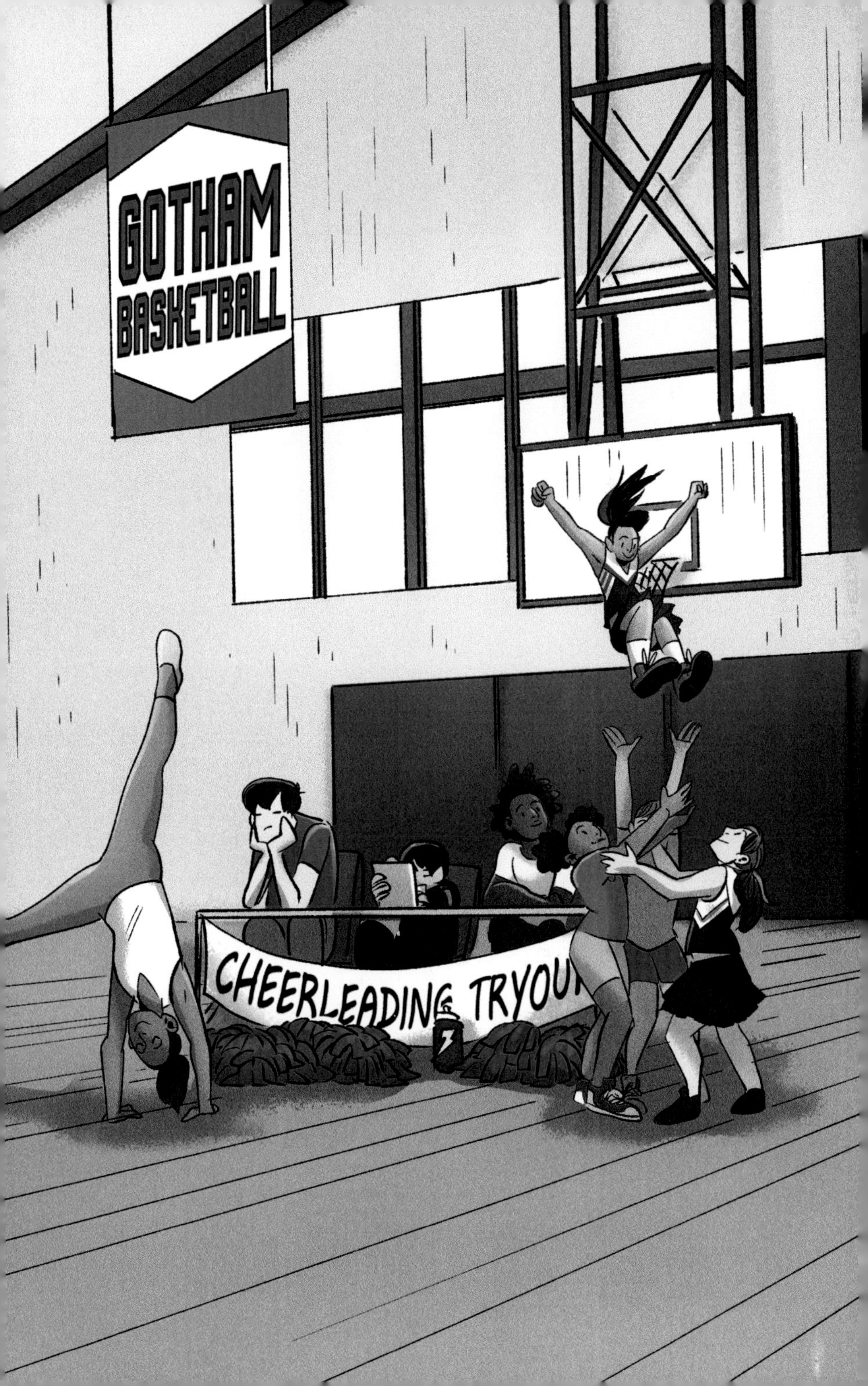
GOTHAM BASKETBALL
CHEERLEADING TRYOU

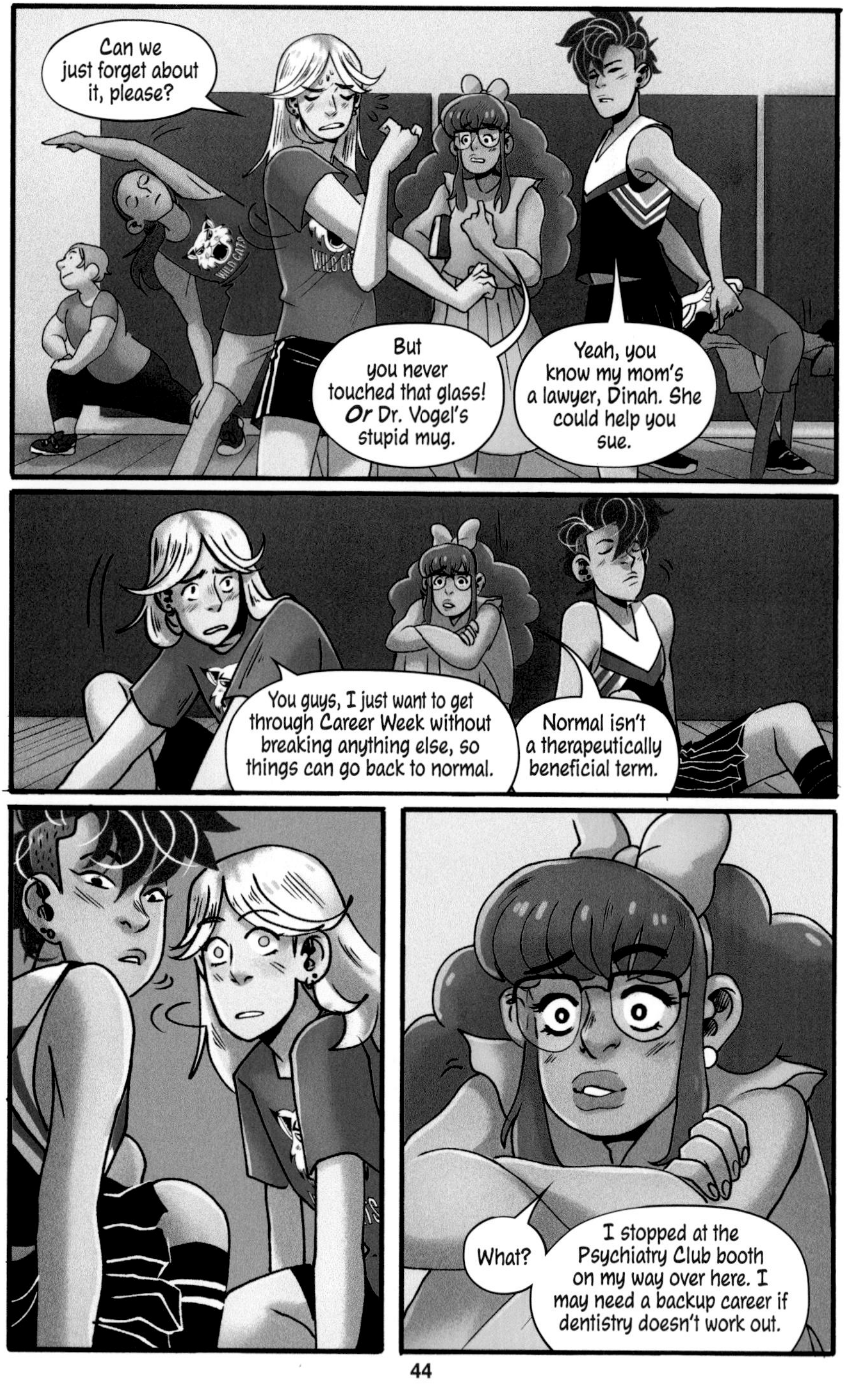

Can we just forget about it, please?
But you never touched that glass! *Or* Dr. Vogel's stupid mug.
Yeah, you know my mom's a lawyer, Dinah. She could help you sue.
You guys, I just want to get through Career Week without breaking anything else, so things can go back to normal.
Normal isn't a therapeutically beneficial term.
What?
I stopped at the Psychiatry Club booth on my way over here. I may need a backup career if dentistry doesn't work out.

breee!!

Who's that?

That's Coach Choi! She decides who makes the team.

She looks scary.

She really does. I'm glad I'm not trying out today.

Gee, thanks.

CHEERLEADING TRYOUTS

WILDCATS

When I call your name, get in line.

Maybe you won't have to go first, Dinah.

I hope not!

WILDCATS

45

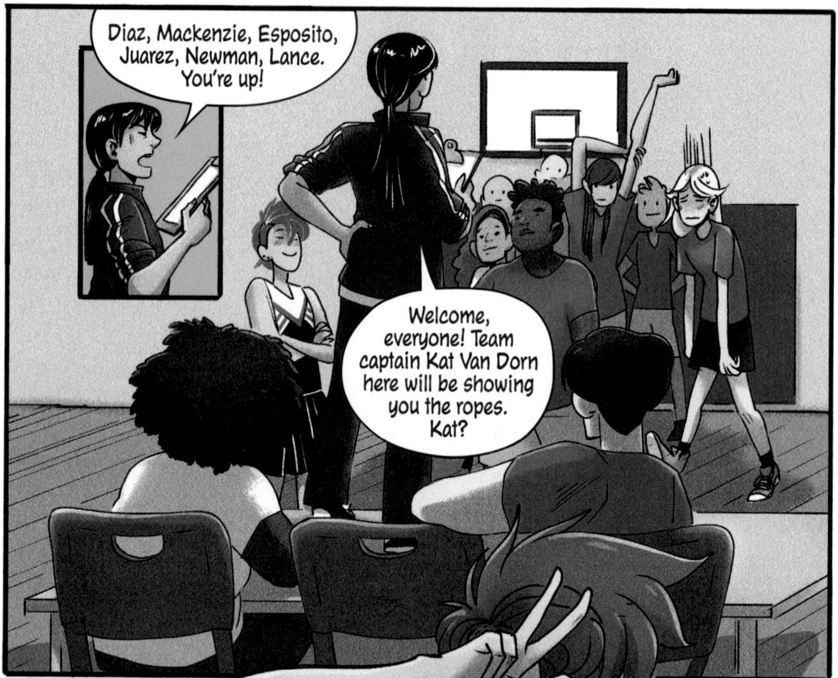
Diaz, Mackenzie, Esposito, Juarez, Newman, Lance. You're up!
Welcome, everyone! Team captain Kat Van Dorn here will be showing you the ropes. Kat?

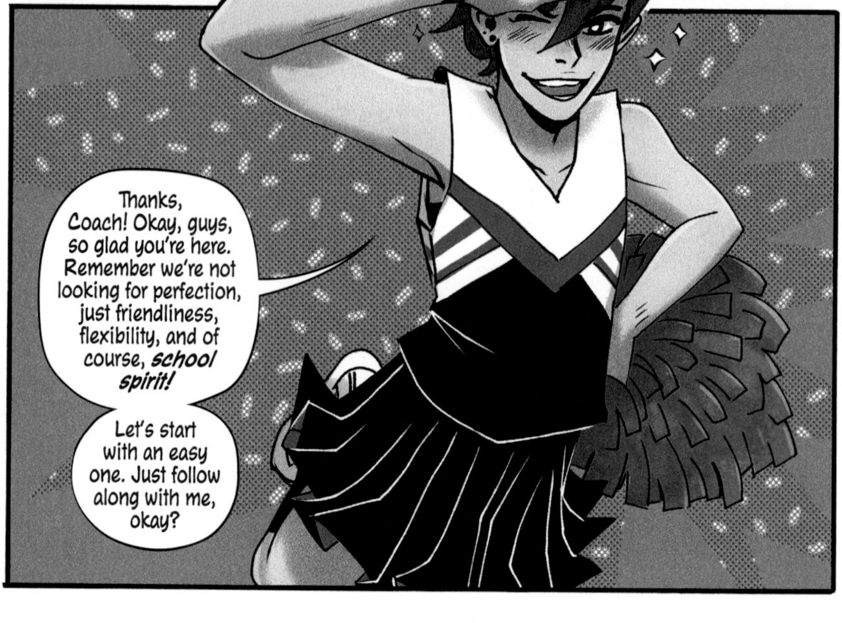
Thanks, Coach! Okay, guys, so glad you're here. Remember we're not looking for perfection, just friendliness, flexibility, and of course, *school spirit!*
Let's start with an easy one. Just follow along with me, okay?

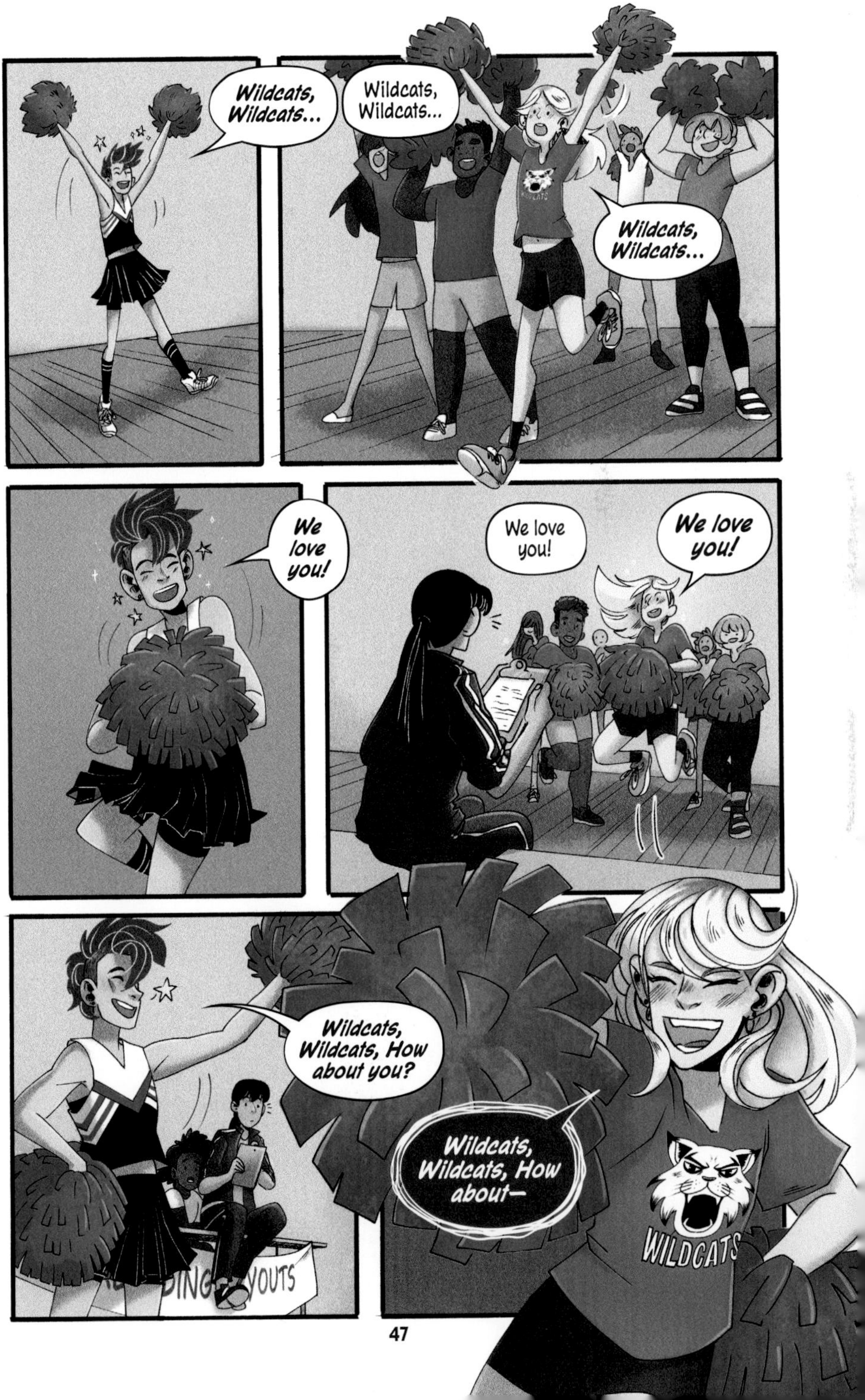
Wildcats, Wildcats...
Wildcats, Wildcats...
Wildcats, Wildcats...
We love you!
We love you!
We love you!
Wildcats, Wildcats, How about you?
Wildcats, Wildcats, How about–
WILDCATS
DING YOUTS

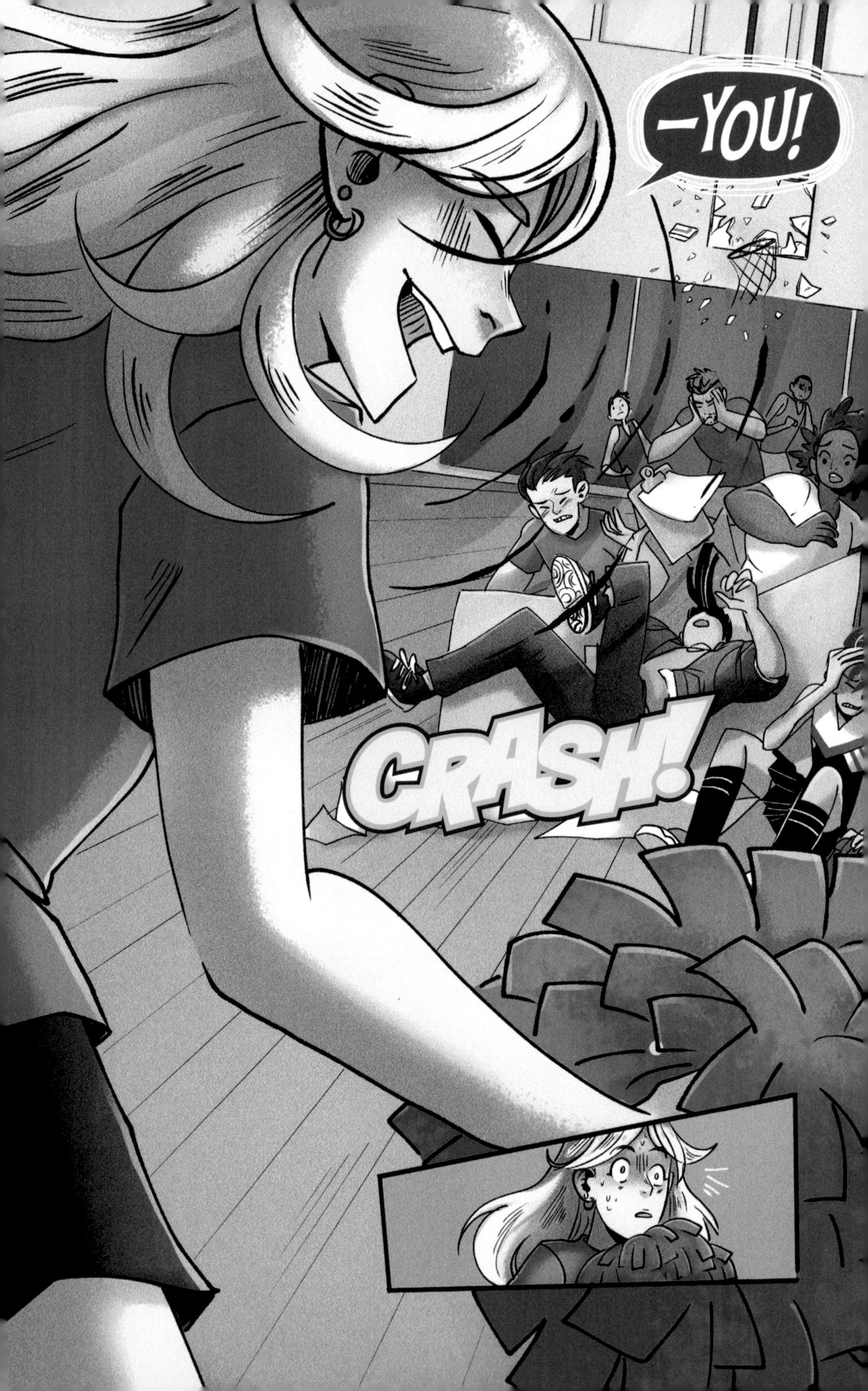
—YOU!
CRASH!

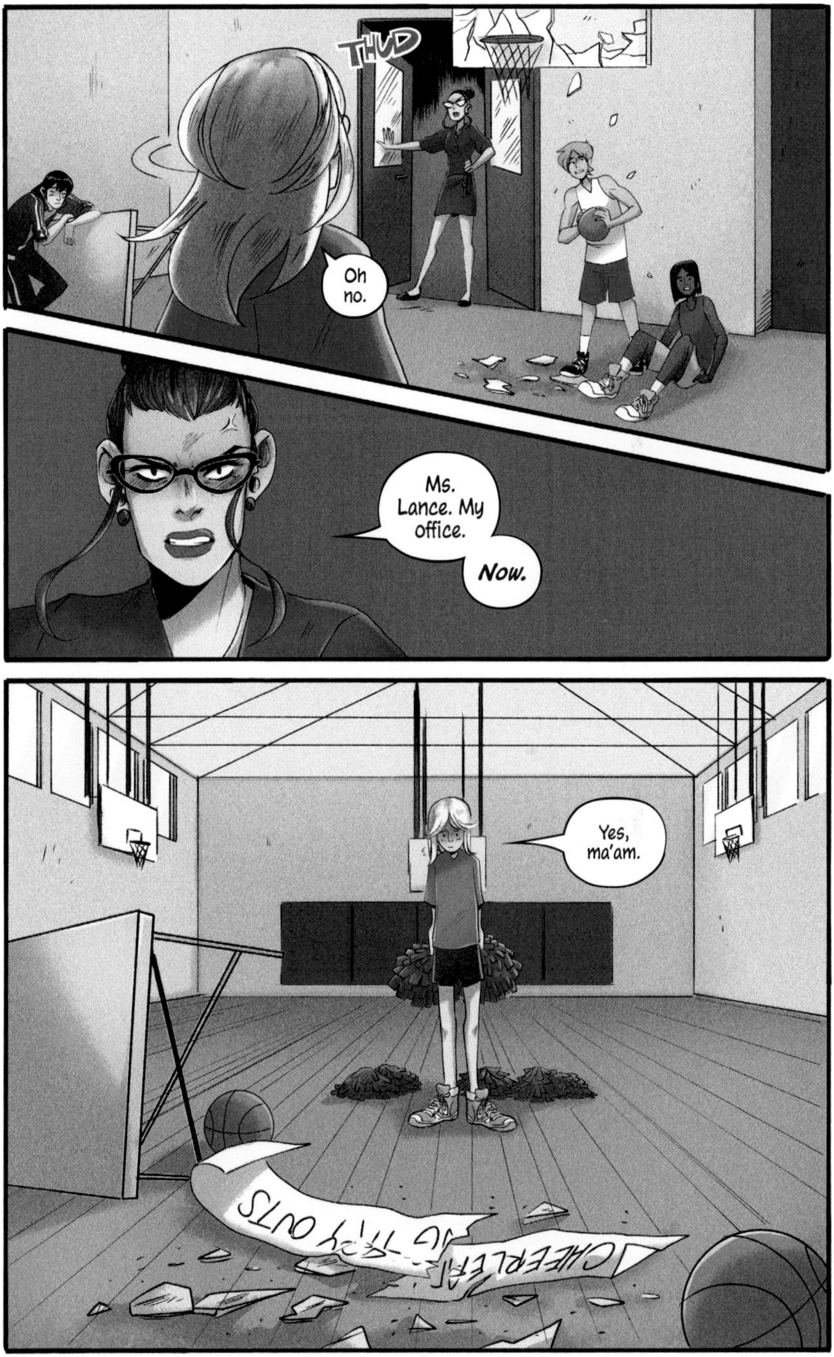
THUD
Oh no.
Ms. Lance. My office.
Now.
Yes, ma'am.

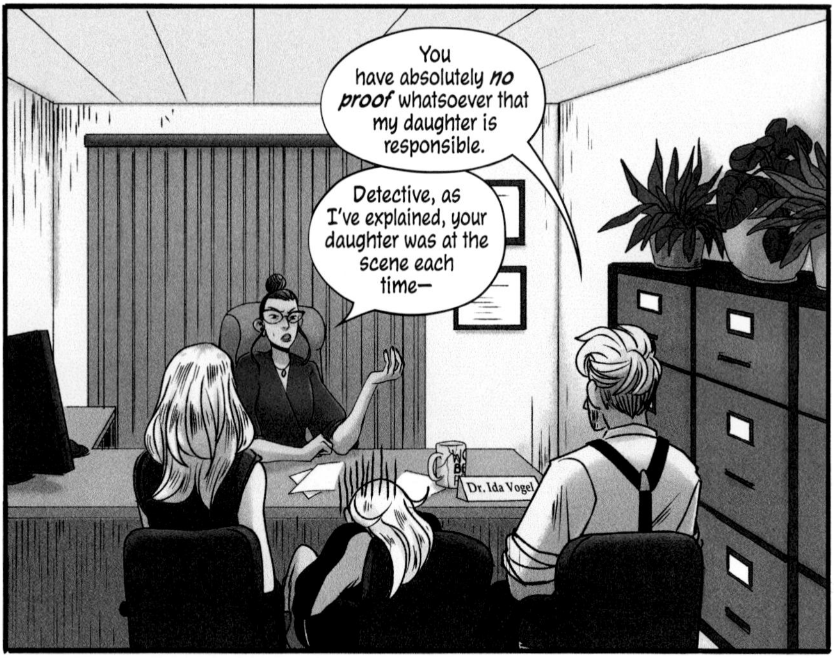
You have absolutely *no proof* whatsoever that my daughter is responsible.
Detective, as I've explained, your daughter was at the scene each time—
Dr. Ida Vogel

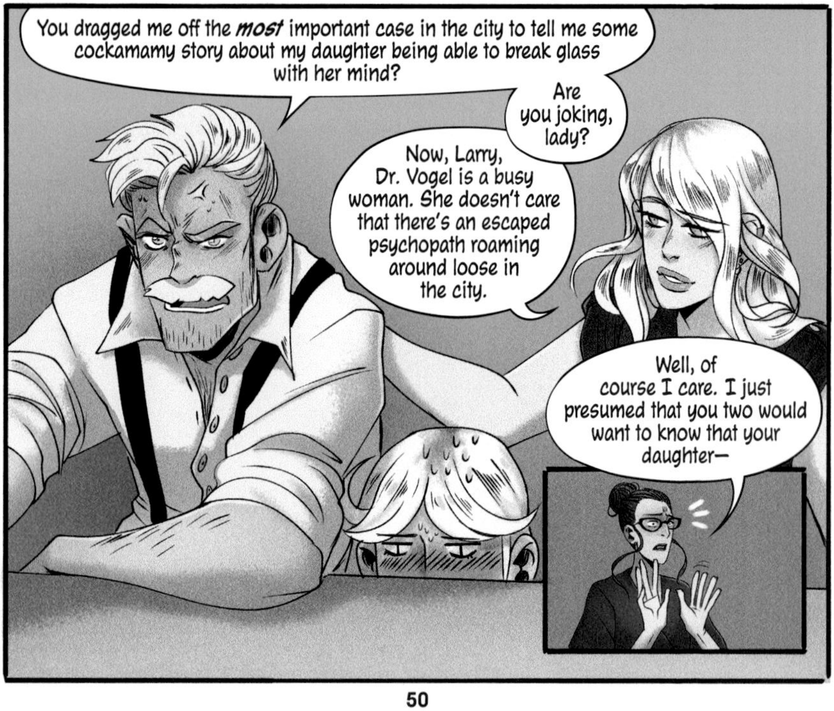
You dragged me off the *most* important case in the city to tell me some cockamamy story about my daughter being able to break glass with her mind?
Are you joking, lady?
Now, Larry, Dr. Vogel is a busy woman. She doesn't care that there's an escaped psychopath roaming around loose in the city.
Well, of course I care. I just presumed that you two would want to know that your daughter—

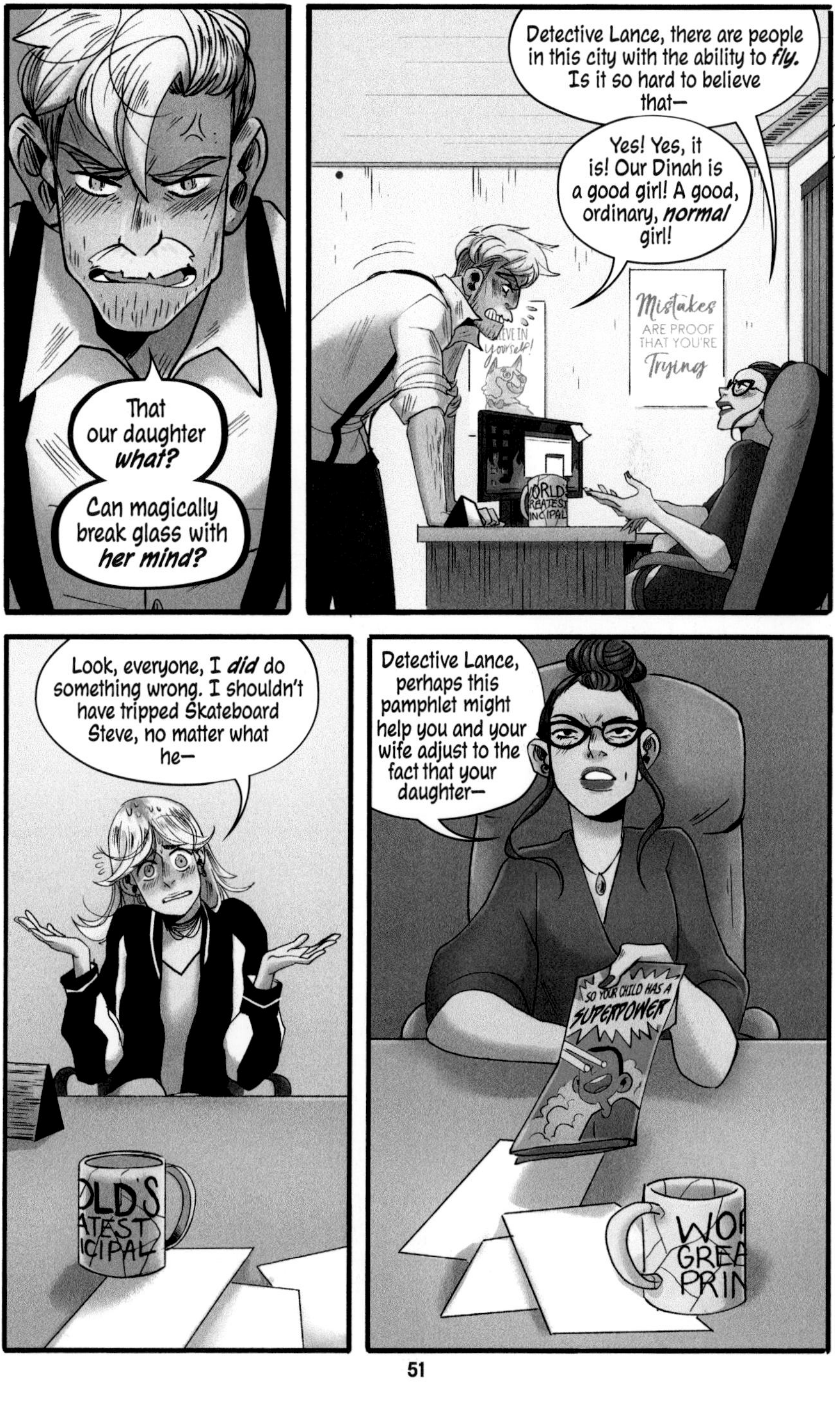
That our daughter *what?*
Can magically break glass with *her mind?*
Detective Lance, there are people in this city with the ability to *fly.* Is it so hard to believe that—
Yes! Yes, it is! Our Dinah is a good girl! A good, ordinary, *normal* girl!
Mistakes ARE PROOF THAT YOU'RE Trying
WORLD'S GREATEST PRINCIPAL
Look, everyone, I *did* do something wrong. I shouldn't have tripped Skateboard Steve, no matter what he—
Detective Lance, perhaps this pamphlet might help you and your wife adjust to the fact that your daughter—
SO YOUR CHILD HAS A SUPERPOWER

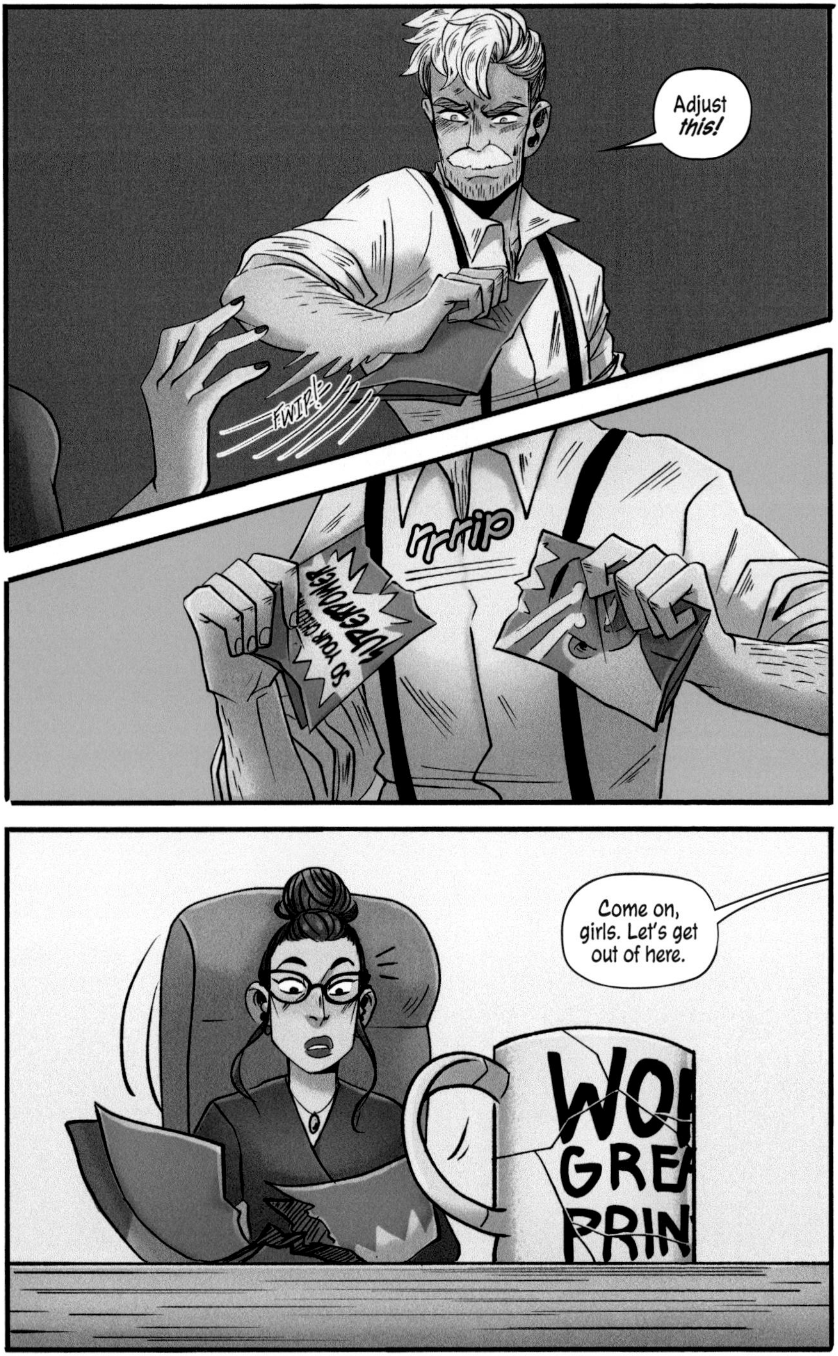
Adjust *this!*
FWIP!
rr-rip
Come on, girls. Let's get out of here.

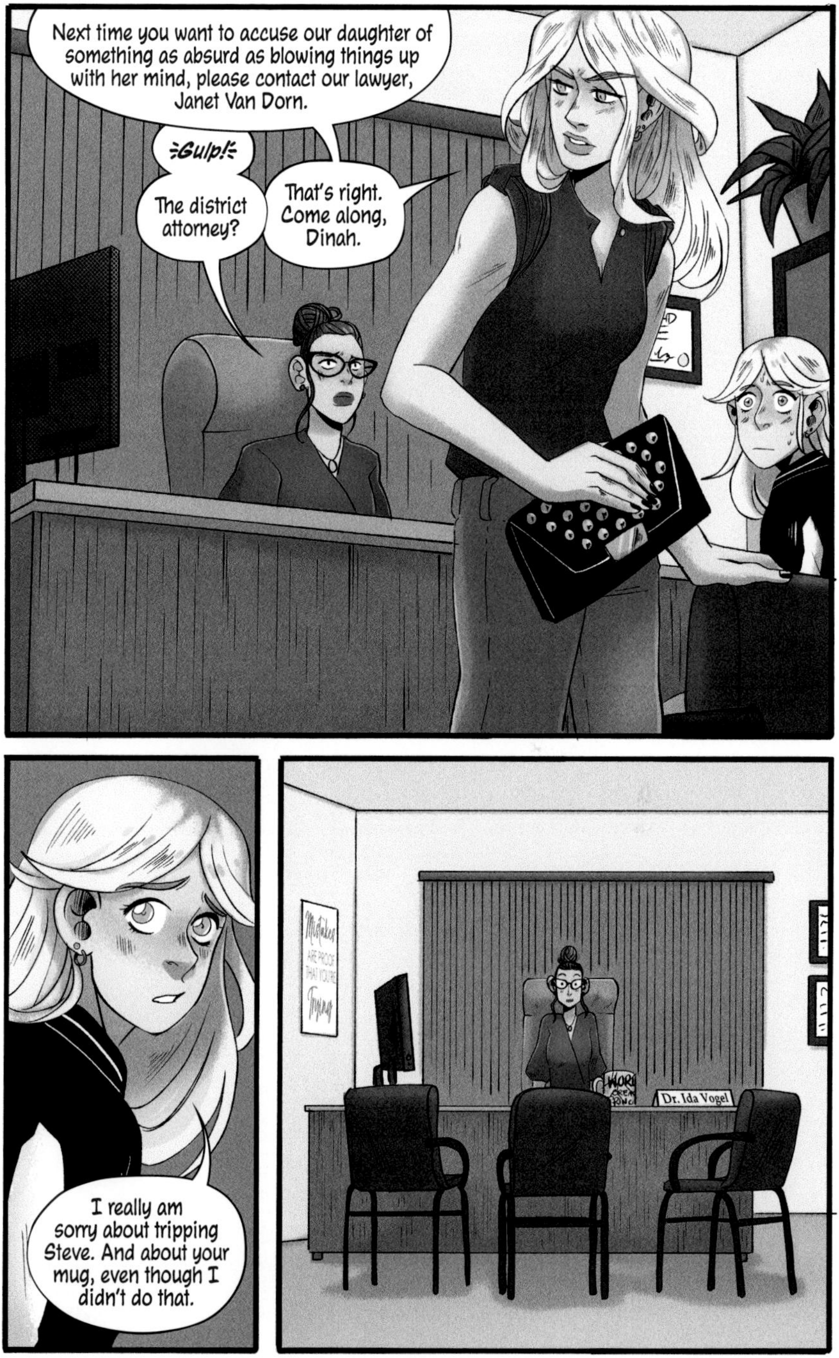

Next time you want to accuse our daughter of something as absurd as blowing things up with her mind, please contact our lawyer, Janet Van Dorn.
Gulp!
The district attorney?
That's right. Come along, Dinah.
Mistakes ARE PROOF THAT YOU'RE Trying
Dr. Ida Vogel
I really am sorry about tripping Steve. And about your mug, even though I didn't do that.

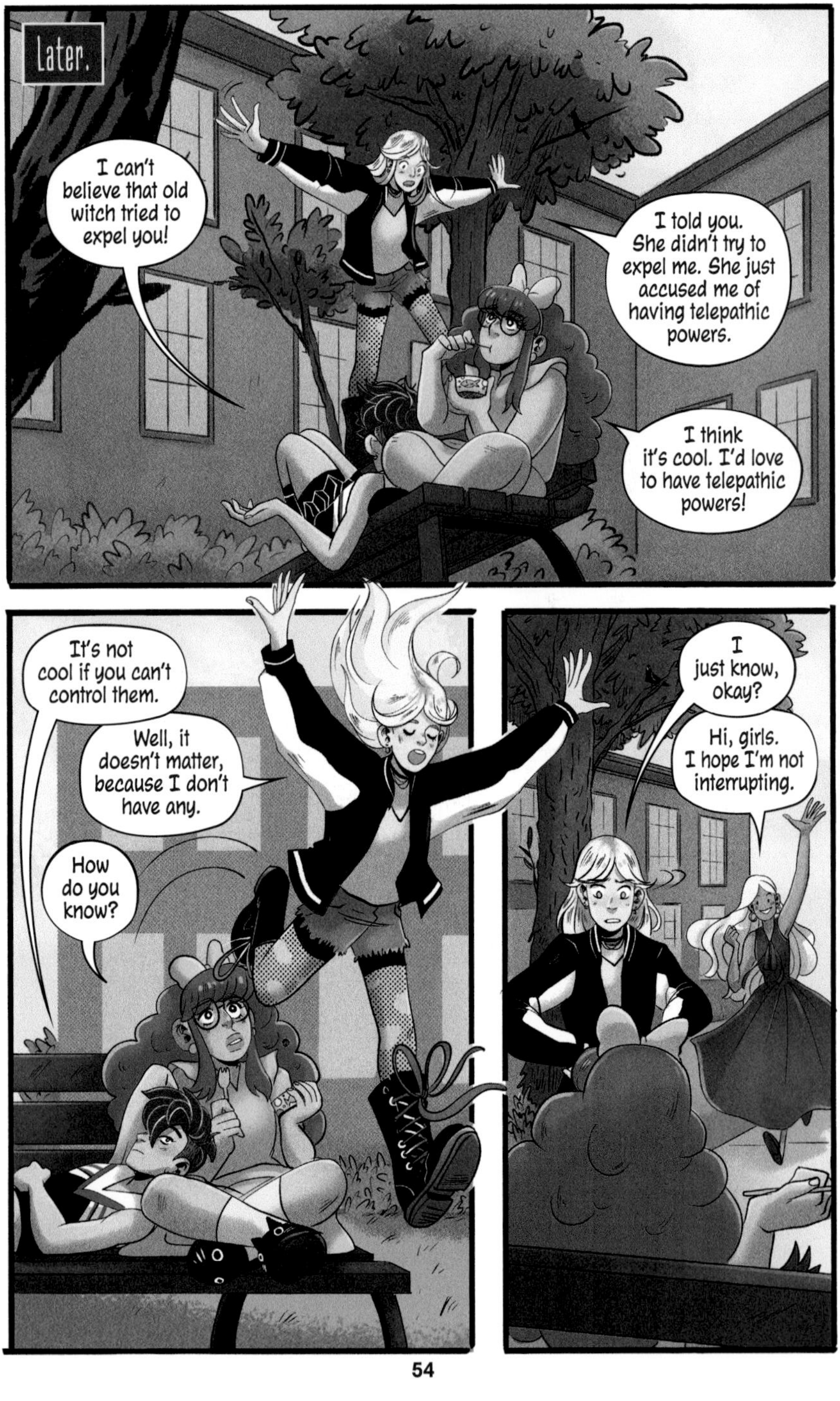
Later.
I can't believe that old witch tried to expel you!
I told you. She didn't try to expel me. She just accused me of having telepathic powers.
I think it's cool. I'd love to have telepathic powers!
It's not cool if you can't control them.
Well, it doesn't matter, because I don't have any.
How do you know?
I just know, okay?
Hi, girls. I hope I'm not interrupting.

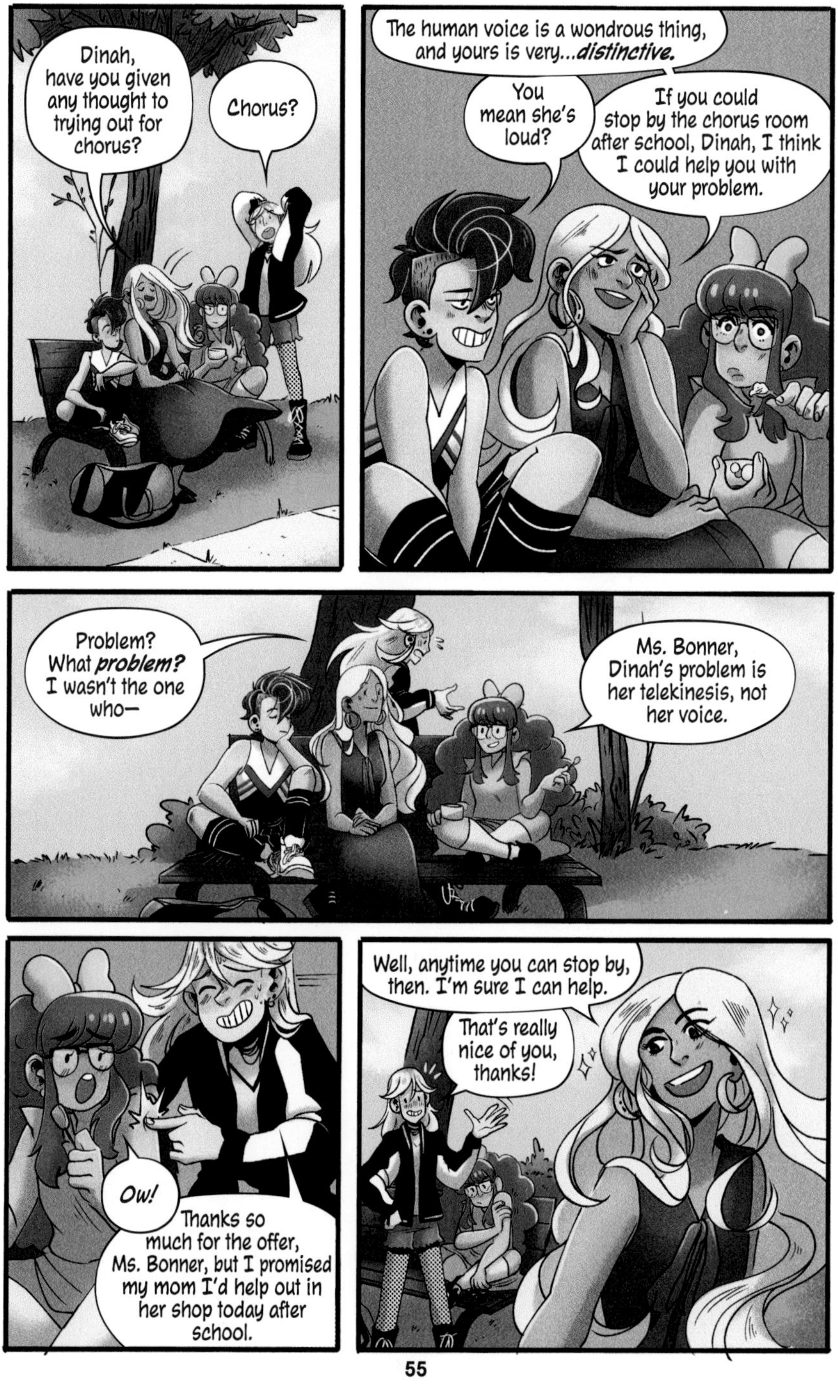
Dinah, have you given any thought to trying out for chorus?
Chorus?
The human voice is a wondrous thing, and yours is very...*distinctive.*
You mean she's loud?
If you could stop by the chorus room after school, Dinah, I think I could help you with your problem.
Problem? What *problem?* I wasn't the one who—
Ms. Bonner, Dinah's problem is her telekinesis, not her voice.
Ow!
Thanks so much for the offer, Ms. Bonner, but I promised my mom I'd help out in her shop today after school.
Well, anytime you can stop by, then. I'm sure I can help.
That's really nice of you, thanks!

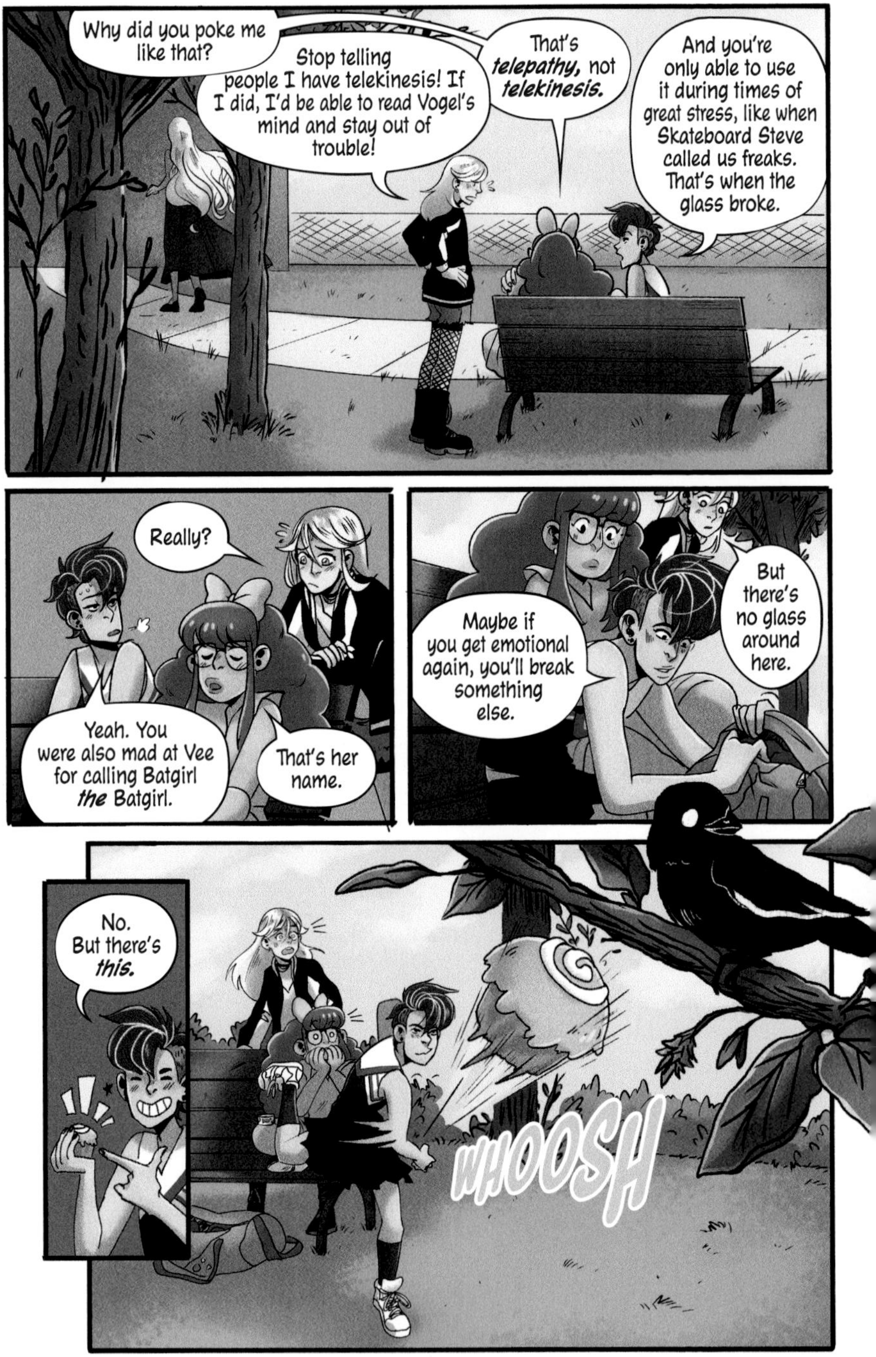
Why did you poke me like that?
Stop telling people I have telekinesis! If I did, I'd be able to read Vogel's mind and stay out of trouble!
That's *telepathy,* not *telekinesis.*
And you're only able to use it during times of great stress, like when Skateboard Steve called us freaks. That's when the glass broke.
Really?
Yeah. You were also mad at Vee for calling Batgirl *the* Batgirl.
That's her name.
Maybe if you get emotional again, you'll break something else.
But there's no glass around here.
No. But there's *this.*
WHOOSH

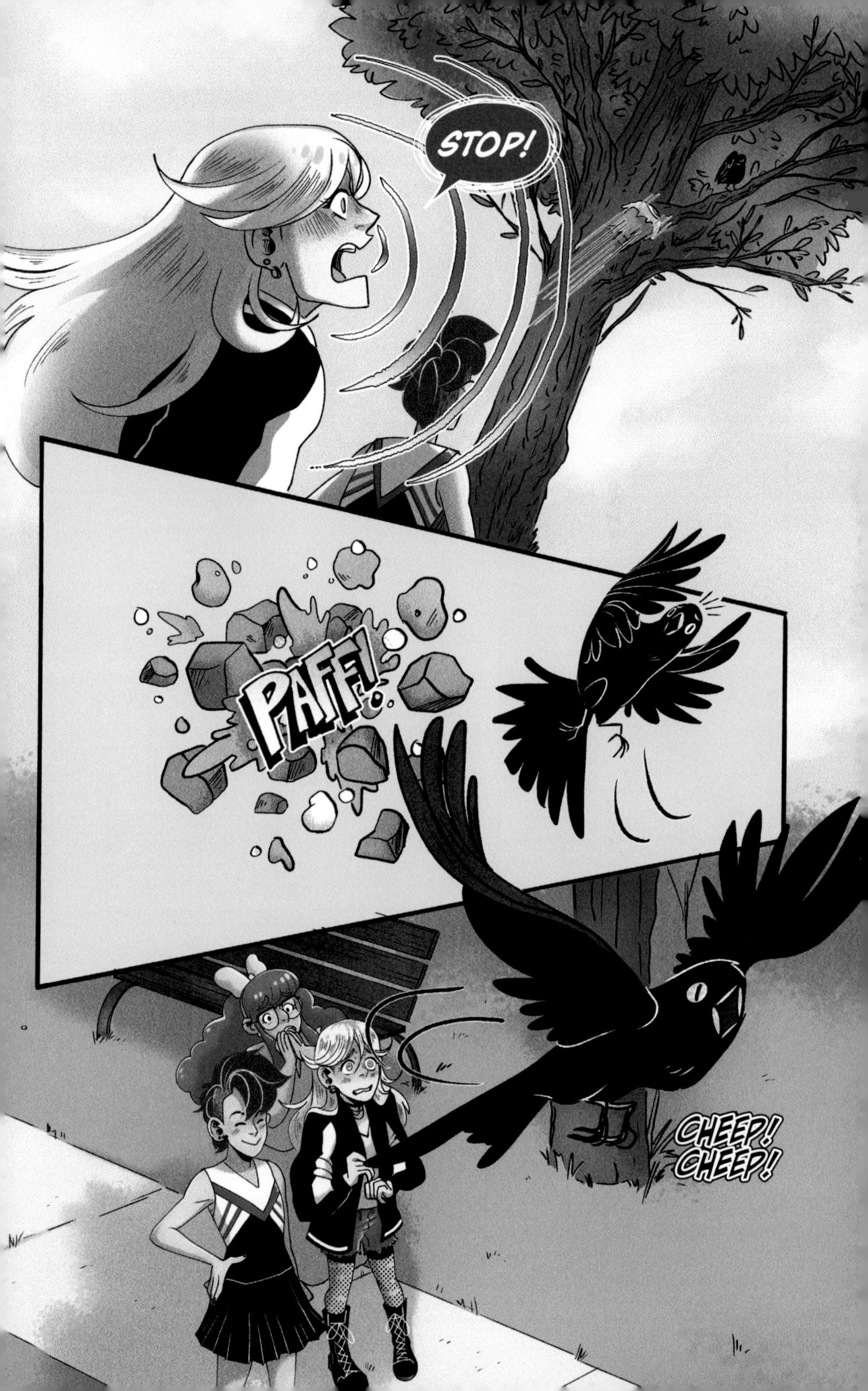
STOP!
PAFF!
CHEEP! CHEEP!

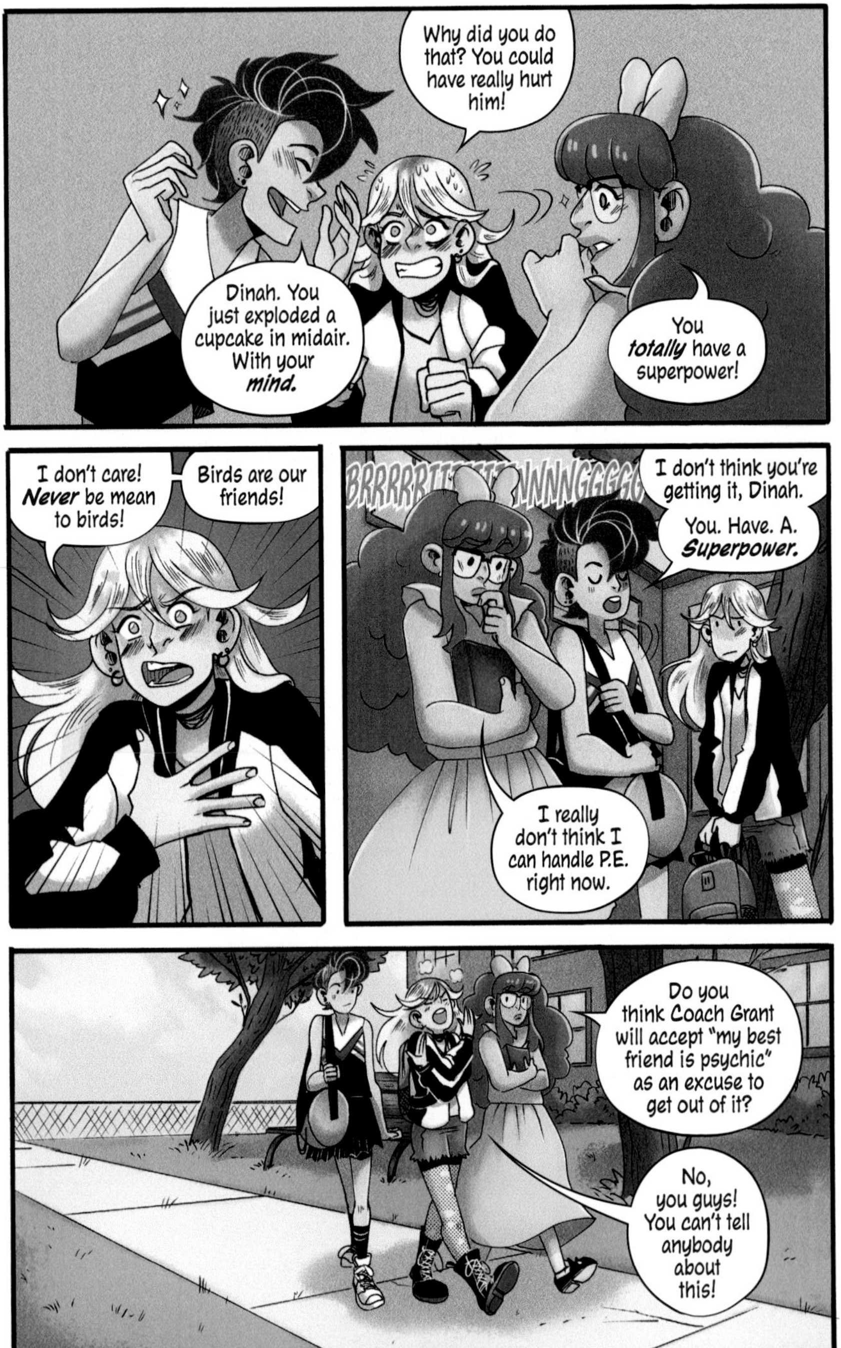
Why did you do that? You could have really hurt him!
Dinah. You just exploded a cupcake in midair. With your *mind.*
You *totally* have a superpower!
I don't care! *Never* be mean to birds!
Birds are our friends!
I don't think you're getting it, Dinah.
You. Have. A. *Superpower.*
I really don't think I can handle P.E. right now.
Do you think Coach Grant will accept "my best friend is psychic" as an excuse to get out of it?
No, you guys! You can't tell anybody about this!

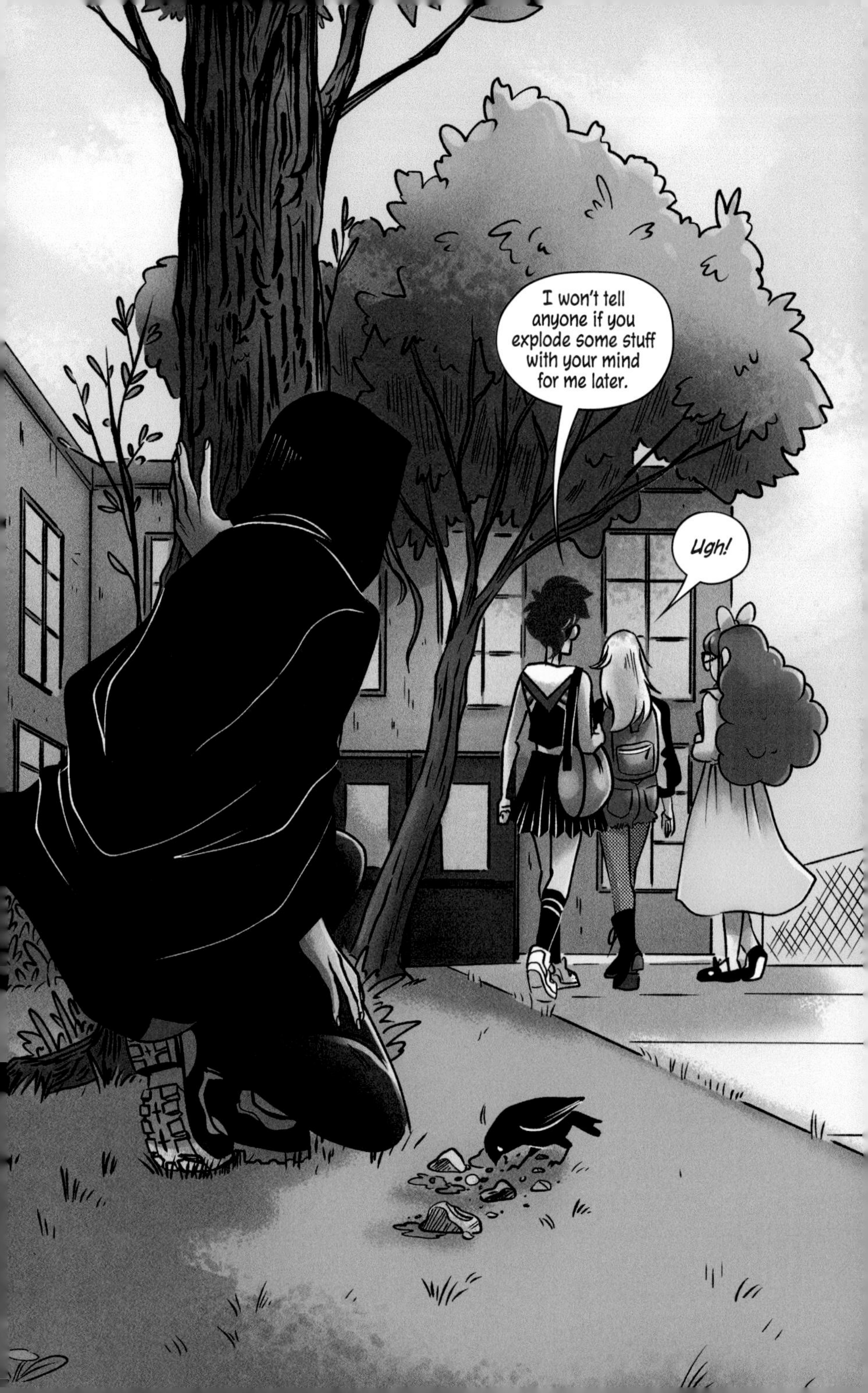
I won't tell anyone if you explode some stuff with your mind for me later.
Ugh!

CHAPTER 4
GONNA BURST INTO FLAME

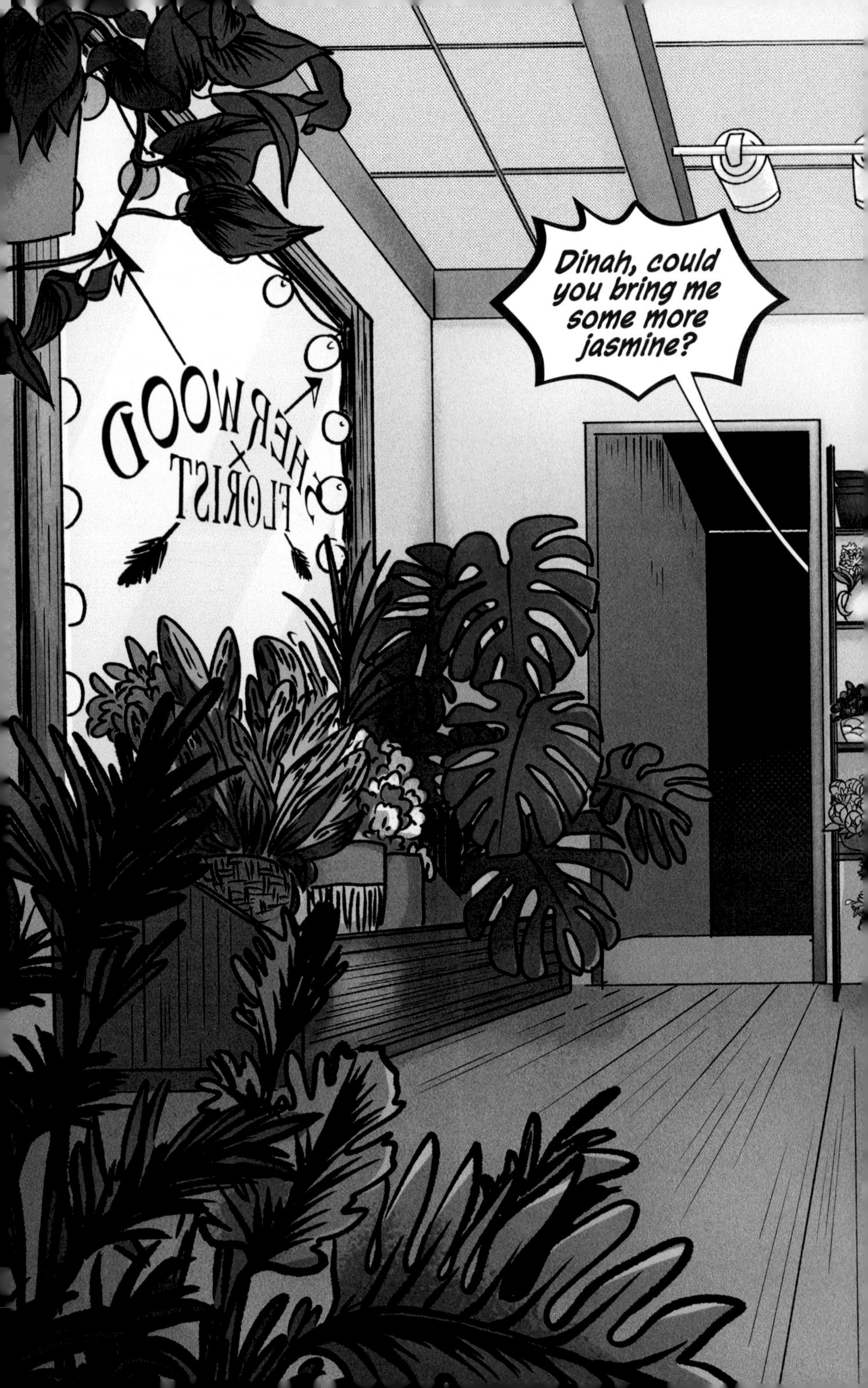
SHERWOOD
FLORIST
Dinah, could you bring me some more jasmine?

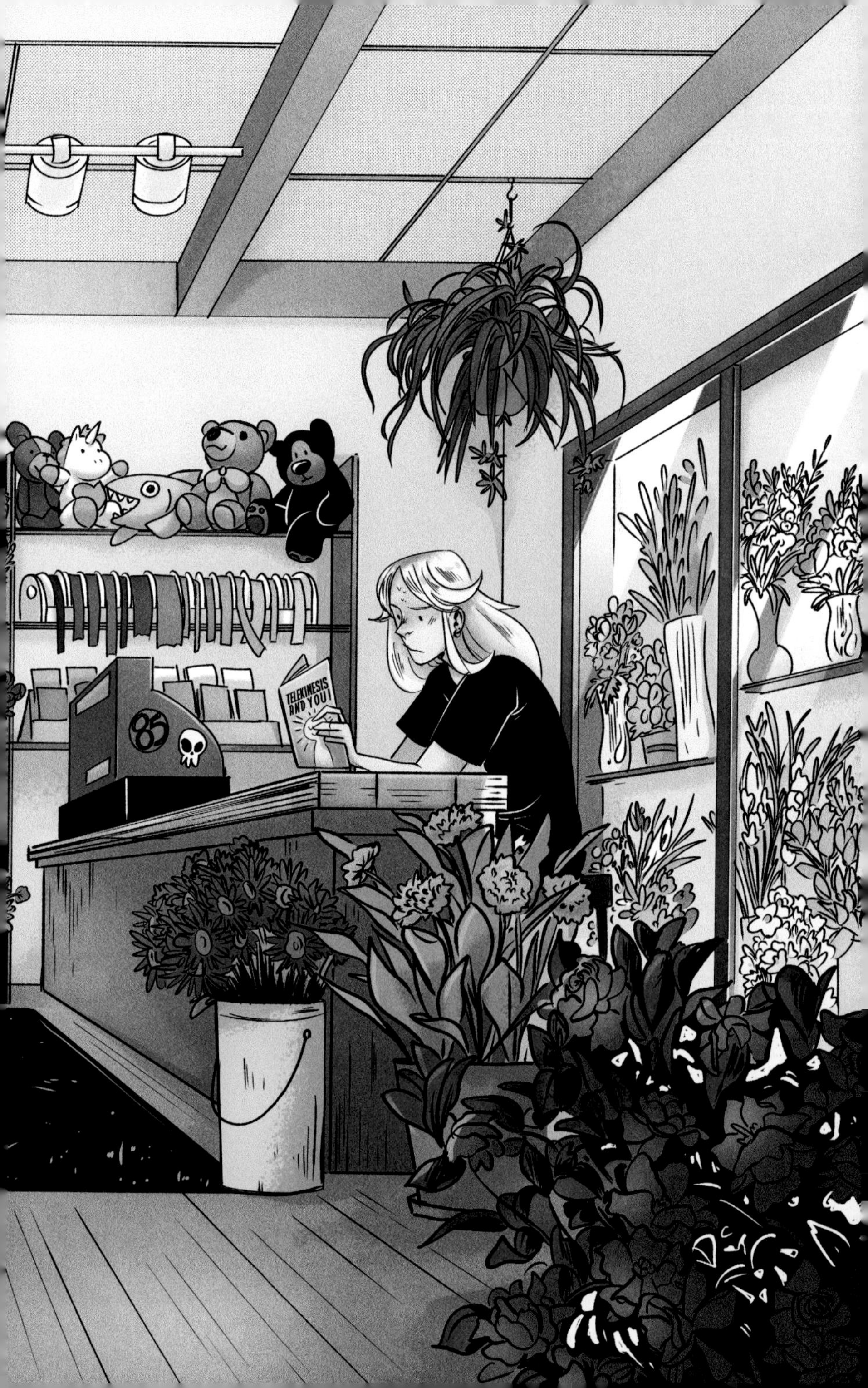
TELEKINESIS AND YOU!

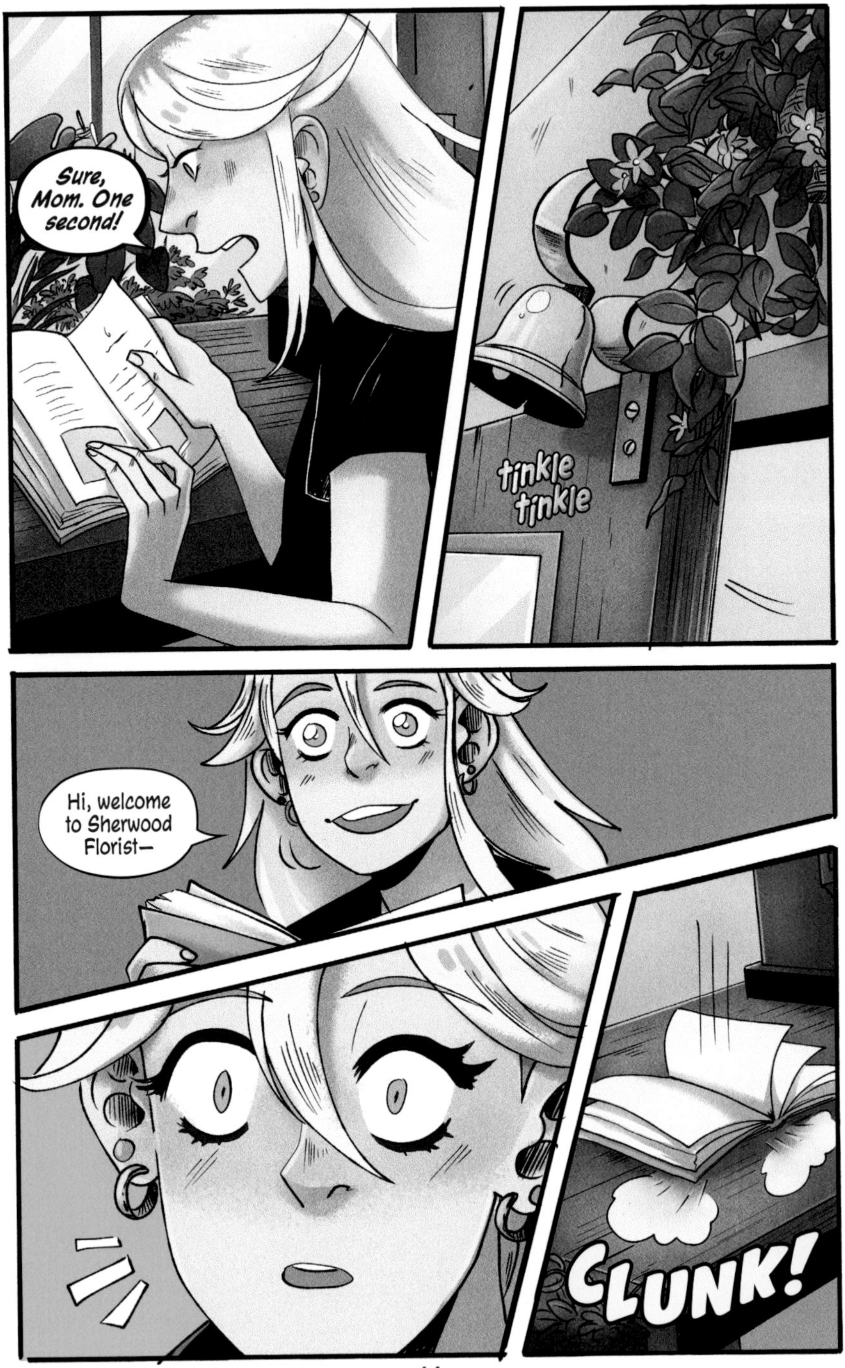
Sure, Mom. One second!
tinkle tinkle
Hi, welcome to Sherwood Florist—
CLUNK!

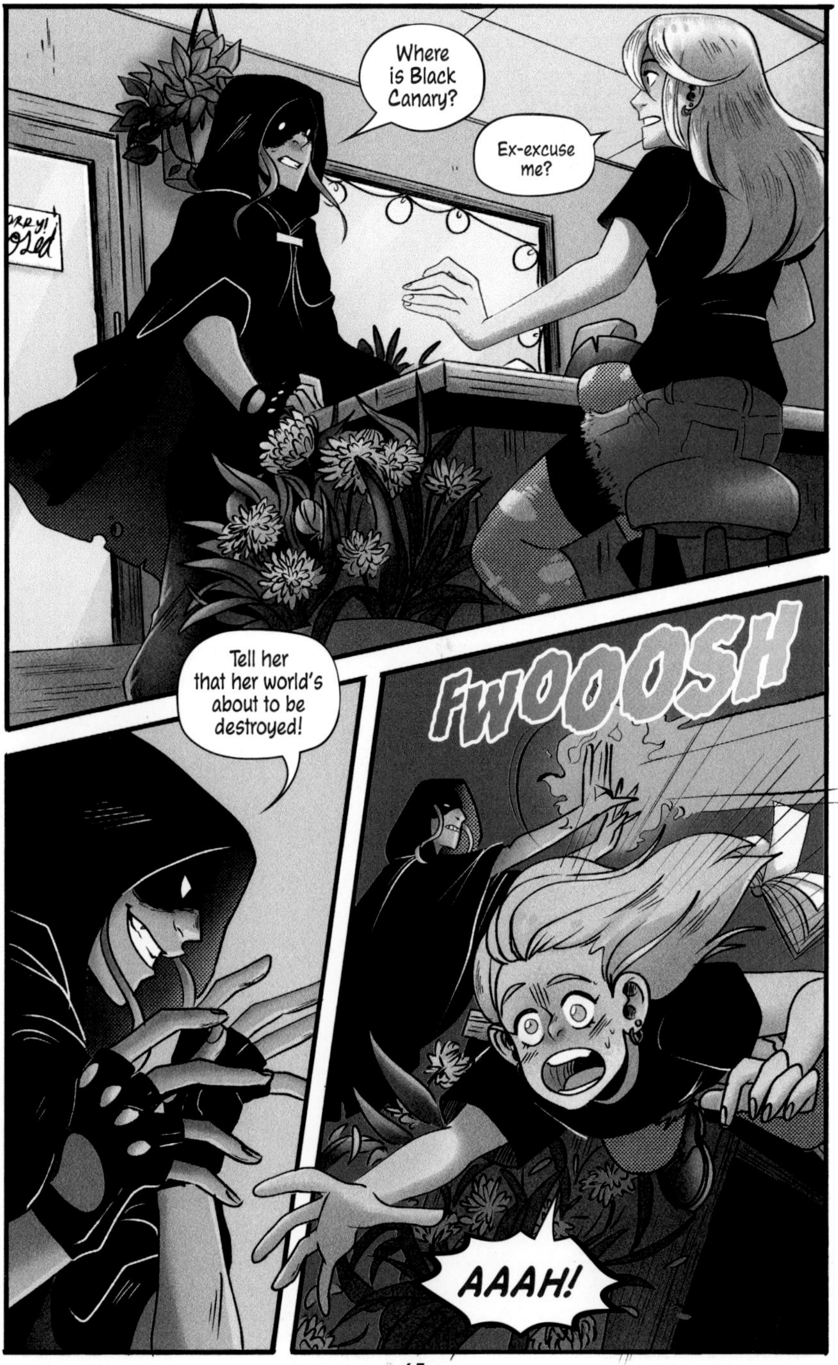
Where is Black Canary?
Ex-excuse me?
Tell her that her world's about to be destroyed!
FWOOOSH
AAAH!

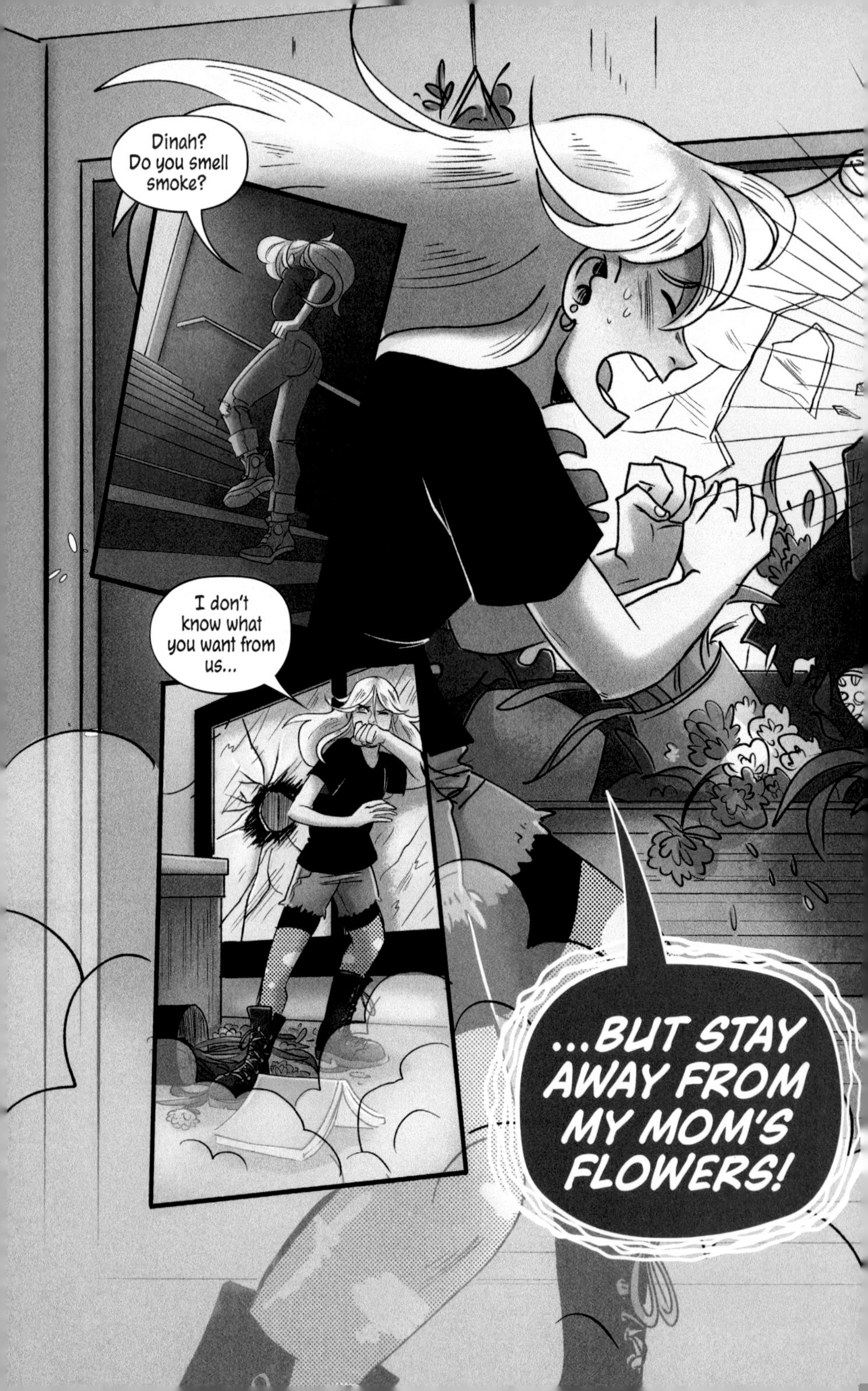
Dinah? Do you smell smoke?
I don't know what you want from us...
...BUT STAY AWAY FROM MY MOM'S FLOWERS!

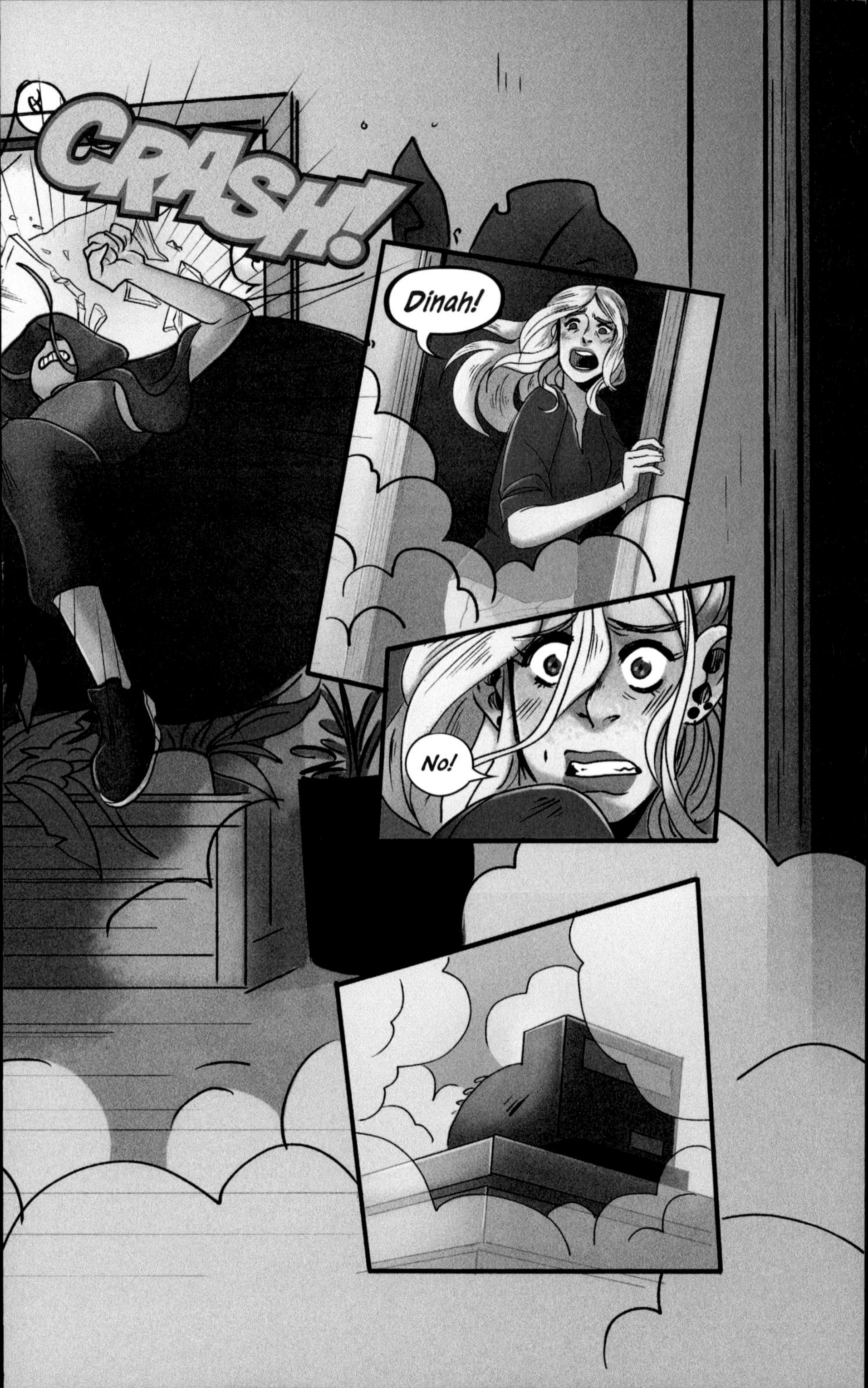
CRASH!
Dinah!
No!

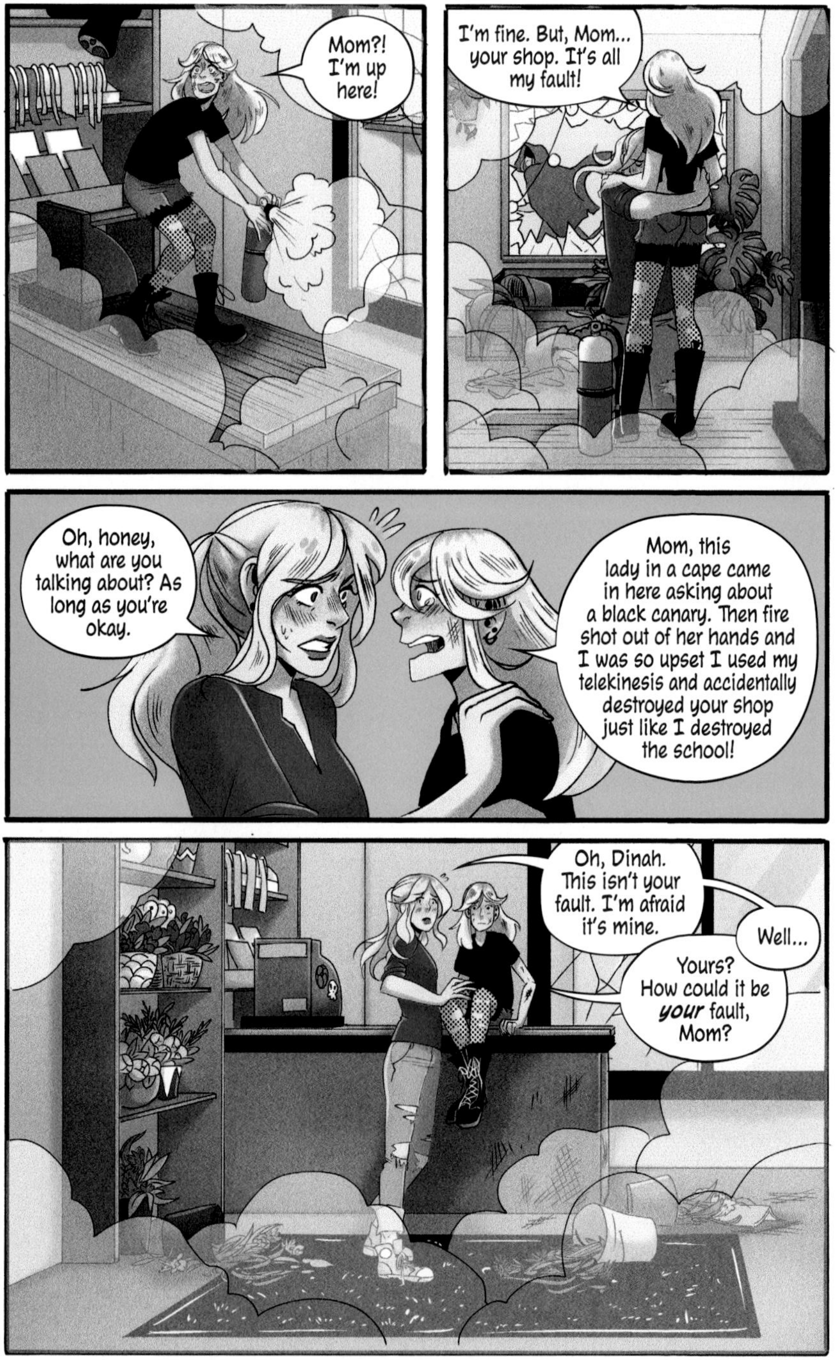
Mom?! I'm up here!
I'm fine. But, Mom... your shop. It's all my fault!
Oh, honey, what are you talking about? As long as you're okay.
Mom, this lady in a cape came in here asking about a black canary. Then fire shot out of her hands and I was so upset I used my telekinesis and accidentally destroyed your shop just like I destroyed the school!
Oh, Dinah. This isn't your fault. I'm afraid it's mine.
Well...
Yours? How could it be *your* fault, Mom?

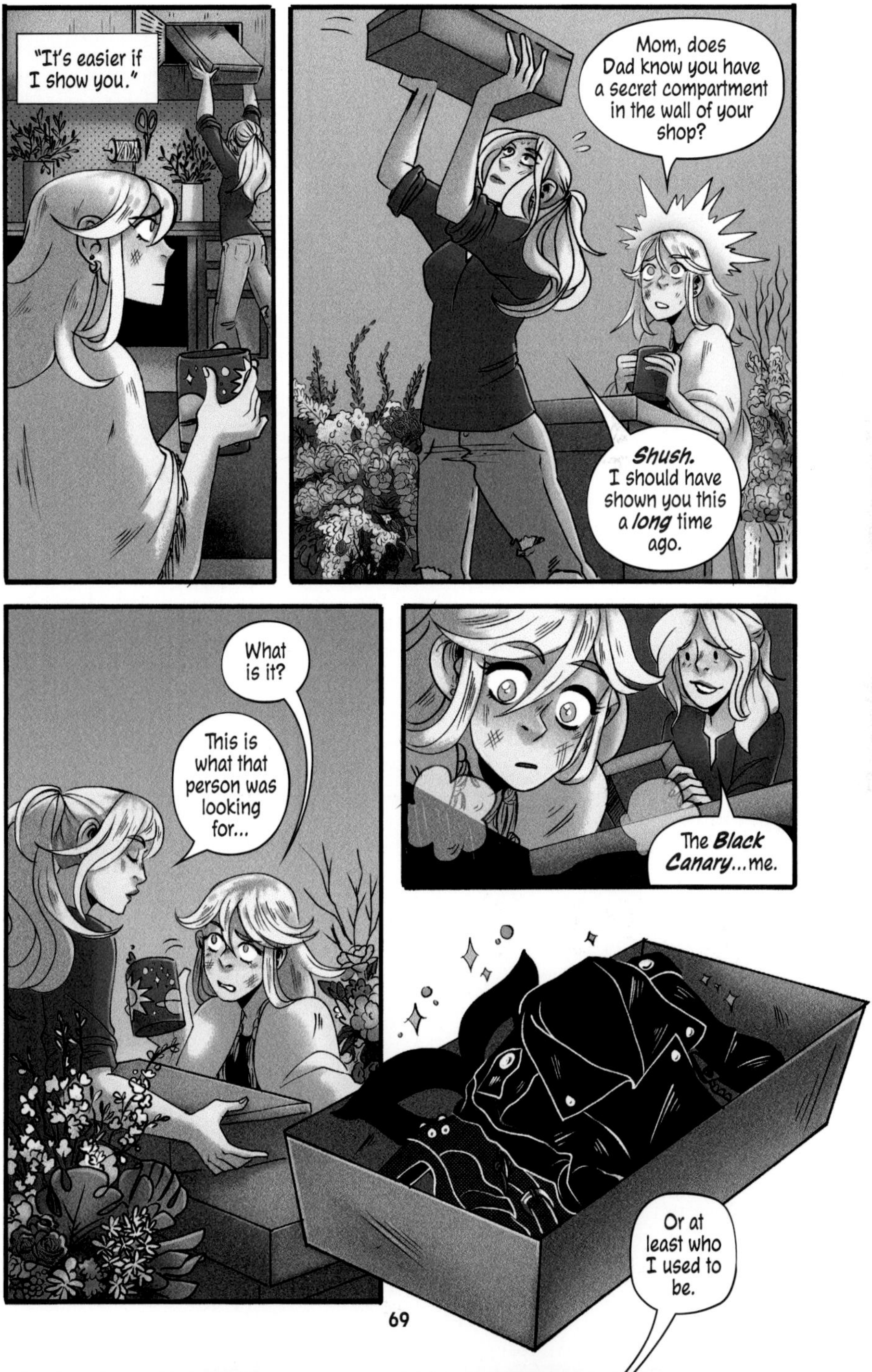
"It's easier if I show you."
Mom, does Dad know you have a secret compartment in the wall of your shop?
Shush. I should have shown you this a *long* time ago.
What is it?
This is what that person was looking for...
The *Black Canary*...me.
Or at least who I used to be.

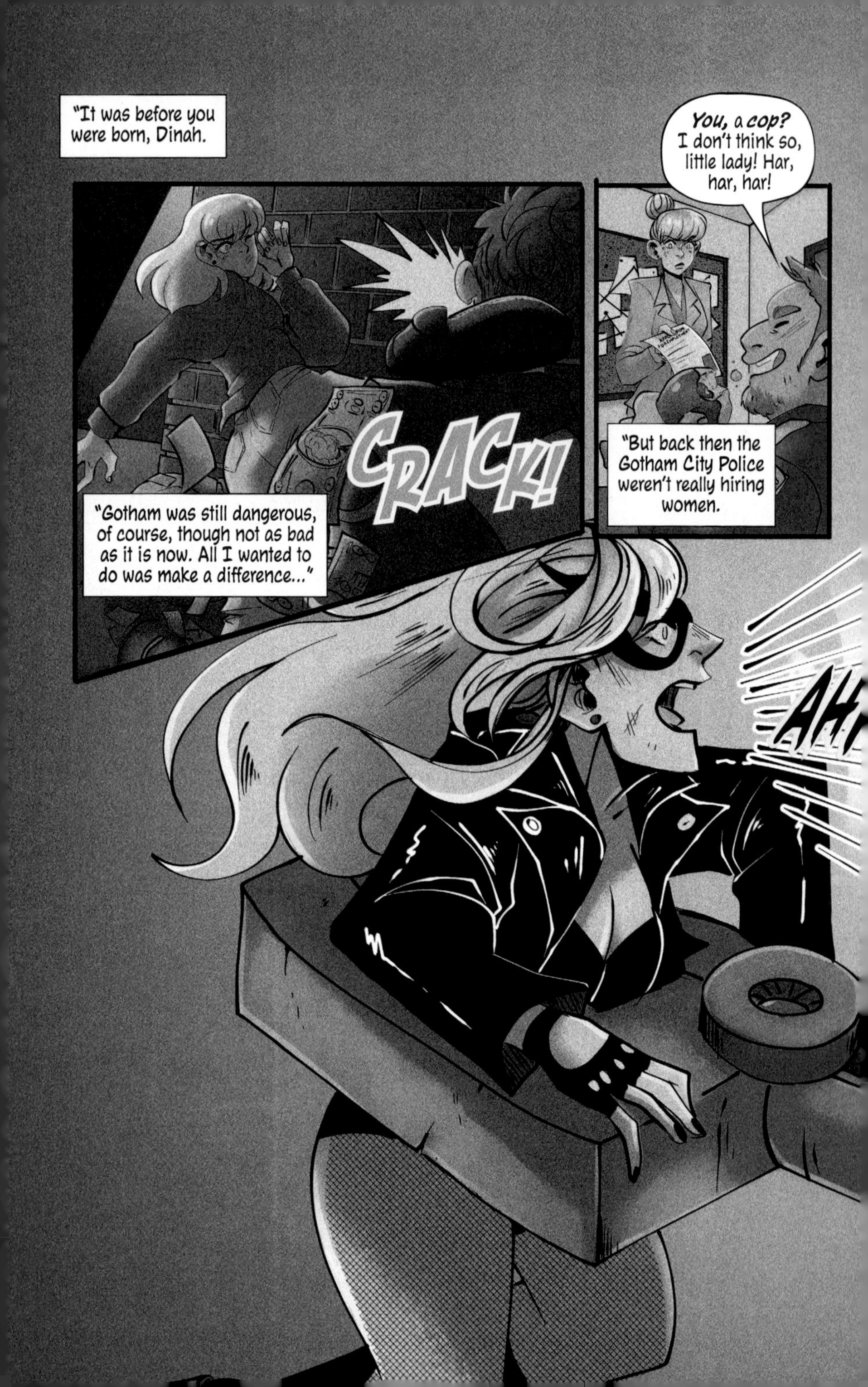
"It was before you were born, Dinah.
"Gotham was still dangerous, of course, though not as bad as it is now. All I wanted to do was make a difference..."
CRACK!
You, a cop? I don't think so, little lady! Har, har, har!
"But back then the Gotham City Police weren't really hiring women.
AH

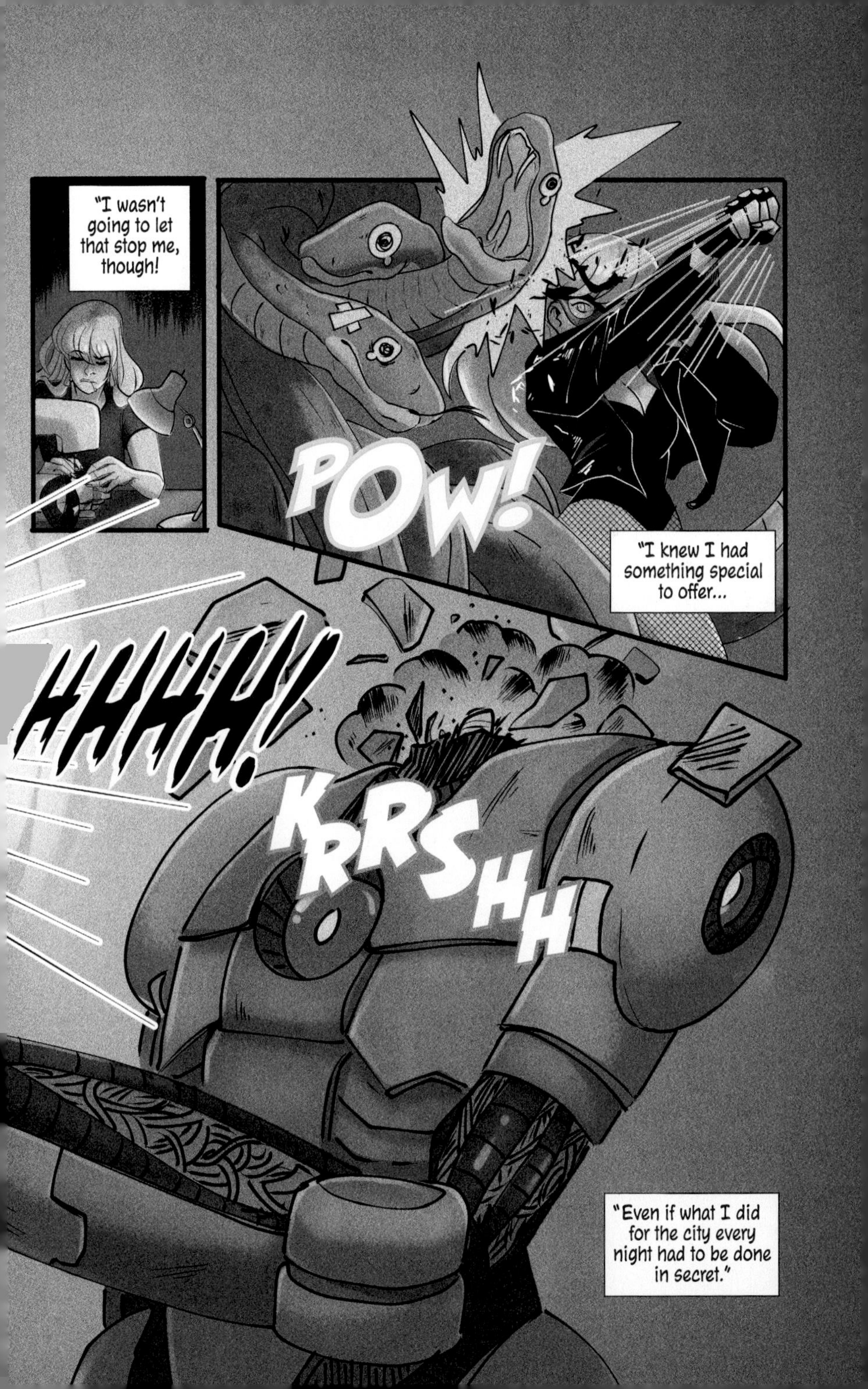
"I wasn't going to let that stop me, though!
POW!
"I knew I had something special to offer...
HHHHH!
KRRSHH
"Even if what I did for the city every night had to be done in secret."

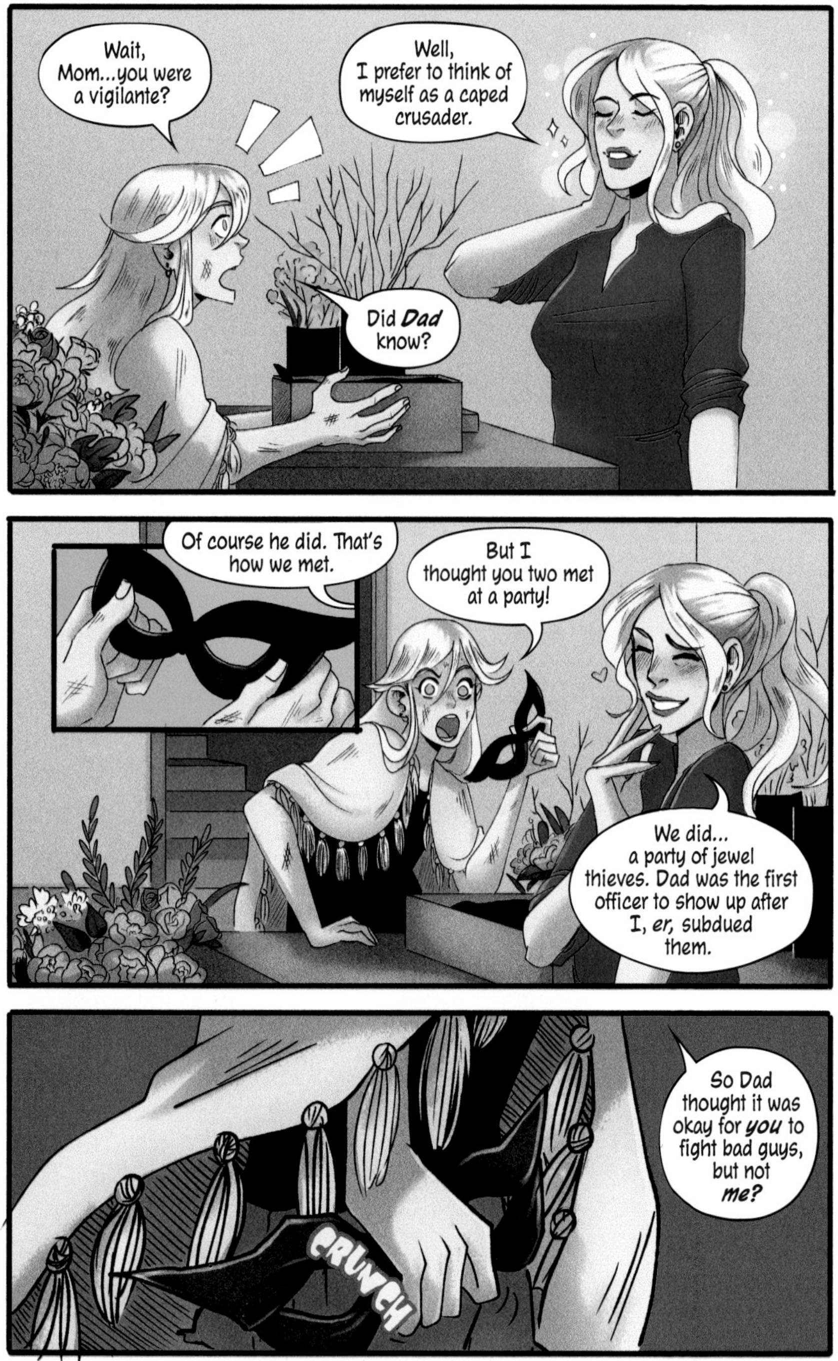
Wait, Mom...you were a vigilante?
Well, I prefer to think of myself as a caped crusader.
Did *Dad* know?
Of course he did. That's how we met.
But I thought you two met at a party!
We did... a party of jewel thieves. Dad was the first officer to show up after I, *er,* subdued them.
So Dad thought it was okay for ***you*** to fight bad guys, but not ***me?***
CRUNCH

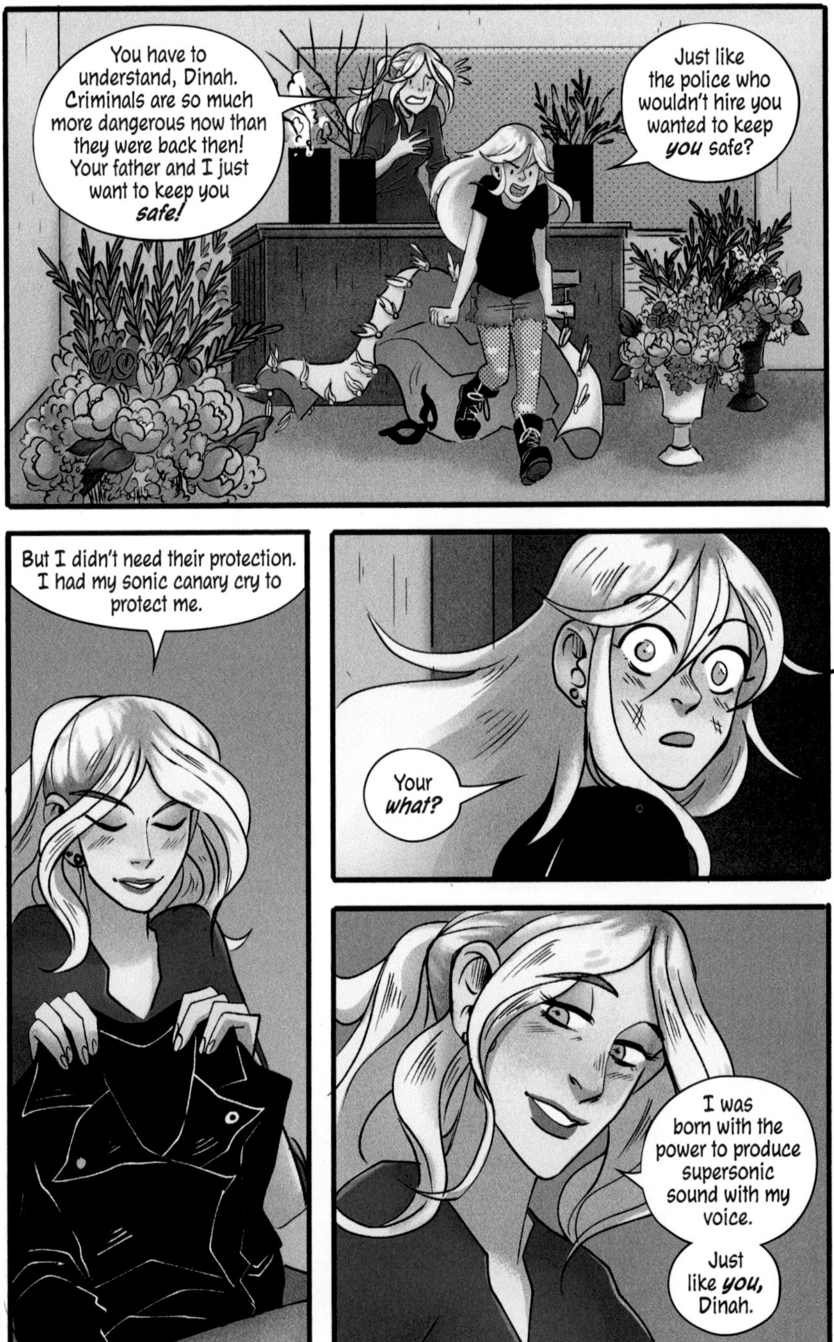
You have to understand, Dinah. Criminals are so much more dangerous now than they were back then! Your father and I just want to keep you *safe!*
Just like the police who wouldn't hire you wanted to keep *you* safe?
But I didn't need their protection. I had my sonic canary cry to protect me.
Your *what?*
I was born with the power to produce supersonic sound with my voice.
Just like *you,* Dinah.

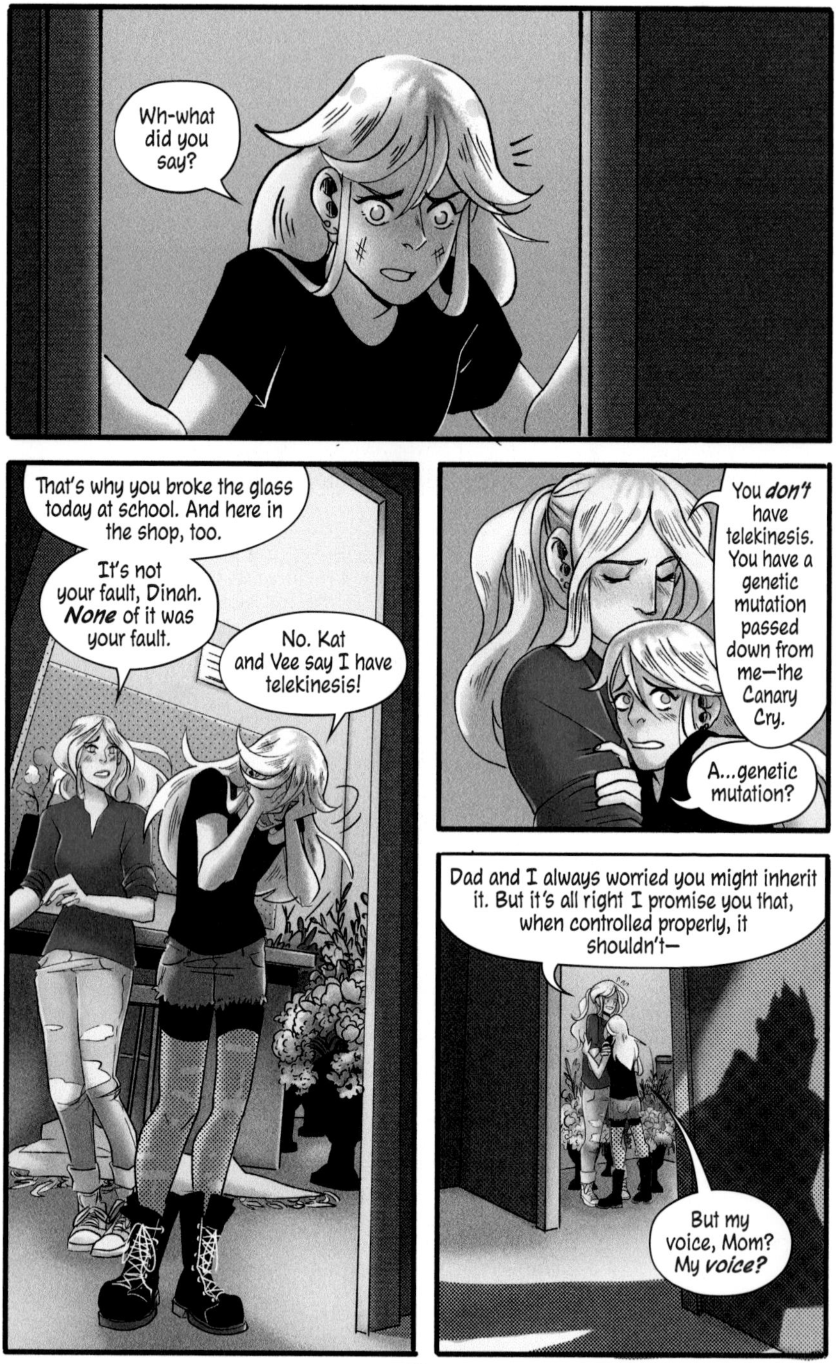
Wh-what did you say?
That's why you broke the glass today at school. And here in the shop, too.
It's not your fault, Dinah. *None* of it was your fault.
No. Kat and Vee say I have telekinesis!
You *don't* have telekinesis. You have a genetic mutation passed down from me—the Canary Cry.
A...genetic mutation?
Dad and I always worried you might inherit it. But it's all right I promise you that, when controlled properly, it shouldn't—
But my voice, Mom? My *voice?*

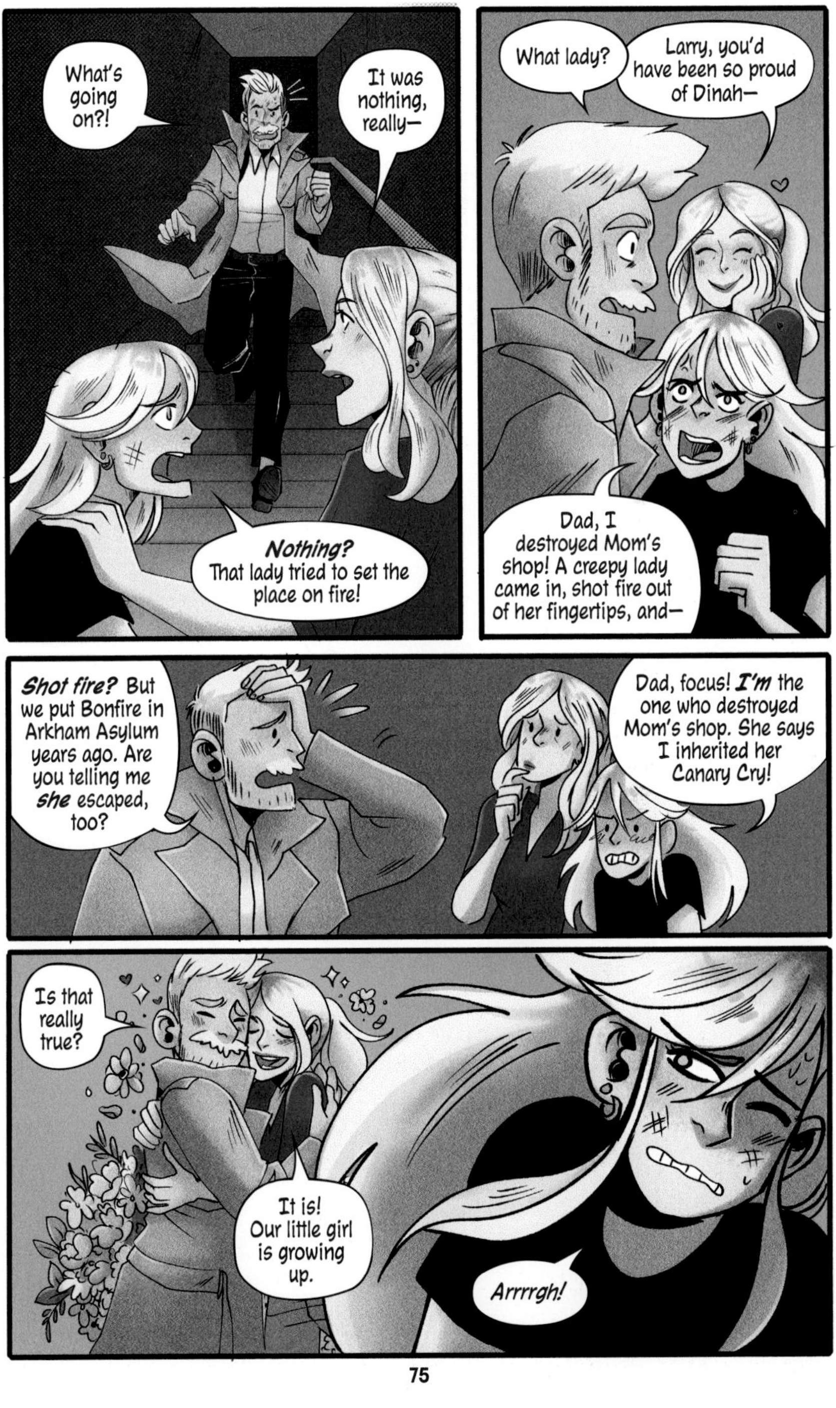
What's going on?!
It was nothing, really—
Nothing? That lady tried to set the place on fire!
What lady?
Larry, you'd have been so proud of Dinah—
Dad, I destroyed Mom's shop! A creepy lady came in, shot fire out of her fingertips, and—
Shot fire? But we put Bonfire in Arkham Asylum years ago. Are you telling me *she* escaped, too?
Dad, focus! *I'm* the one who destroyed Mom's shop. She says I inherited her Canary Cry!
Is that really true?
It is! Our little girl is growing up.
Arrrrgh!

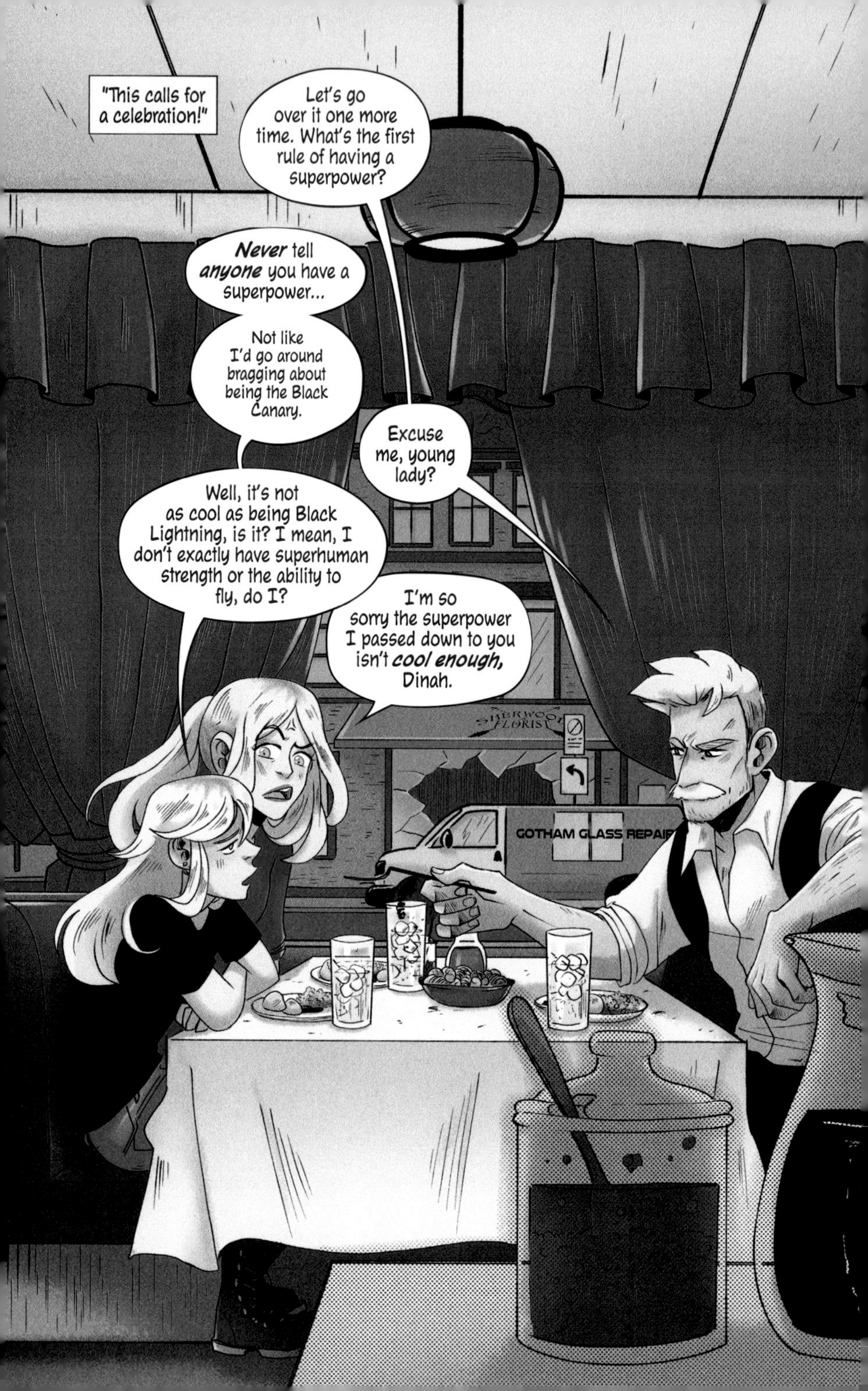
"This calls for a celebration!"
Let's go over it one more time. What's the first rule of having a superpower?
Never tell *anyone* you have a superpower...
Not like I'd go around bragging about being the Black Canary.
Excuse me, young lady?
Well, it's not as cool as being Black Lightning, is it? I mean, I don't exactly have superhuman strength or the ability to fly, do I?
I'm so sorry the superpower I passed down to you isn't *cool enough,* Dinah.
GOTHAM GLASS REPAIR

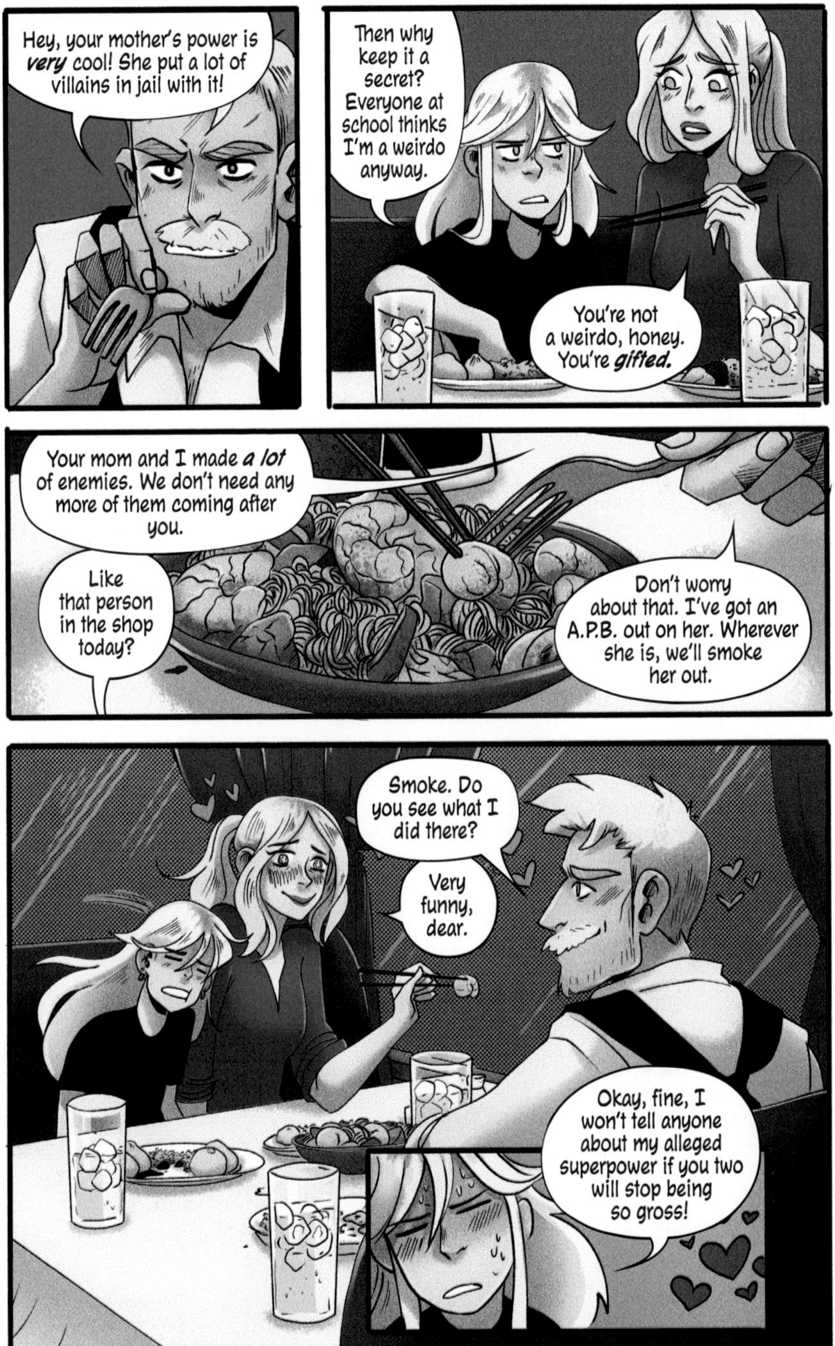
Hey, your mother's power is *very* cool! She put a lot of villains in jail with it!
Then why keep it a secret? Everyone at school thinks I'm a weirdo anyway.
You're not a weirdo, honey. You're *gifted.*
Your mom and I made *a lot* of enemies. We don't need any more of them coming after you.
Like that person in the shop today?
Don't worry about that. I've got an A.P.B. out on her. Wherever she is, we'll smoke her out.
Smoke. Do you see what I did there?
Very funny, dear.
Okay, fine, I won't tell anyone about my alleged superpower if you two will stop being so gross!

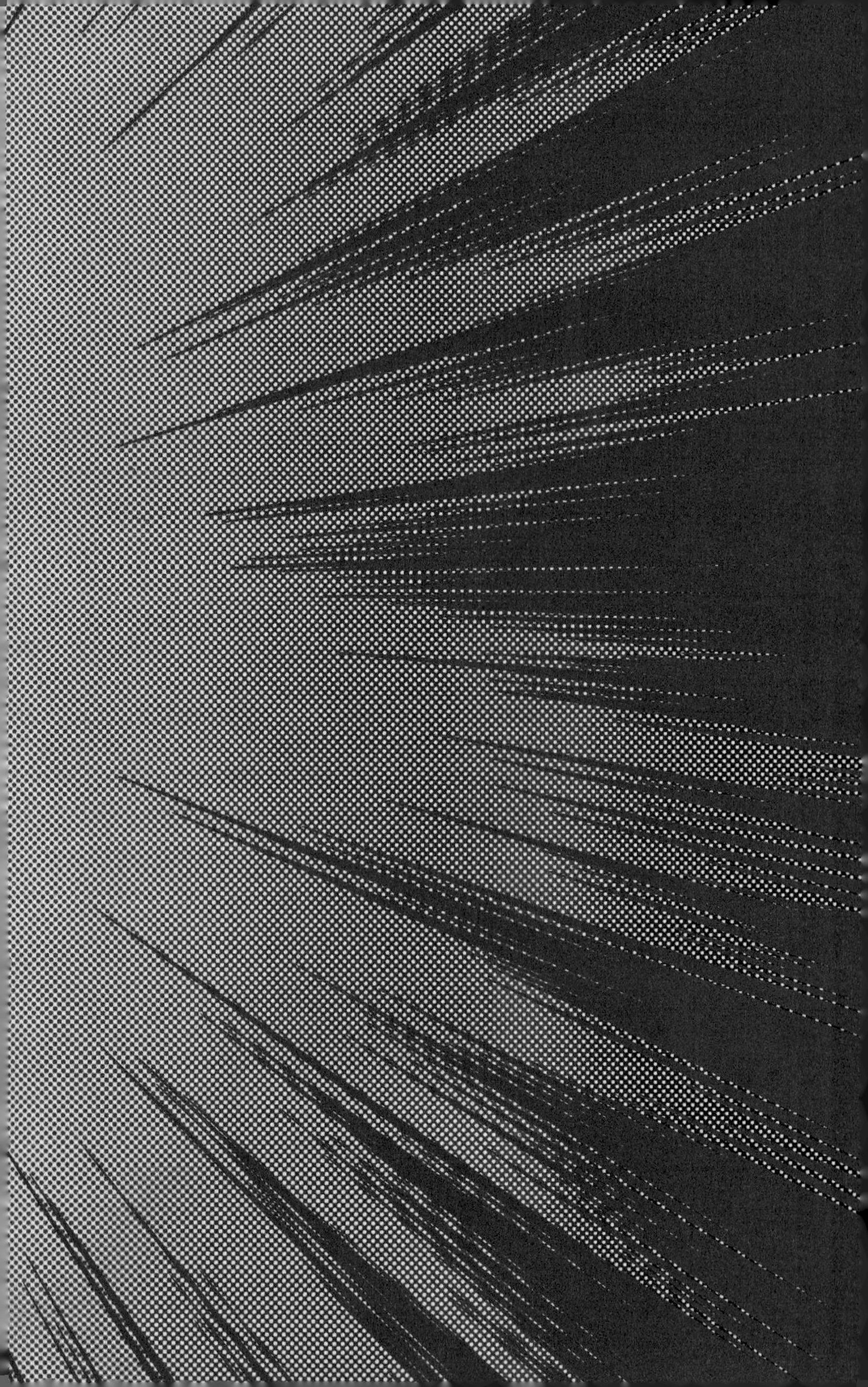

CHAPTER 5
YOU'RE WEIRD
BUT NOT A WEIRDO

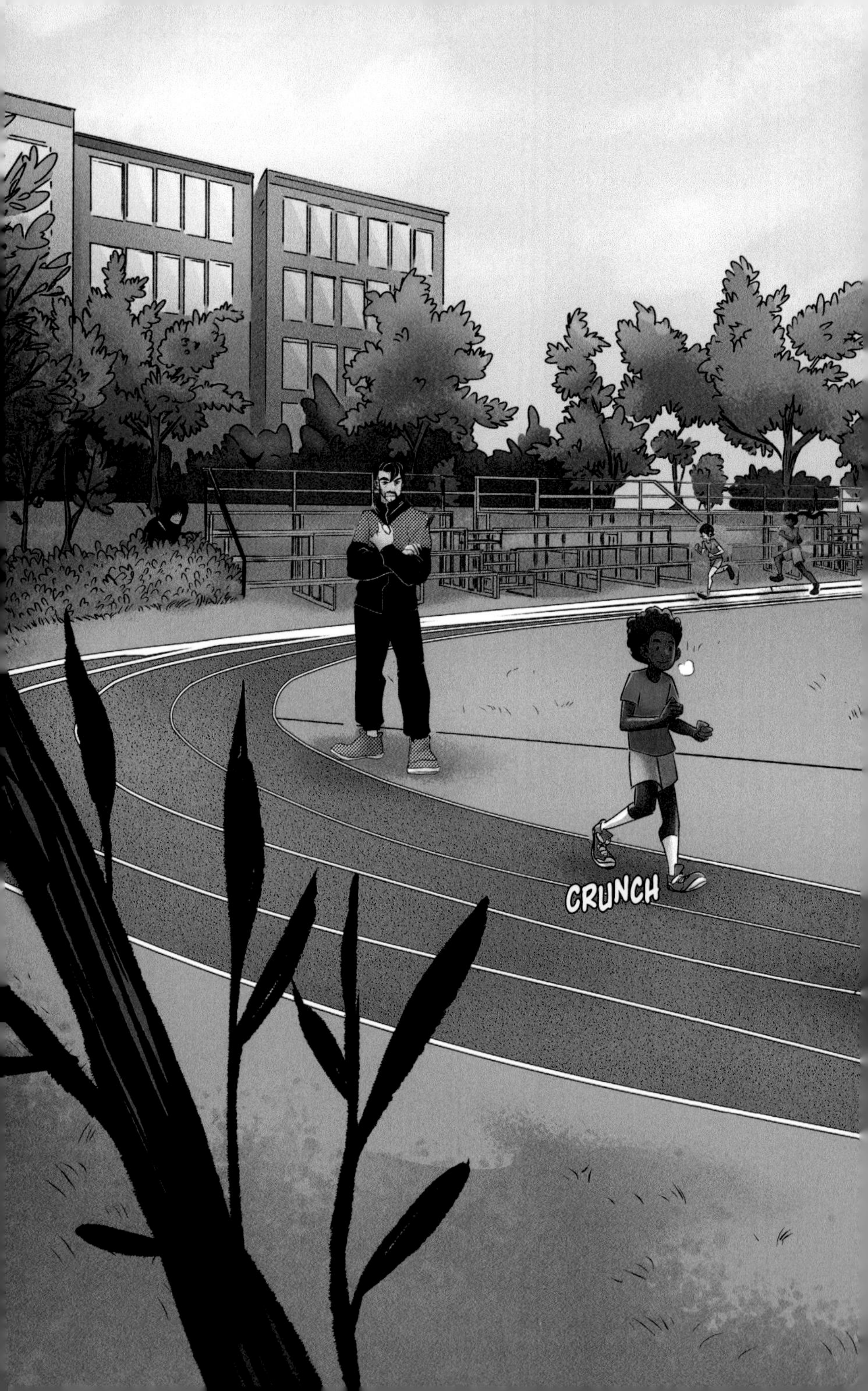
CRUNCH

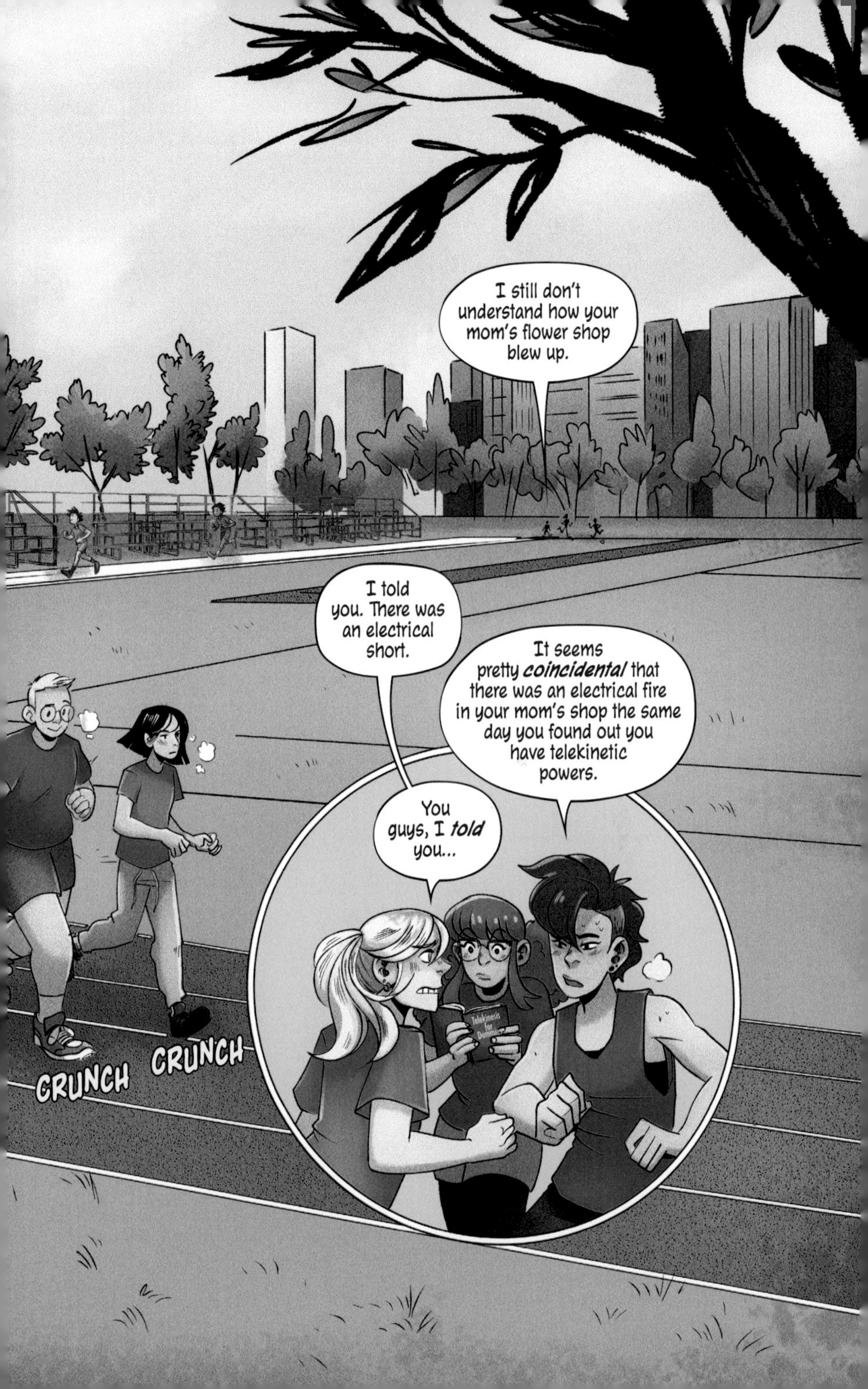
I still don't understand how your mom's flower shop blew up.
I told you. There was an electrical short.
It seems pretty *coincidental* that there was an electrical fire in your mom's shop the same day you found out you have telekinetic powers.
You guys, I *told* you...
Telekinesis for Dummies
CRUNCH
CRUNCH

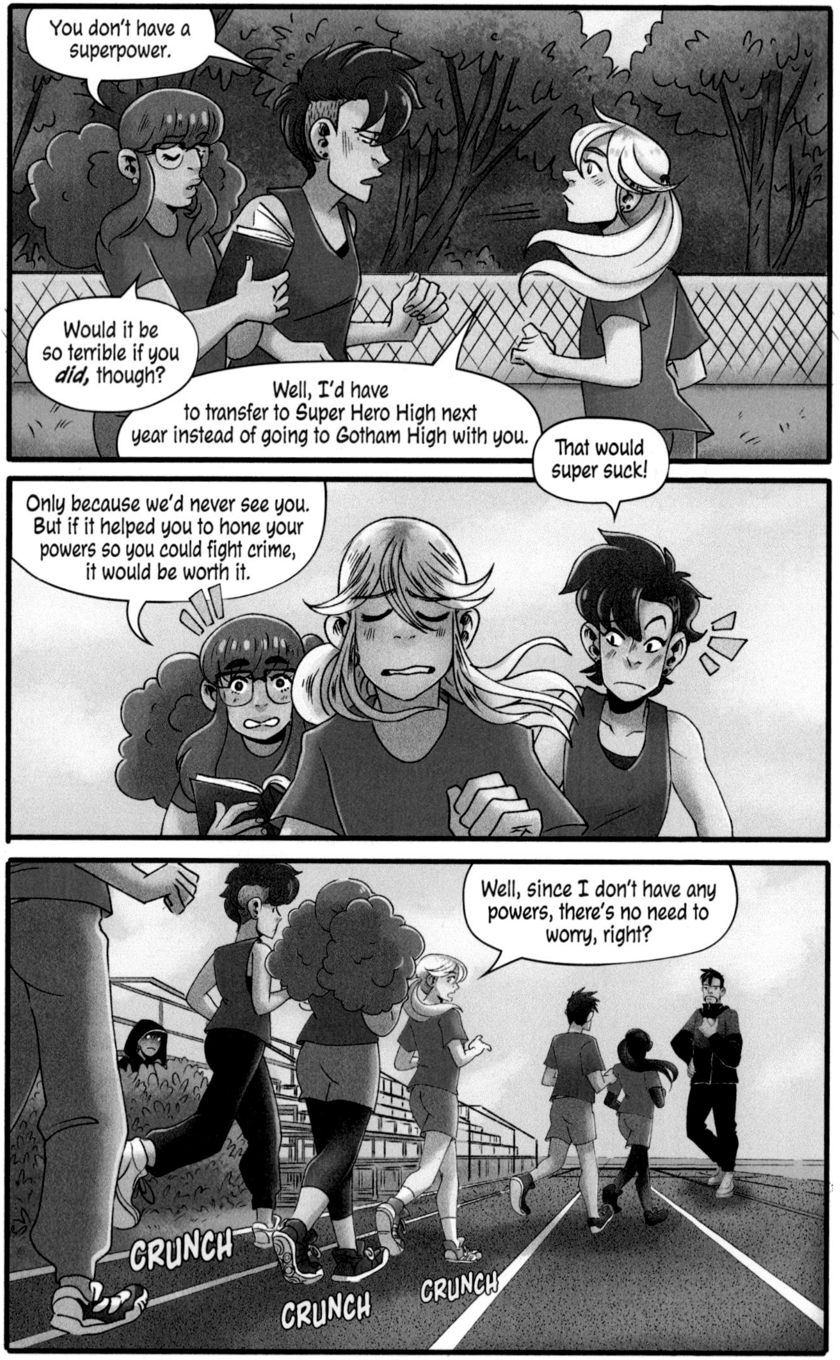
You don't have a superpower.
Would it be so terrible if you *did,* though?
Well, I'd have to transfer to Super Hero High next year instead of going to Gotham High with you.
That would super suck!
Only because we'd never see you. But if it helped you to hone your powers so you could fight crime, it would be worth it.
Well, since I don't have any powers, there's no need to worry, right?
CRUNCH
CRUNCH
CRUNCH

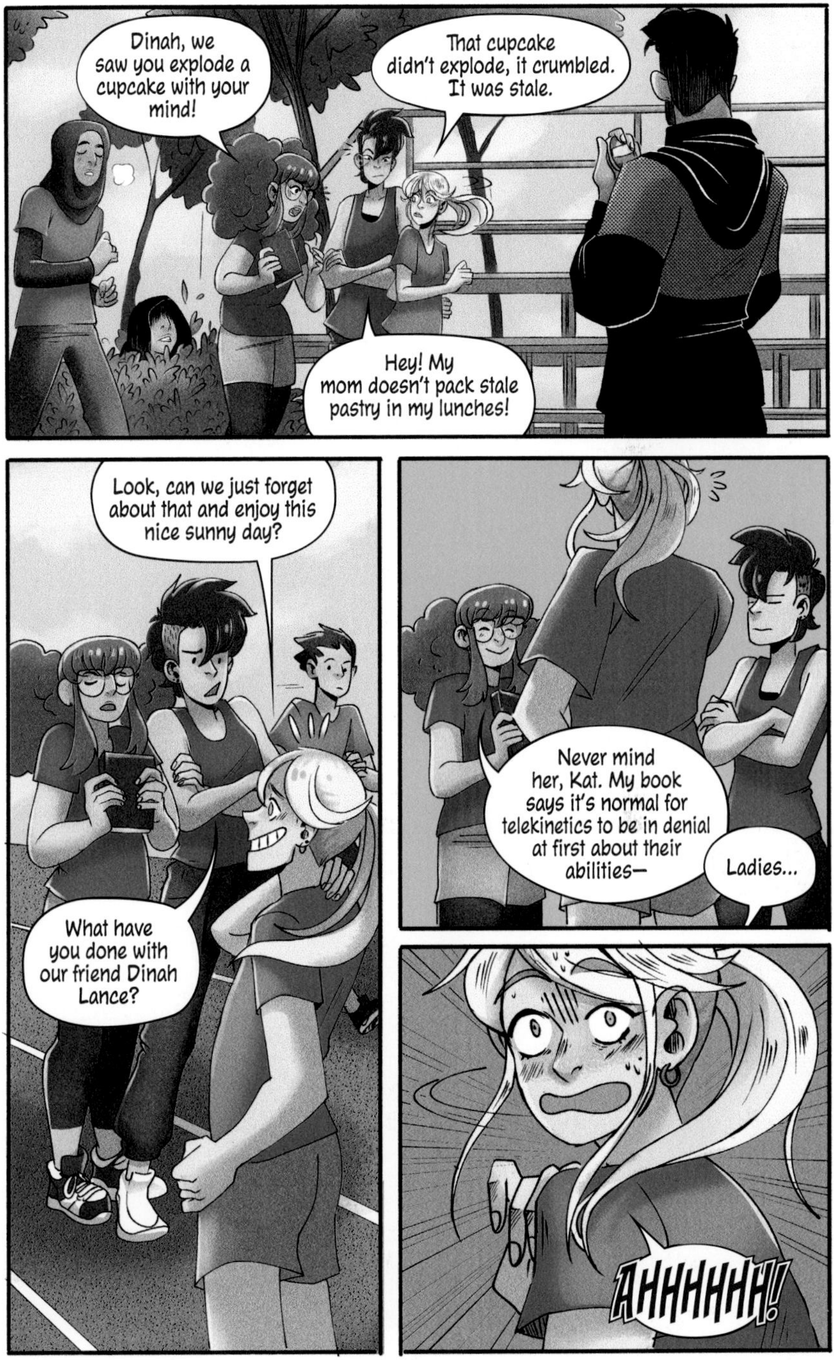
Dinah, we saw you explode a cupcake with your mind!
That cupcake didn't explode, it crumbled. It was stale.
Hey! My mom doesn't pack stale pastry in my lunches!
Look, can we just forget about that and enjoy this nice sunny day?
What have you done with our friend Dinah Lance?
Never mind her, Kat. My book says it's normal for telekinetics to be in denial at first about their abilities—
Ladies...
AHHHHH!

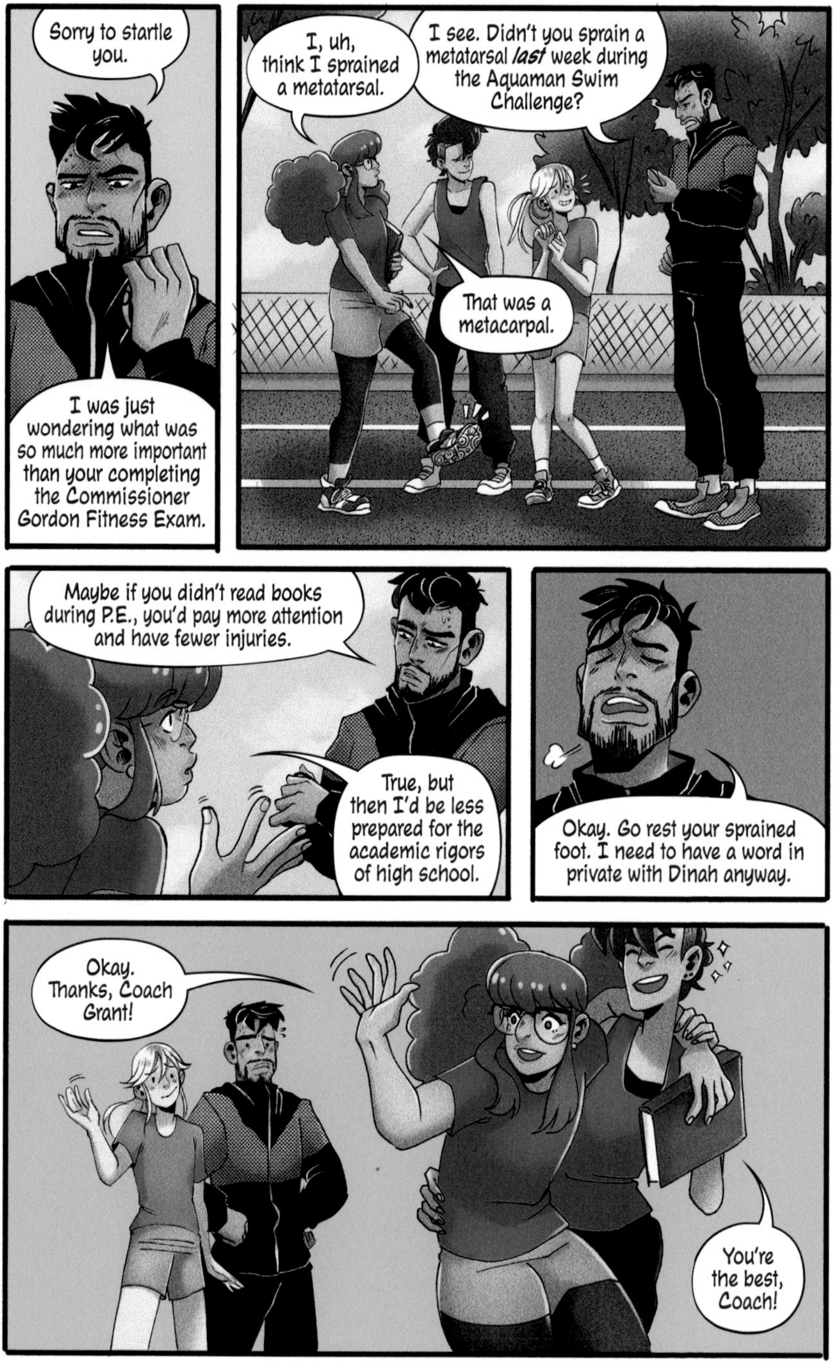
Sorry to startle you.
I was just wondering what was so much more important than your completing the Commissioner Gordon Fitness Exam.
I, uh, think I sprained a metatarsal.
I see. Didn't you sprain a metatarsal *last* week during the Aquaman Swim Challenge?
That was a metacarpal.
Maybe if you didn't read books during P.E., you'd pay more attention and have fewer injuries.
True, but then I'd be less prepared for the academic rigors of high school.
Okay. Go rest your sprained foot. I need to have a word in private with Dinah anyway.
Okay. Thanks, Coach Grant!
You're the best, Coach!

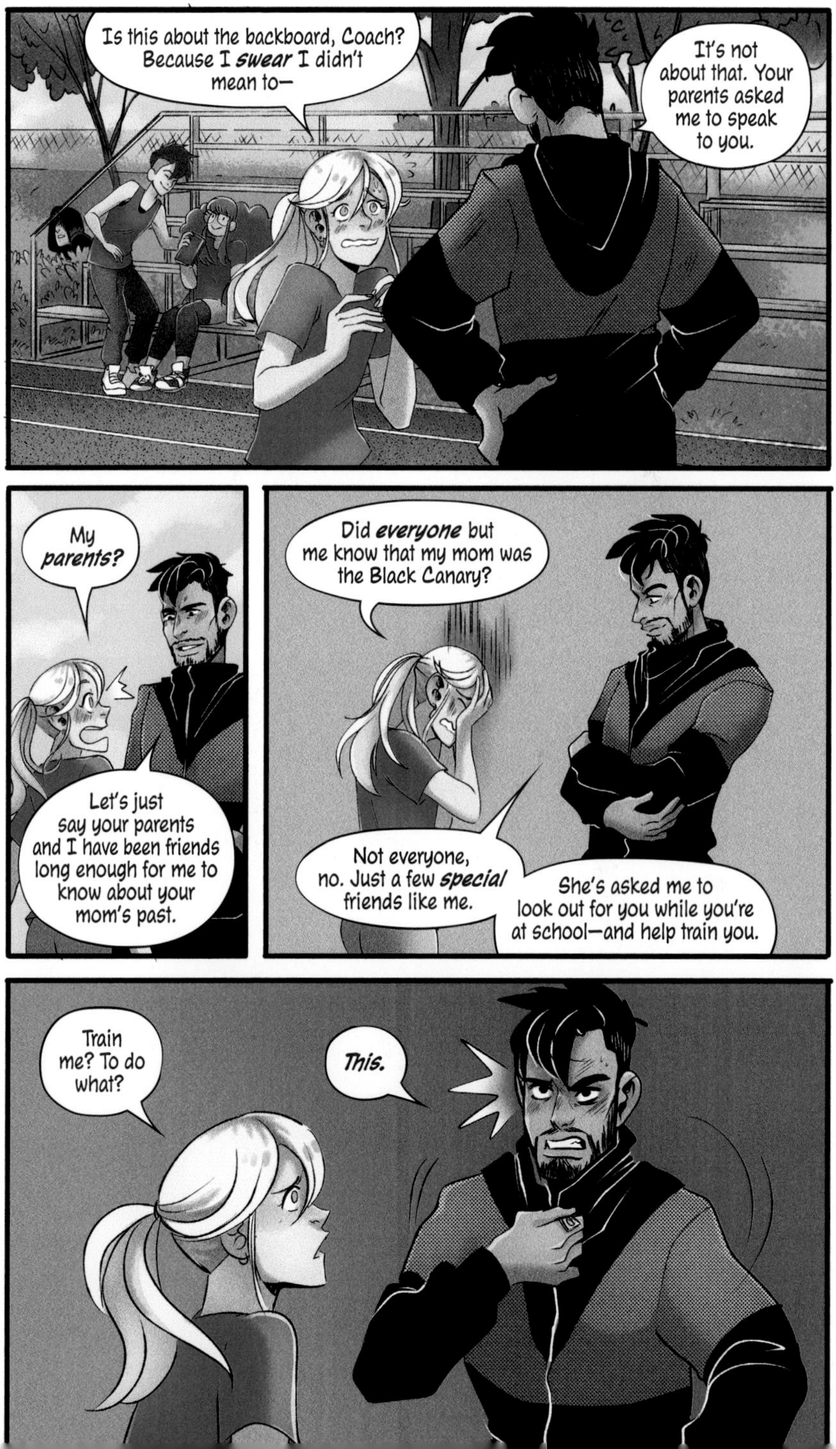
Is this about the backboard, Coach? Because I *swear* I didn't mean to—
It's not about that. Your parents asked me to speak to you.
My *parents?*
Let's just say your parents and I have been friends long enough for me to know about your mom's past.
Did *everyone* but me know that my mom was the Black Canary?
Not everyone, no. Just a few *special* friends like me.
She's asked me to look out for you while you're at school—and help train you.
Train me? To do what?
This.

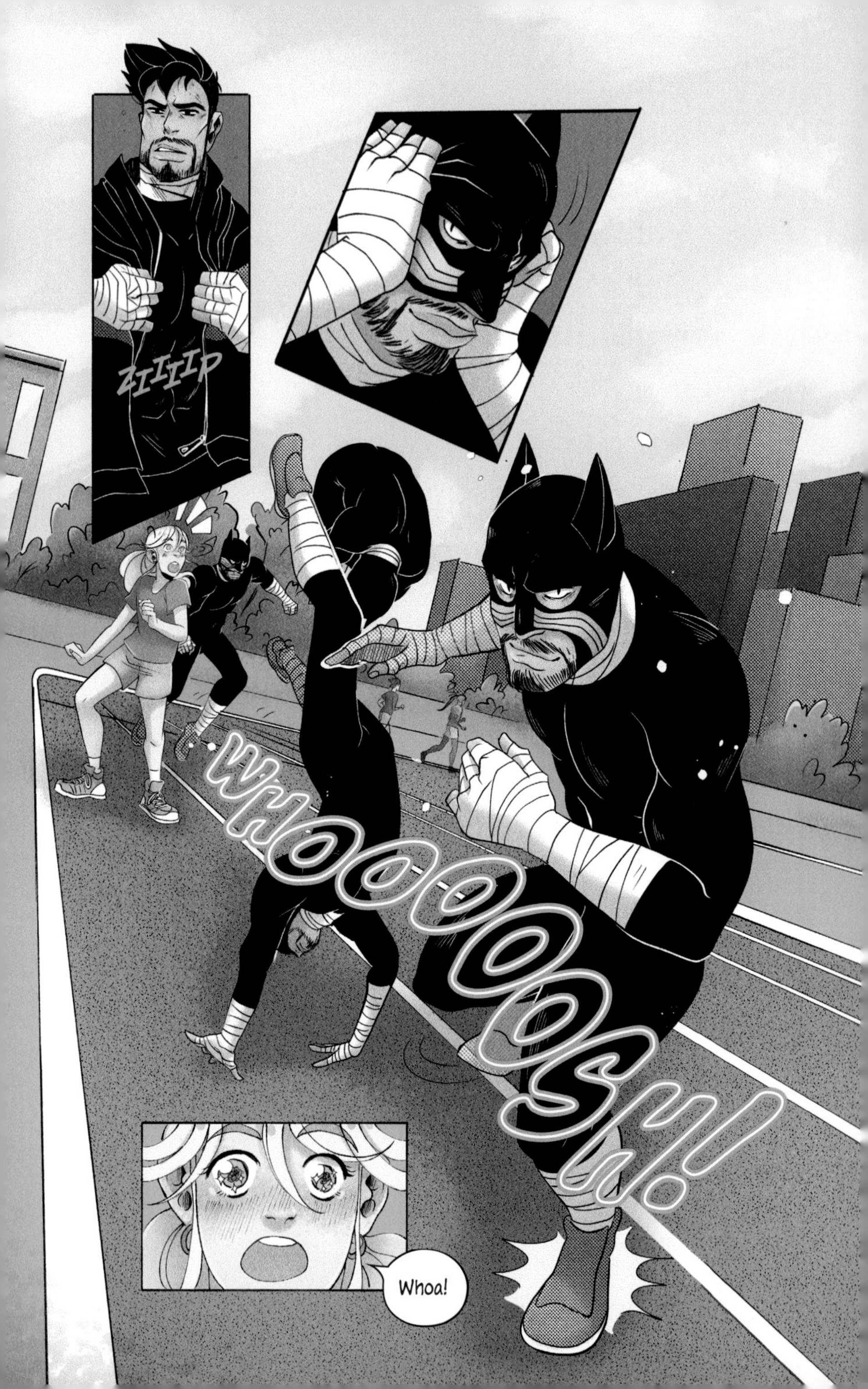
ZIIIIP
WHOOOOOSH!
Whoa!

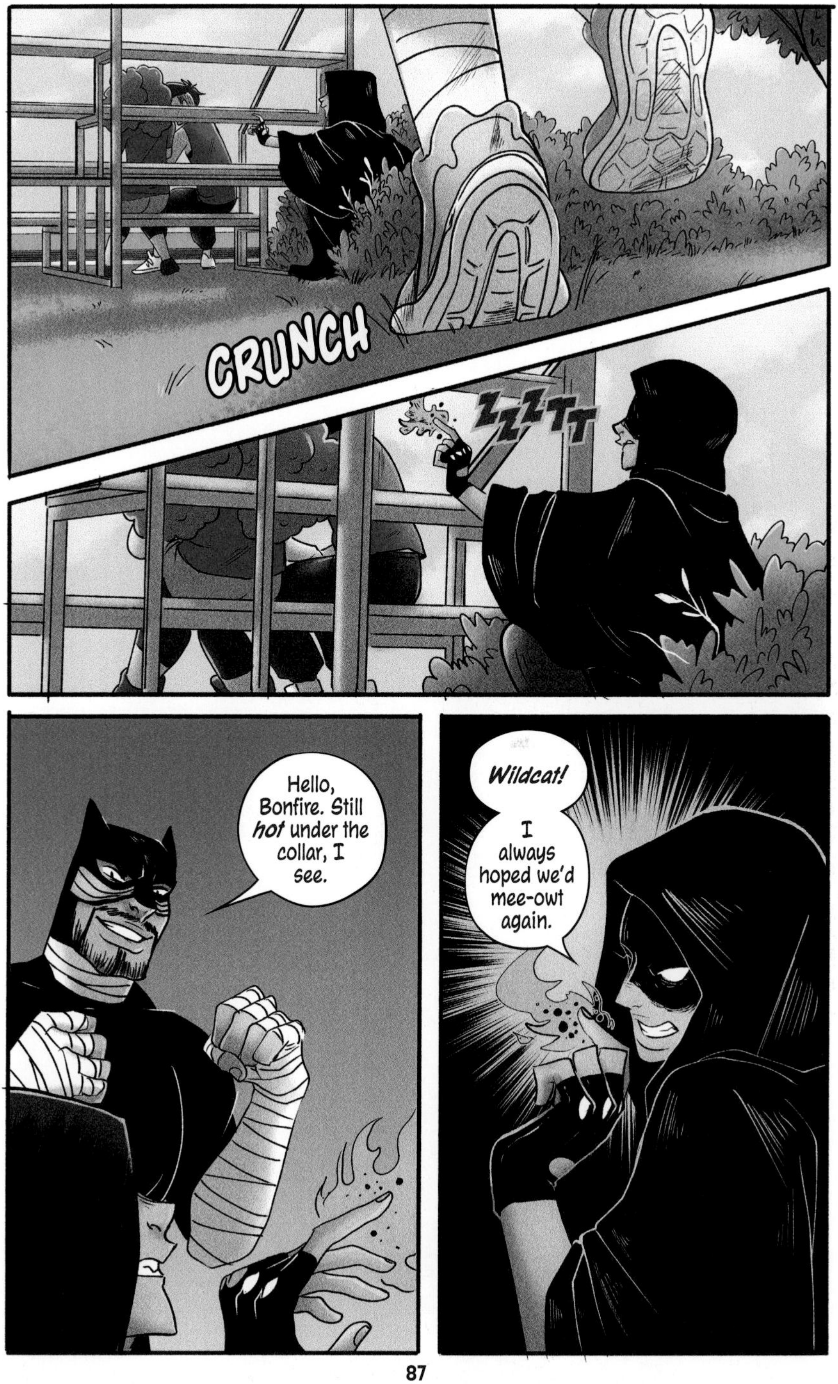
CRUNCH
ZZZTT
Hello, Bonfire. Still *hot* under the collar, I see.
Wildcat!
I always hoped we'd mee-owt again.

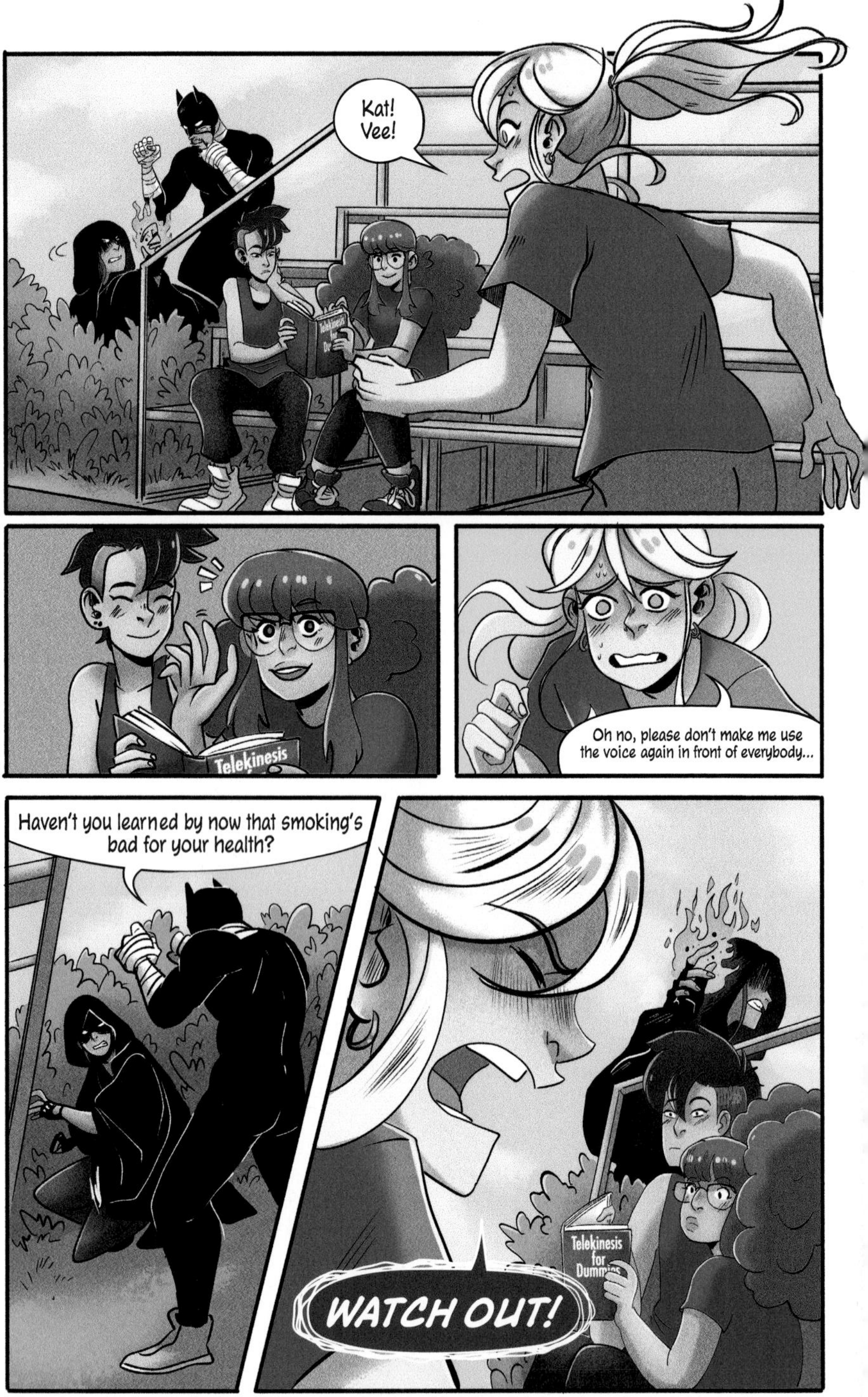
Kat!
Vee!
Telekinesis for Dummies
Telekinesis
Oh no, please don't make me use the voice again in front of everybody...
Haven't you learned by now that smoking's bad for your health?
WATCH OUT!
Telekinesis for Dummies

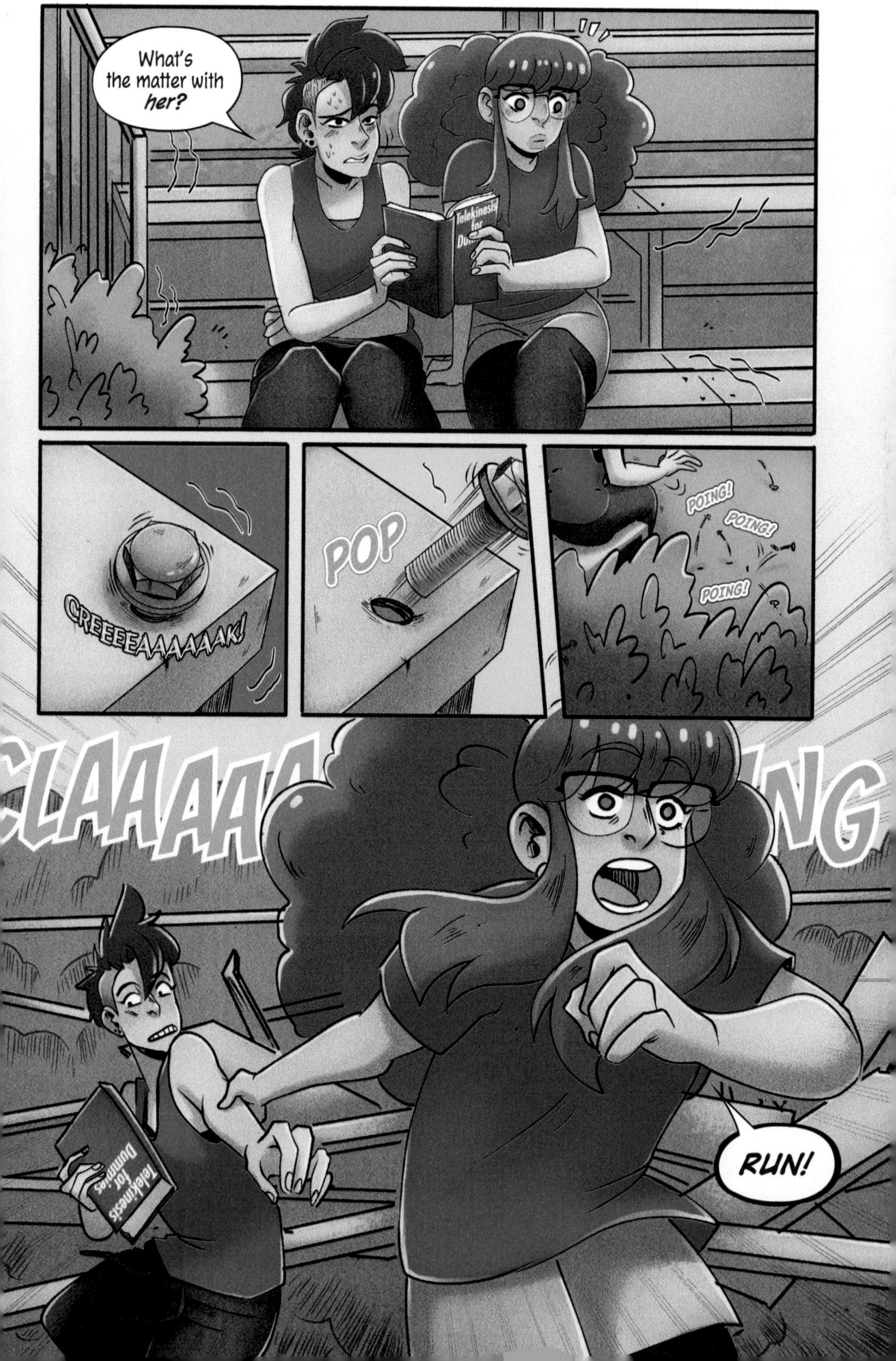
What's the matter with *her?*
Telekinesis for Dum...
CREEEEAAAAAAK!
POP
POING!
POING!
POING!
CLAAAA...NG
Telekinesis for Dummies
RUN!

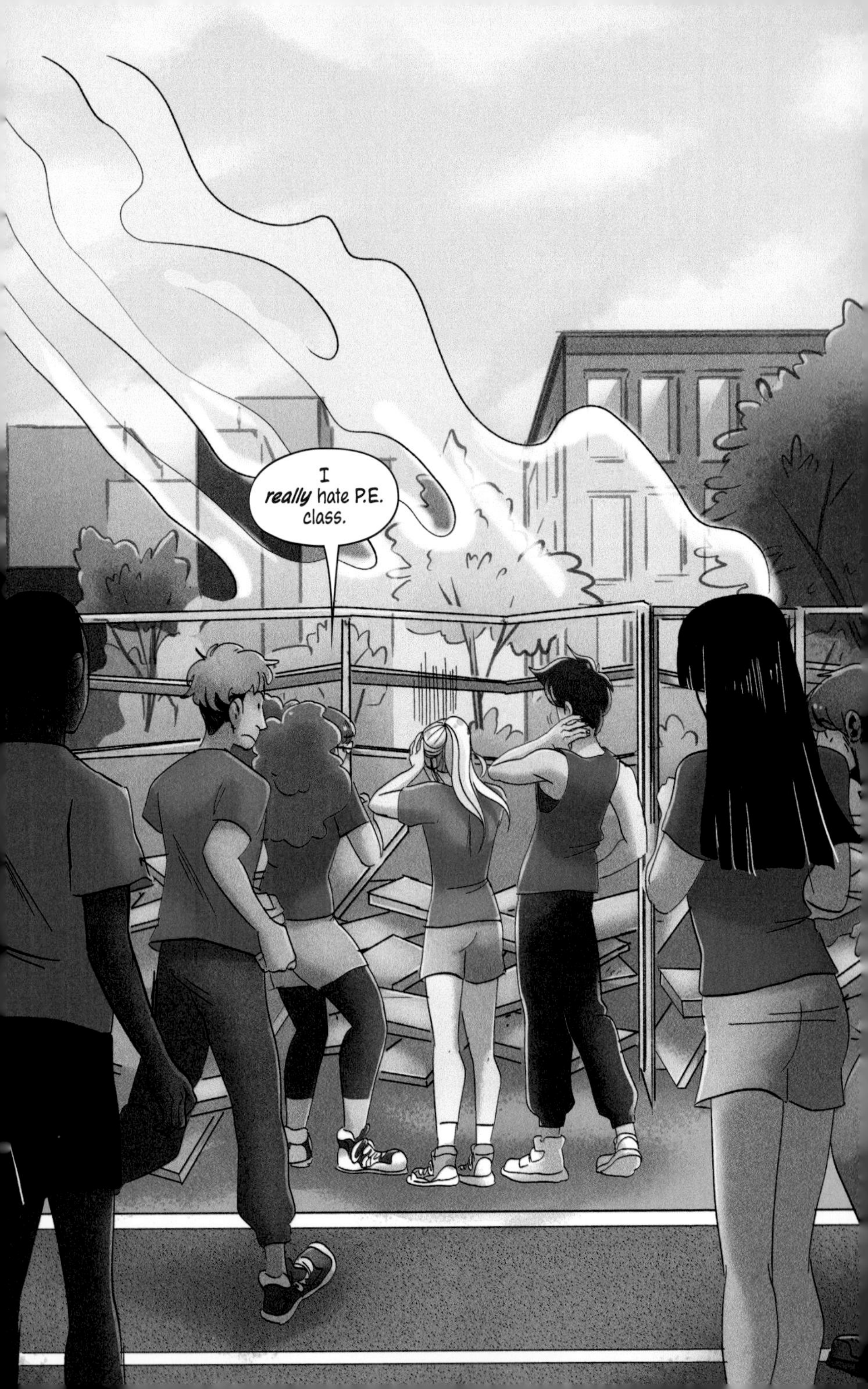
I *really* hate P.E. class.

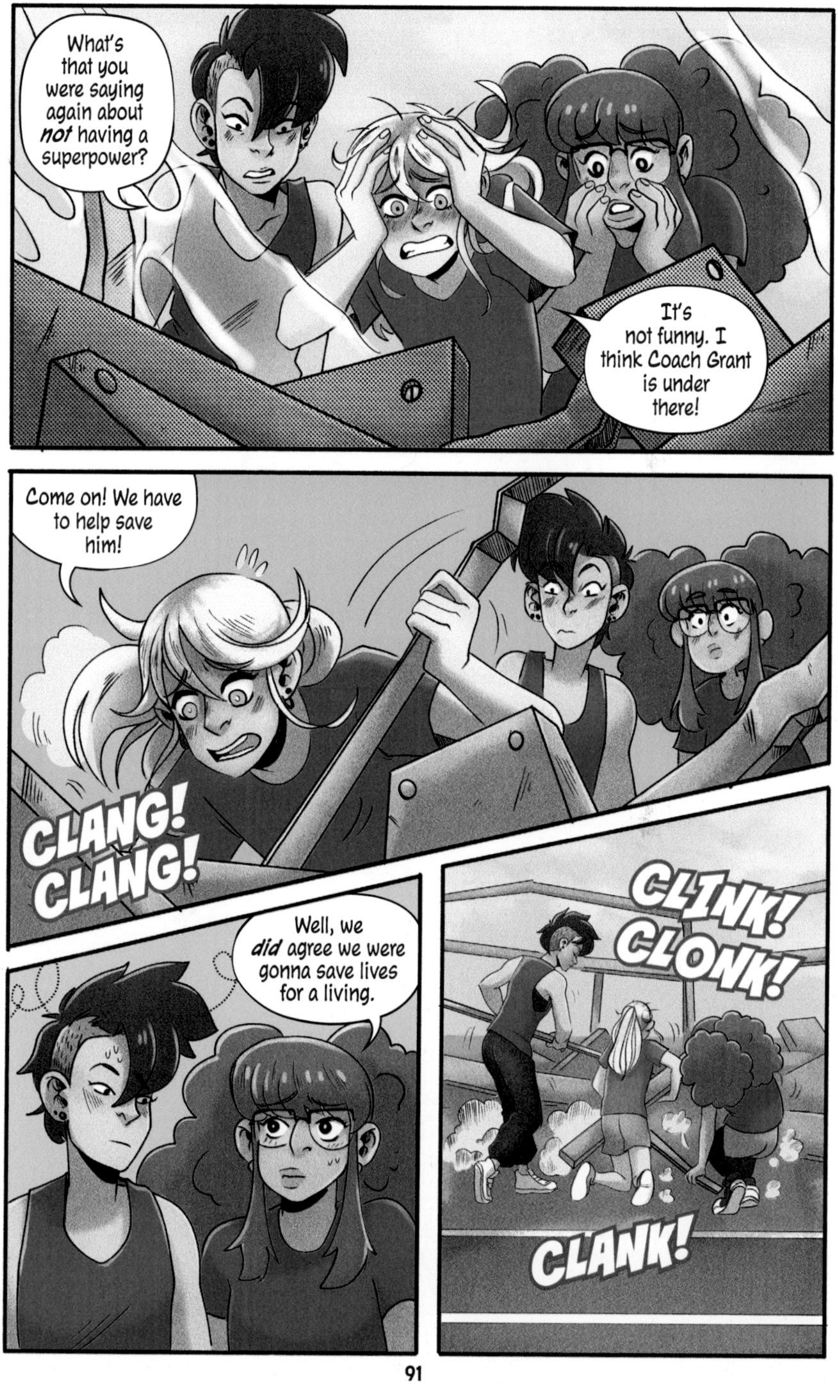
What's that you were saying again about *not* having a superpower?
It's not funny. I think Coach Grant is under there!
Come on! We have to help save him!
CLANG! CLANG!
CLINK! CLONK!
Well, we *did* agree we were gonna save lives for a living.
CLANK!

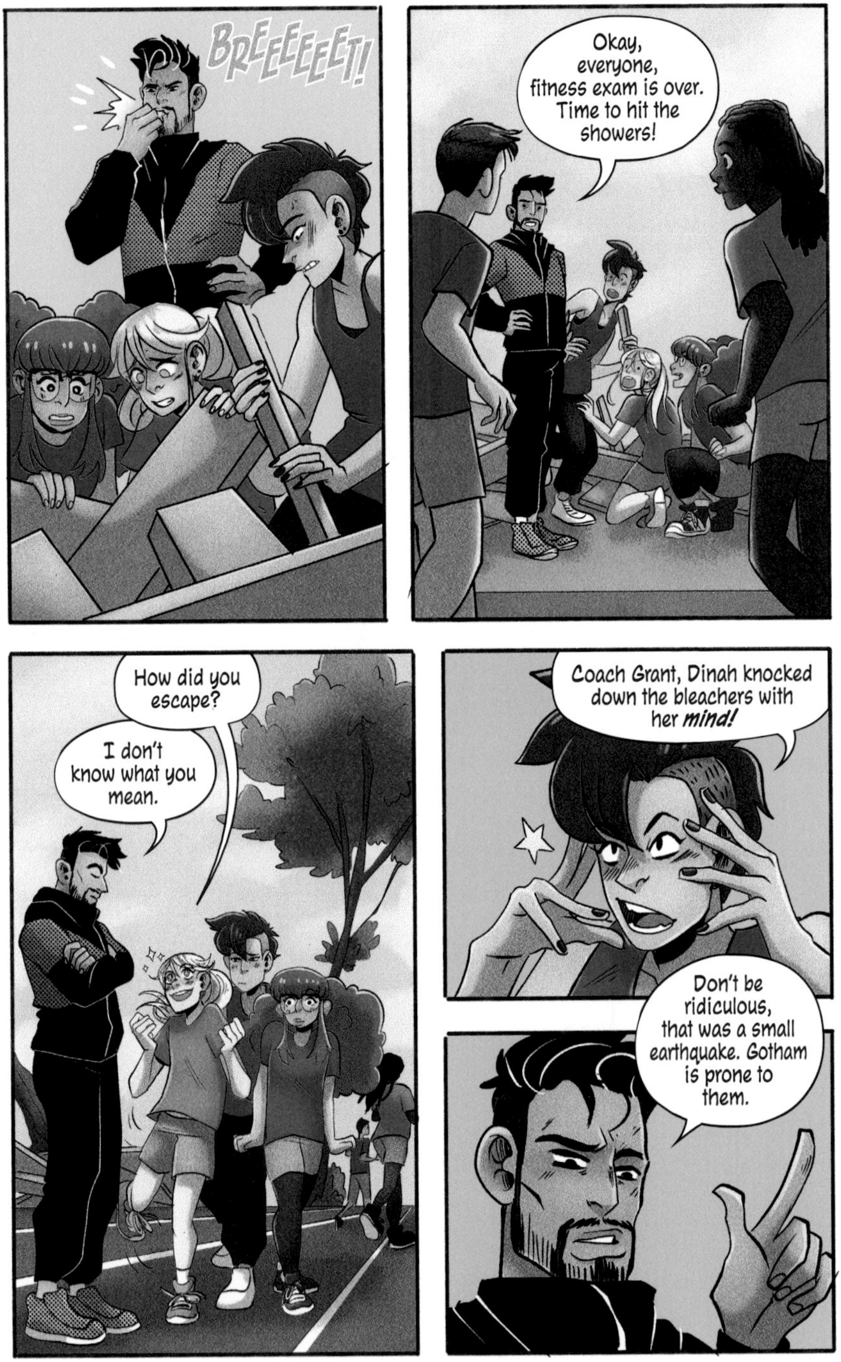

BREEEEEET!
Okay, everyone, fitness exam is over. Time to hit the showers!
How did you escape?
I don't know what you mean.
Coach Grant, Dinah knocked down the bleachers with her *mind!*
Don't be ridiculous, that was a small earthquake. Gotham is prone to them.

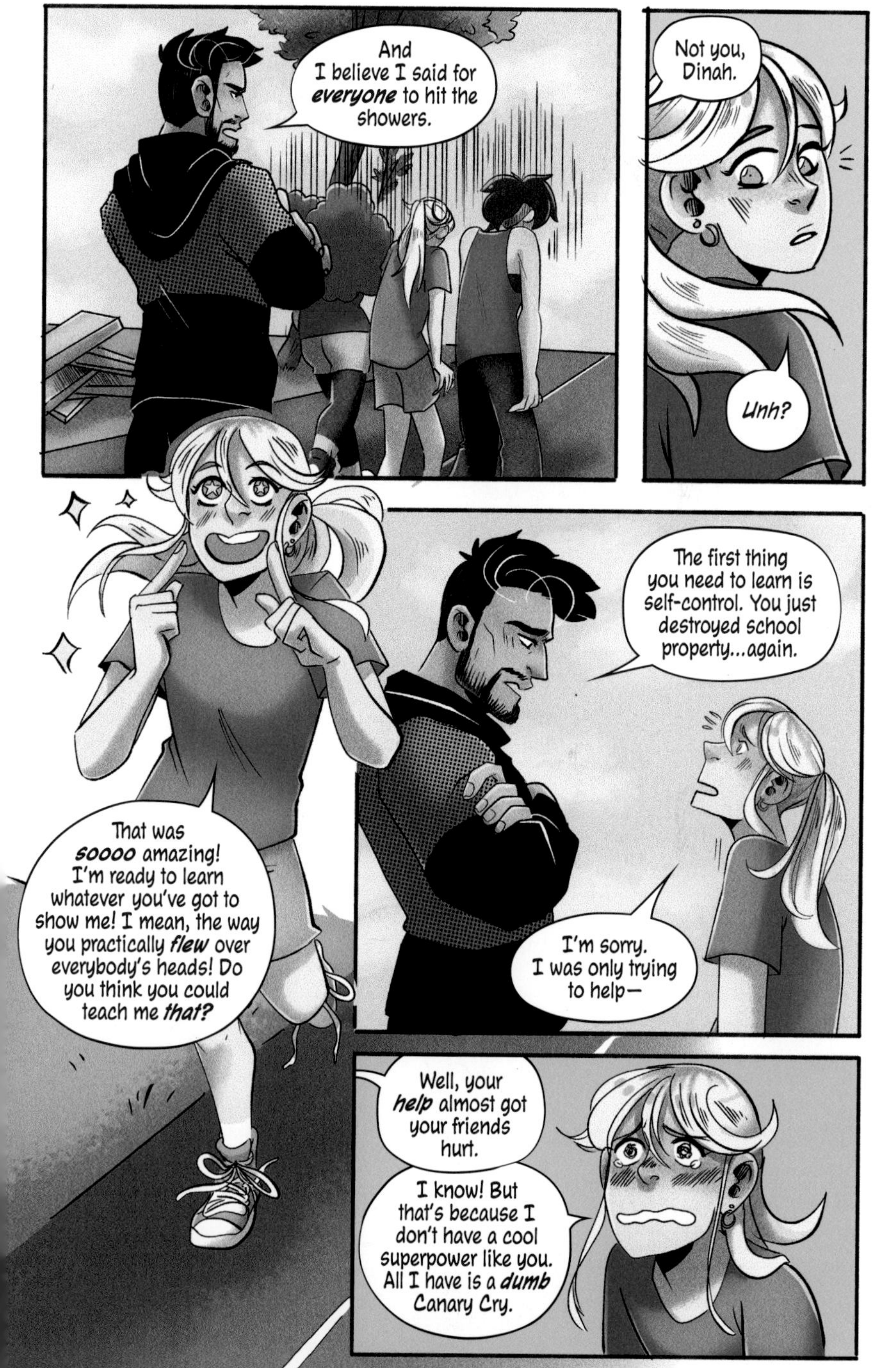
And I believe I said for *everyone* to hit the showers.
Not you, Dinah.
Unh?
That was *soooo* amazing! I'm ready to learn whatever you've got to show me! I mean, the way you practically *flew* over everybody's heads! Do you think you could teach me *that?*
The first thing you need to learn is self-control. You just destroyed school property...again.
I'm sorry. I was only trying to help—
Well, your *help* almost got your friends hurt.
I know! But that's because I don't have a cool superpower like you. All I have is a *dumb* Canary Cry.

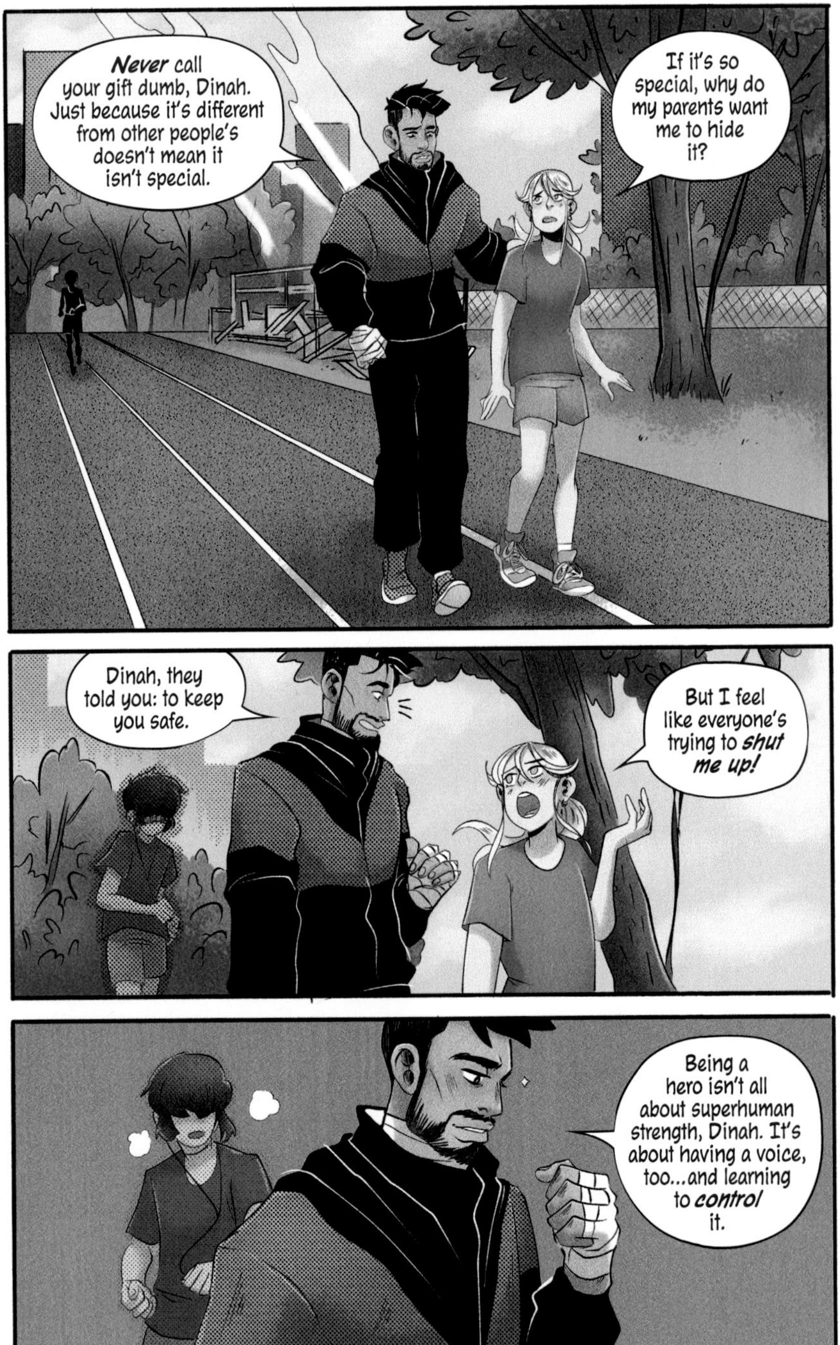
Never call your gift dumb, Dinah. Just because it's different from other people's doesn't mean it isn't special.
If it's so special, why do my parents want me to hide it?
Dinah, they told you: to keep you safe.
But I feel like everyone's trying to *shut me up!*
Being a hero isn't all about superhuman strength, Dinah. It's about having a voice, too...and learning to *control* it.

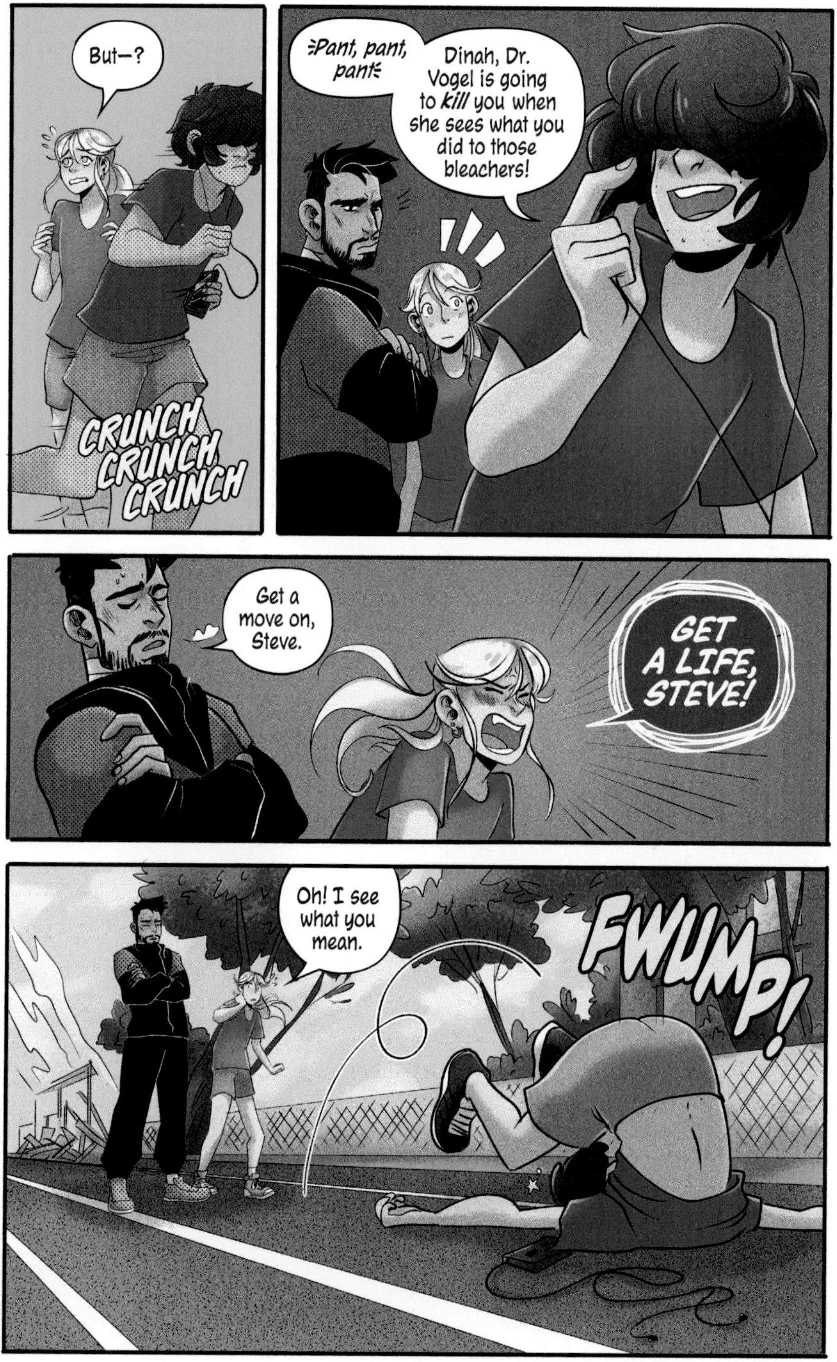
But—?
CRUNCH CRUNCH CRUNCH
Pant, pant, pant
Dinah, Dr. Vogel is going to kill you when she sees what you did to those bleachers!
Get a move on, Steve.
GET A LIFE, STEVE!
Oh! I see what you mean.
FWUMP!

CHAPTER 6
BURNING DOWN THE HOUSE

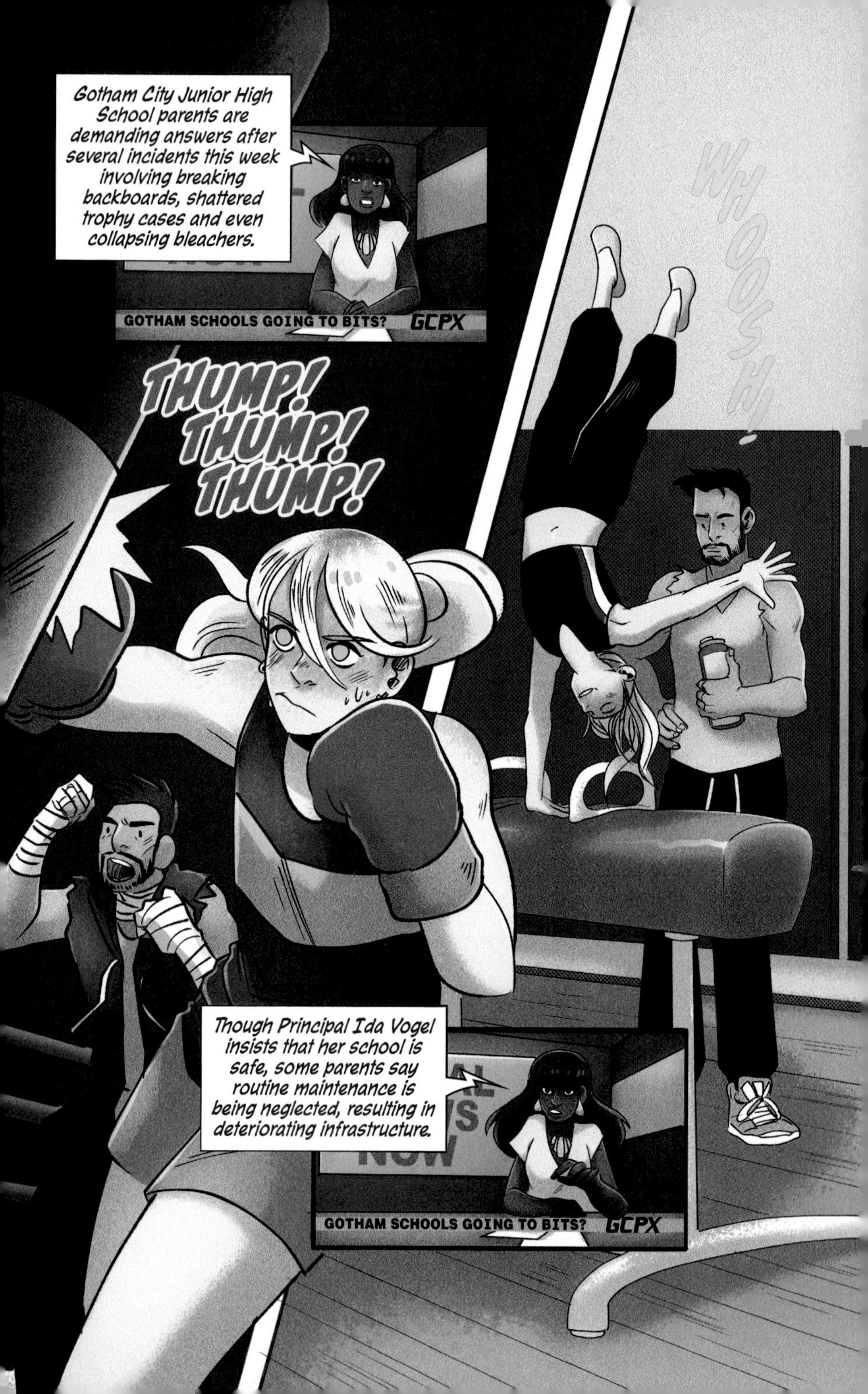
Gotham City Junior High School parents are demanding answers after several incidents this week involving breaking backboards, shattered trophy cases and even collapsing bleachers.
GOTHAM SCHOOLS GOING TO BITS?
GCPX
WHOOSH!
THUMP! THUMP! THUMP!
Though Principal Ida Vogel insists that her school is safe, some parents say routine maintenance is being neglected, resulting in deteriorating infrastructure.
GOTHAM SCHOOLS GOING TO BITS?
GCPX

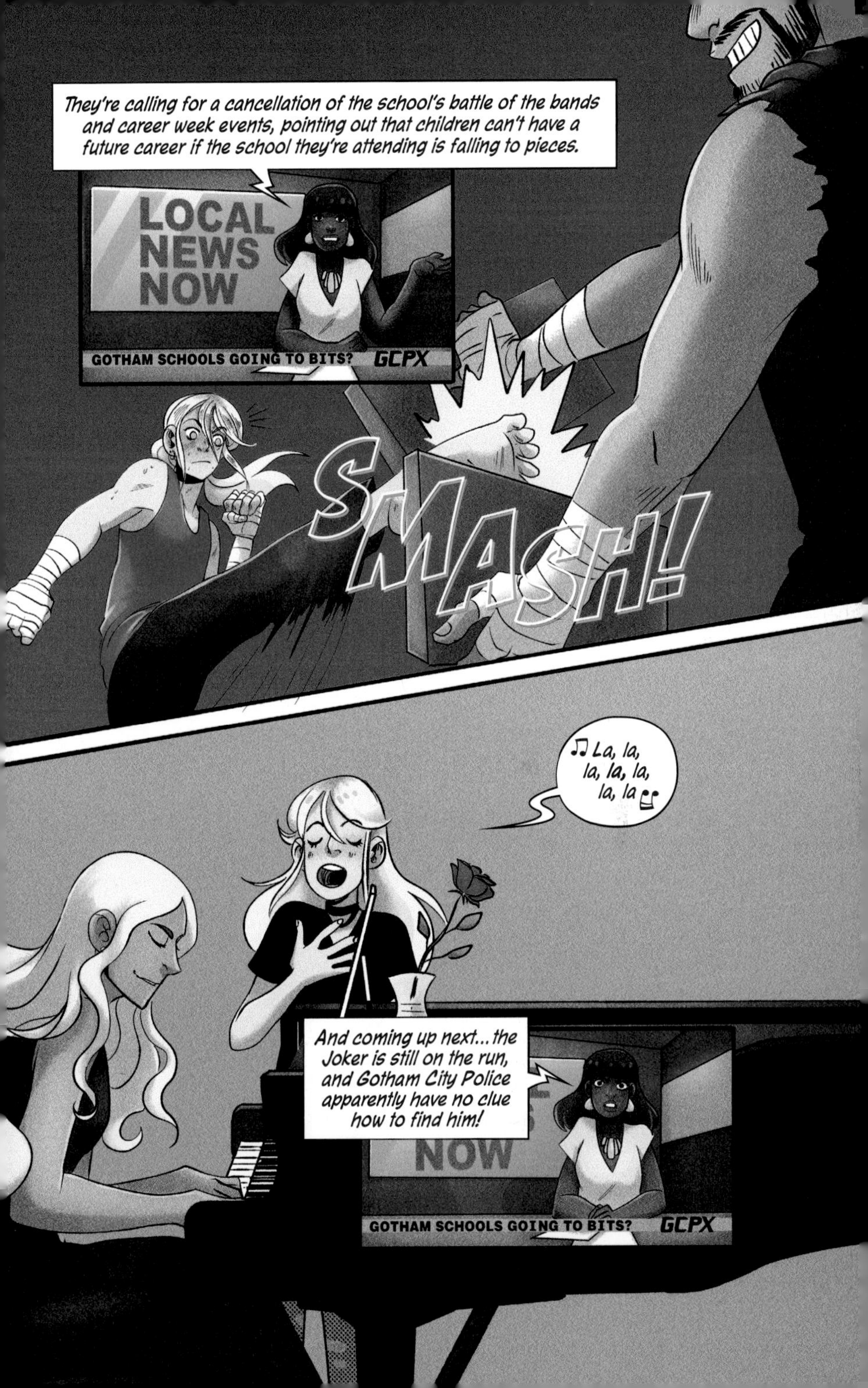
They're calling for a cancellation of the school's battle of the bands and career week events, pointing out that children can't have a future career if the school they're attending is falling to pieces.
LOCAL NEWS NOW
GOTHAM SCHOOLS GOING TO BITS?
GCPX
SMASH!
♫ La, la, la, la, la, la, la ♫
And coming up next... the Joker is still on the run, and Gotham City Police apparently have no clue how to find him!
NOW
GOTHAM SCHOOLS GOING TO BITS?
GCPX

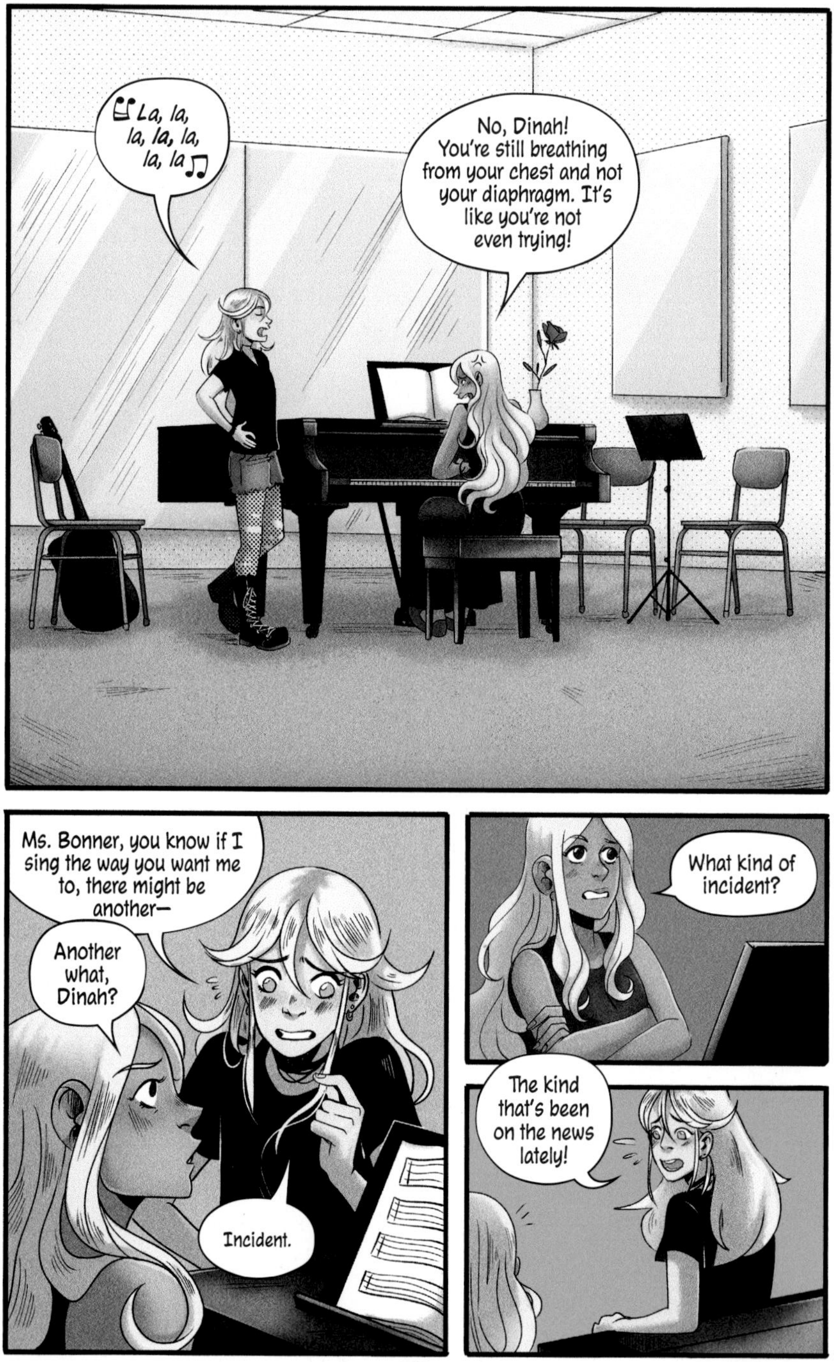
La, la, la, la, la, la, la
No, Dinah! You're still breathing from your chest and not your diaphragm. It's like you're not even trying!
Ms. Bonner, you know if I sing the way you want me to, there might be another—
Another what, Dinah?
Incident.
What kind of incident?
The kind that's been on the news lately!

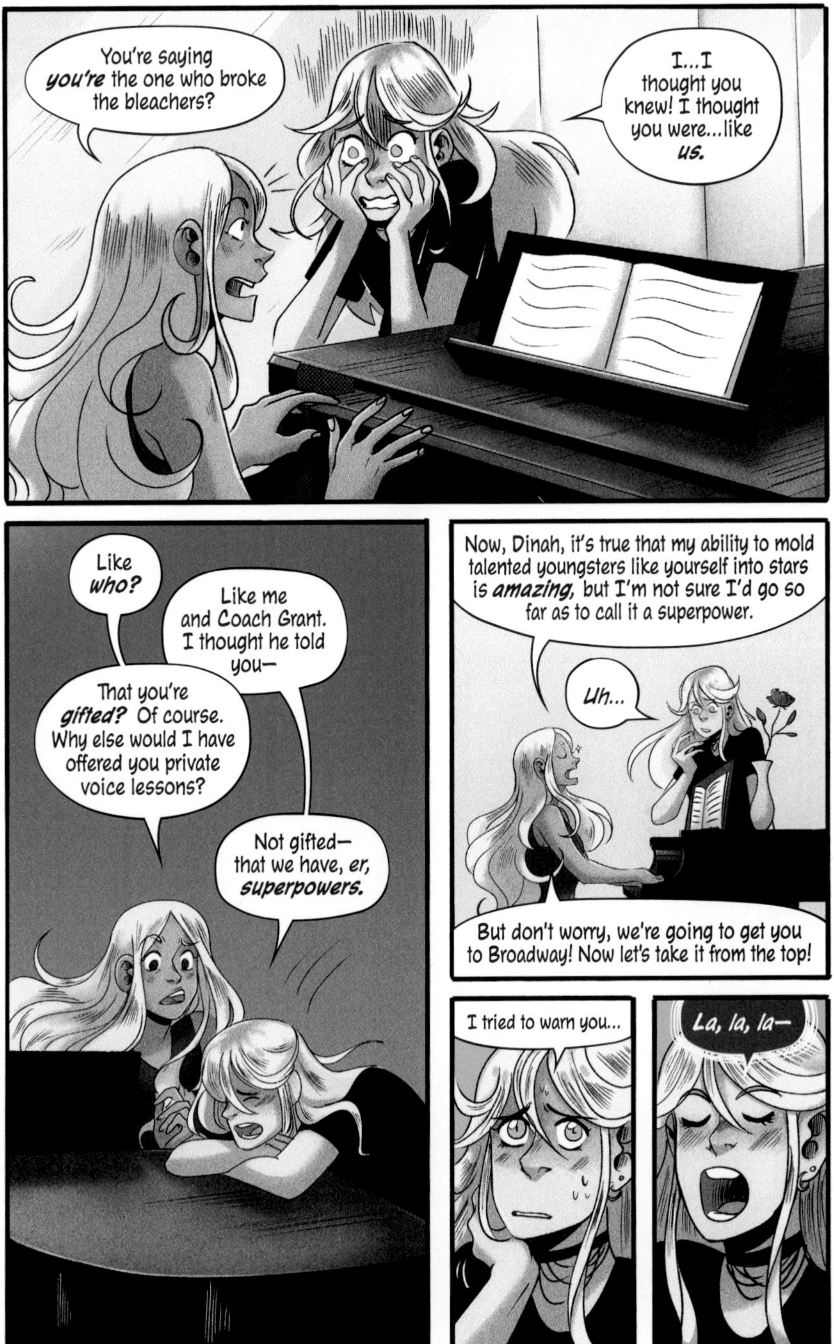
You're saying *you're* the one who broke the bleachers?
I...I thought you knew! I thought you were...like *us.*
Like *who?*
Like me and Coach Grant. I thought he told you—
That you're *gifted?* Of course. Why else would I have offered you private voice lessons?
Not gifted— that we have, er, *superpowers.*
Now, Dinah, it's true that my ability to mold talented youngsters like yourself into stars is *amazing,* but I'm not sure I'd go so far as to call it a superpower.
Uh...
But don't worry, we're going to get you to Broadway! Now let's take it from the top!
I tried to warn you...
La, la, la—

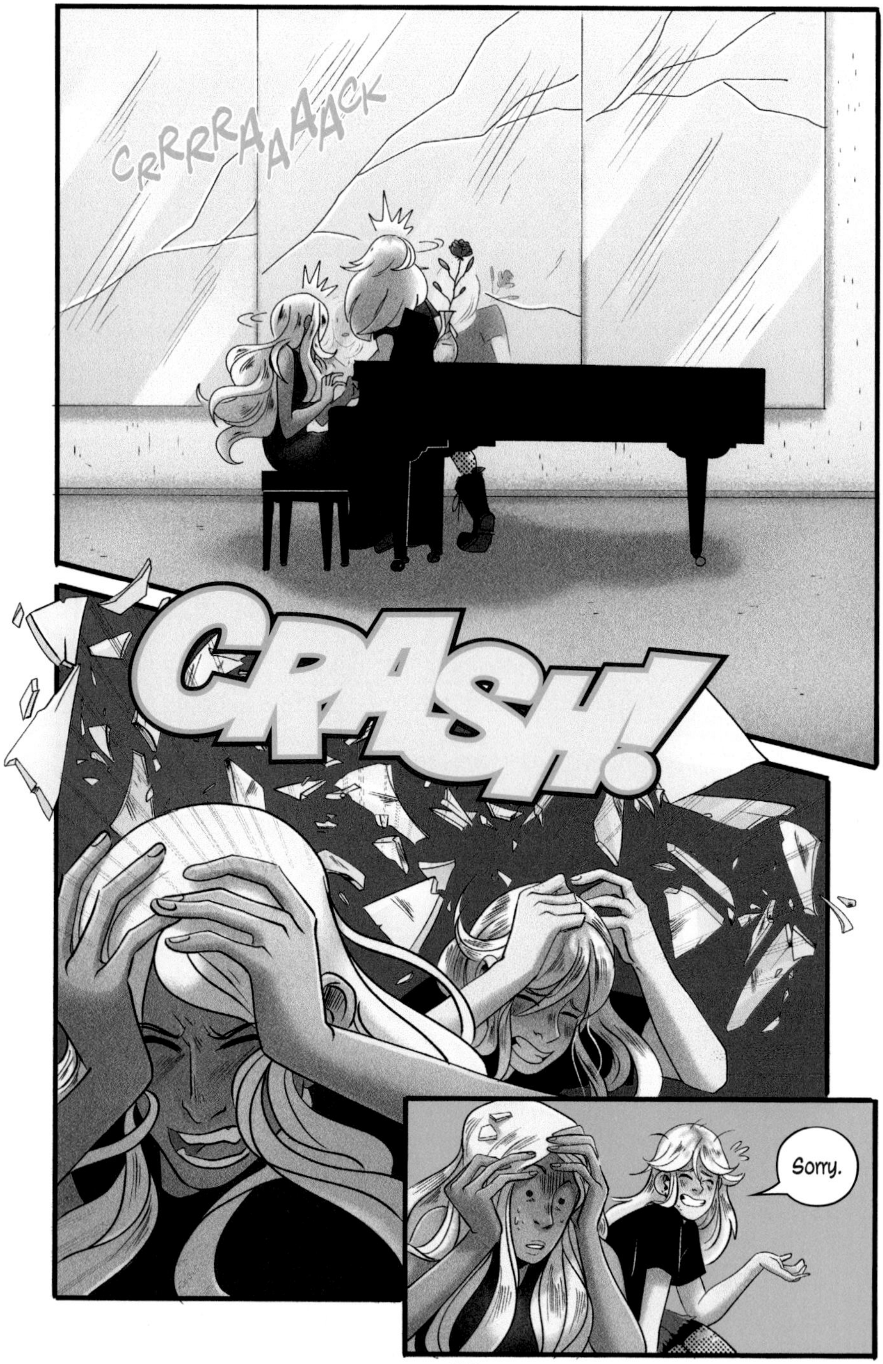
CRRRRAAAACK
CRASH!
Sorry.

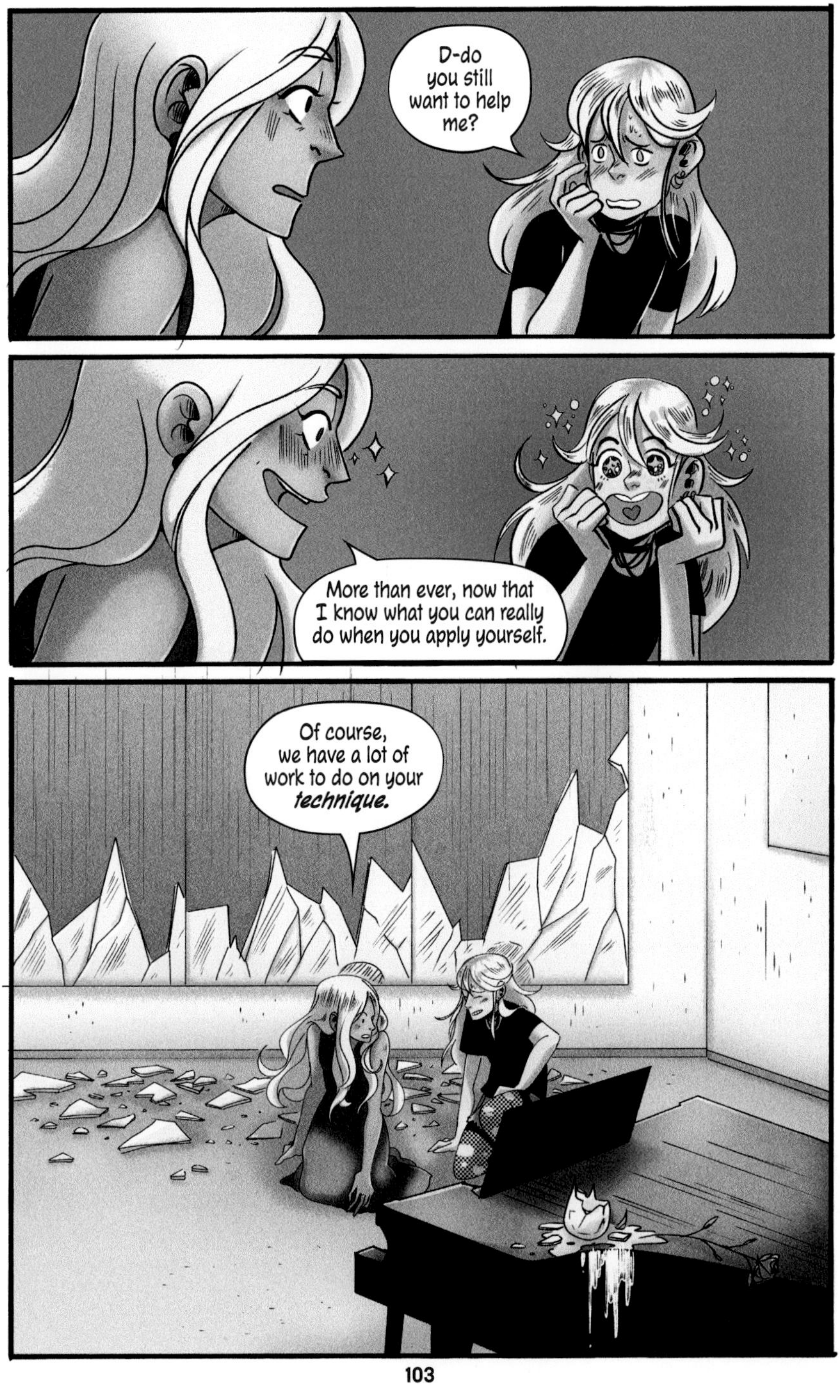
D-do you still want to help me?
More than ever, now that I know what you can really do when you apply yourself.
Of course, we have a lot of work to do on your *technique.*

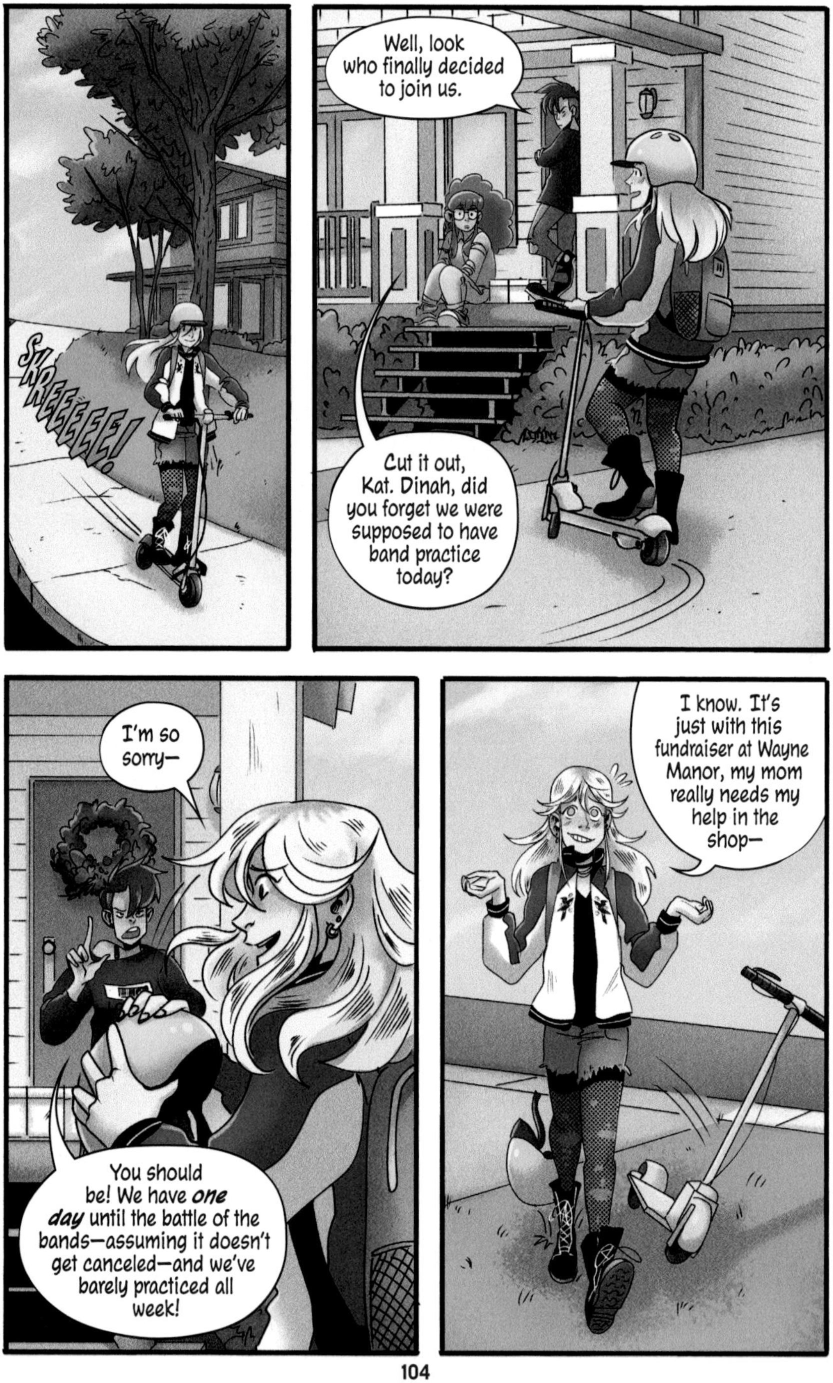
SKREEEEE!
Well, look who finally decided to join us.
Cut it out, Kat. Dinah, did you forget we were supposed to have band practice today?
I'm so sorry—
You should be! We have ***one day*** until the battle of the bands—assuming it doesn't get canceled—and we've barely practiced all week!
I know. It's just with this fundraiser at Wayne Manor, my mom really needs my help in the shop—

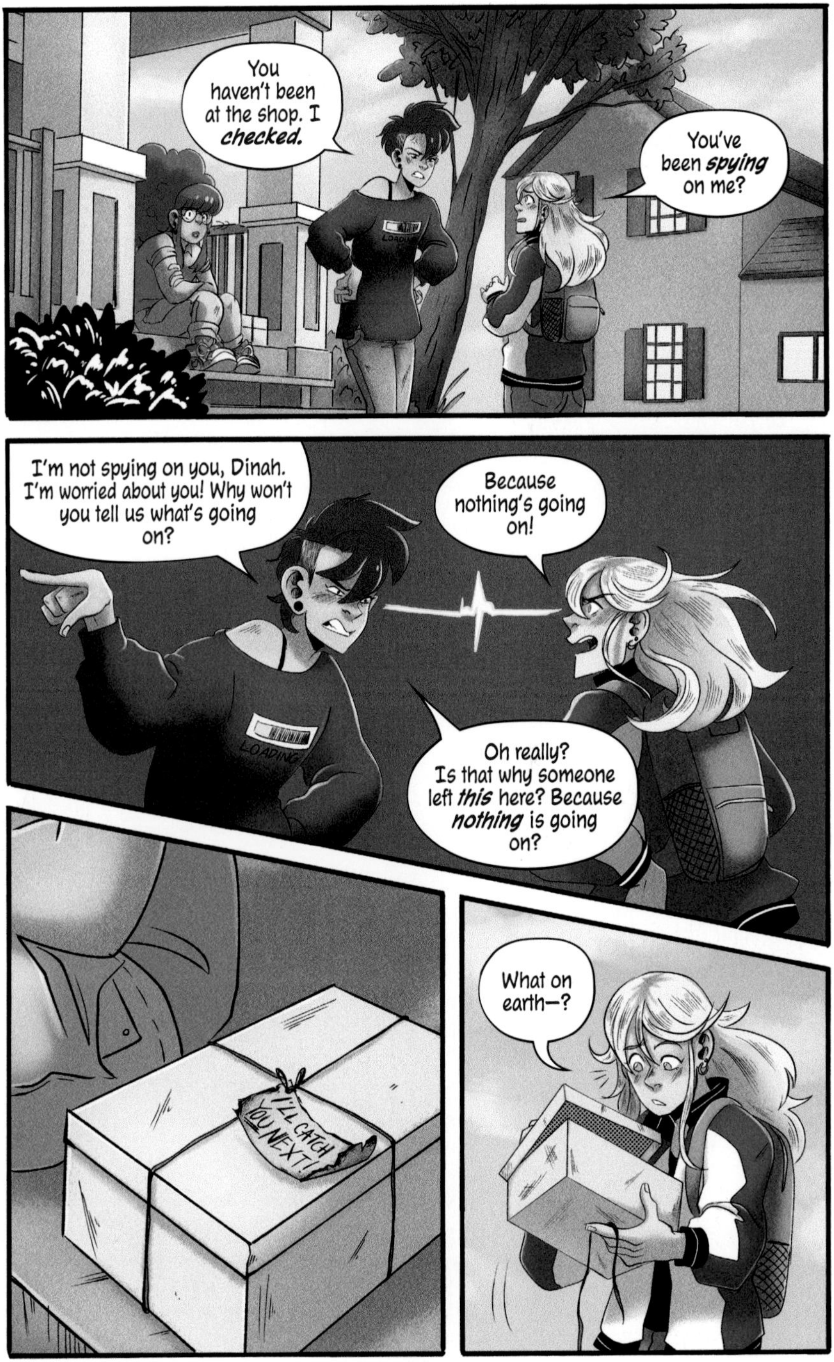
You haven't been at the shop. I *checked.*
You've been *spying* on me?
I'm not spying on you, Dinah. I'm worried about you! Why won't you tell us what's going on?
Because nothing's going on!
Oh really? Is that why someone left *this* here? Because *nothing* is going on?
I'LL CATCH YOU NEXT!
What on earth—?

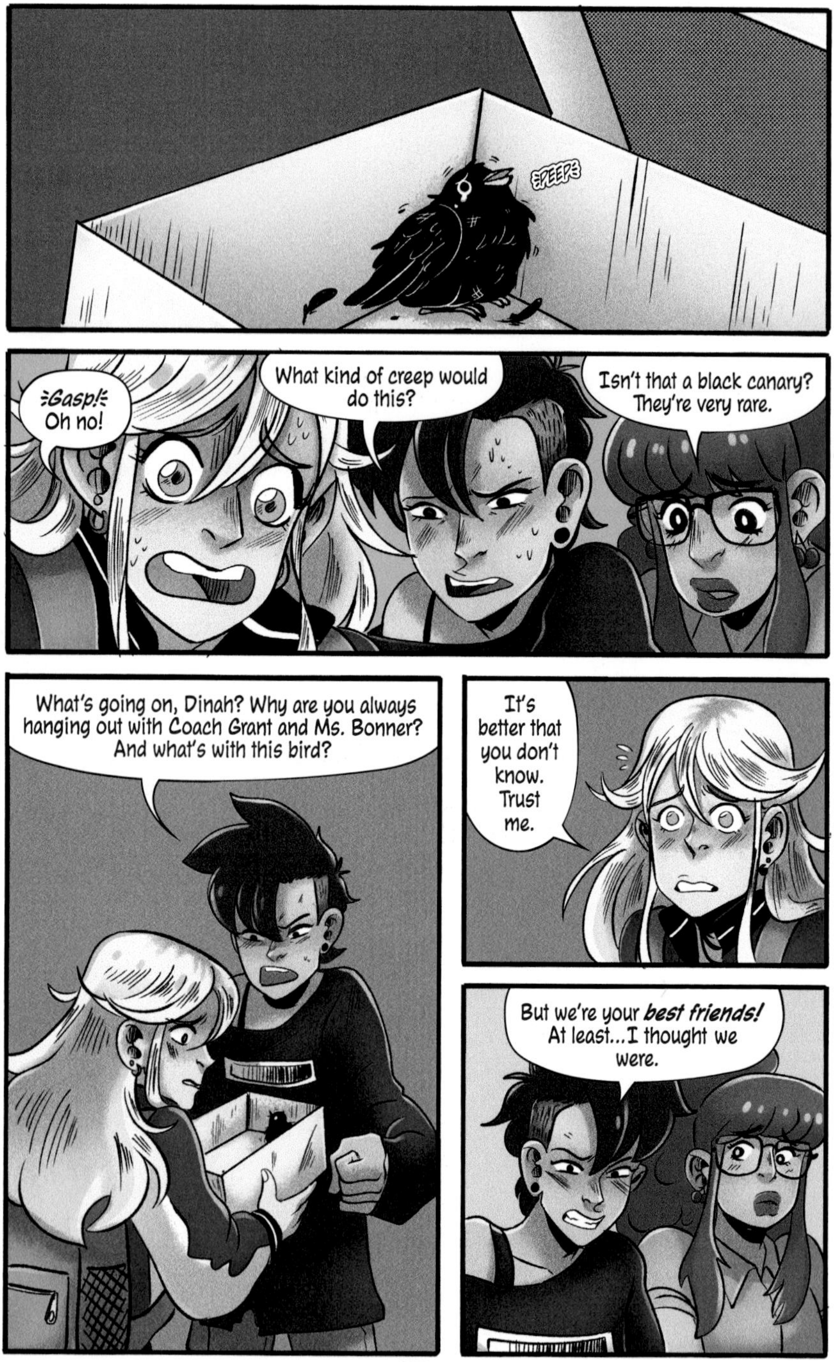
PEEP
Gasp! Oh no!
What kind of creep would do this?
Isn't that a black canary? They're very rare.
What's going on, Dinah? Why are you always hanging out with Coach Grant and Ms. Bonner? And what's with this bird?
It's better that you don't know. Trust me.
But we're your best friends! At least...I thought we were.

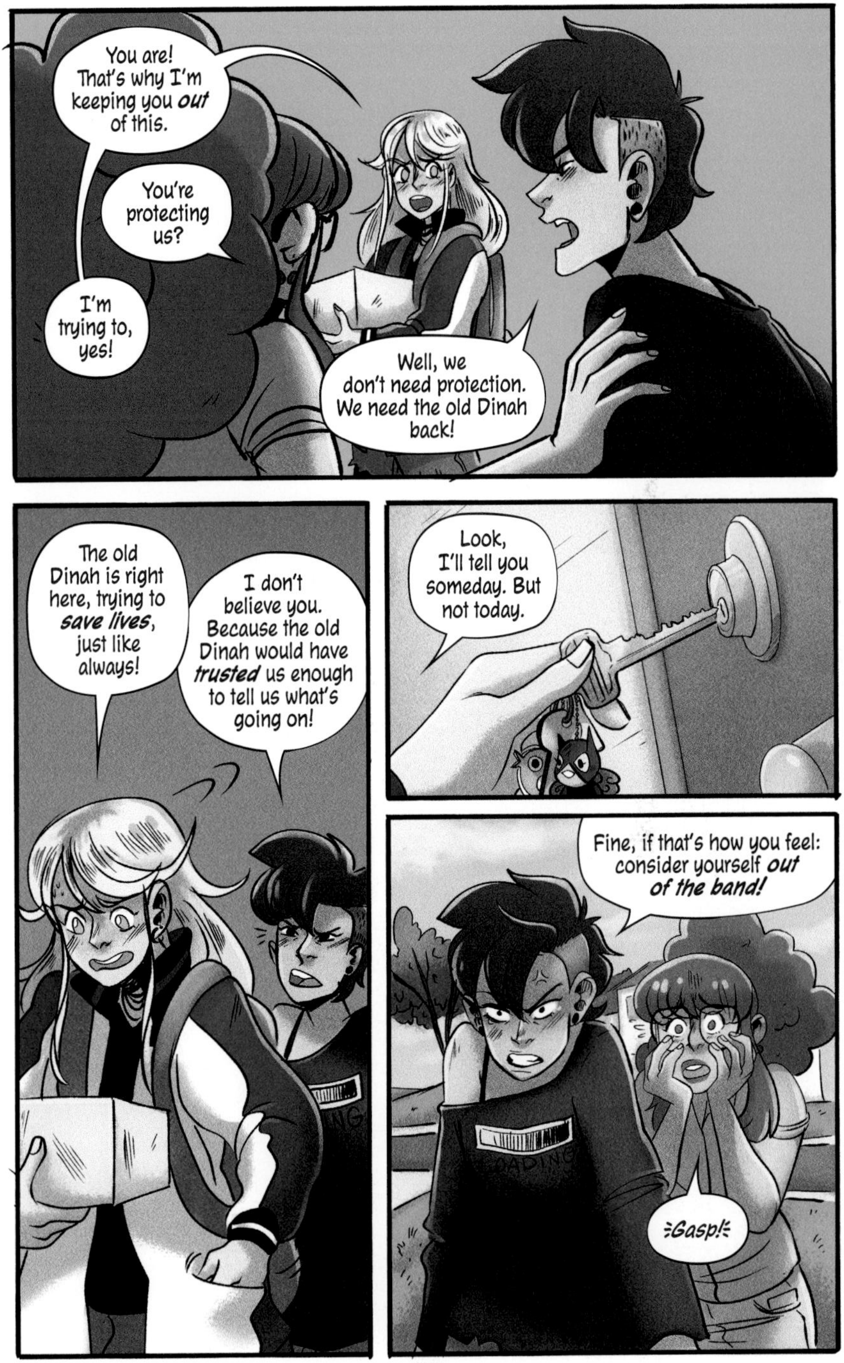
You are! That's why I'm keeping you *out* of this.
You're protecting us?
I'm trying to, yes!
Well, we don't need protection. We need the old Dinah back!
The old Dinah is right here, trying to ***save lives***, just like always!
I don't believe you. Because the old Dinah would have ***trusted*** us enough to tell us what's going on!
Look, I'll tell you someday. But not today.
Fine, if that's how you feel: consider yourself ***out of the band!***
Gasp!

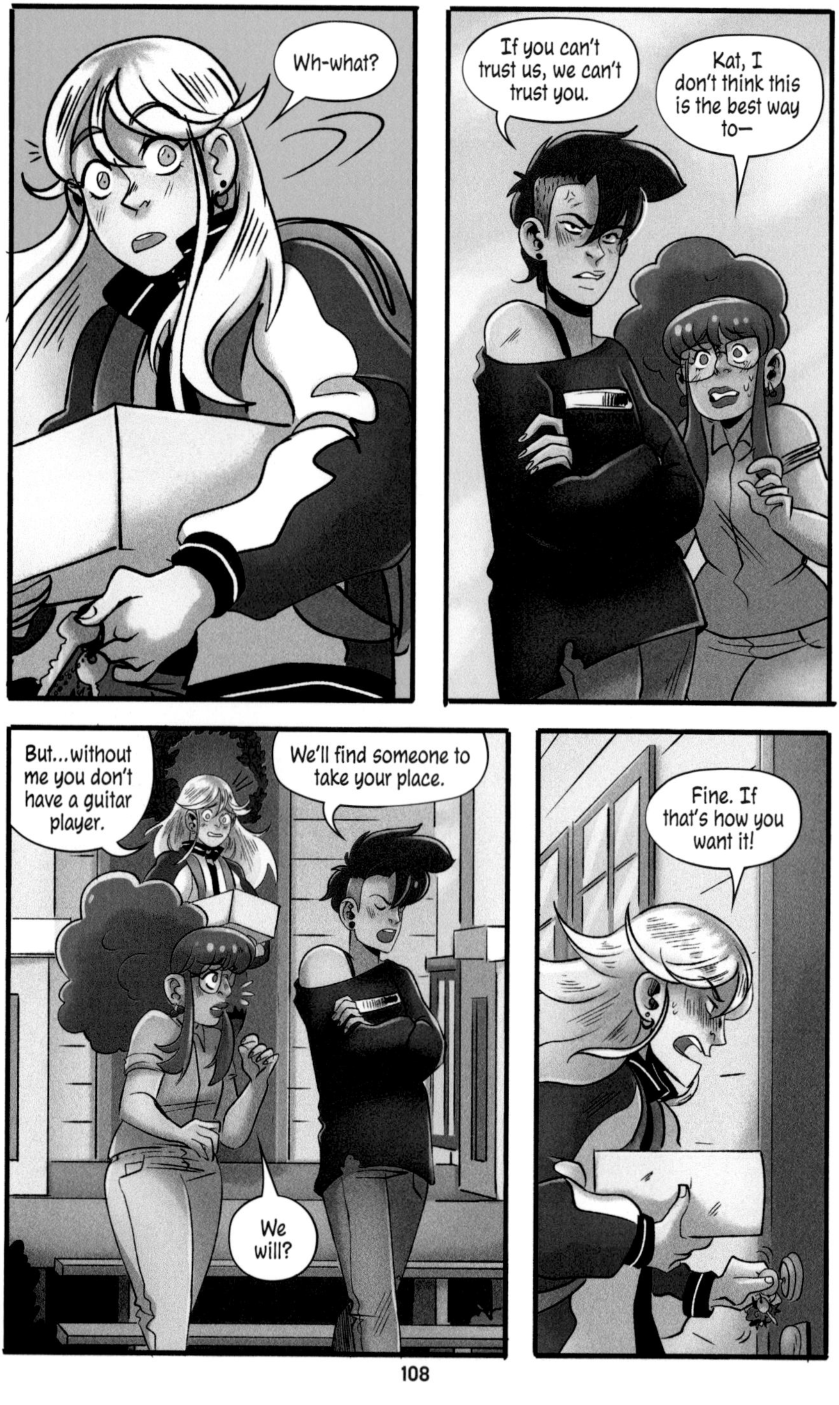
Wh-what?
If you can't trust us, we can't trust you.
Kat, I don't think this is the best way to—
But...without me you don't have a guitar player.
We'll find someone to take your place.
We will?
Fine. If that's how you want it!

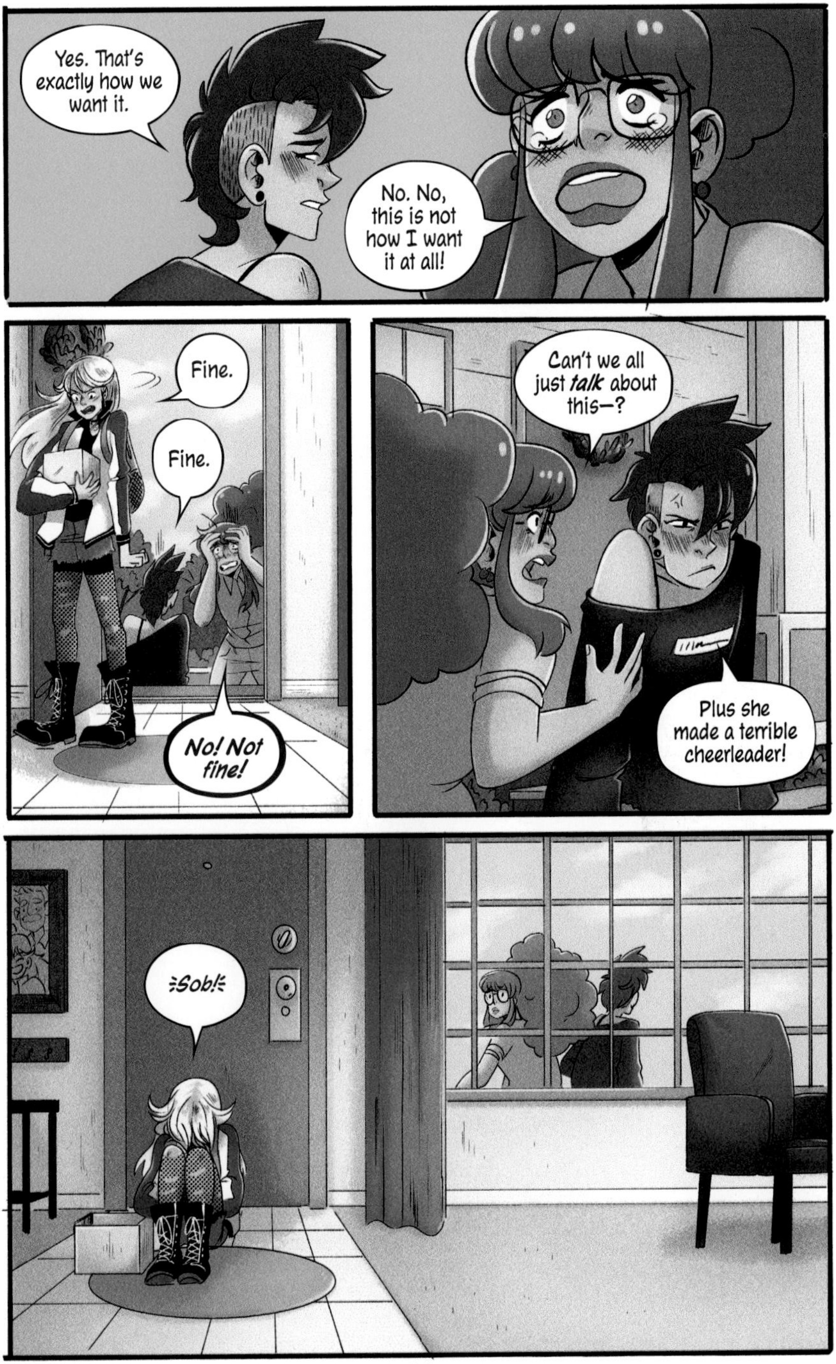
Yes. That's exactly how we want it.
No. No, this is not how I want it at all!
Fine.
Fine.
No! Not fine!
Can't we all just *talk* about this—?
Plus she made a terrible cheerleader!
Sob!

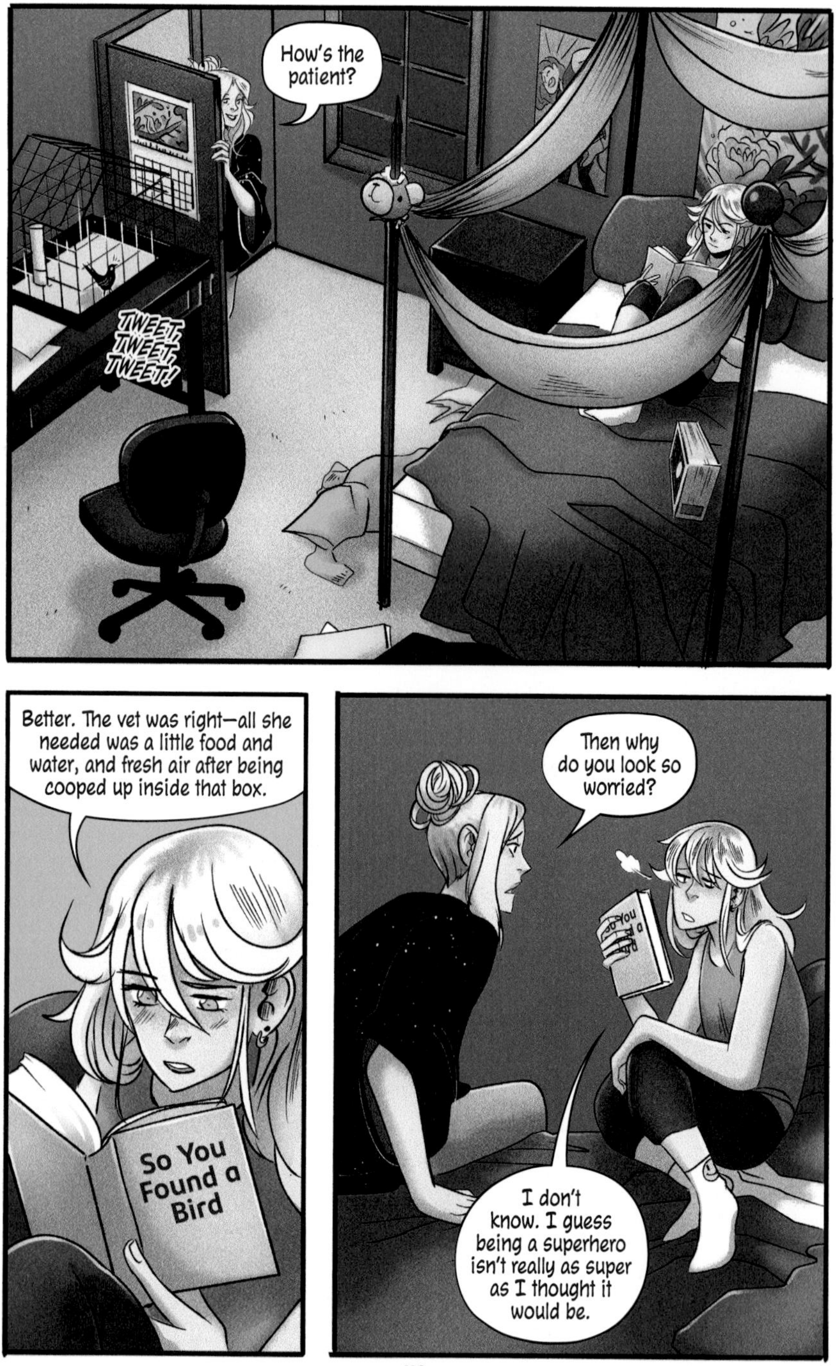
How's the patient?
TWEET, TWEET, TWEET!
Better. The vet was right—all she needed was a little food and water, and fresh air after being cooped up inside that box.
So You Found a Bird
Then why do you look so worried?
I don't know. I guess being a superhero isn't really as super as I thought it would be.

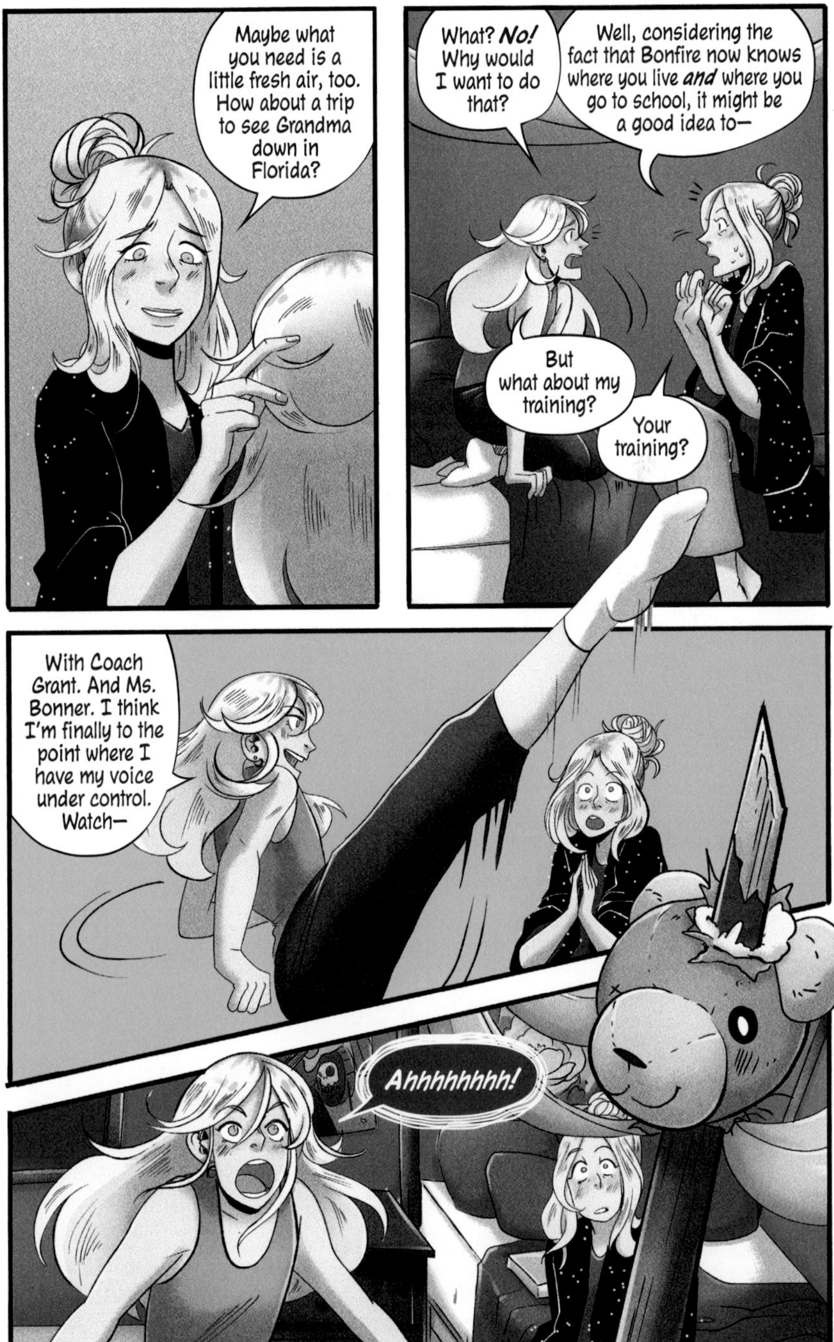
Maybe what you need is a little fresh air, too. How about a trip to see Grandma down in Florida?
What? No! Why would I want to do that?
Well, considering the fact that Bonfire now knows where you live and where you go to school, it might be a good idea to—
But what about my training?
Your training?
With Coach Grant. And Ms. Bonner. I think I'm finally to the point where I have my voice under control. Watch—
Ahhhhhhhh!

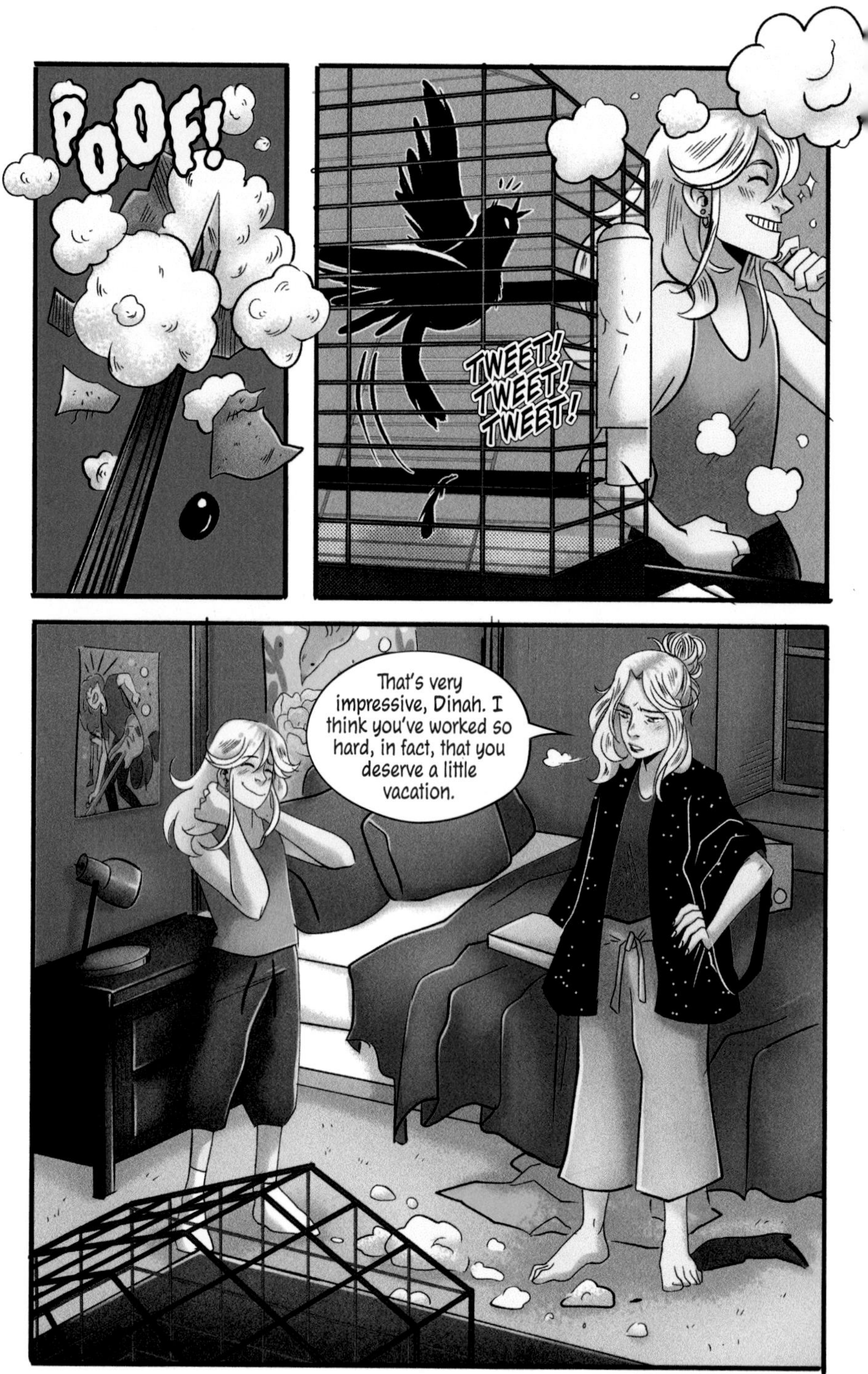
POOF!
TWEET! TWEET! TWEET!
That's very impressive, Dinah. I think you've worked so hard, in fact, that you deserve a little vacation.

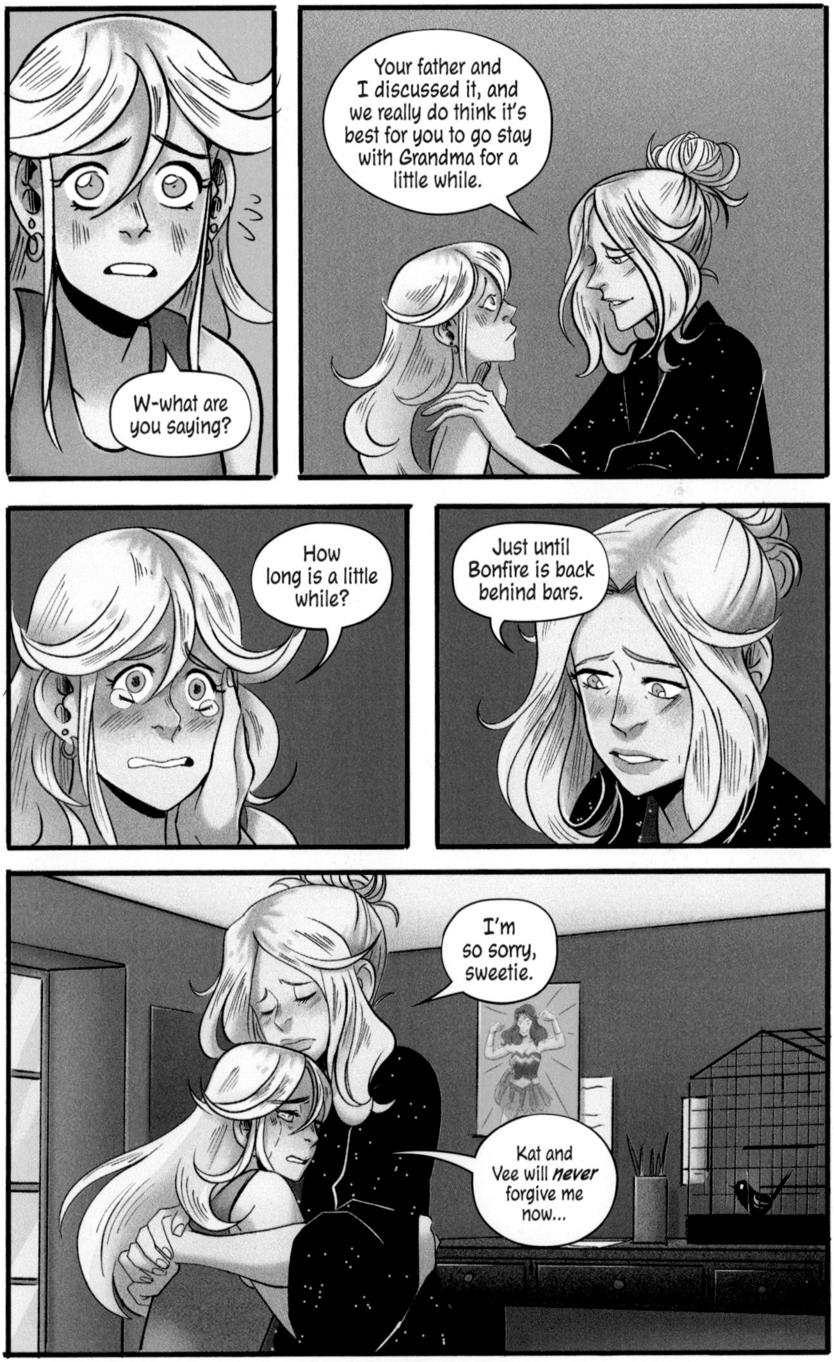
W-what are you saying?
Your father and I discussed it, and we really do think it's best for you to go stay with Grandma for a little while.
How long is a little while?
Just until Bonfire is back behind bars.
I'm so sorry, sweetie.
Kat and Vee will *never* forgive me now...

CHAPTER 7
GONNA SAVE THE WORLD

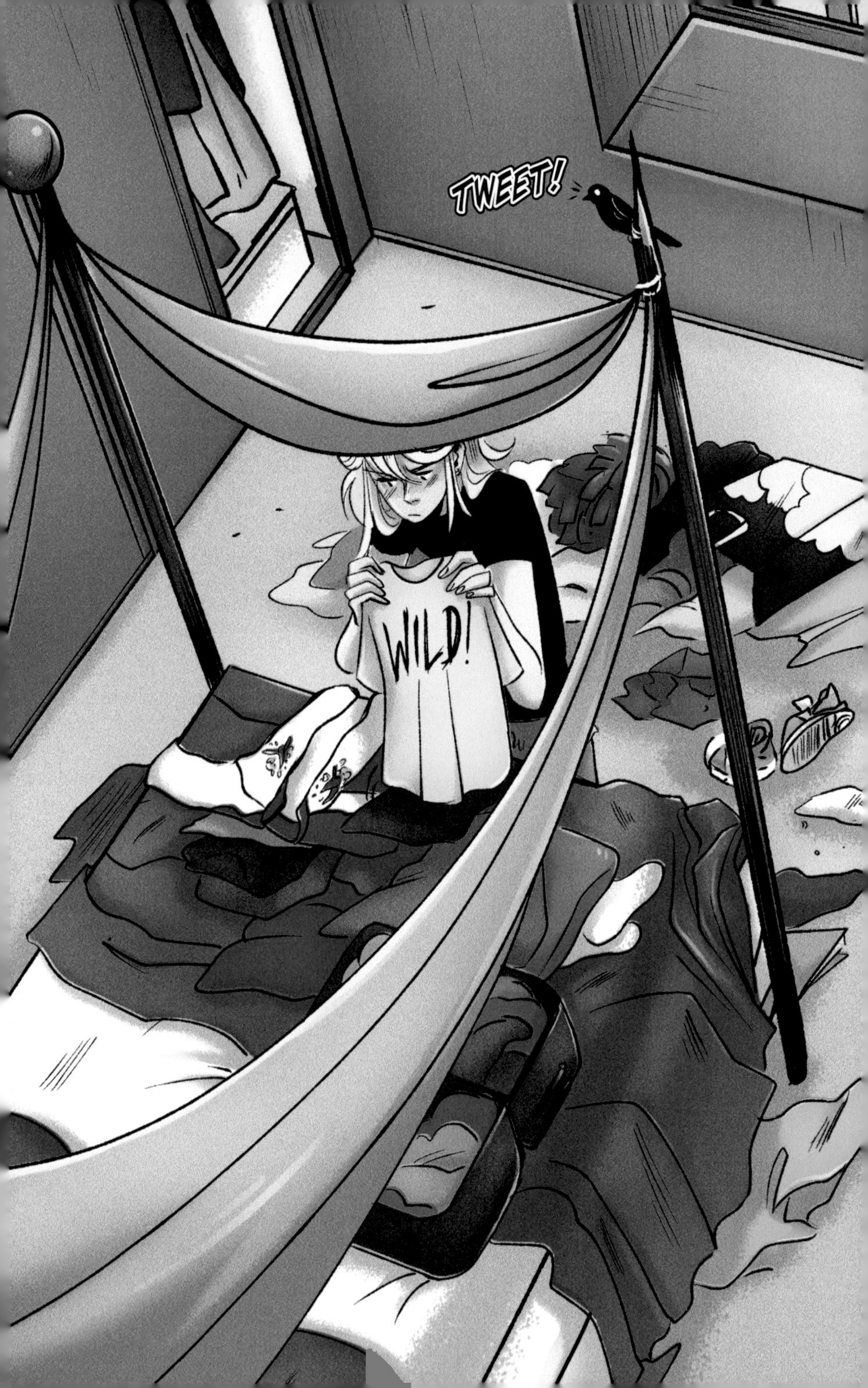
TWEET!
WILD!

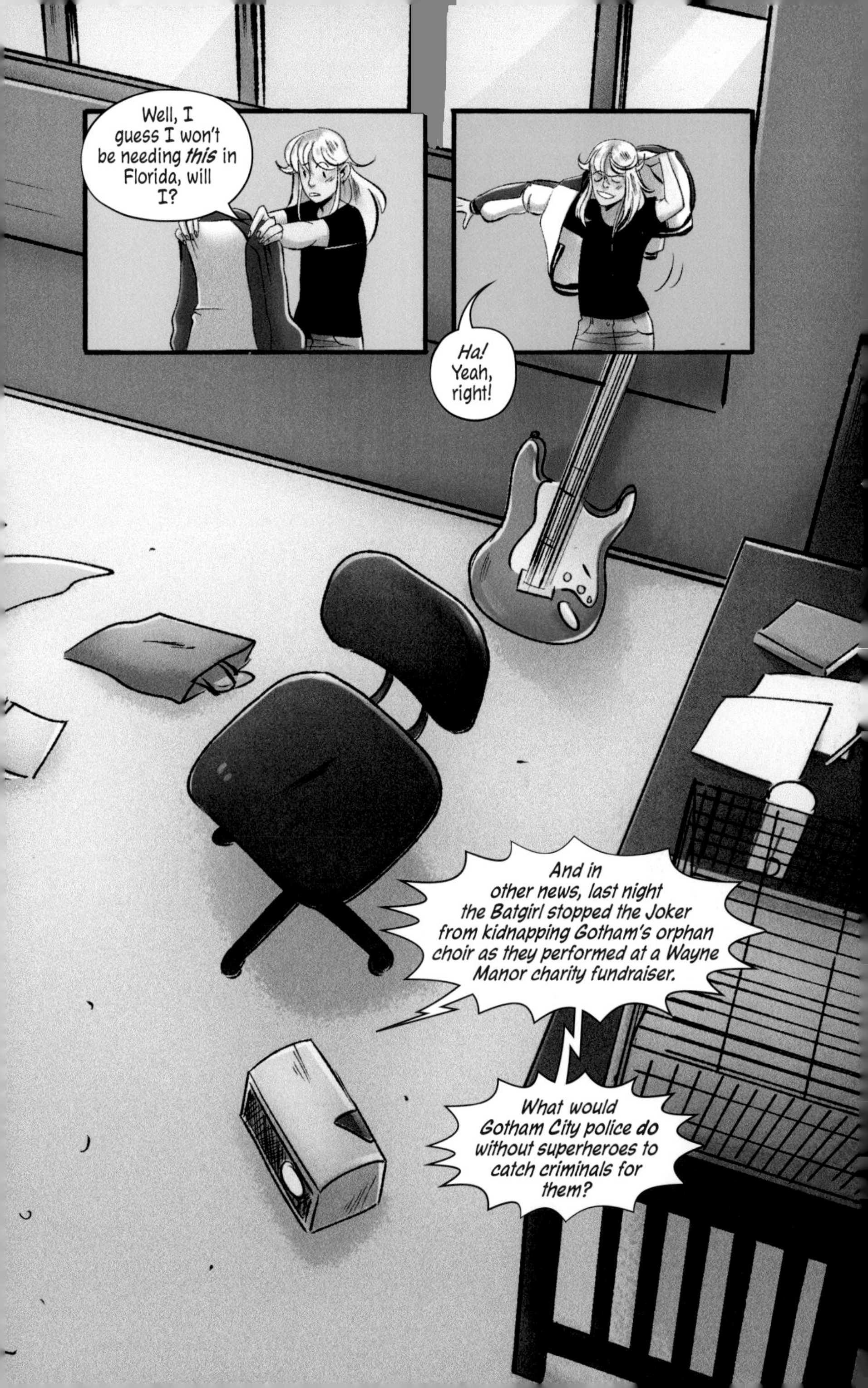
Well, I guess I won't be needing *this* in Florida, will I?
Ha! Yeah, right!
And in other news, last night the Batgirl stopped the Joker from kidnapping Gotham's orphan choir as they performed at a Wayne Manor charity fundraiser.
What would Gotham City police *do* without superheroes to catch criminals for them?

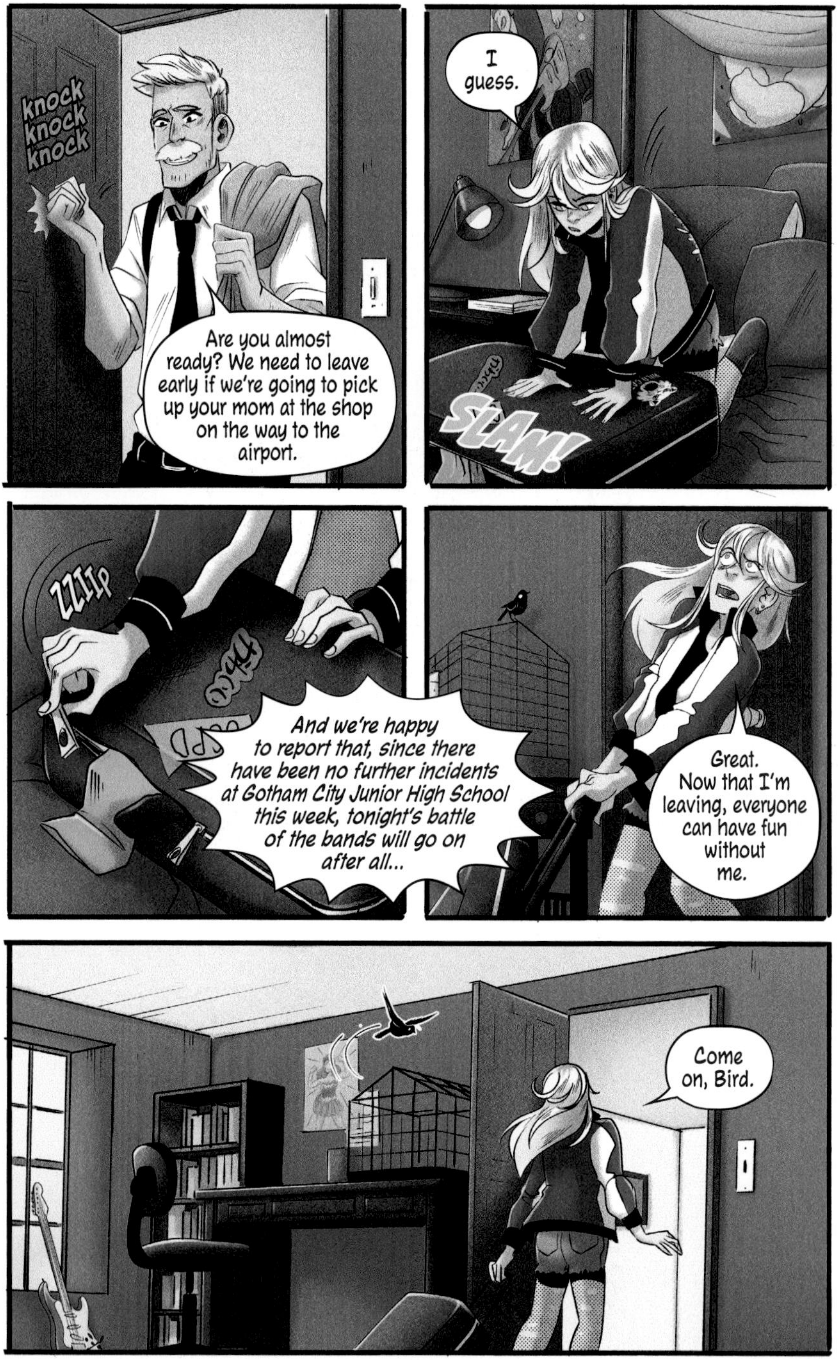
knock knock knock
Are you almost ready? We need to leave early if we're going to pick up your mom at the shop on the way to the airport.
I guess.
SLAM!
ZZZIP
And we're happy to report that, since there have been no further incidents at Gotham City Junior High School this week, tonight's battle of the bands will go on after all...
Great. Now that I'm leaving, everyone can have fun without me.
Come on, Bird.

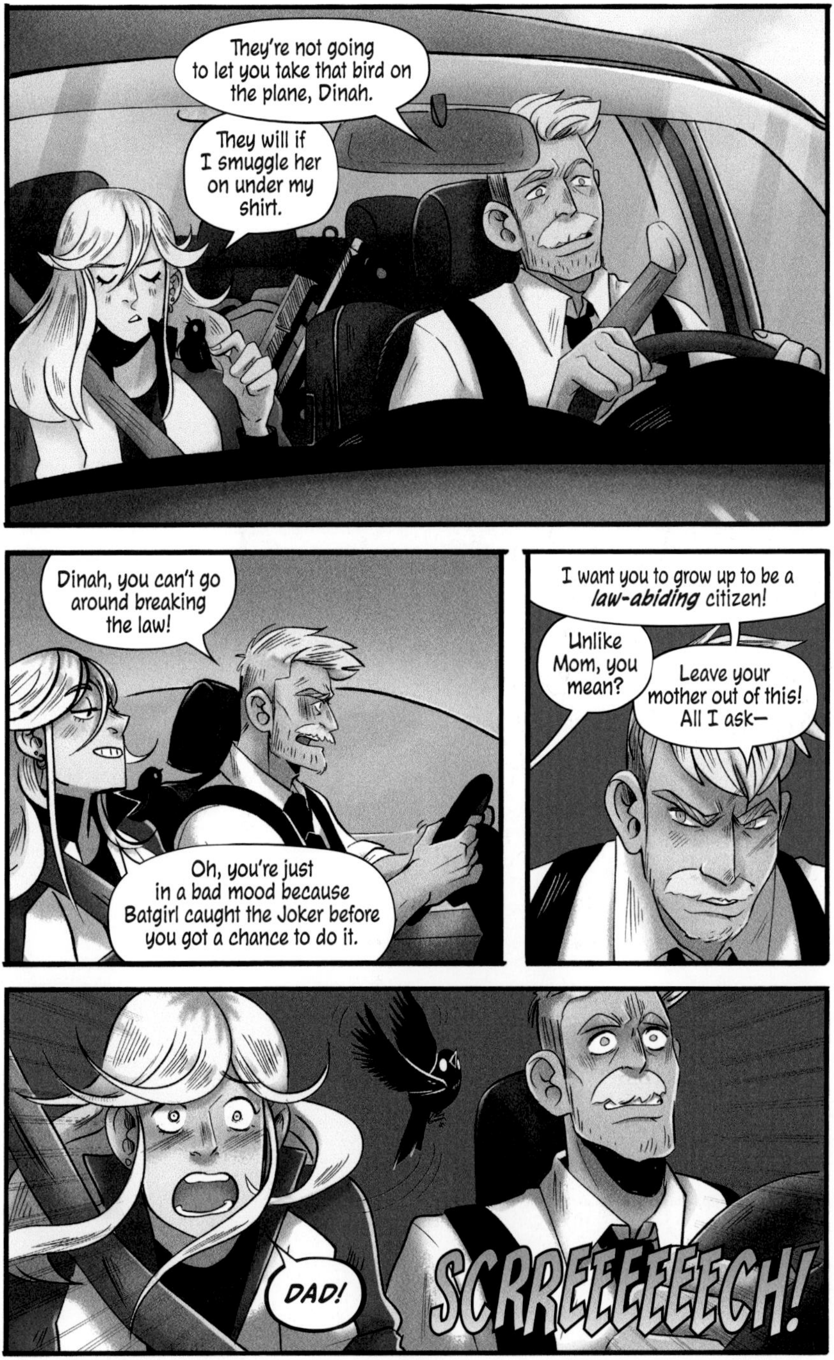
They're not going to let you take that bird on the plane, Dinah.
They will if I smuggle her on under my shirt.
Dinah, you can't go around breaking the law!
Oh, you're just in a bad mood because Batgirl caught the Joker before you got a chance to do it.
I want you to grow up to be a *law-abiding* citizen!
Unlike Mom, you mean?
Leave your mother out of this! All I ask—
DAD!
SCRREEEEEEECH!

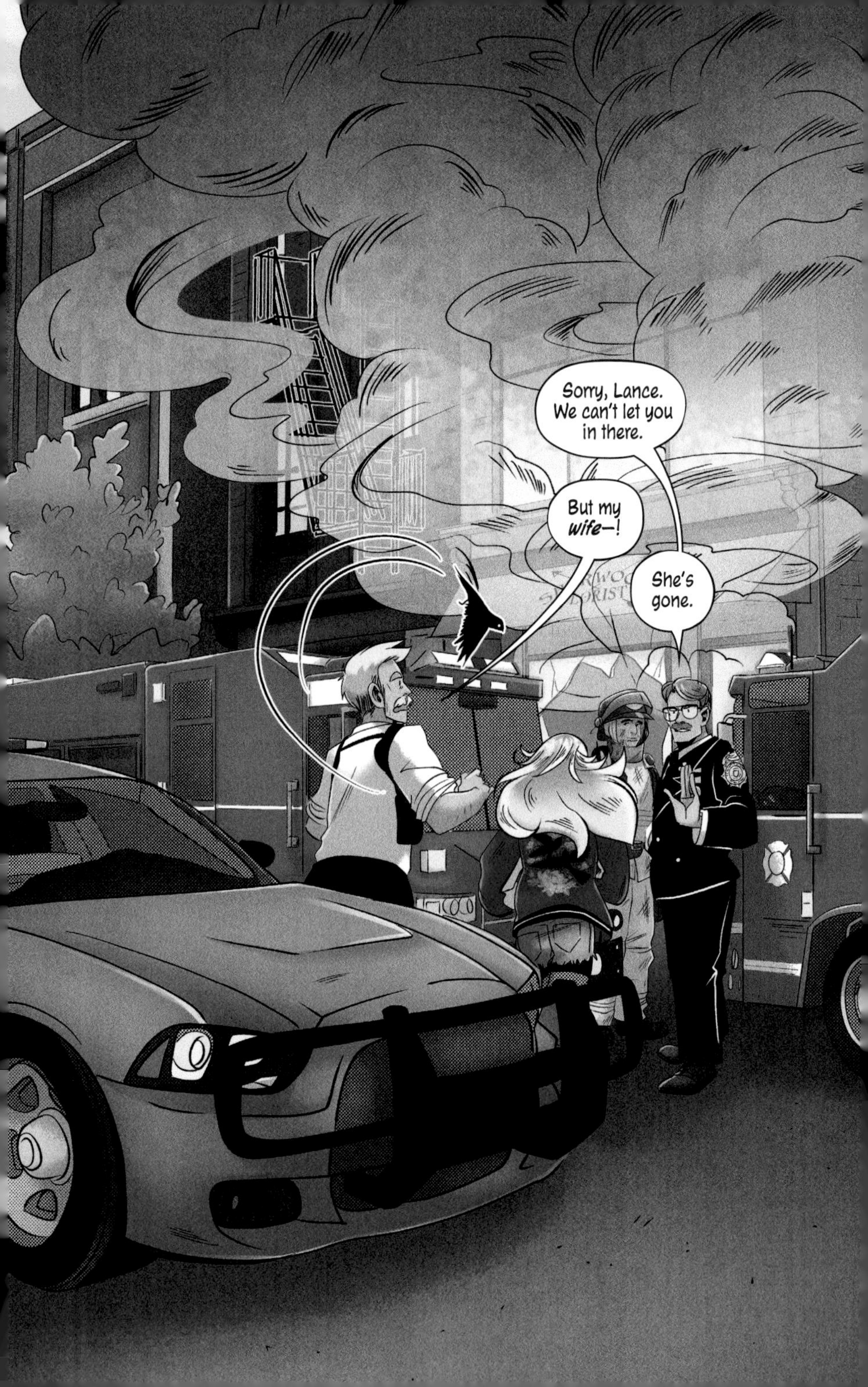
Sorry, Lance. We can't let you in there.
But my *wife*—!
She's gone.

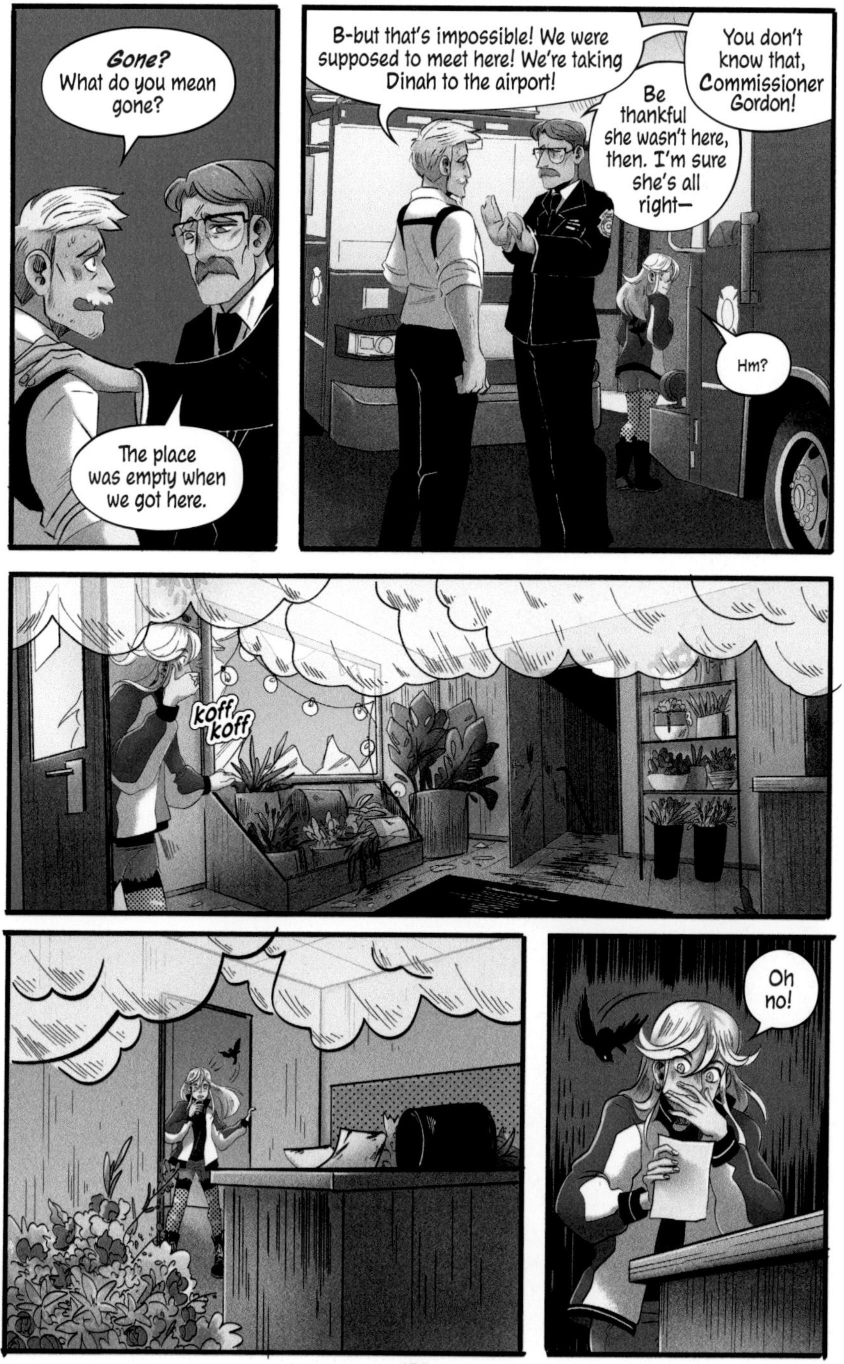
Gone? What do you mean gone?
The place was empty when we got here.
B-but that's impossible! We were supposed to meet here! We're taking Dinah to the airport!
Be thankful she wasn't here, then. I'm sure she's all right—
You don't know that, Commissioner Gordon!
Hm?
koff koff
Oh no!

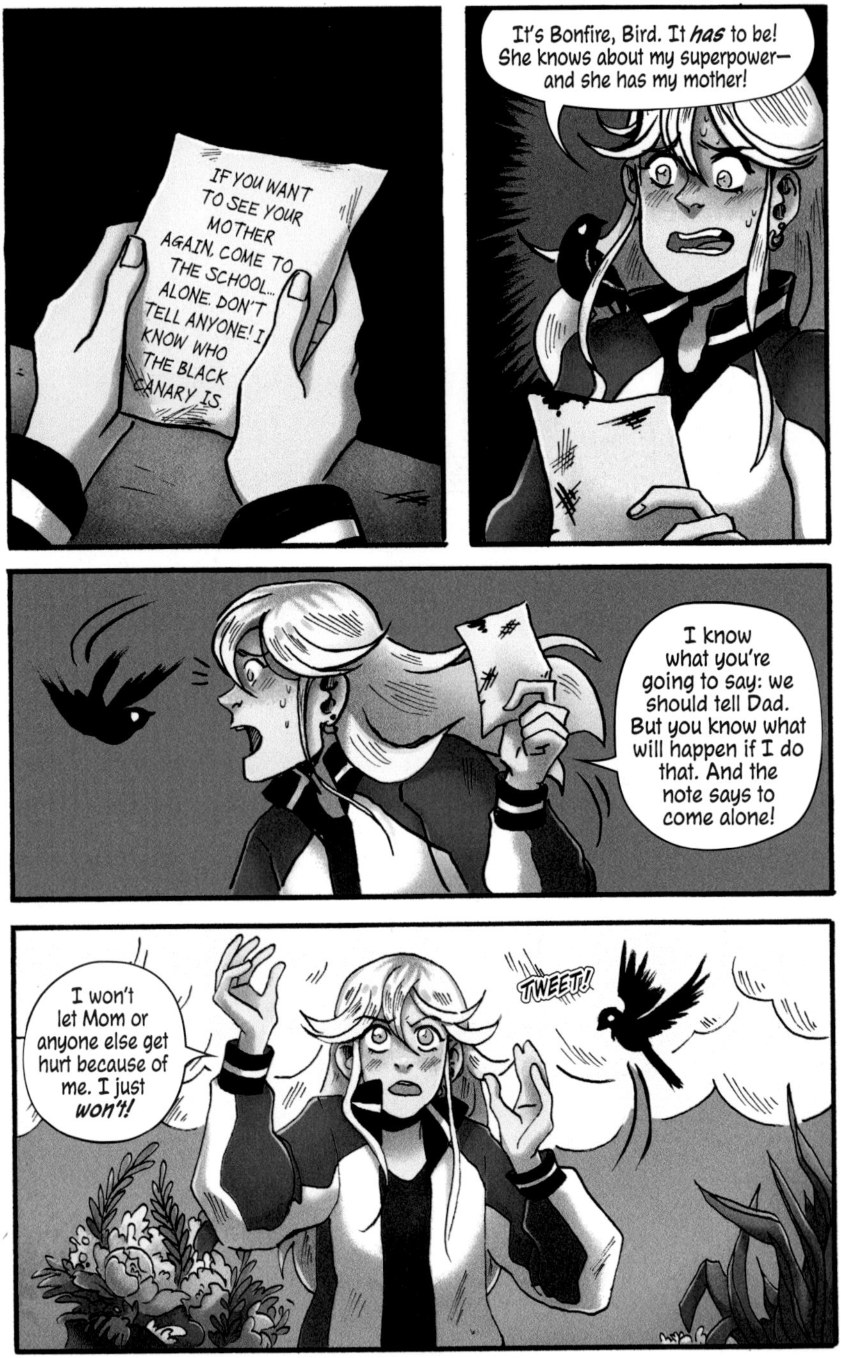
IF YOU WANT TO SEE YOUR MOTHER AGAIN, COME TO THE SCHOOL... ALONE. DON'T TELL ANYONE! I KNOW WHO THE BLACK CANARY IS.
It's Bonfire, Bird. It *has* to be! She knows about my superpower—and she has my mother!
I know what you're going to say: we should tell Dad. But you know what will happen if I do that. And the note says to come alone!
I won't let Mom or anyone else get hurt because of me. I just *won't!*
TWEET!

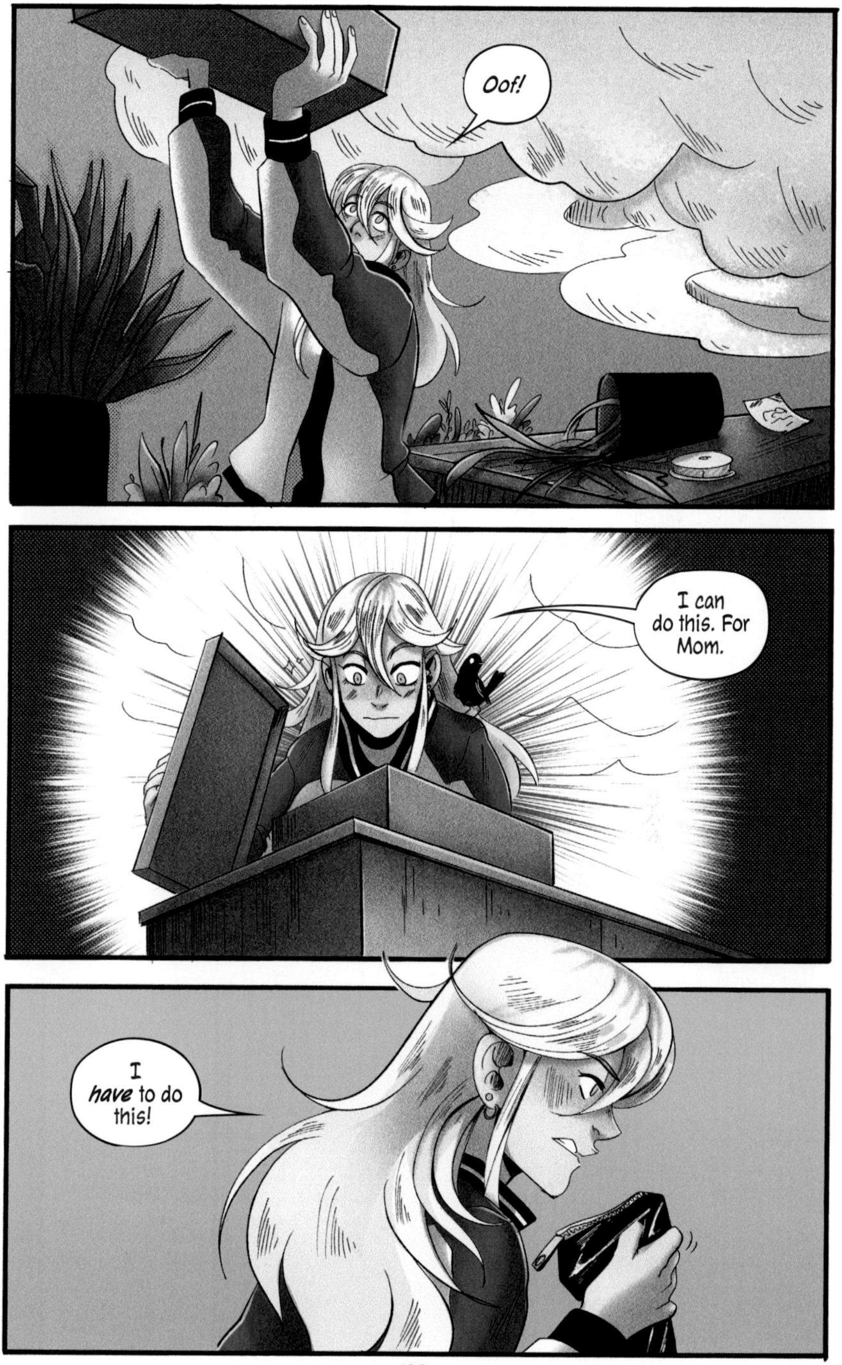
Oof!
I can do this. For Mom.
I *have* to do this!

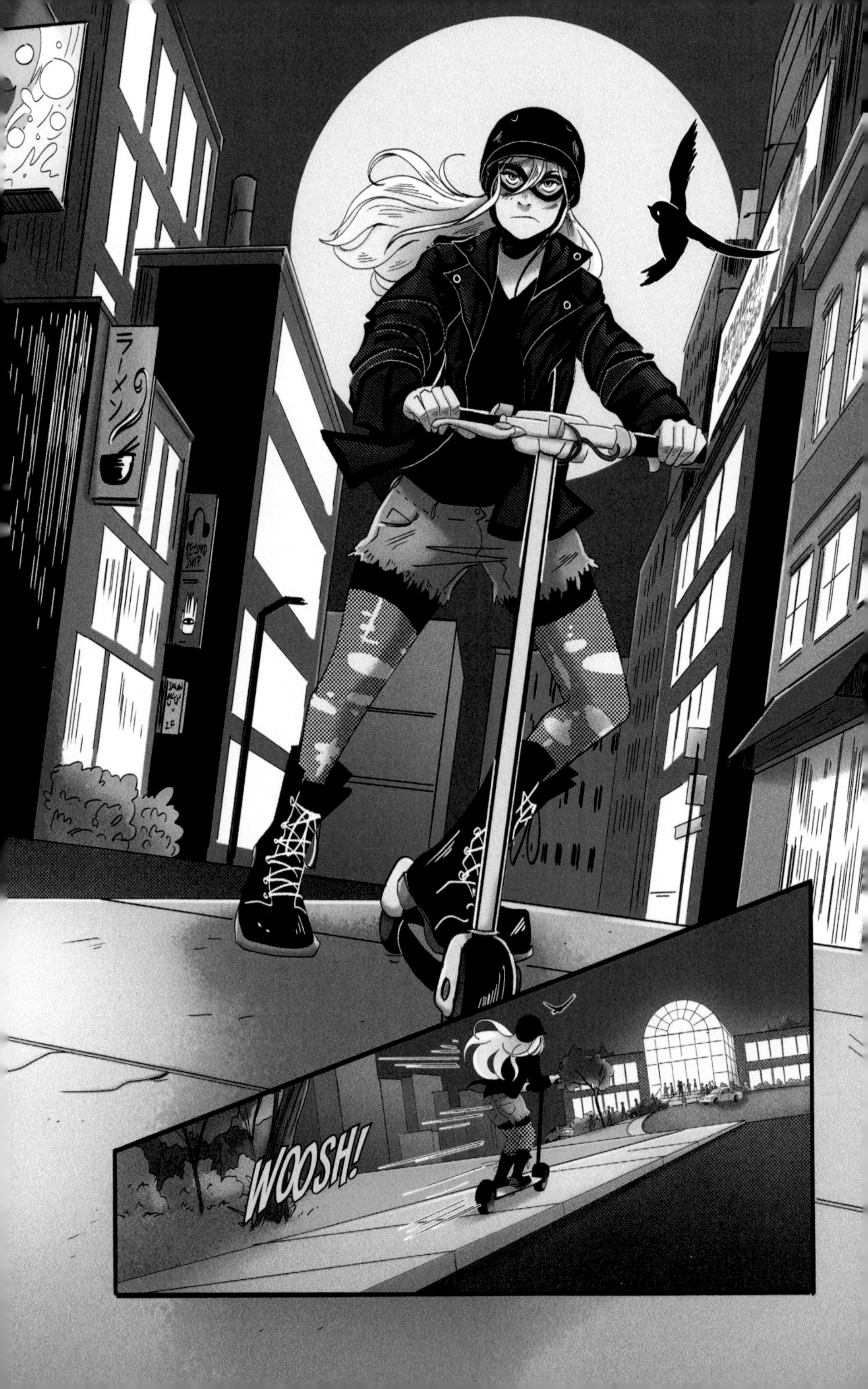
ラーメン
RECORD SHOP
SALON
2F
WOOSH!

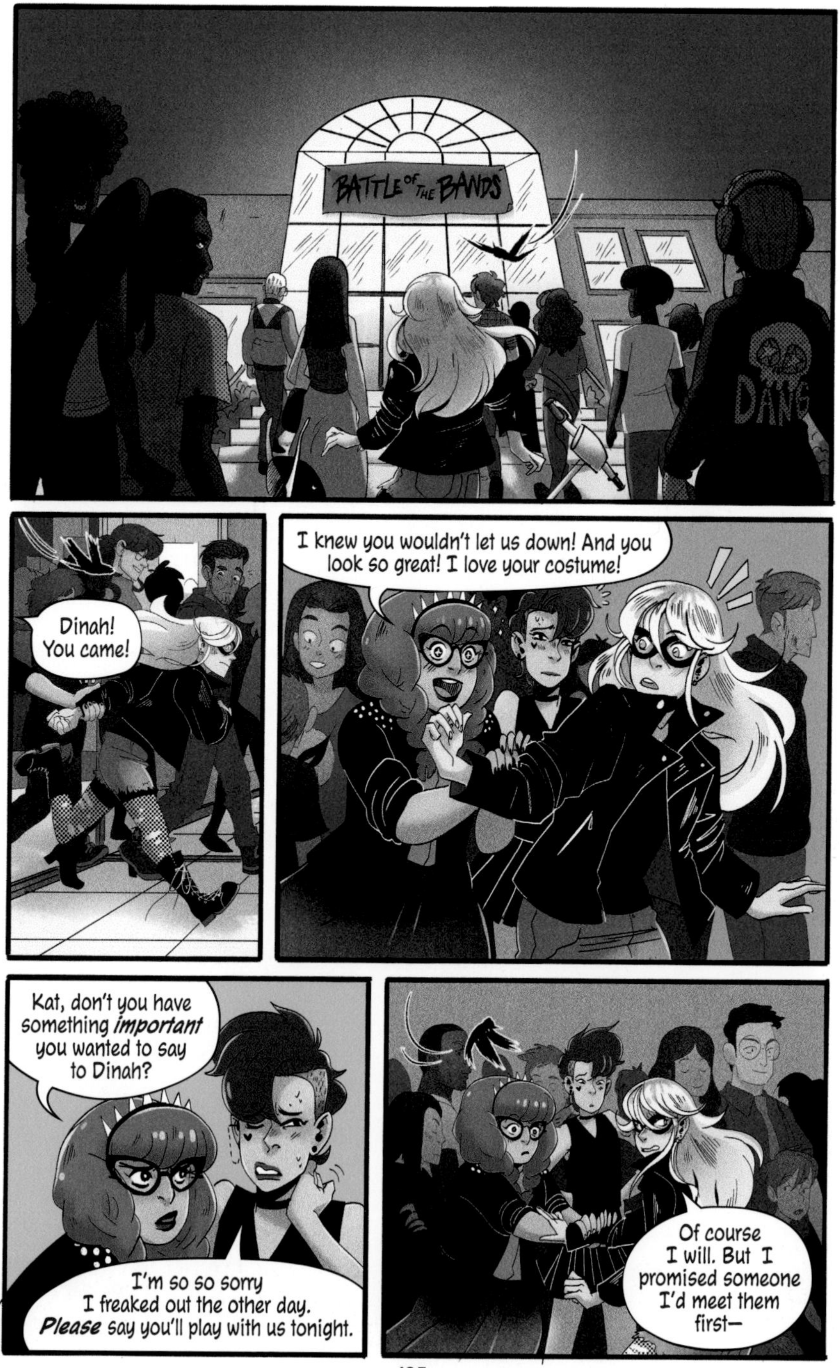
BATTLE OF THE BANDS
DANG
Dinah! You came!
I knew you wouldn't let us down! And you look so great! I love your costume!
Kat, don't you have something *important* you wanted to say to Dinah?
I'm so so sorry I freaked out the other day. *Please* say you'll play with us tonight.
Of course I will. But I promised someone I'd meet them first—

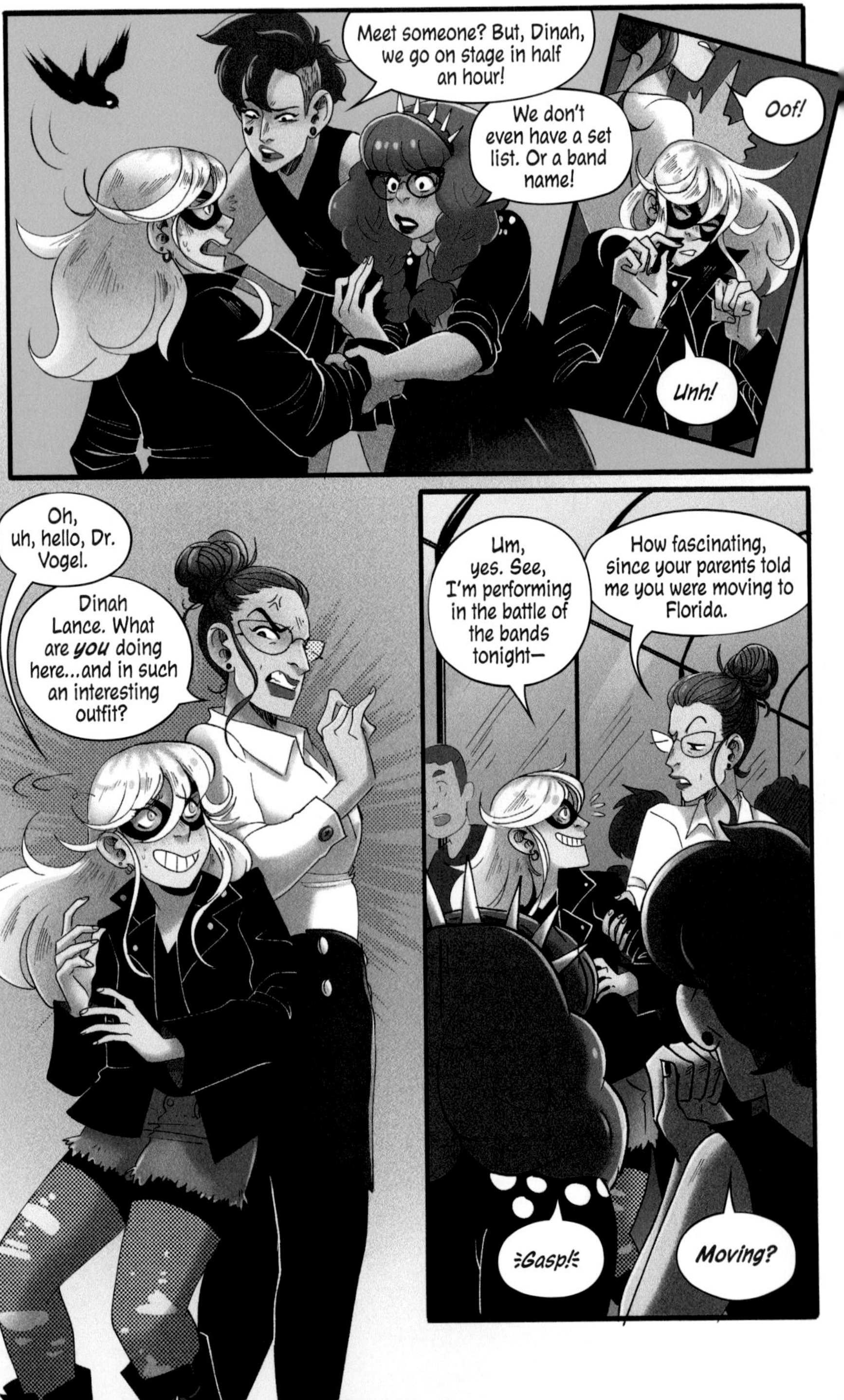
Meet someone? But, Dinah, we go on stage in half an hour!
We don't even have a set list. Or a band name!
Oof!
Unh!
Oh, uh, hello, Dr. Vogel.
Dinah Lance. What are *you* doing here...and in such an interesting outfit?
Um, yes. See, I'm performing in the battle of the bands tonight—
How fascinating, since your parents told me you were moving to Florida.
Gasp!
Moving?

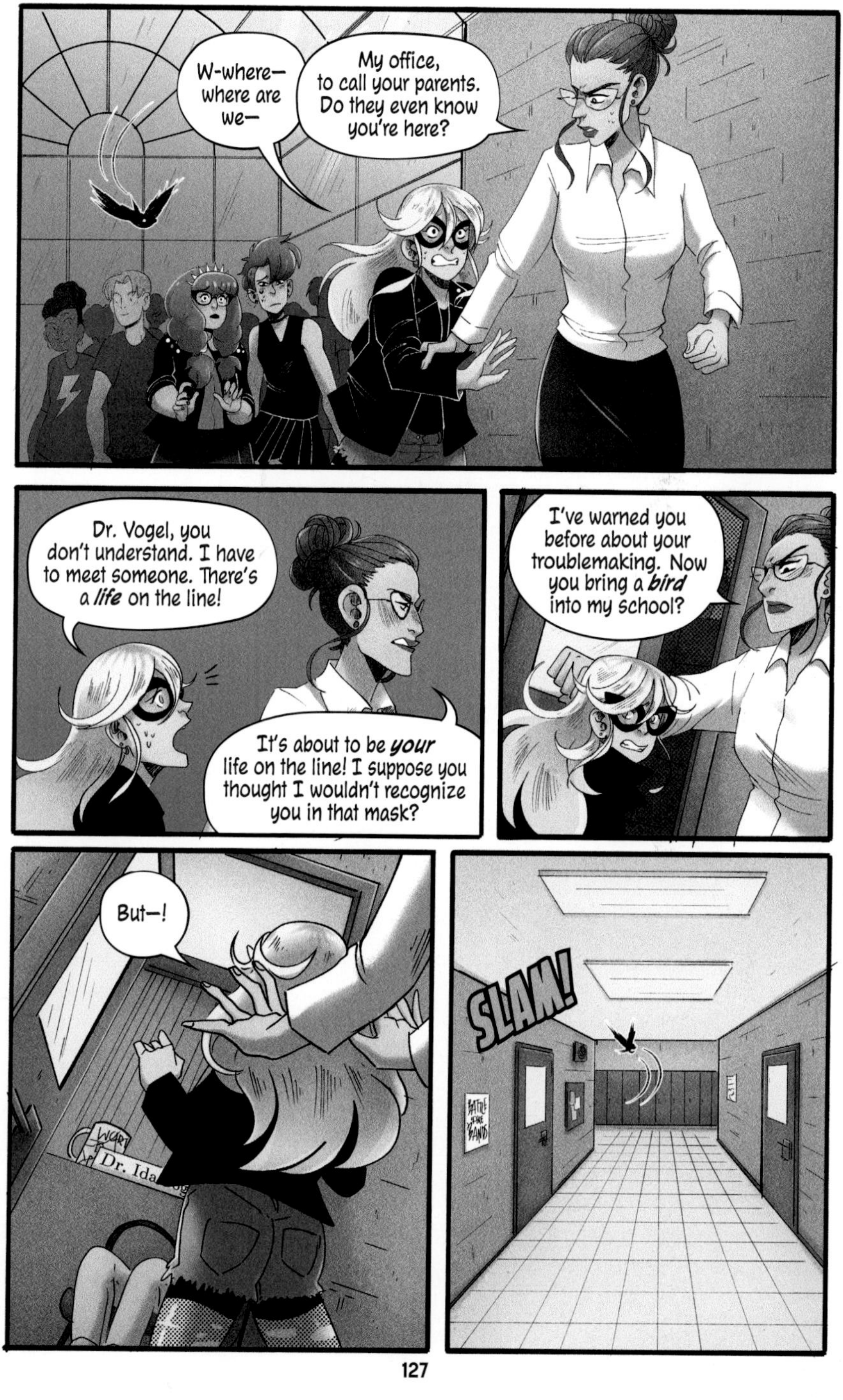
W-where— where are we—
My office, to call your parents. Do they even know you're here?
Dr. Vogel, you don't understand. I have to meet someone. There's a *life* on the line!
It's about to be ***your*** life on the line! I suppose you thought I wouldn't recognize you in that mask?
I've warned you before about your troublemaking. Now you bring a ***bird*** into my school?
But—!
Dr. Ida
SLAM!
BATTLE OF THE BANDS

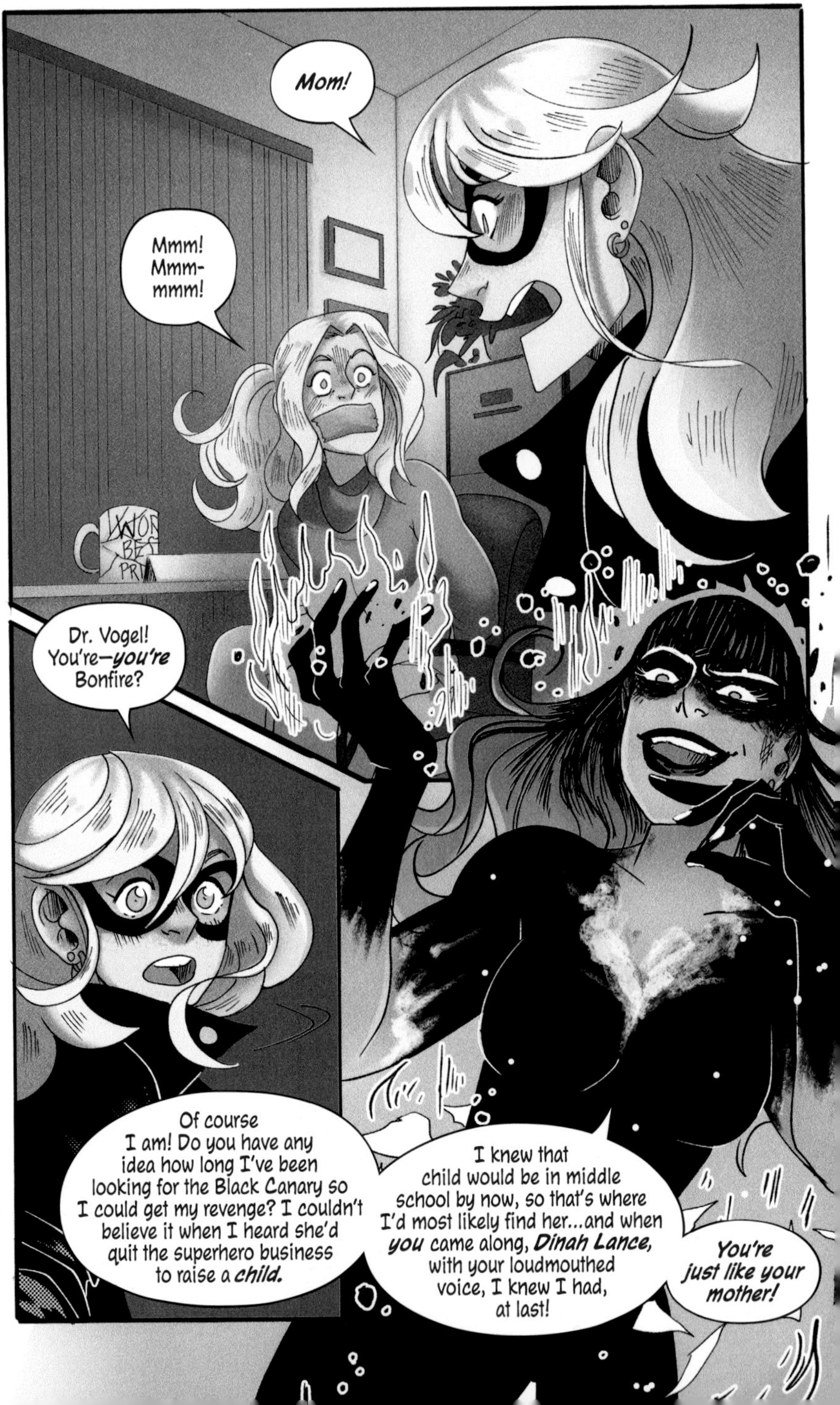
Mom!
Mmm! Mmm-mmm!
Dr. Vogel! You're—*you're* Bonfire?
Of course I am! Do you have any idea how long I've been looking for the Black Canary so I could get my revenge? I couldn't believe it when I heard she'd quit the superhero business to raise a *child.*
I knew that child would be in middle school by now, so that's where I'd most likely find her...and when *you* came along, *Dinah Lance,* with your loudmouthed voice, I knew I had, at last!
You're just like your mother!
WOR BES PRI

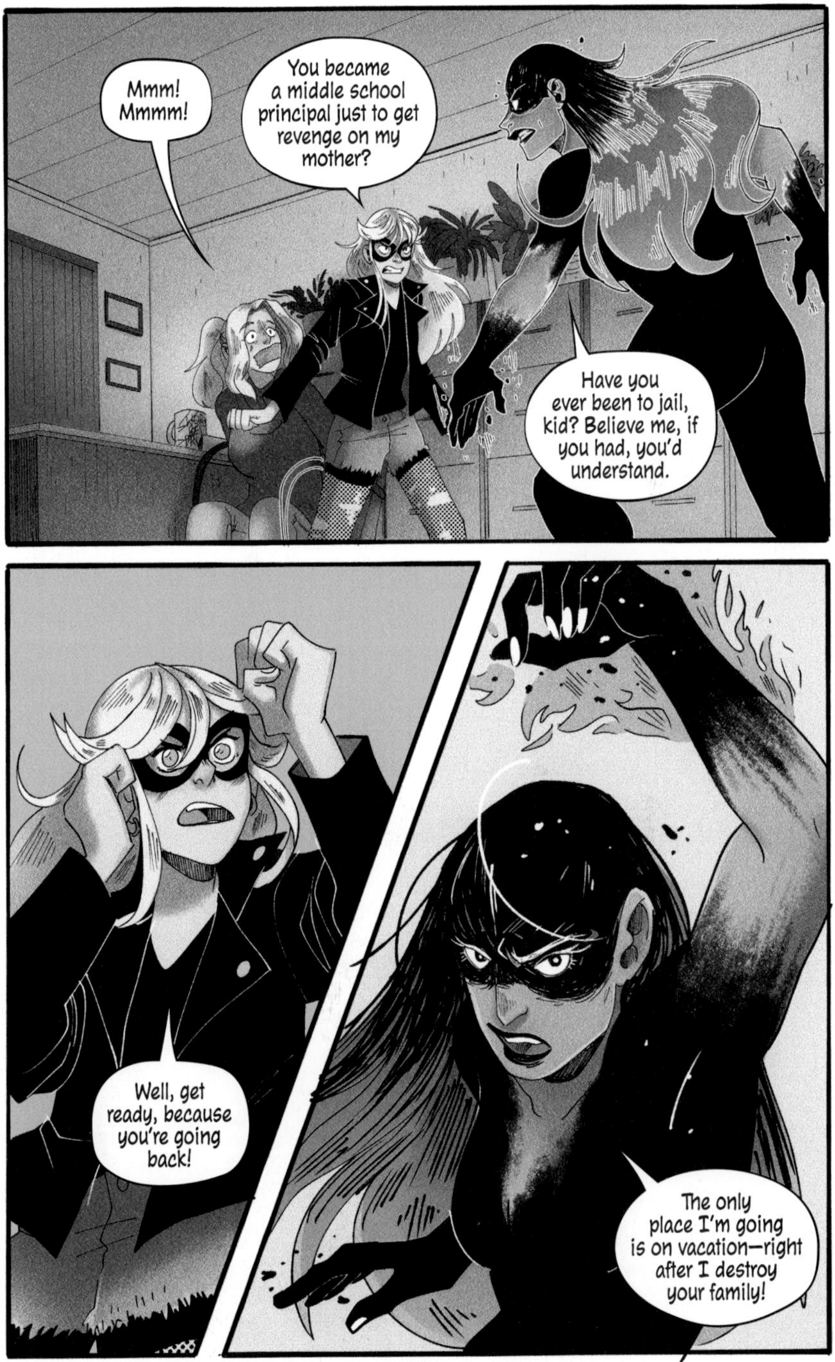
Mmm! Mmmm!
You became a middle school principal just to get revenge on my mother?
Have you ever been to jail, kid? Believe me, if you had, you'd understand.
Well, get ready, because you're going back!
The only place I'm going is on vacation—right after I destroy your family!

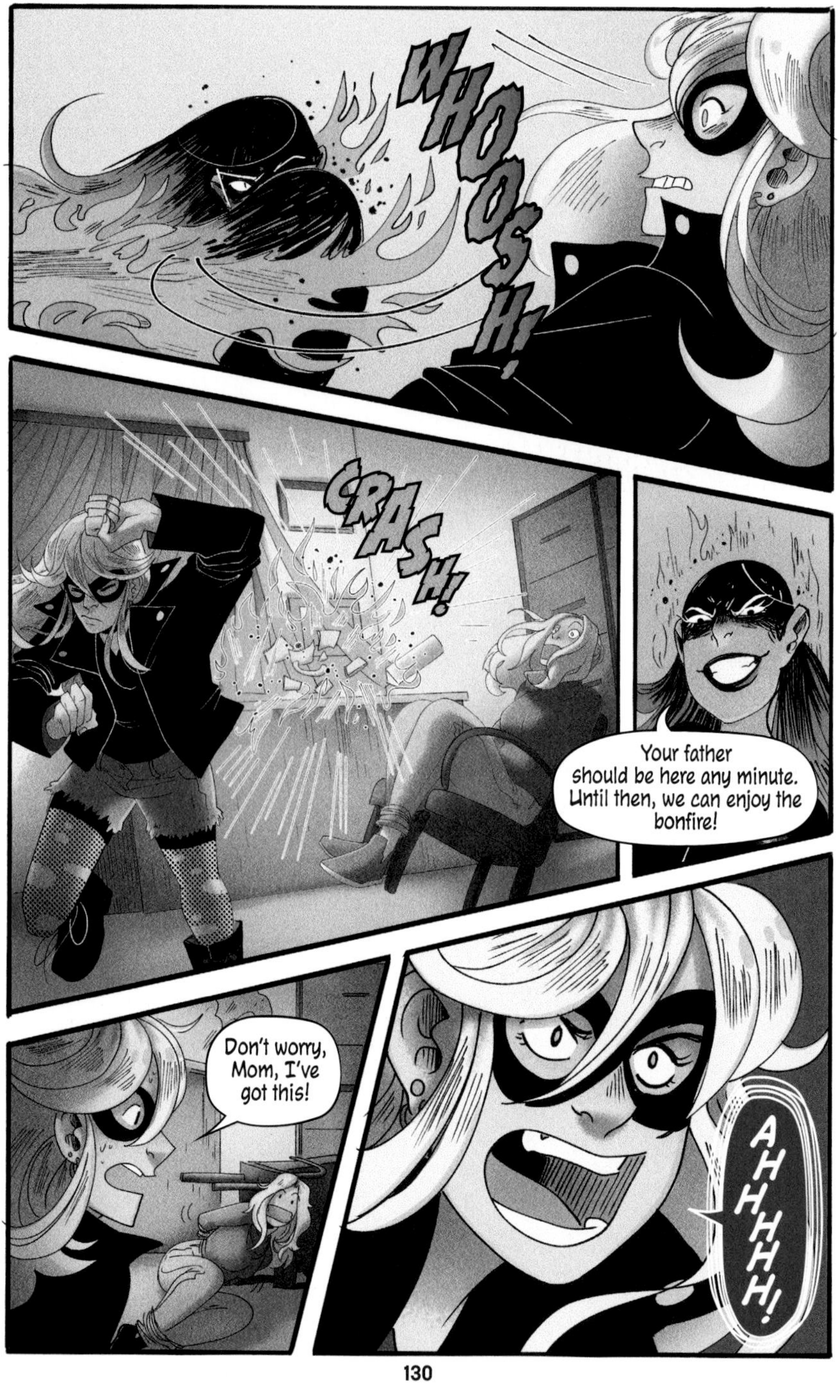
WHOOSH!
CRASH!
Your father should be here any minute. Until then, we can enjoy the bonfire!
Don't worry, Mom, I've got this!
AHHHHH!

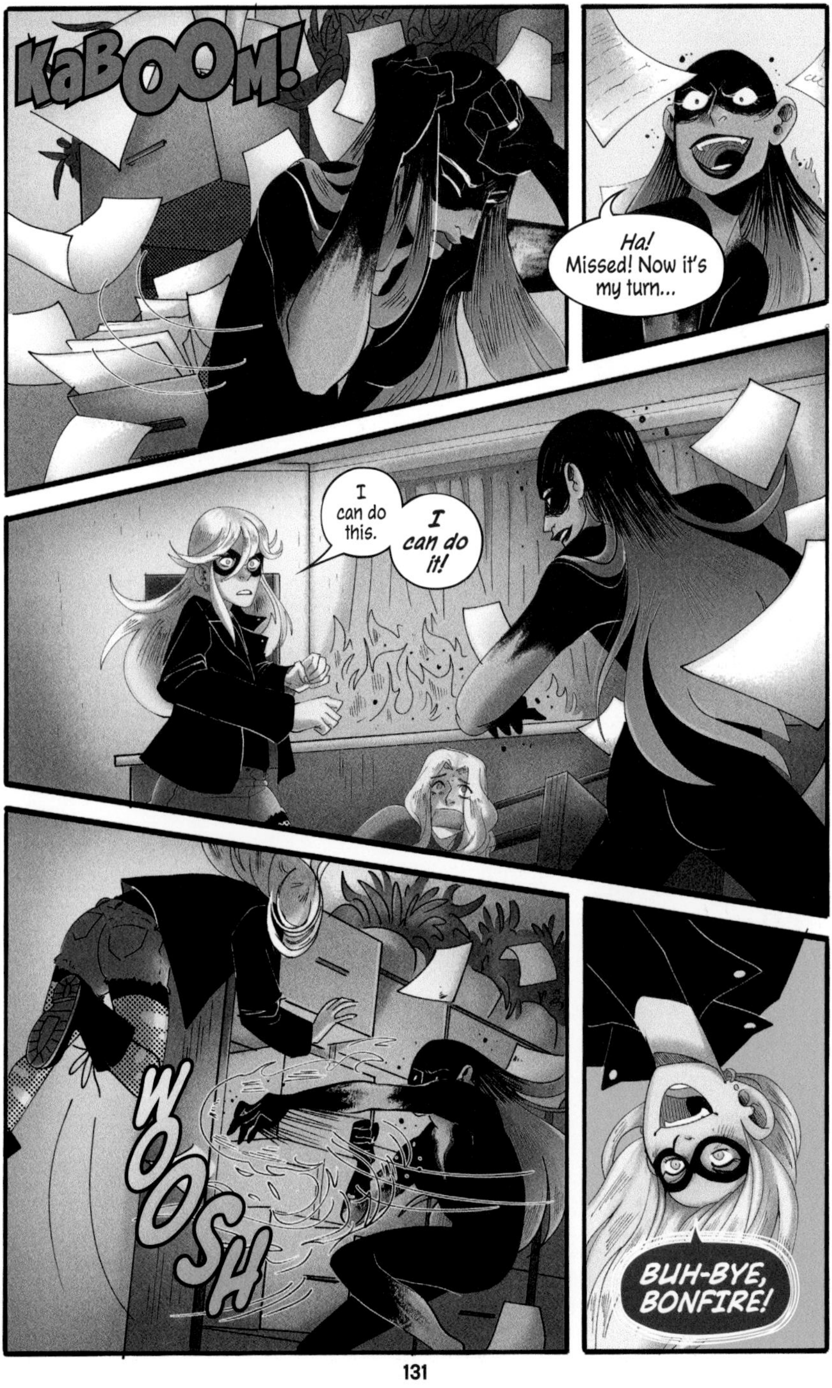

KaBOOM!
Ha! Missed! Now it's my turn...
I can do this.
I can do it!
WOOSH
BUH-BYE, BONFIRE!

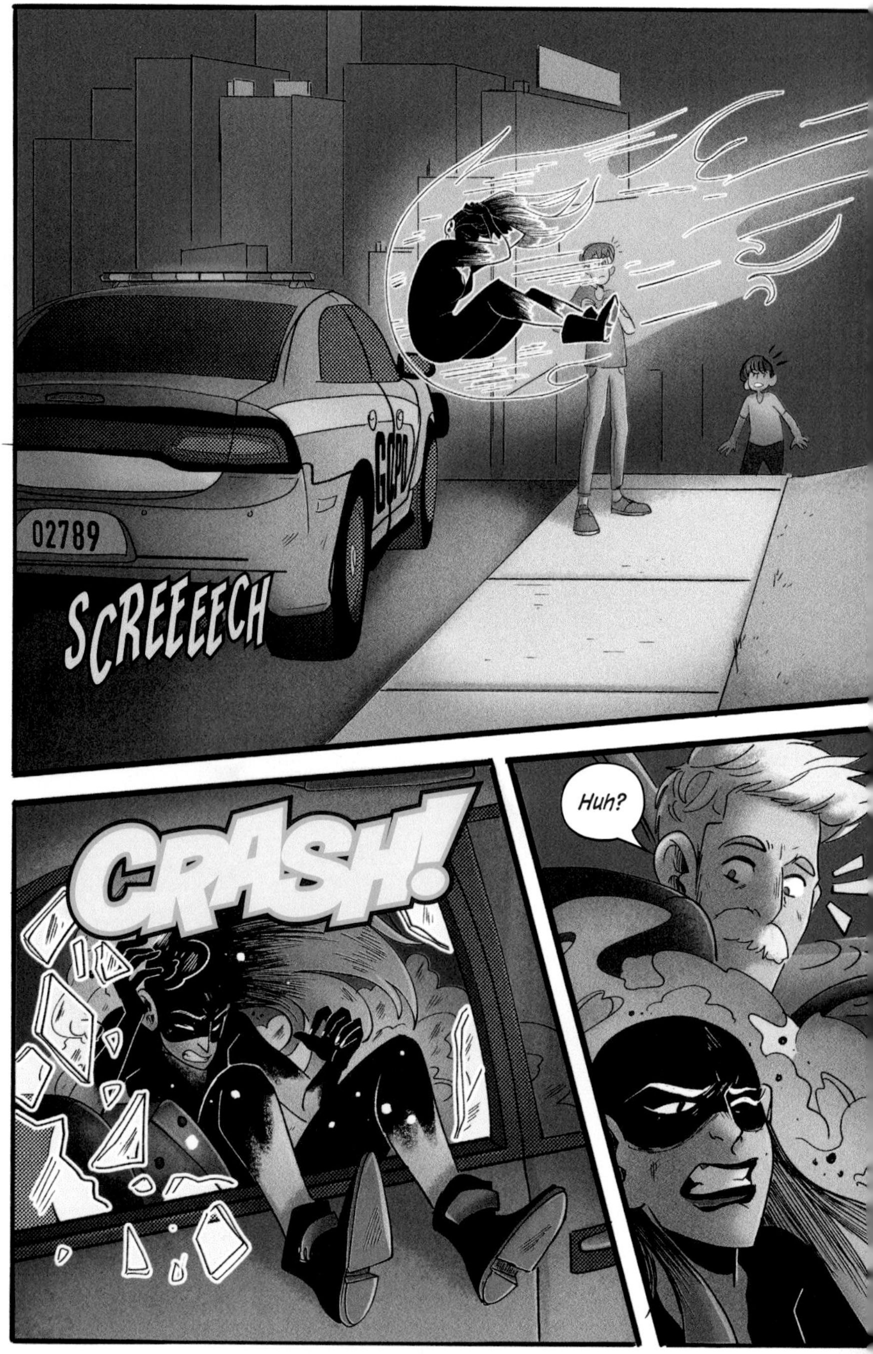
02789
GCPD
SCREEEECH
CRASH!
Huh?

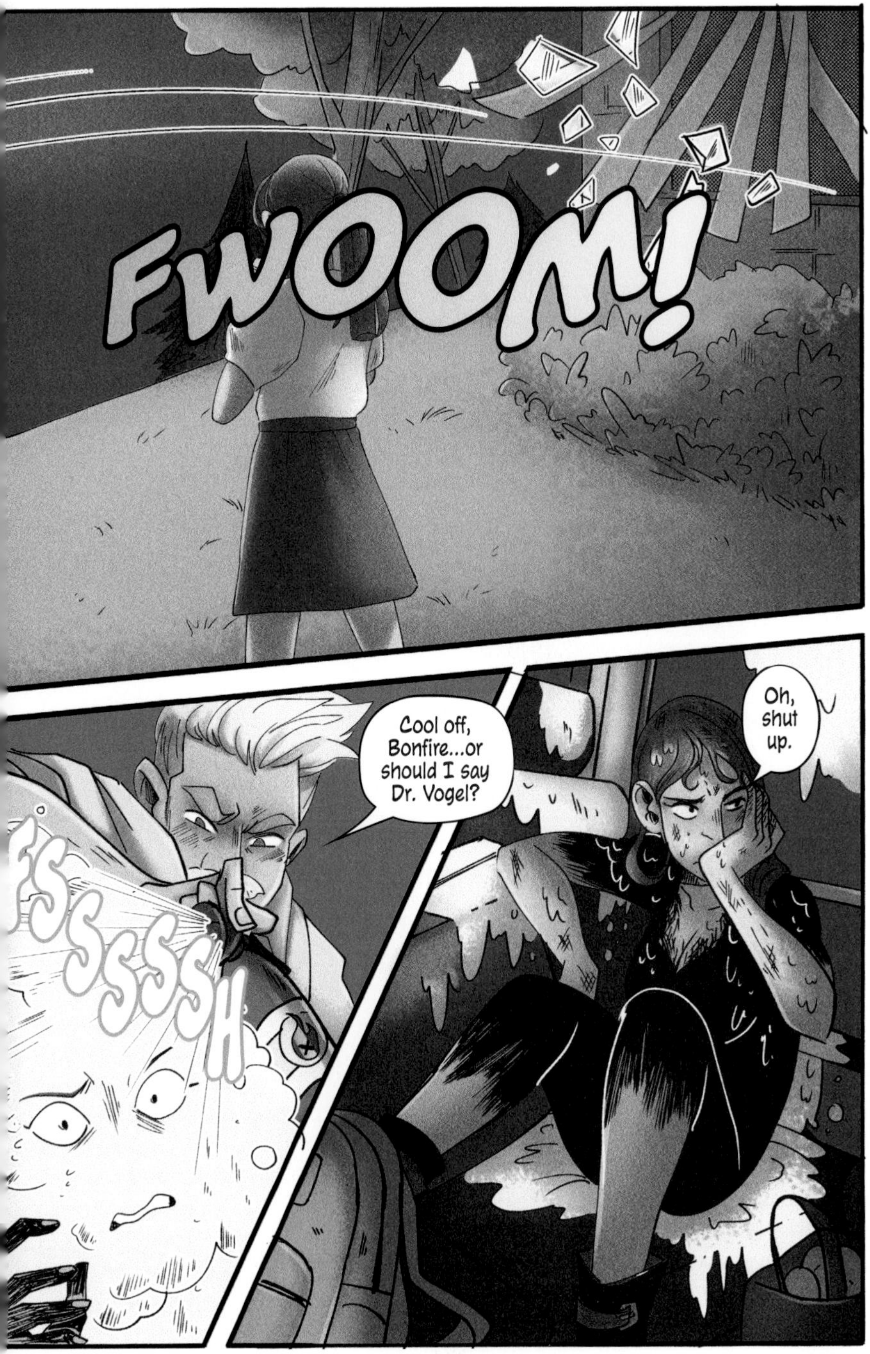
FWOOM!
Cool off, Bonfire...or should I say Dr. Vogel?
Oh, shut up.

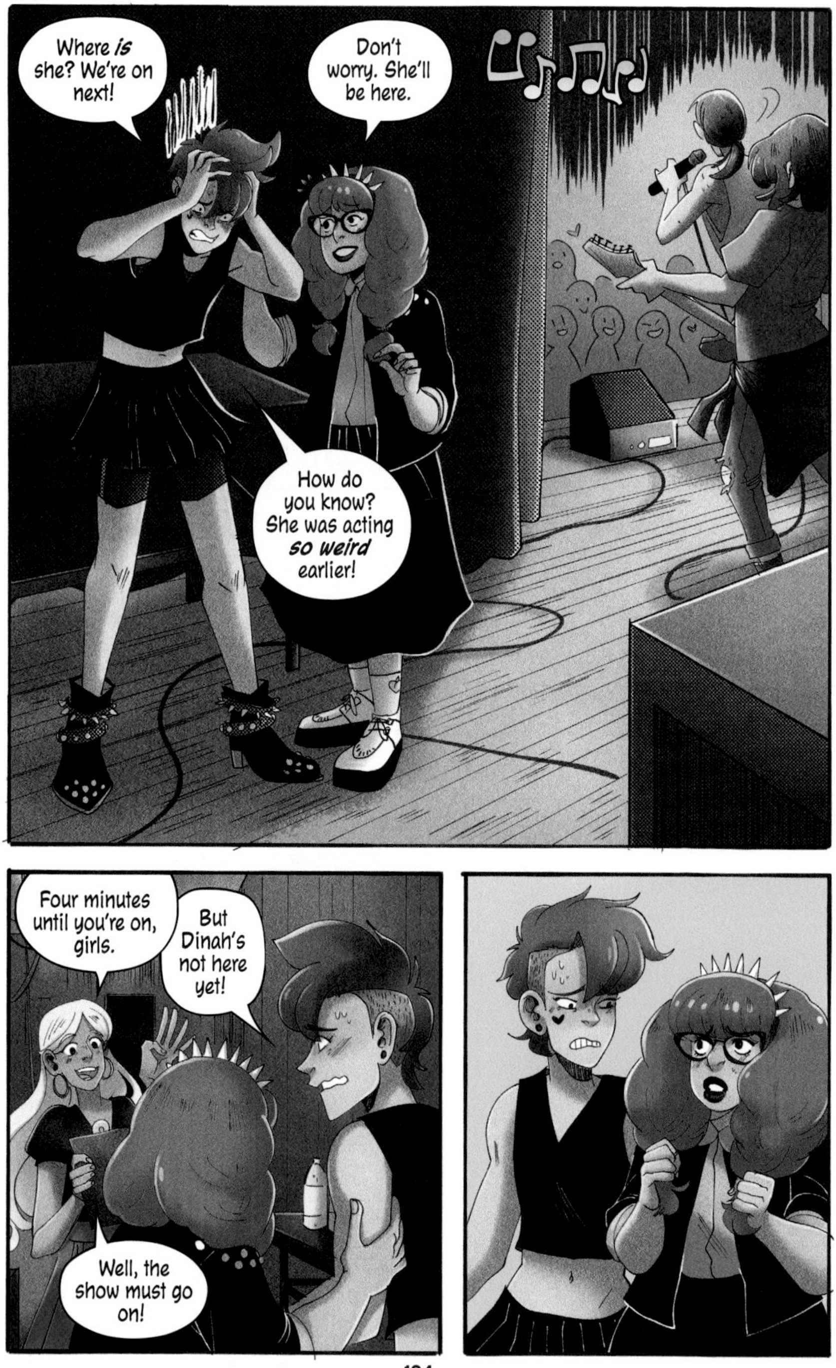
Where *is* she? We're on next!
Don't worry. She'll be here.
How do you know? She was acting ***so weird*** earlier!
Four minutes until you're on, girls.
But Dinah's not here yet!
Well, the show must go on!

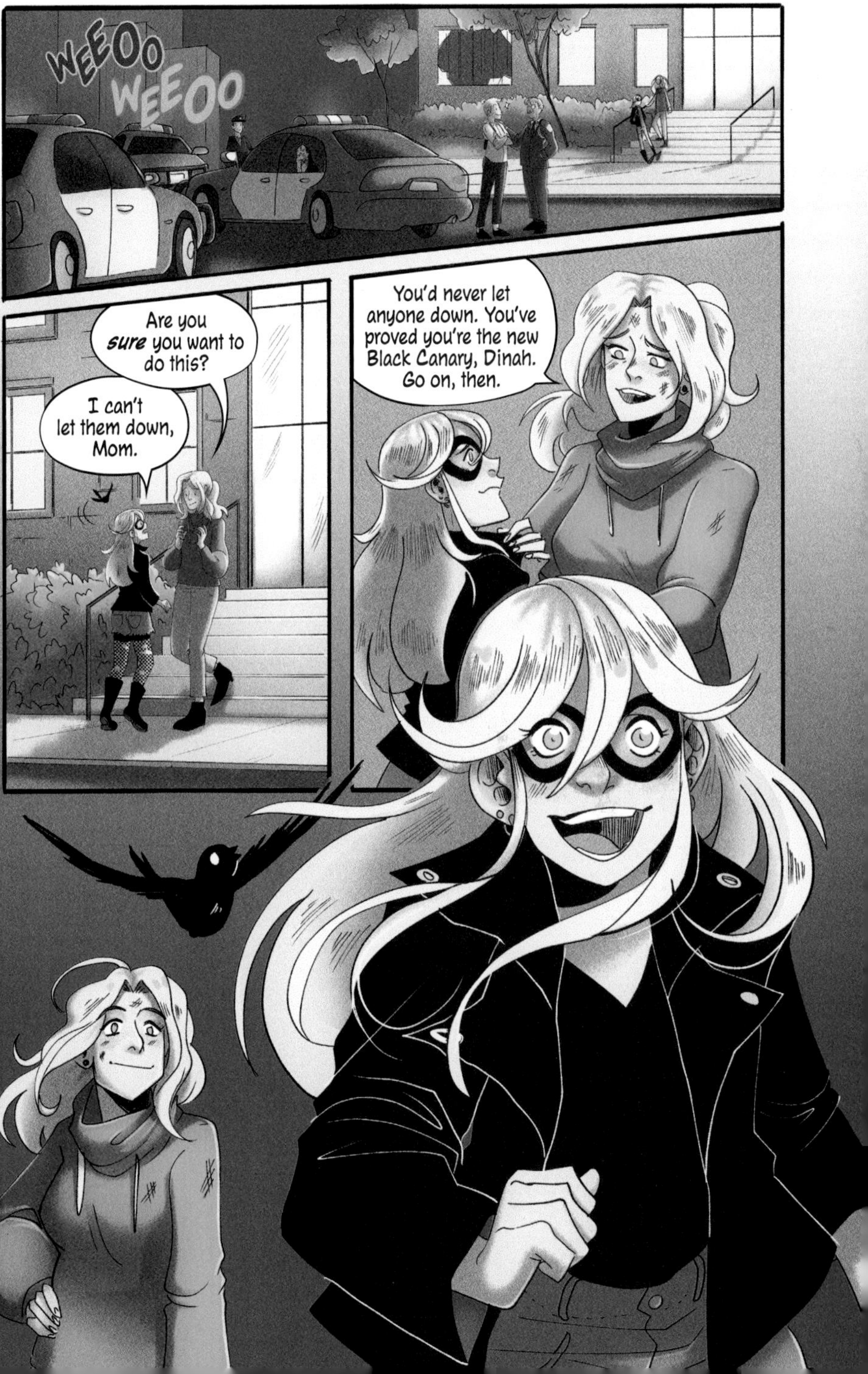
WEEOO
WEEOO
Are you *sure* you want to do this?
I can't let them down, Mom.
You'd never let anyone down. You've proved you're the new Black Canary, Dinah. Go on, then.

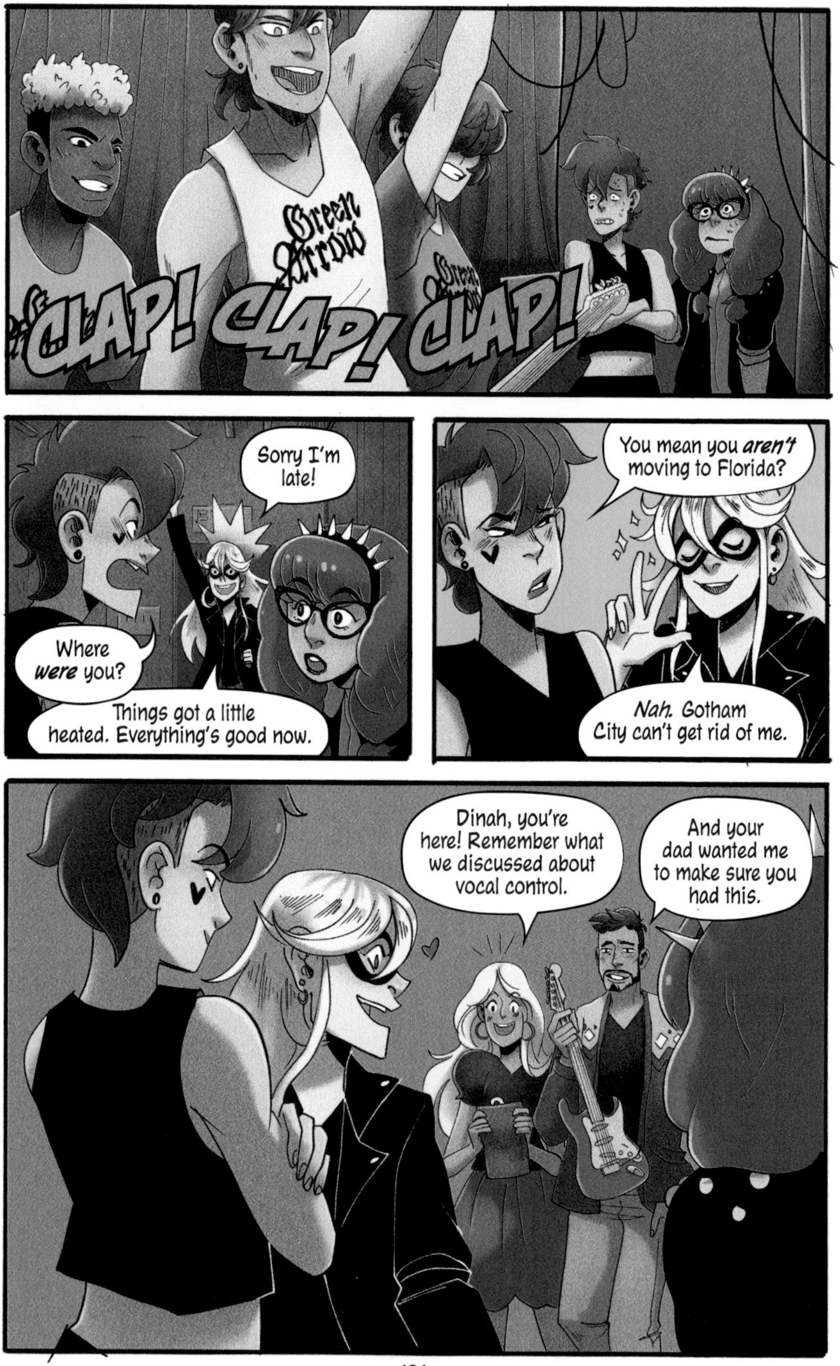
CLAP! CLAP! CLAP!
Sorry I'm late!
Where *were* you?
Things got a little heated. Everything's good now.
You mean you *aren't* moving to Florida?
Nah. Gotham City can't get rid of me.
Dinah, you're here! Remember what we discussed about vocal control.
And your dad wanted me to make sure you had this.

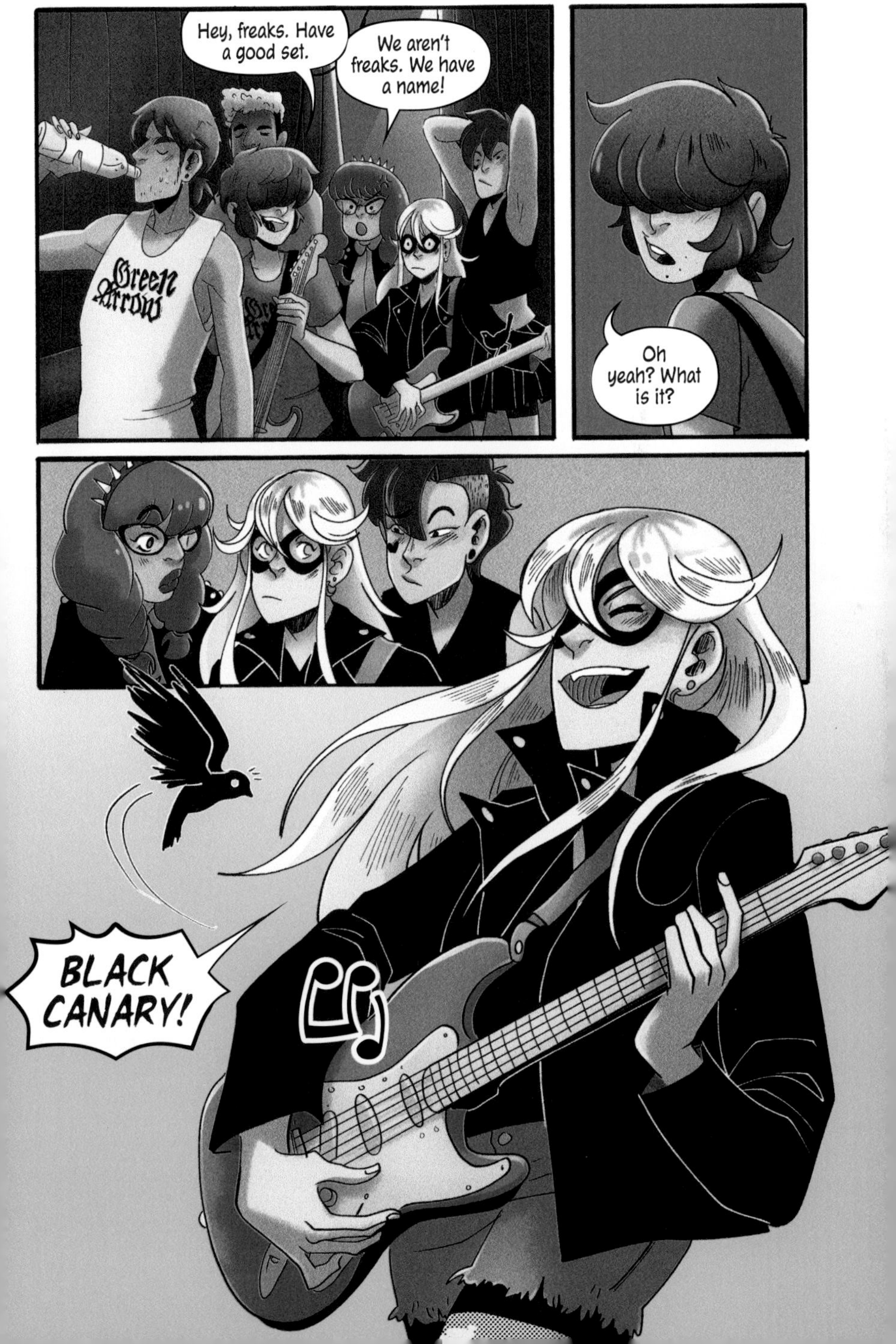
Hey, freaks. Have a good set.
We aren't freaks. We have a name!
Green Arrow
Oh yeah? What is it?
BLACK CANARY!

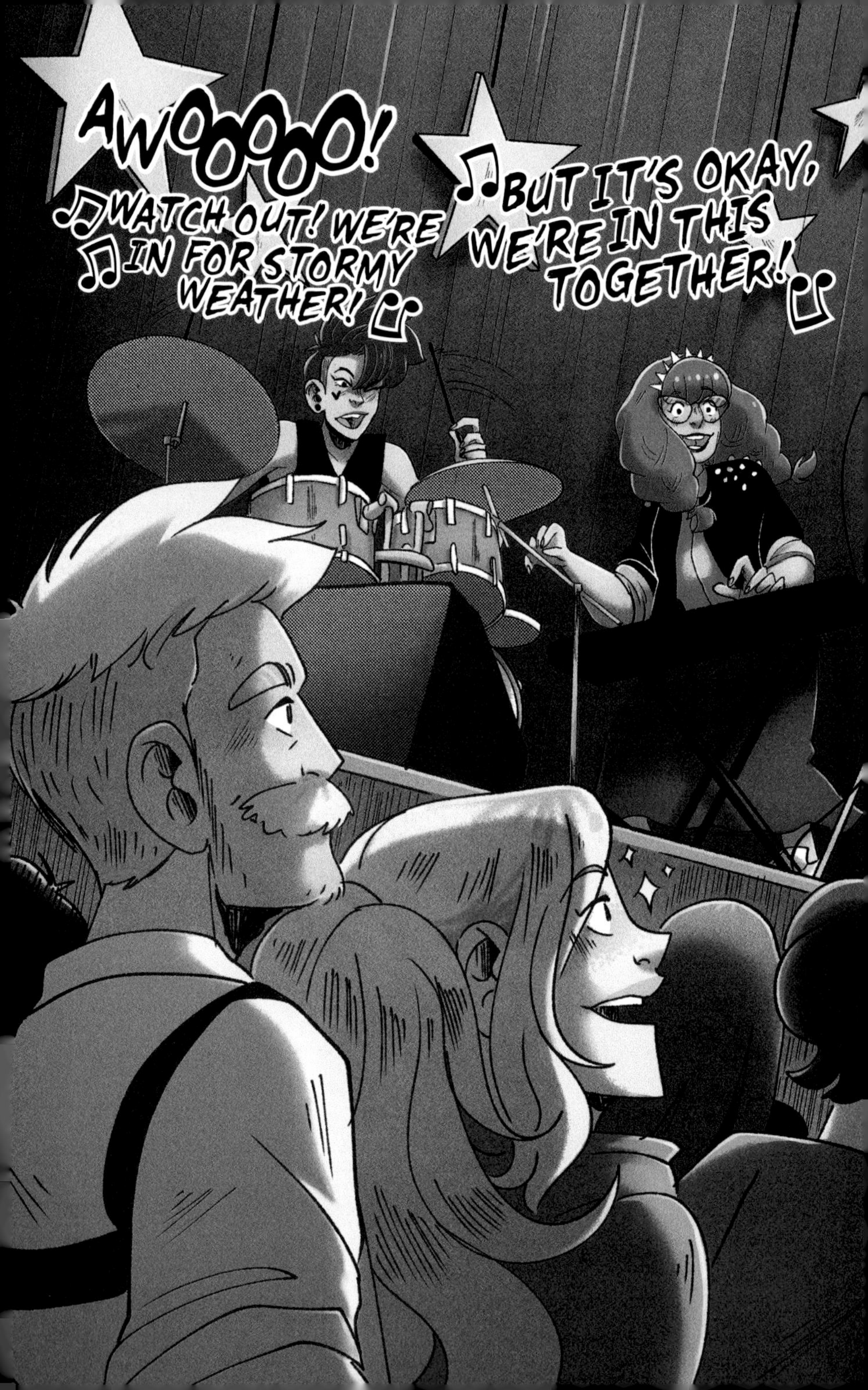
AWOOOOOO!
♫WATCH OUT! WE'RE IN FOR STORMY WEATHER!♫
♫BUT IT'S OKAY, WE'RE IN THIS TOGETHER!♫

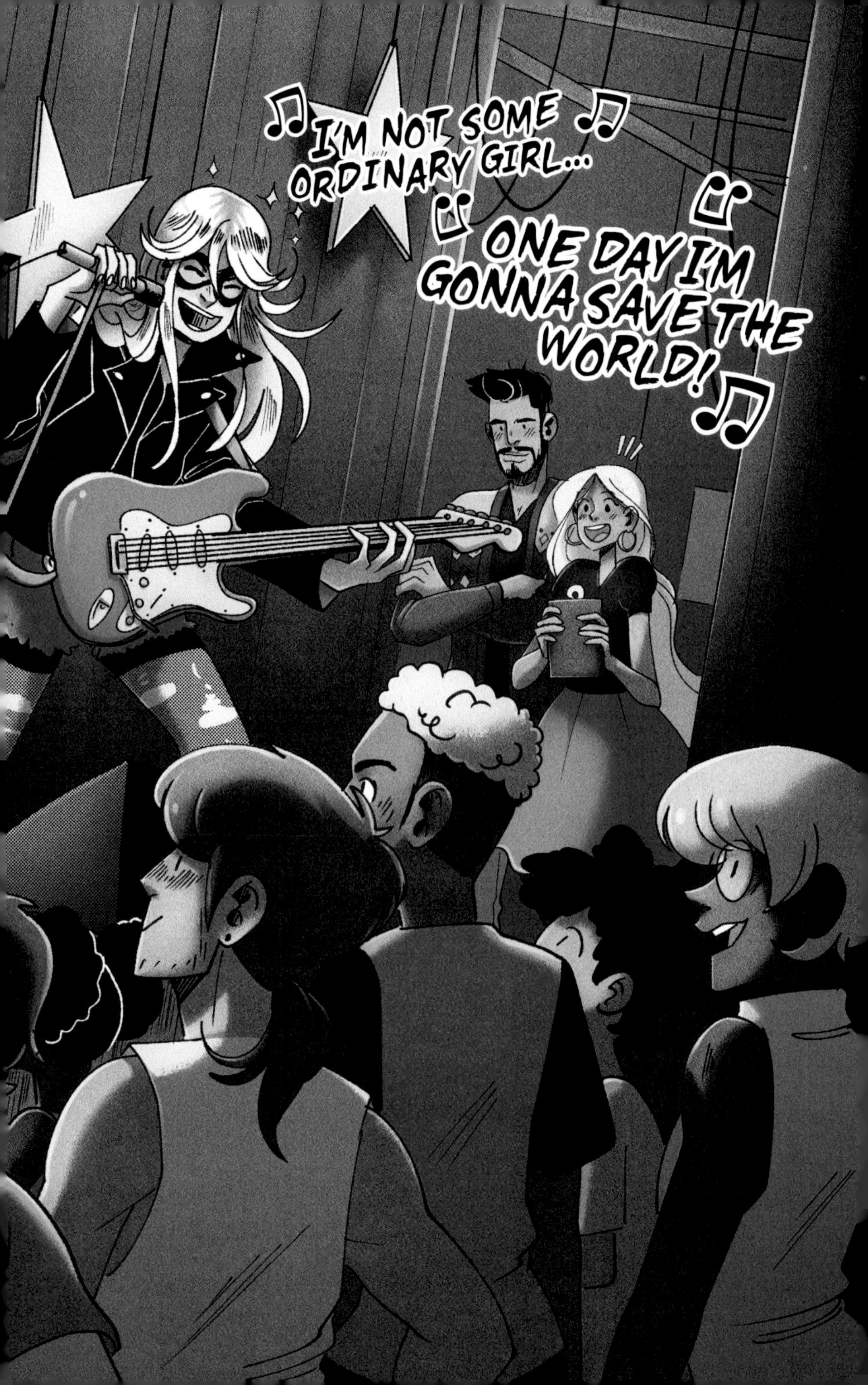
I'M NOT SOME ORDINARY GIRL...
ONE DAY I'M GONNA SAVE THE WORLD!

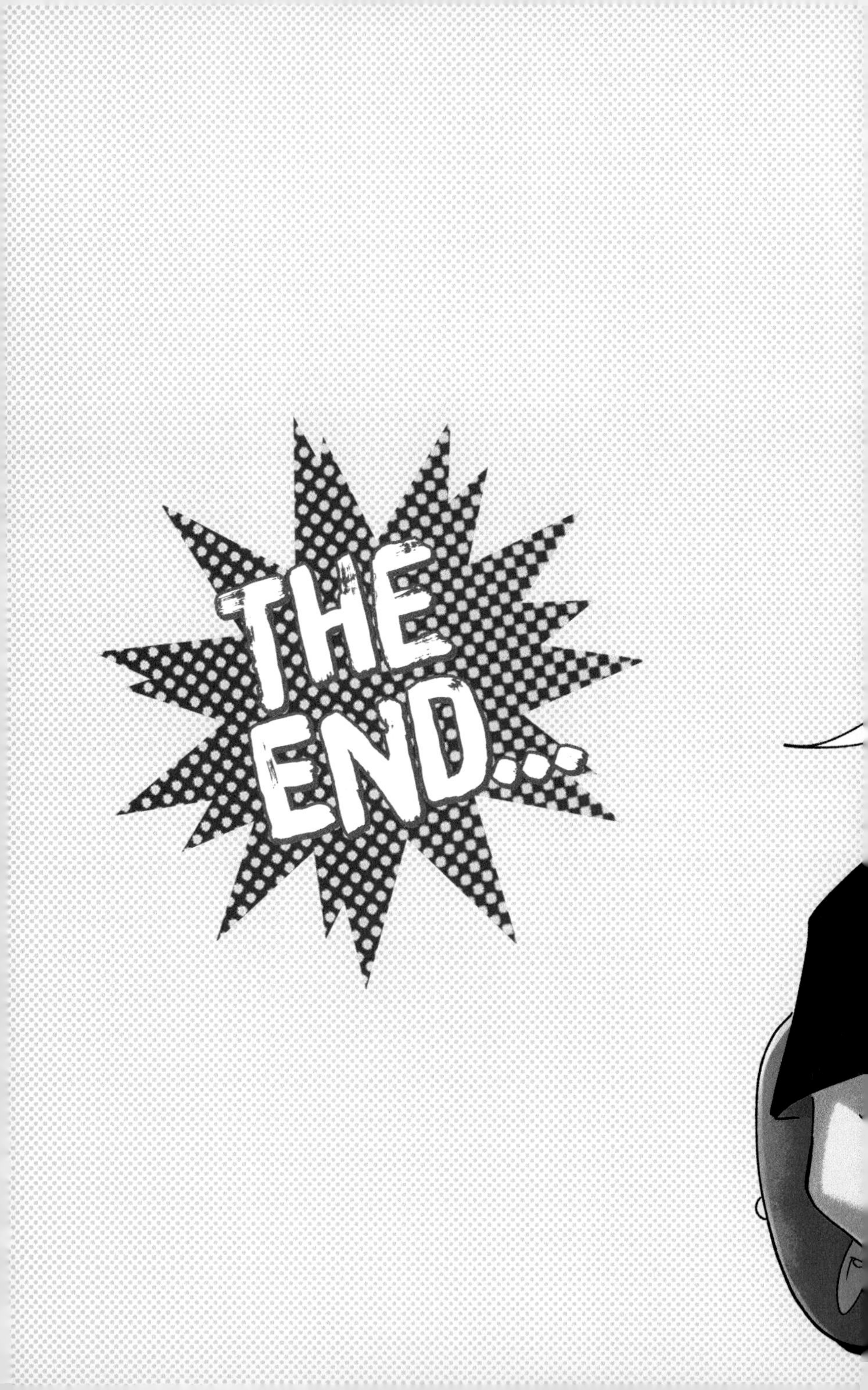
THE END...

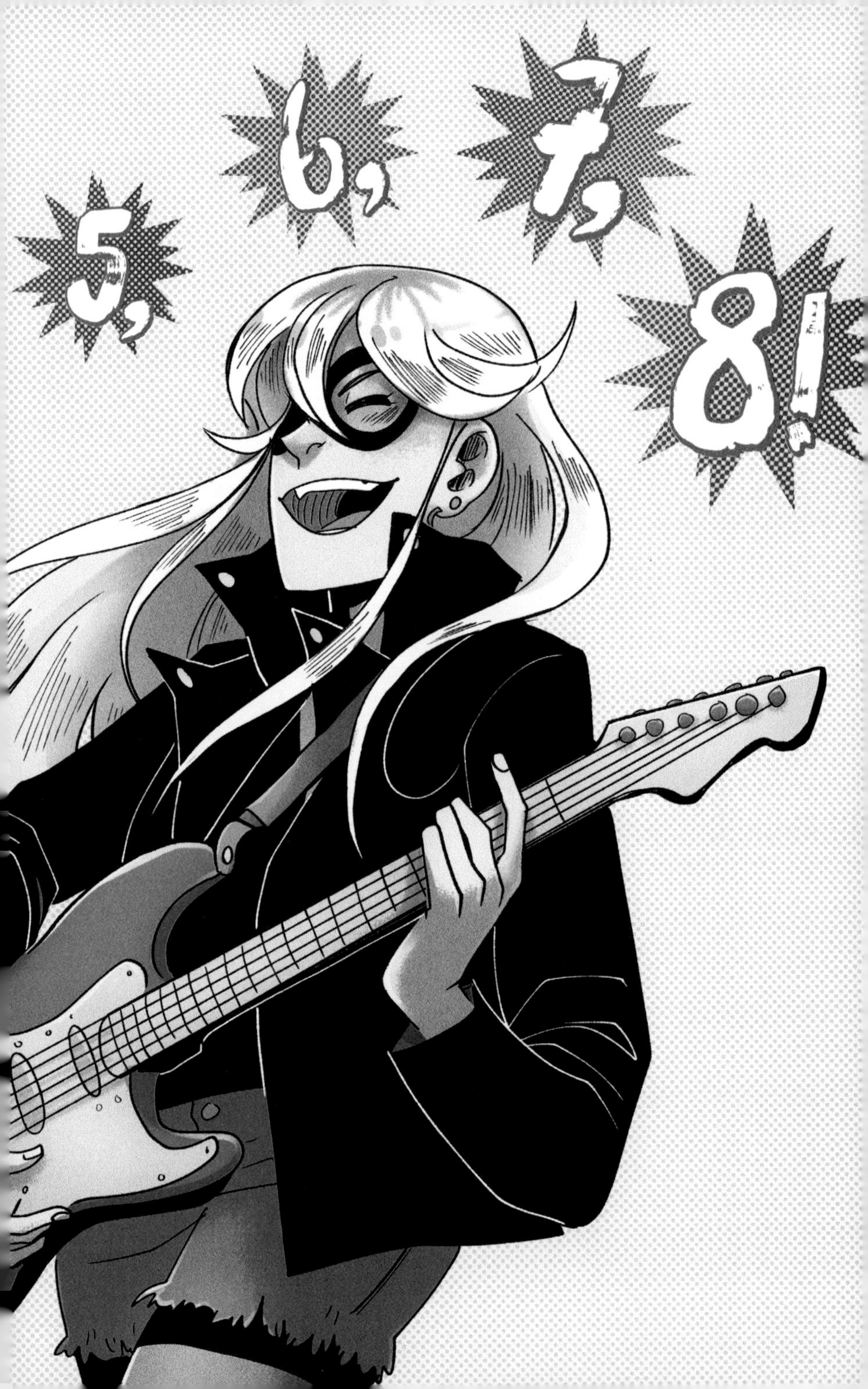
5, 6, 7, 8!

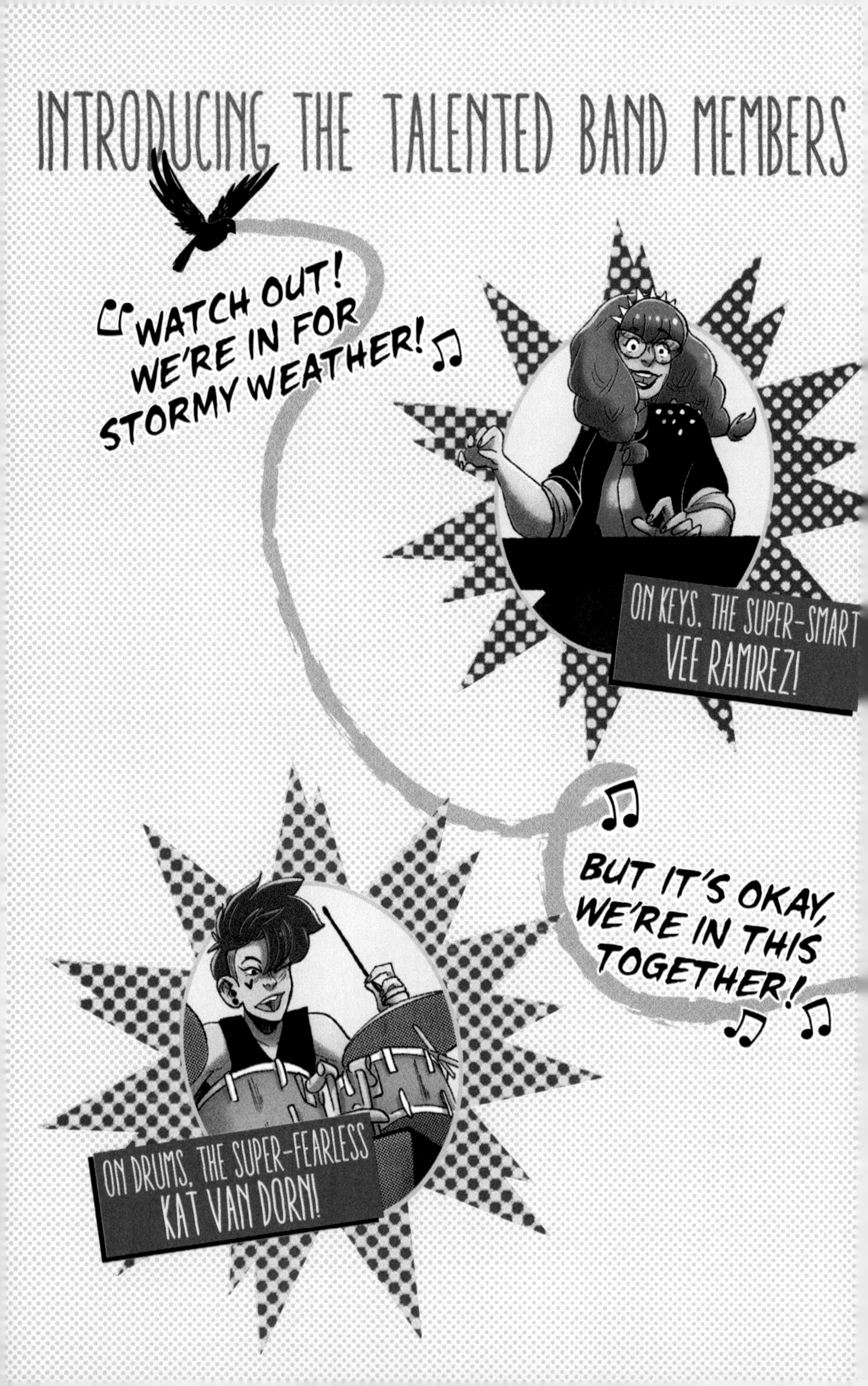
INTRODUCING THE TALENTED BAND MEMBERS
WATCH OUT! WE'RE IN FOR STORMY WEATHER!
ON KEYS, THE SUPER-SMART VEE RAMIREZ!
BUT IT'S OKAY, WE'RE IN THIS TOGETHER!
ON DRUMS, THE SUPER-FEARLESS KAT VAN DORN!

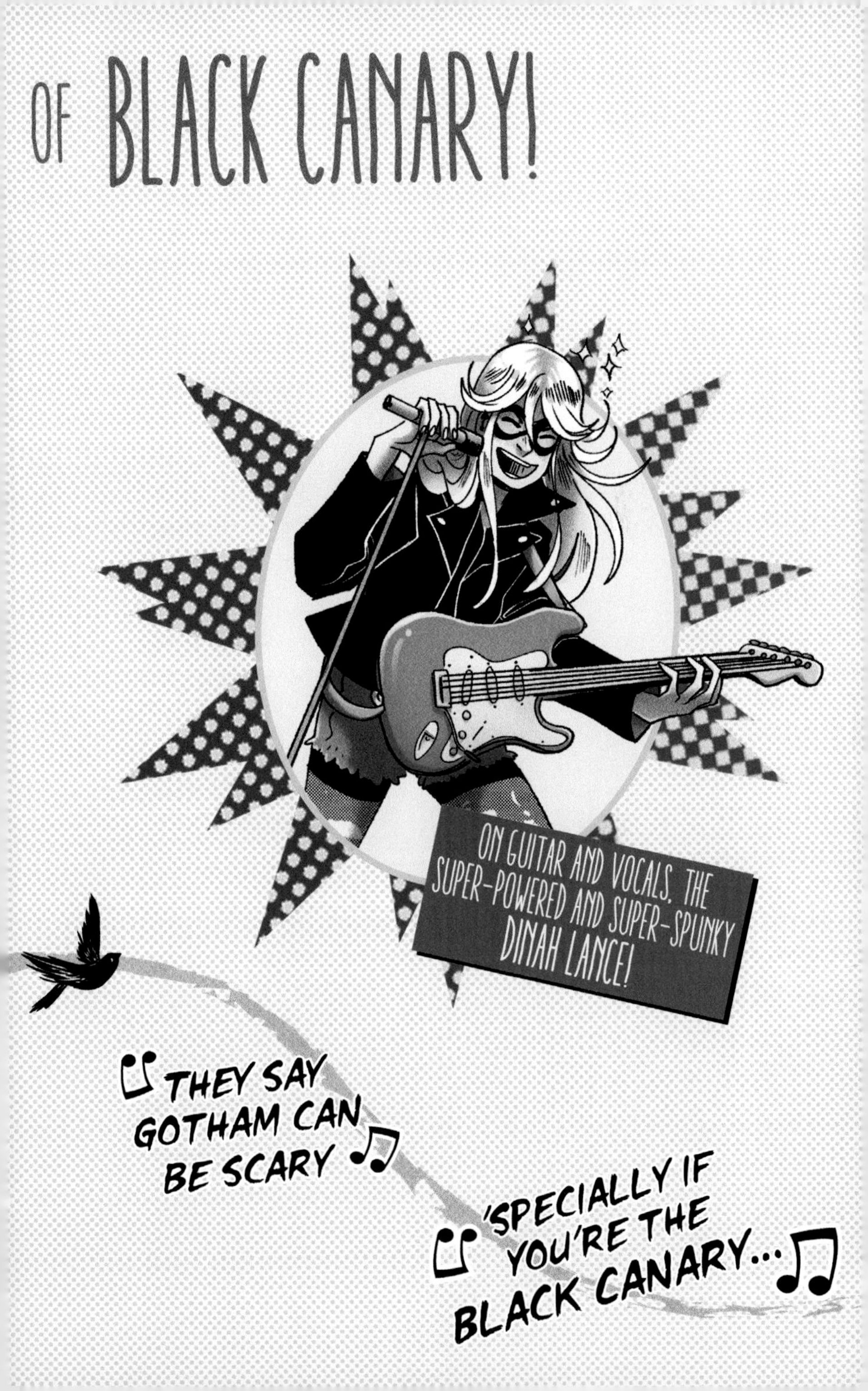
OF BLACK CANARY!
ON GUITAR AND VOCALS, THE SUPER-POWERED AND SUPER-SPUNKY DINAH LANCE!
THEY SAY GOTHAM CAN BE SCARY
'SPECIALLY IF YOU'RE THE BLACK CANARY...

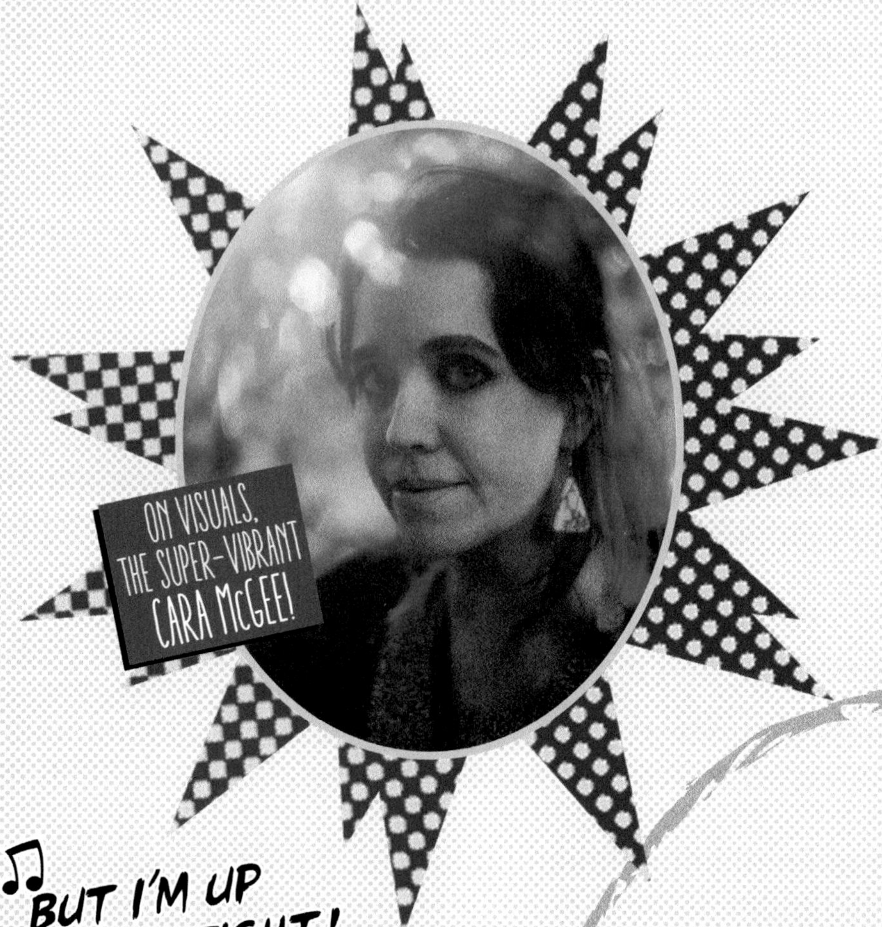
ON VISUALS, THE SUPER-VIBRANT CARA McGEE!

BUT I'M UP FOR THE FIGHT! PUSH ME AND I'LL IGNITE!

Cara McGee is a BFA graduate of SCAD's sequential art program. Since graduating in 2010, she has worked on a number of personal minicomics, as well as comics, covers, and illustrations for companies like BOOM!, DC Comics, IDW, and Cards Against Humanity. She currently lives in the woods in the middle of nowhere and travels as much as her schedule allows.

"I'M NOT SOME ORDINARY GIRL...

"I'M GONNA SAVE THE WORLD!

Meg Cabot is an award-winning author. Her books for adults, teens, and tweens have included multiple #1 *New York Times* bestsellers, selling well over 25 million copies worldwide. Cabot's *Princess Diaries* series has been published in more than 38 countries and was made into two hit films by Disney. She is also the author of the popular *Mediator* series and the *Heather Wells* mystery series. Meg was born in Indiana during the Chinese astrological year of the Fire Horse, a notoriously unlucky sign, but has been working hard ever since to give herself a happy ending. She currently lives in Key West with her husband.

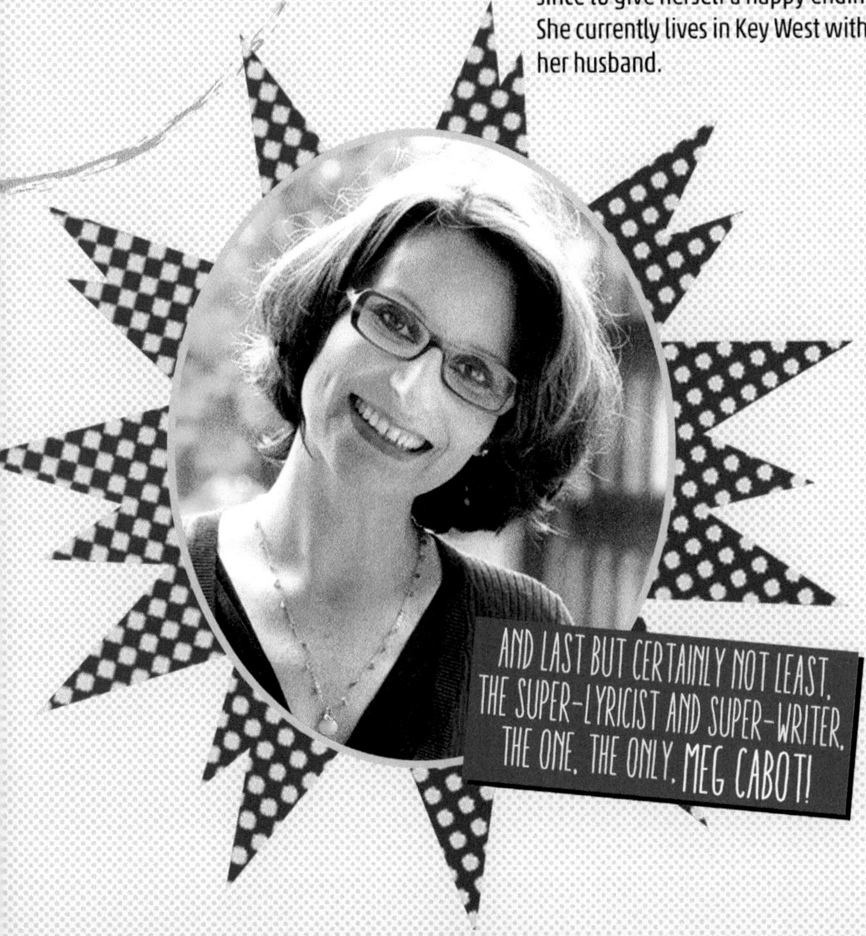
AND LAST BUT CERTAINLY NOT LEAST,
THE SUPER-LYRICIST AND SUPER-WRITER,
THE ONE, THE ONLY, MEG CABOT!

From **Minh Lê**, award-winning author of
Drawn Together and *Let Me Finish!*,
and illustrator **Andie Tong** comes
the story of thirteen-year-old Tai Pham,
the newest member of a group of space cops
known as the **Green Lanterns!**

When Tai's world expands beyond his wildest imagination,
he must decide what kind of hero he wants to be:
Will he learn to soar above his insecurities,
or will the past keep him grounded?

Read on for a special sneak preview of
GREEN LANTERN: LEGACY
On sale January 21, 2020,
and available for preorder now!

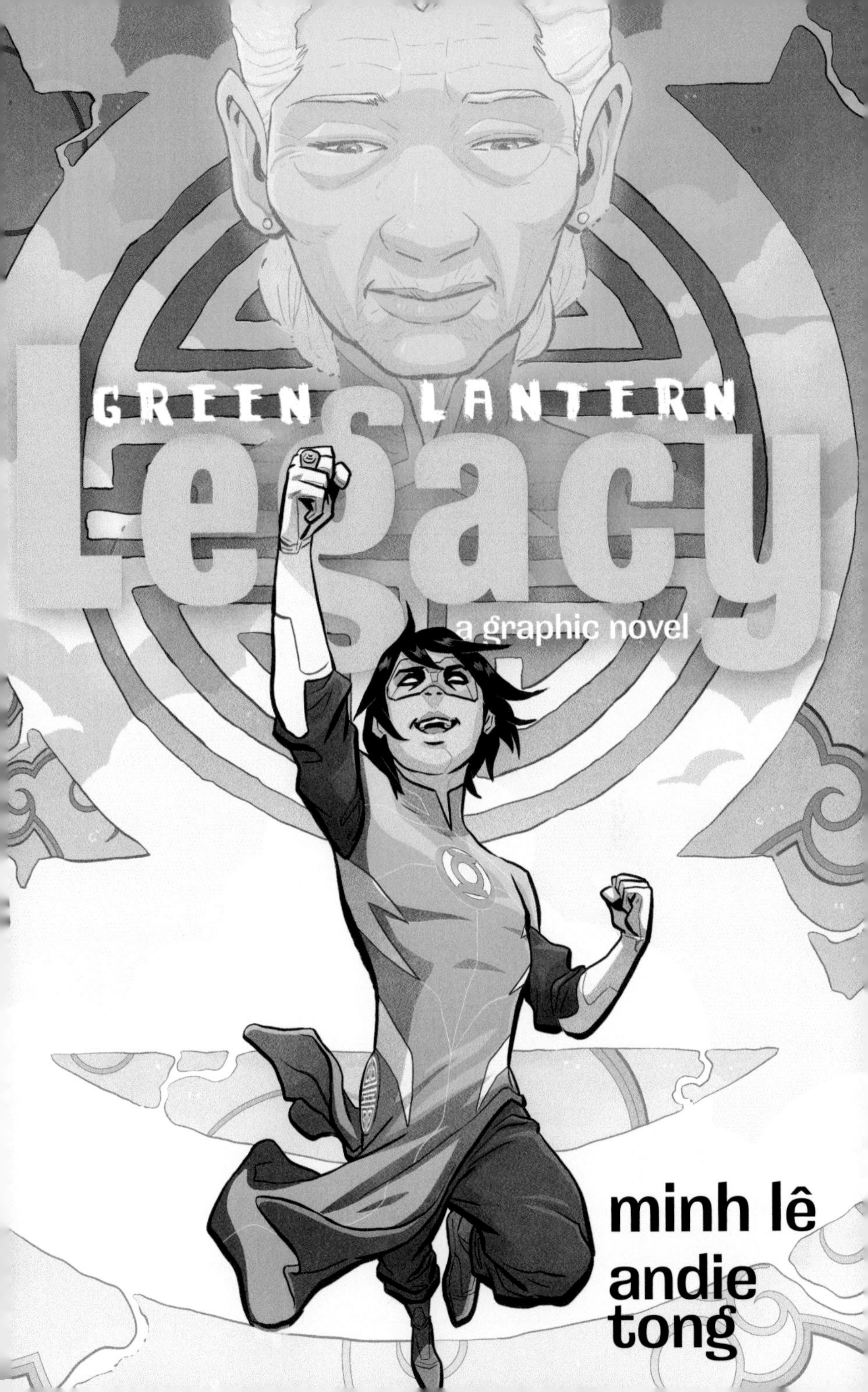
GREEN LANTERN
Legacy
a graphic novel
minh lê
andie tong

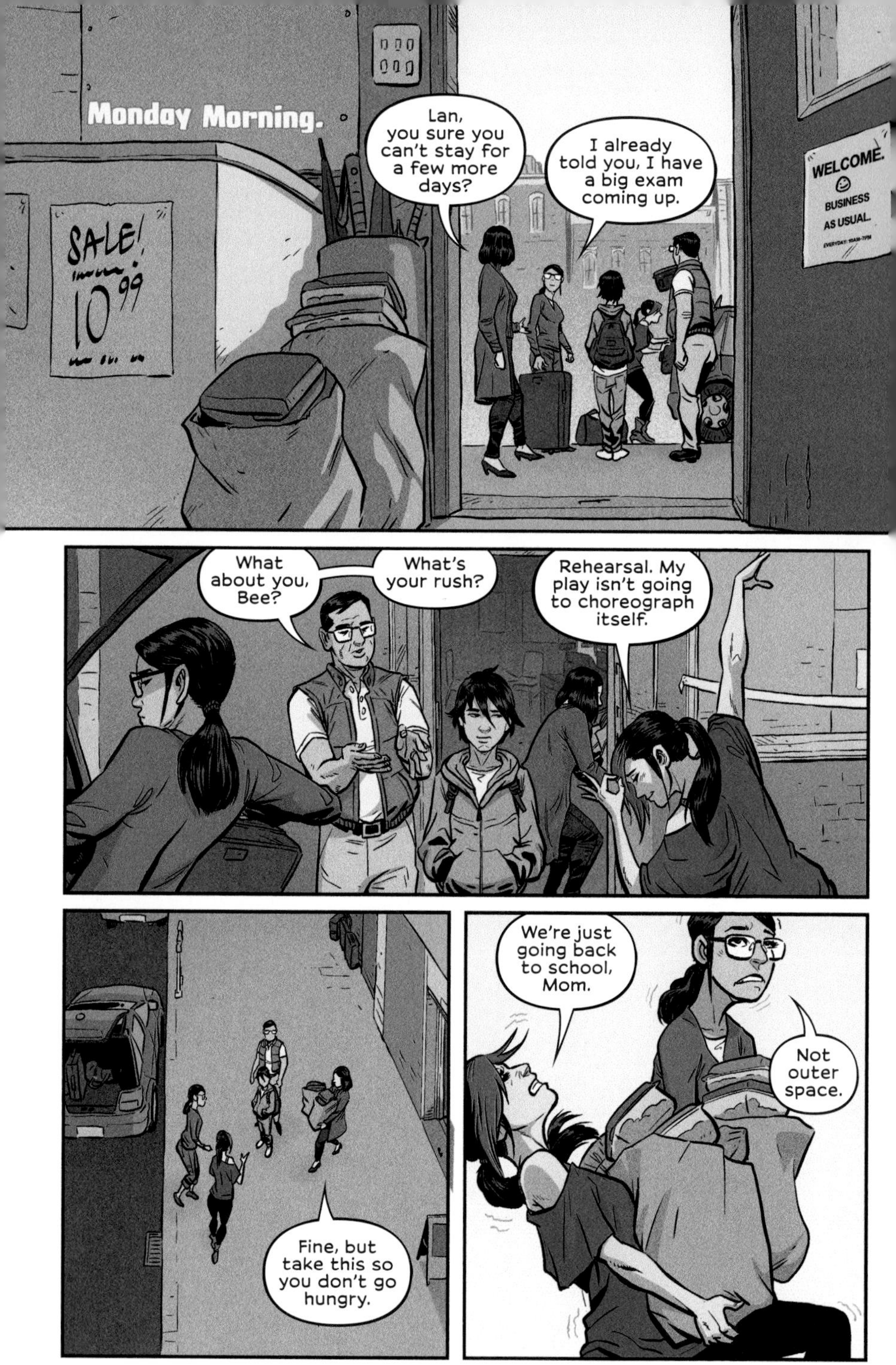
Monday Morning.
SALE! 10.99
Lan, you sure you can't stay for a few more days?
I already told you, I have a big exam coming up.
WELCOME. BUSINESS AS USUAL.
What about you, Bee?
What's your rush?
Rehearsal. My play isn't going to choreograph itself.
Fine, but take this so you don't go hungry.
We're just going back to school, Mom.
Not outer space.

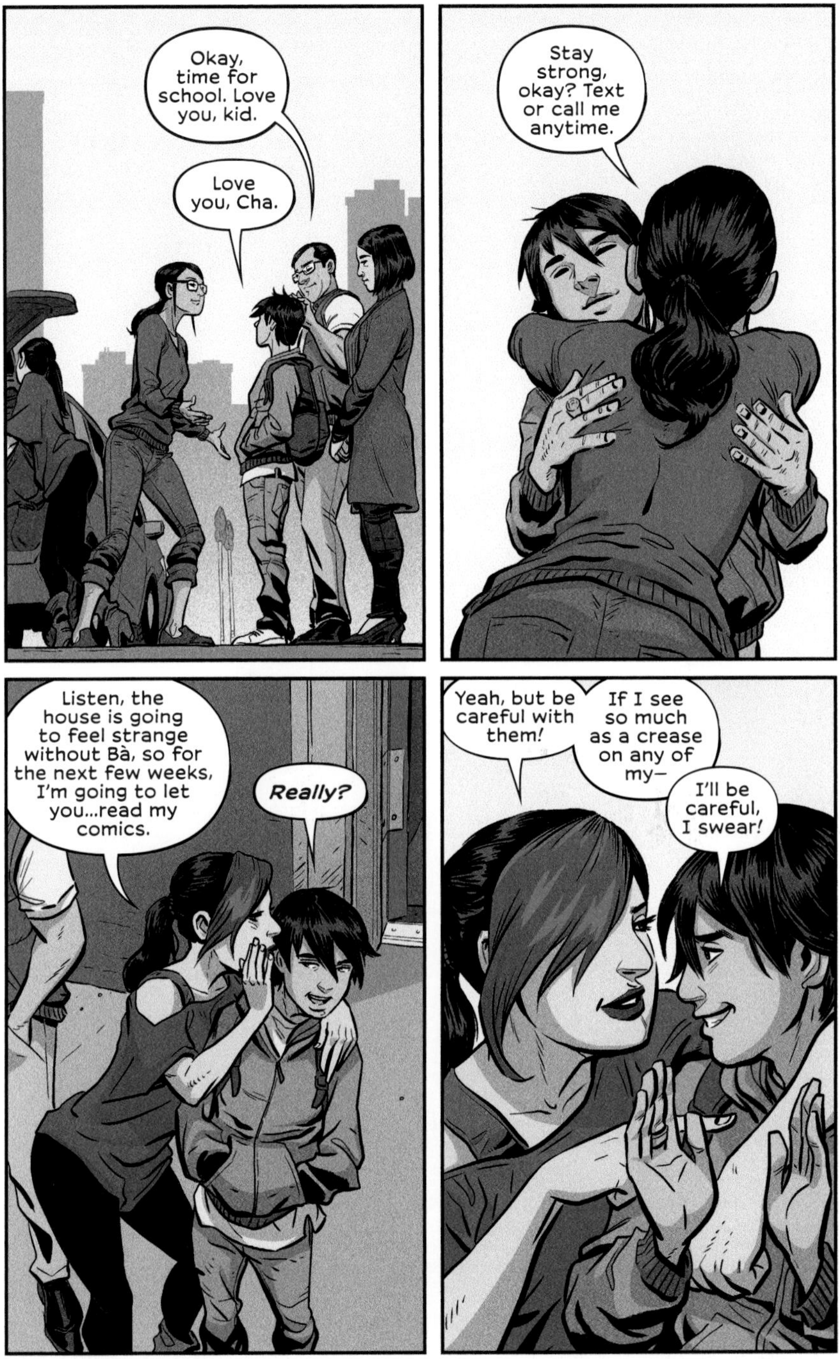
Okay, time for school. Love you, kid.
Love you, Cha.
Stay strong, okay? Text or call me anytime.
Listen, the house is going to feel strange without Bà, so for the next few weeks, I'm going to let you...read my comics.
Really?
Yeah, but be careful with them!
If I see so much as a crease on any of my—
I'll be careful, I swear!

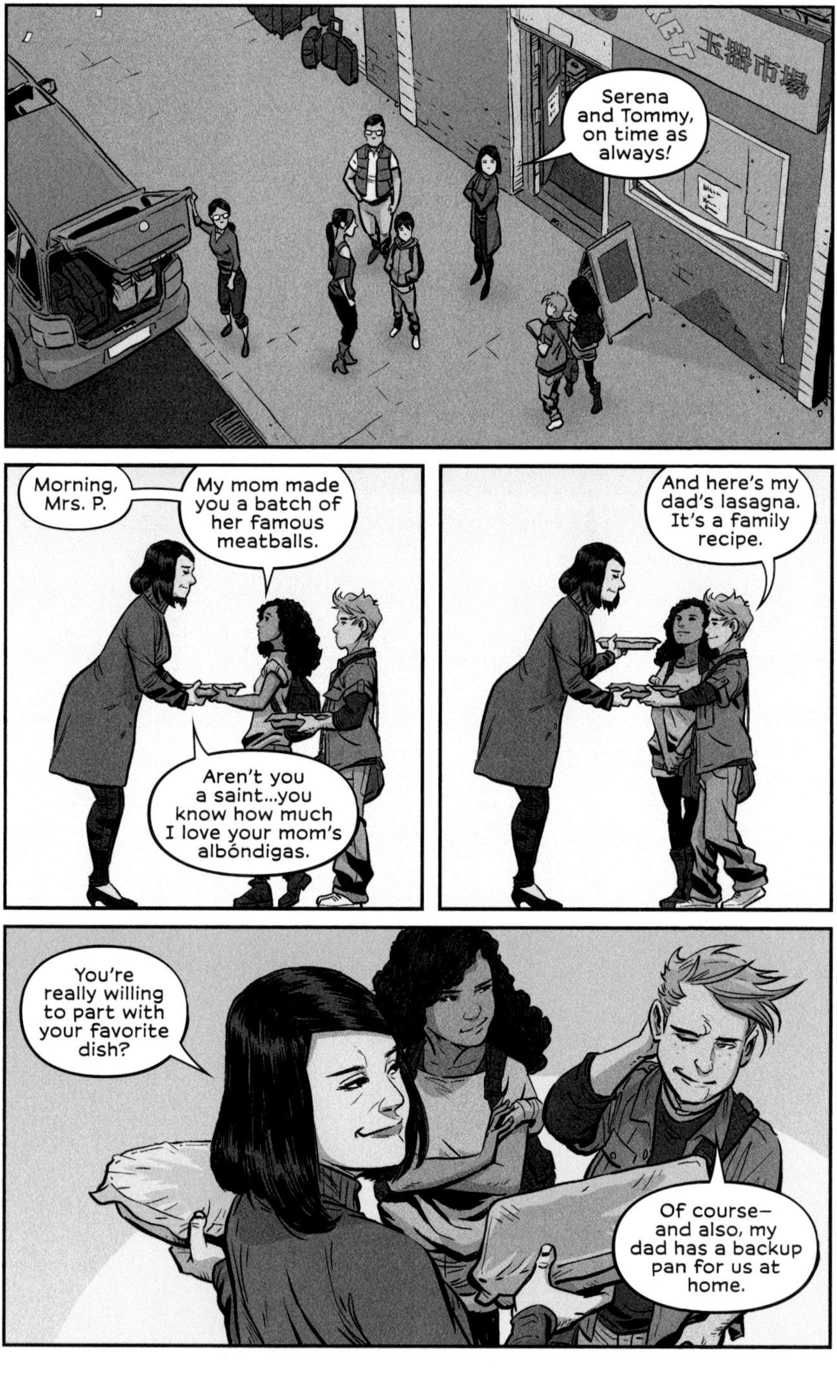
玉器市場
Serena and Tommy, on time as always!
Morning, Mrs. P.
My mom made you a batch of her famous meatballs.
Aren't you a saint...you know how much I love your mom's albóndigas.
And here's my dad's lasagna. It's a family recipe.
You're really willing to part with your favorite dish?
Of course— and also, my dad has a backup pan for us at home.

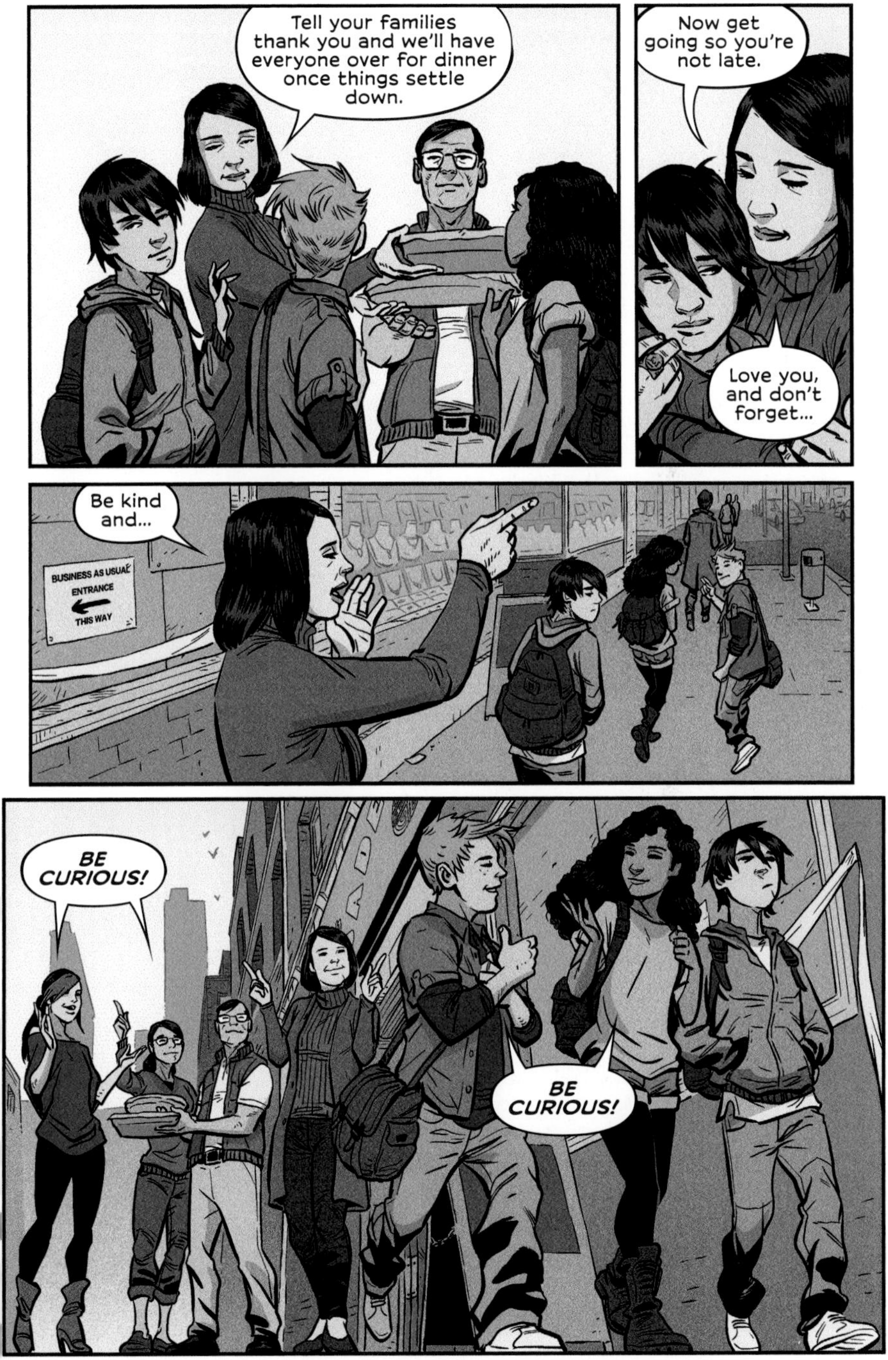

Tell your families thank you and we'll have everyone over for dinner once things settle down.
Now get going so you're not late.
Love you, and don't forget...
Be kind and...
BUSINESS AS USUAL ENTRANCE THIS WAY
BE CURIOUS!
BE CURIOUS!

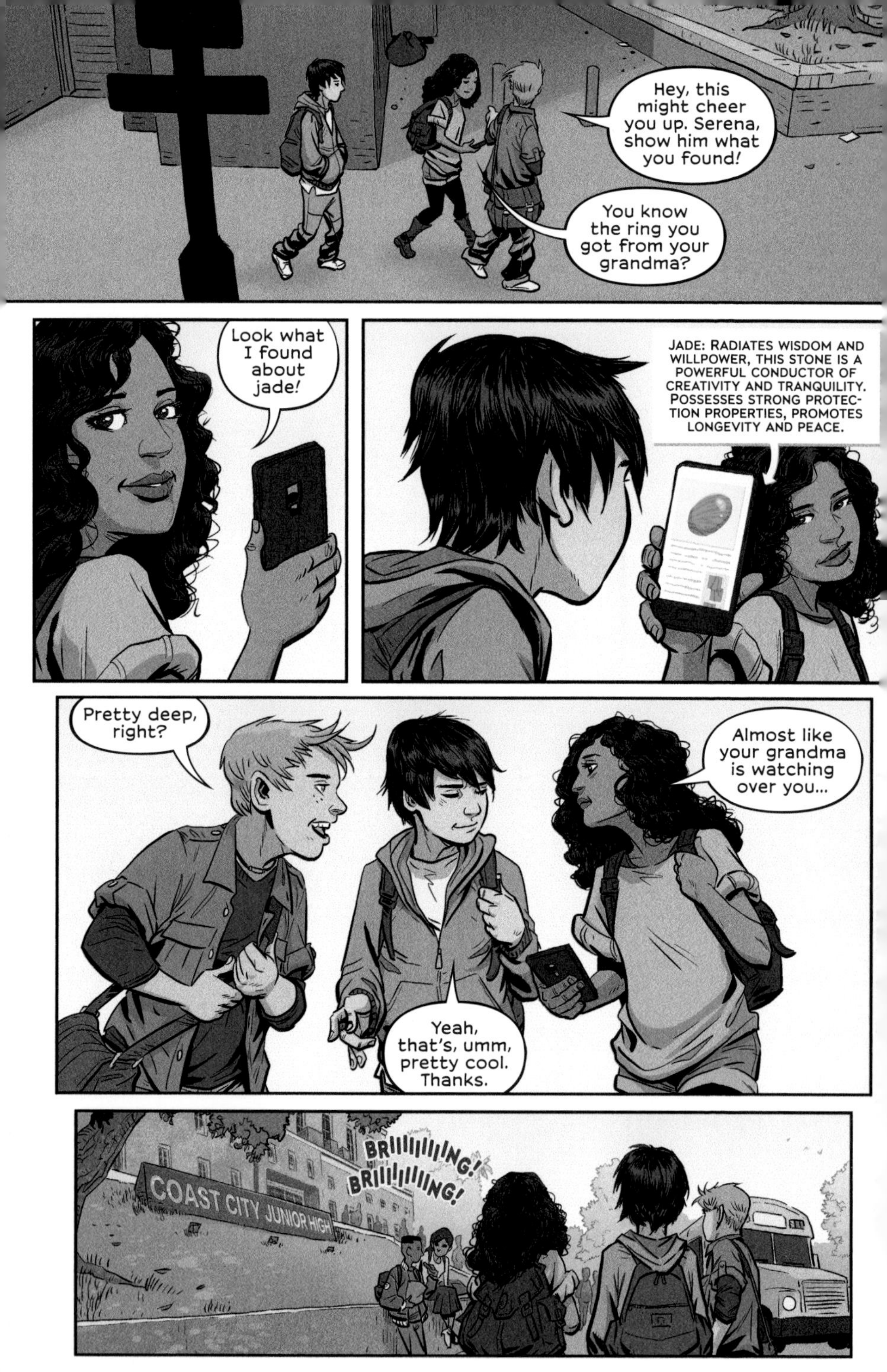

Hey, this might cheer you up. Serena, show him what you found!
You know the ring you got from your grandma?
Look what I found about jade!
JADE: RADIATES WISDOM AND WILLPOWER, THIS STONE IS A POWERFUL CONDUCTOR OF CREATIVITY AND TRANQUILITY. POSSESSES STRONG PROTECTION PROPERTIES, PROMOTES LONGEVITY AND PEACE.
Pretty deep, right?
Almost like your grandma is watching over you...
Yeah, that's, umm, pretty cool. Thanks.
COAST CITY JUNIOR HIGH
BRIIIIIIING! BRIIIIIIING!

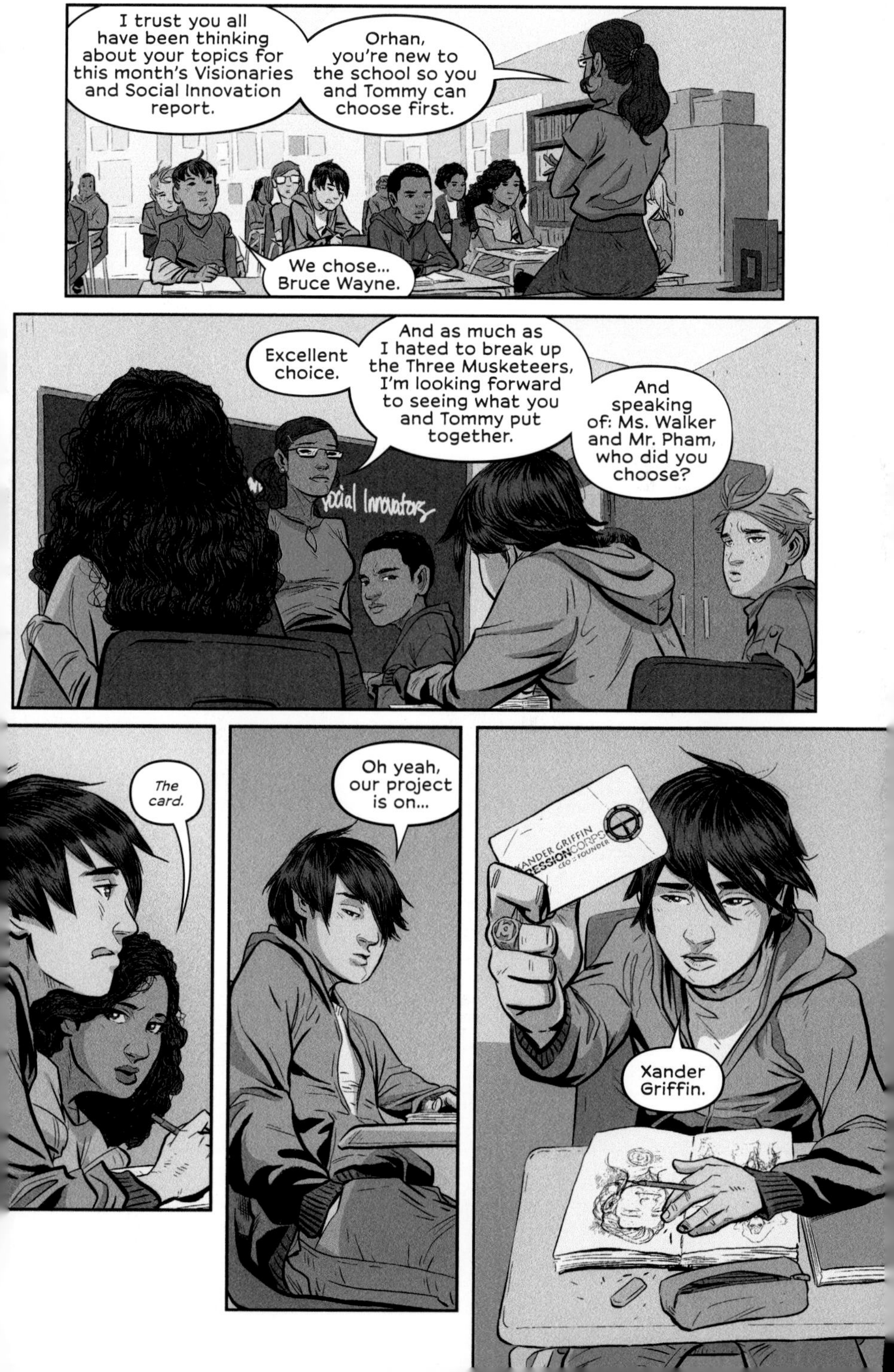
I trust you all have been thinking about your topics for this month's Visionaries and Social Innovation report.
Orhan, you're new to the school so you and Tommy can choose first.
We chose... Bruce Wayne.
Excellent choice.
And as much as I hated to break up the Three Musketeers, I'm looking forward to seeing what you and Tommy put together.
And speaking of: Ms. Walker and Mr. Pham, who did you choose?
Social Innovators
The card.
Oh yeah, our project is on...
XANDER GRIFFIN
CEO & FOUNDER
Xander Griffin.

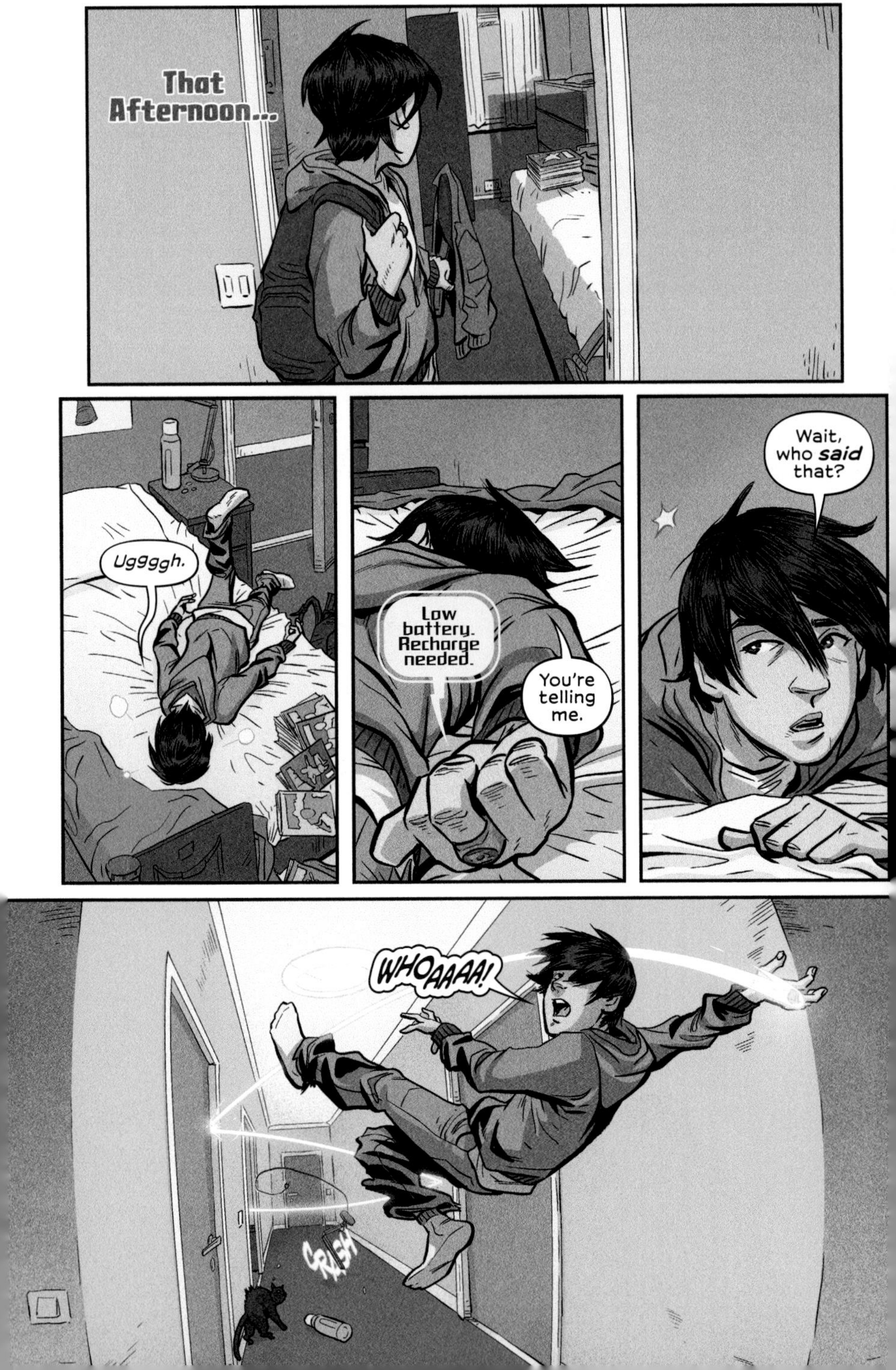
That Afternoon...
Uggggh.
Low battery. Recharge needed.
You're telling me.
Wait, who said that?
WHOAAAA!
CRASH

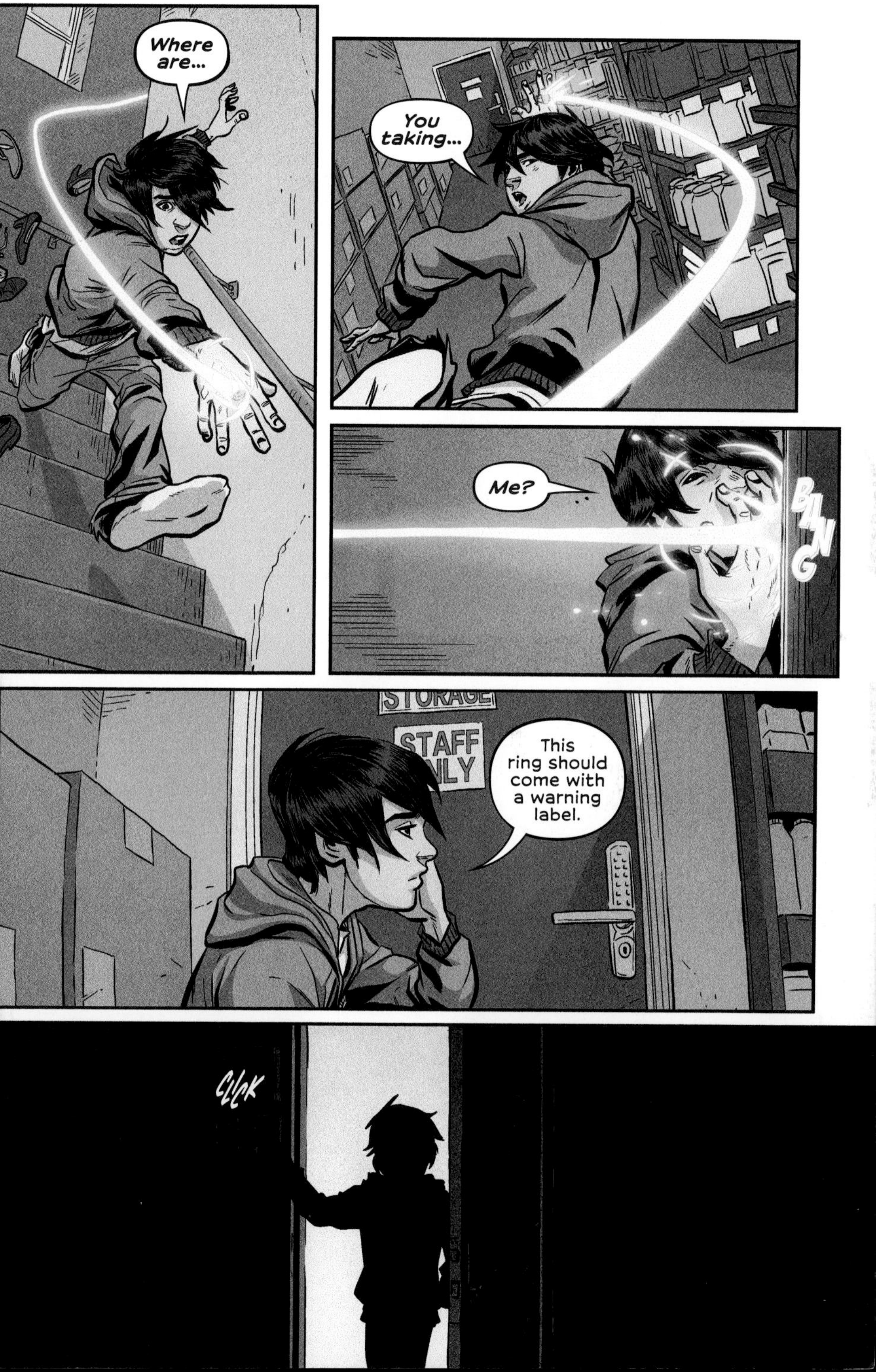
Where are...
You taking...
Me?
BLANG
STORAGE
STAFF ONLY
This ring should come with a warning label.
CLICK

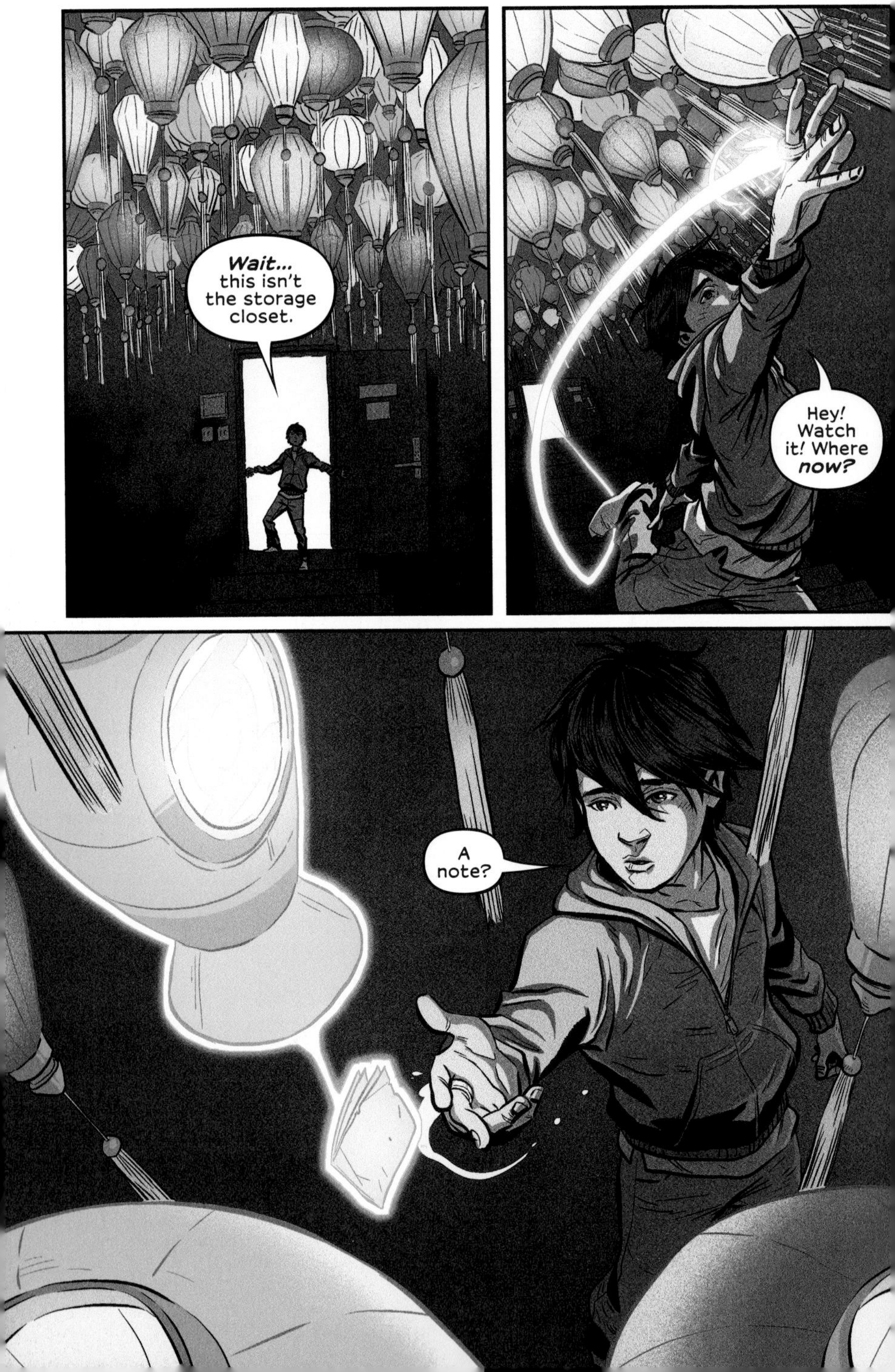
Wait... this isn't the storage closet.
Hey! Watch it! Where now?
A note?

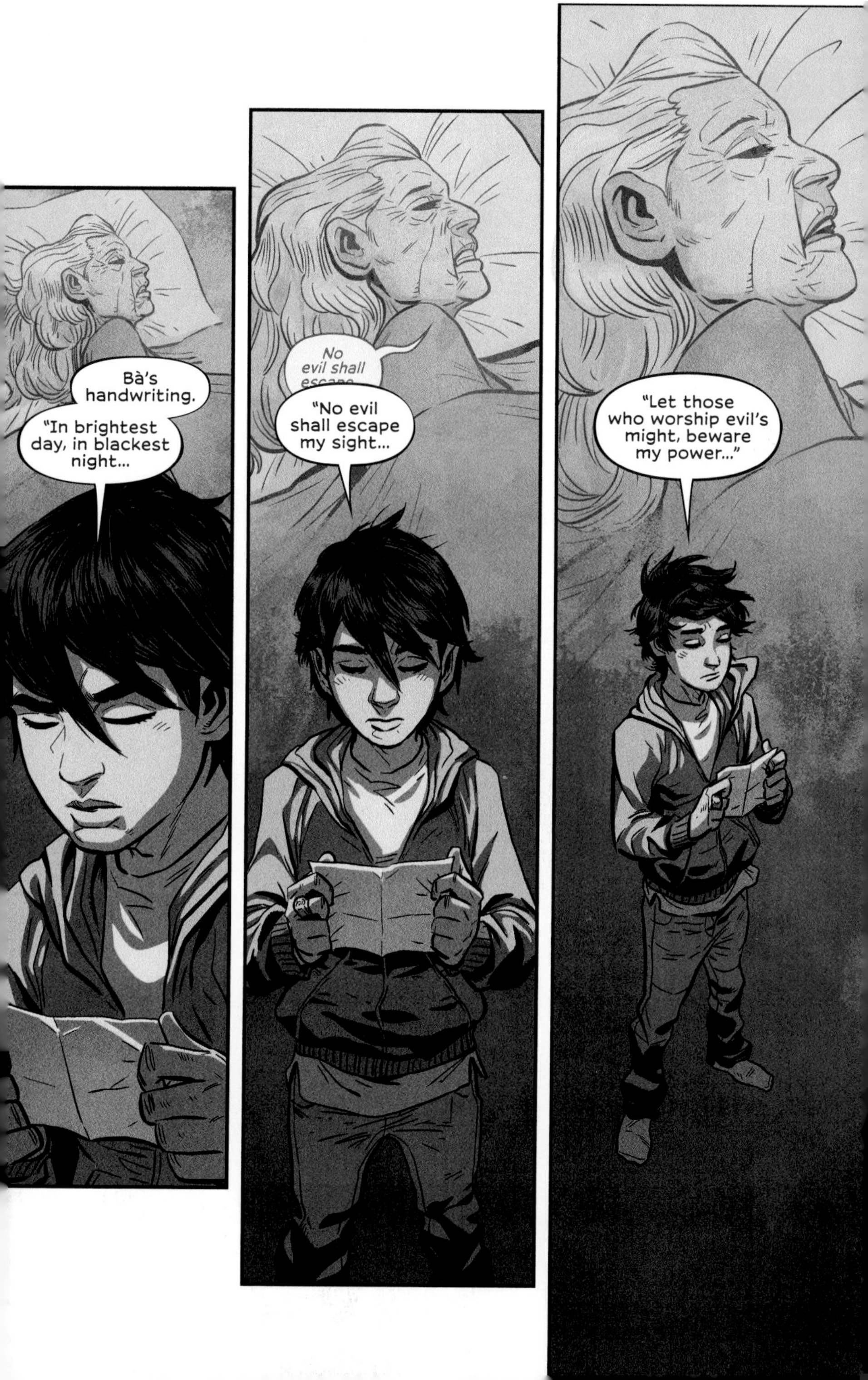
Bà's handwriting.
"In brightest day, in blackest night...
No evil shall
"No evil shall escape my sight...
"Let those who worship evil's might, beware my power..."

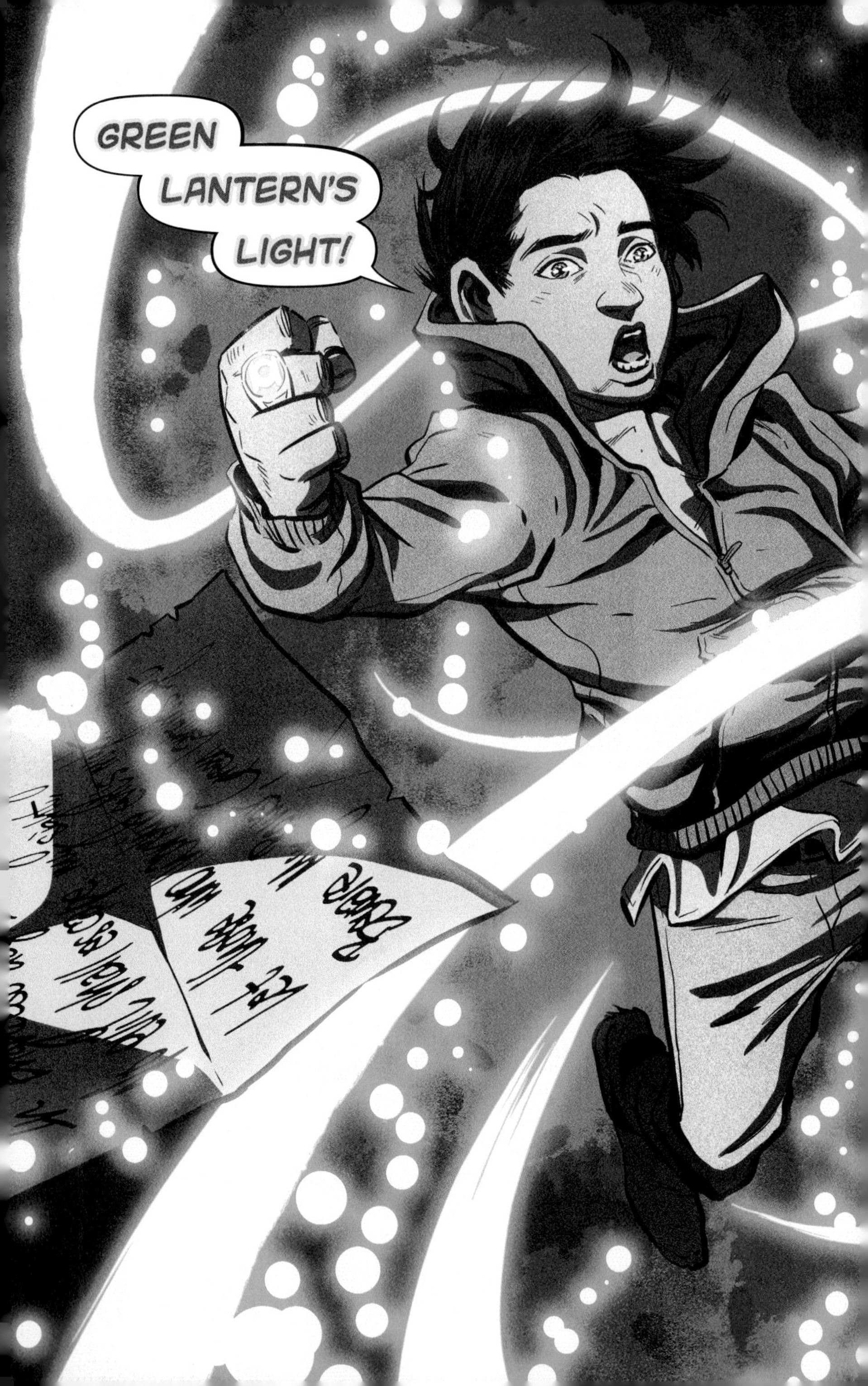
GREEN LANTERN'S LIGHT!

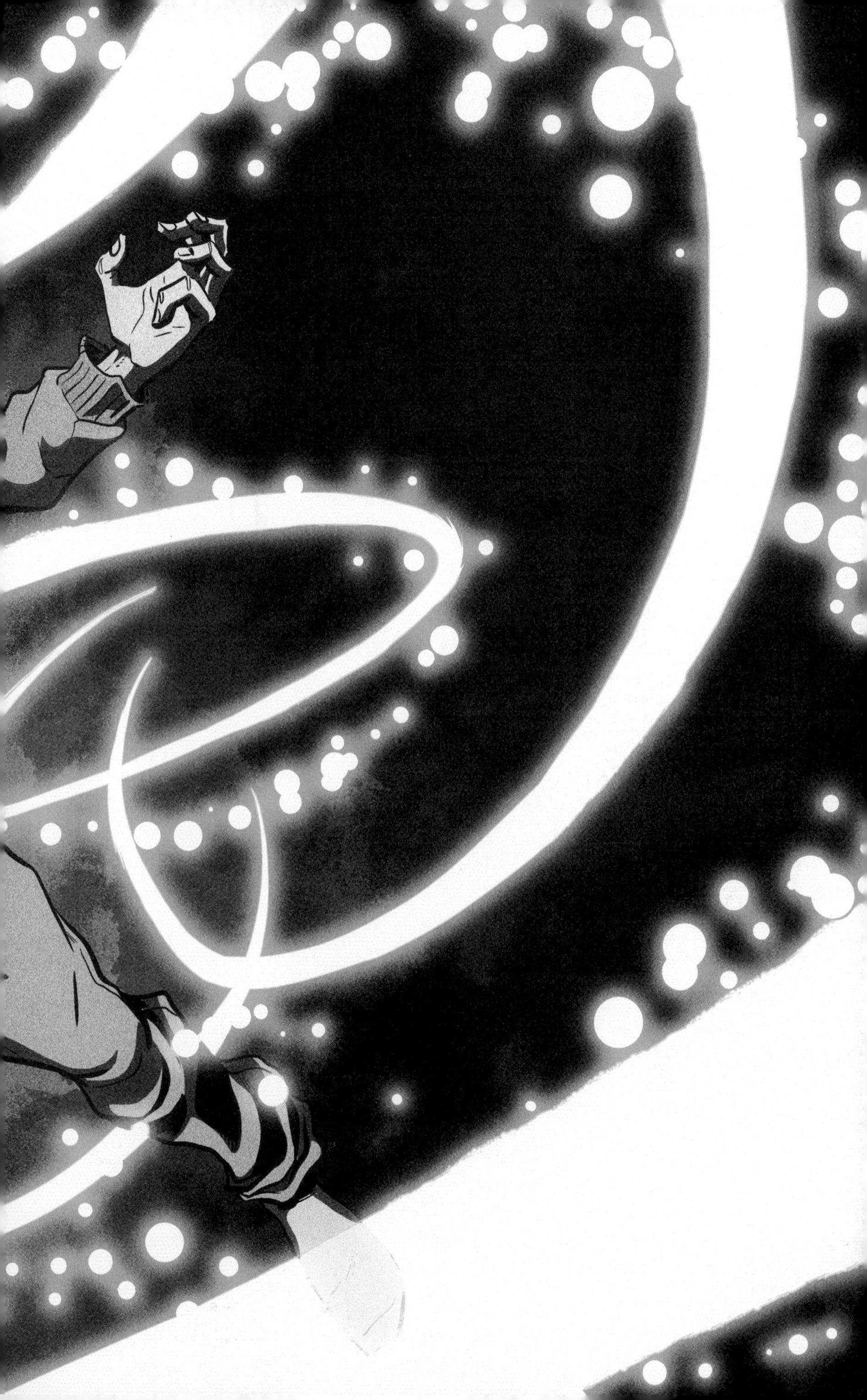

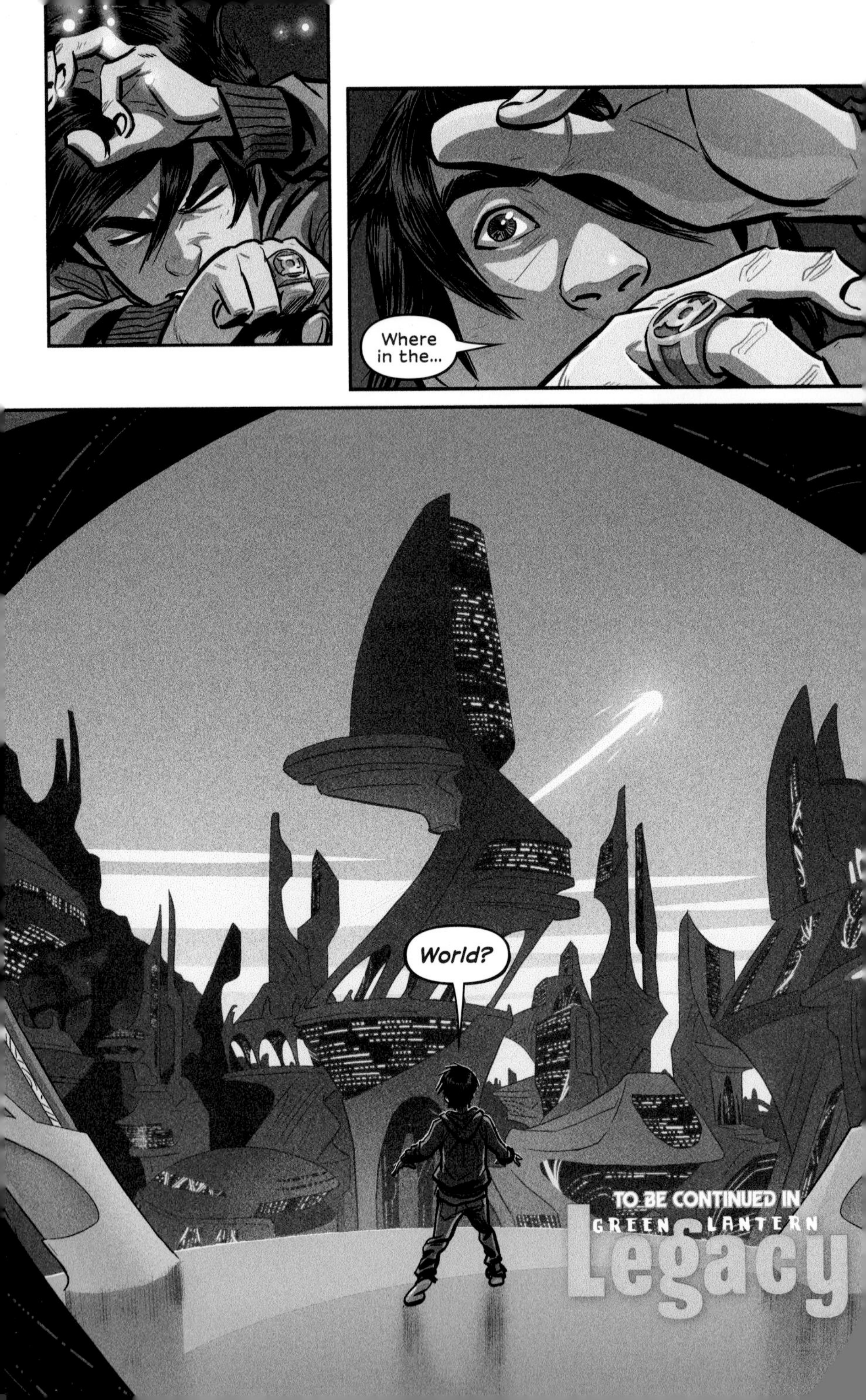
Where in the...
World?
TO BE CONTINUED IN
GREEN LANTERN
Legacy